Elizabeth Whitmer

019/110

Aloha Rainbow

by
Elizabeth Whitmer

Second Edition
or
Revised Edition

Bloomington, IN Milton Keynes, UK

AuthorHouse™
1663 Liberty Drive, Suite 200
Bloomington, IN 47403
www.authorhouse.com
Phone: 1-800-839-8640

AuthorHouse™ UK Ltd.
500 Avebury Boulevard
Central Milton Keynes, MK9 2BE
www.authorhouse.co.uk
Phone: 08001974150

With the exception of historical figures, this book is entirely fictitious. Any resemblance to any persons, dead or living, is purely a coincidence.

© 2007 Elizabeth Whitmer. All rights reserved.

No part of this book may be reproduced, stored in a retrieval system, or transmitted by any means without the written permission of the author.

First published by AuthorHouse 12/6/2007

ISBN: 978-1-4259-7360-5 (e)
ISBN: 978-1-4259-7359-9 (sc)
ISBN: 978-1-4259-8225-6 (hc)

Library of Congress Control Number: 2006909405

Printed in the United States of America
Bloomington, Indiana

This book is printed on acid-free paper.

*Cover photo – original image copyright Steve Alterman.
Rainbow digitally added.*

To my parents, who set my sights high but made sure my feet were planted firmly on the ground.

Table of Contents

Prologue: xi
Complications

1. Place Of Refuge 1
   Pu`uhonua Road and Honuanau Bay

2. Caregiver 11
   La`Ohana Inn and Livia's Memories

3. Kuhuna 39
   Chakra and Aye's Beach Shack

4. Mele Kalikimaka 51
   Queens' Stables and The Establishment

5. Old News and New 75
   South Kona

6. Hukilau and Barbecue 107
   Hookena Beach and La`Ohana Inn

7. Orchid Cove 121
   Seaside Cliffs near the Beach Shack

8. The Good Doctor's Doctor 147
   La`Ohana Inn and Waimea

9. Caretaker's Cottage 163
   The Inn's Cottage and Queens' Stables

10. Birthday In Waikiki 173
    Honolulu, Waikiki, and Kaneohe

11. Work Hard. Play Hard 187
    Hilo and Waimea

12. Poliahu 205
    Caretaker's Cottage

13. Hockey Visitors 215
    The Inn and Kohala Coast Golf Courses

14. Accident At Captain Cook 225
    Old Kaawaloa Road and Kealakekua Bay

15. Fantasy Auction 251
    La`Ohana Inn and Waimea

16. Orchid Of Hilo 269
    Ma's Shop and Old Hilo

17. Power Of Attorney 291
    La`Ohana Inn and Queens' Stables

18. `Ohana 307
    Kona

19. Death Of a Queen 337
    Caretaker's Cottage and Beach Shack

20. Aloha `Oe 353
    La`Ohana Inn

21. Clambake 367
    Kohala Coast and Mauna Kea Resort

    Epilogue: 371
    Michigan and Kona

Prologue:

Someone asked why I wrote this book. Here is my best short answer.

Life would be dull without complications. In 1976 I visited the World Trade Center and looked down on the Statue of Liberty. Times were hard then too. Oddly enough – I was lucky to have had older parents who witnessed the 1930's Depression. Like their generation, the very next year we were forced to leave our small town and move to a city for jobs. Even before 9/11/2001 many professionals teetered on the line between middle and lower class, and pathways to hard won freedoms and perks were slowly eroding. Realizing the cogs of democracy would not turn without their tax base – some individuals stood up, dusted themselves off, and resorted to the ways and means that brought their ancestors to what is now this great United States. Let the greedy and the obsessed never forget heroic acts of civil disobedience and shouts of "Let's roll!"

Not a call to arms or an endorsement for vigilantes, this novel tells how a handful of spoiled yet enterprising Kids of the Sixties, spit out Big Business' pabulum, sold what they could, kissed their families goodbye, and moved on — finding something real and laughing a bit in the process.

Main Characters:

Livia Hinman – Hoosier. Tired teacher and pink collar automotive worker. Kick Ice Bear's backup goalie. Groundskeeper and owner of La'Ohana Inn.

Catherine Patrice Kievers – Native suburban Detroiter of Russian heritage. True to her namesakes. Kick Ice Bear's lead goalie. Inn's manager and owner.

Margaret Anne Brown, M.D. – Detroit surgeon. Played defense for Dartmouth, The Blades, and Kick Ice Bears. Volunteers, and runs Kona's ER. Inn's owner.

Tom Smith – Displaced teacher. Manager and partner at Queens' Stables.

Tim Boki – Hawaiian blacksmith and farrier. Owns Queens' Stables.

Chakra Kuhanamana – Elderly Hawaiian. Quilts with Cate. Sister of Aye.

Aye Noelani – Elderly Hawaiian. Livia's gardening buddy. Brother of Chakra.

Ma Loa Hakkalani – Mysterious Hawaiian woman from Hilo.

Richard Header, D.V.M. and M.D. – Dates Margaret. Beastialist. Pedophile.

Chapter 1: Place Of Refuge

The old road to Honaunau Bay veered sharply West. Something flashed in the rearview mirror, and a horse trailer buffeted the car before swerving back, nearly missing a small row of mailboxes. Her fine-boned hands steeled their grip, as the car hugged the asphalt rimming back lots of tiny Manini Beach. Catherine watched truck and trailer float down the gentle undulations over the vast sea plain. Blowing her breath, she relaxed her shoulders and sighed, "'Tween Time," as a beautiful sky-blue-pink anchored a very long day.

That afternoon, she talked her way past the guards, at Keauhou. Continuing uphill along the old battlegrounds near Kainaliu, she turned south on Highway 11 searching the old storefronts along the few miles to Kealakekua, before passing the hospital turnoff and heading down Napoopoo Road. Livia carried a sophisticated cell phone. Looking down at the on-board GoGalaxy, Cate flipped the device off, thinking, "So much for GPS tracking."

Now, the evening star pulsed high above a thin, peachy glow. The truck and trailer sat near the stop sign, its left turn signal quietly blinking. Her jaw slacked as the gorgeous driver hopped down to the pavement and grabbed the emergency flasher off the roof. Eyes flashing above a fabulous grin, he hopped back in and pulled away.

Marveling, at the lack of scattered cinders, she watched as truck and trailer disappeared into low forest and vegetation. Not until then, did it occur to her. What fire? She'd smelled no smoke.

So few places left to look — she continued to the bay. Her head throbbed. That dull, ebbing 'Hurry' evolved to a skin-prickling mantra. So she hummed. As a hockey goalie, it always calmed her and sharpened her focus.

No matter. The day's events played through.

Back on the mainland, her best friend's aunt died this morning. Now, Livia was missing.

Stop it. Find her. Her poor night vision strained at every black detail. Livia always noted how the woody dense heliotrope clung to this shoreline.

Catherine's head bobbed as she chanted. "See movement; find detail. See movement; find detail..." Like tracking a puck — except the ice glared, the play more defined. Her back stiffened as she took the last curve and pulled onto the twenty-foot black sea shelf. Releasing her seatbelt, she glanced down at the clock. It was almost the time of day when Livia left two nights ago, for business in Hilo.

Catherine had recognized this as a day of sorrow, way before sunrise. Moments before noon, Livia rang the inn's house phone — quickly followed by a booming voice from the upstairs hallway.

Perfect timing: the Big Texan, in Suite 3A, must have heard enough of his wife's complaints: The Kona Mall's luau is too expensive; the Mauna Kea Resort's clambake is too far. Leaning hard on the check-in desk, he continued his litany until Livia's voice interrupted, "Catie Pat! I'll get there as soon as I can. Couple of rest stops, and I should be in Kona by late afternoon." That was it; the phone went dead.

The light sea breeze snapped her back. Honaunau's dark waters lapped beneath the running board, as Cate forced a few deep breaths, pulled down the mirror, and stole a quick glance north. Tears welled. Pure habit - searching for rainbows - ever since Livia read about the triple one that followed Hawaii's King Kamehameha III's death.

"Catie Pat," she'd say, "One morning, you'll see a rainbow over the sea, but we may have to visit the windward coast for that." Well, that was no longer a prerequisite. Each witnessed a tiny lovely arc this morning.

At the moment mountains were barely discernable let alone rainbows. The last sandpiper, which had been standing rigidly still, hopped along the highest flat rock then flew away. So dry was this past summer, that on many a fine evening, Lilinoe's towering mists failed to dress Hualalai's summits.

A huge wave crashed below. Cate's chin shot up, to the full drama of the distant shore. Stark and serene — no wonder the Ancients chose this as their Place of Refuge. She and Livia discovered it that first week in Kona. Actually, Livia insisted they come here. This shoreline was her best bet. She hissed, "Shoulda come here first!" Swift head shake and she calmed herself whispering, "No, any earlier and Livia would have stopped for supper — avoiding the late afternoon sun."

Her heart tighened and fluttered. "Anxiety attack!" her mind raced. "Breath!" and she inhaled. Till her nostrils burned sucked salt air, and she began scratching at an uneven chip of paint from the racing mirror, Cate noticed more stars blinking above the horizon. The cool mountain air sent the last tiny black crabs scampering, from the somber waves that lapped the rocks and asphalt. Lightly slapping her cheek, her eyes settled to their business and devoured the national park's every detail. Up front was Keoneele Cove, calm tidal pool and home of Honu, Great Green Sea Turtle (her aumakua, or guardian). Not 100 feet away, at the cove's near distant shore, rose two massive totems. Grimacing and flanked by the Mighty Pacific, they marked the ancient Pu'uhonua, ancient place of refuge, but no Livia.

The Laredo leaned as she pulled a sharp U-turn and parked adjacent the public boat launch. Sunset passed; the 911 call imminent. Ironically, it would be no lie to report Livia as missing the required twenty-four hours. Cell phone snatched, from the dash, she pressed ON. Familiar buzz– and she hit Speed Dial. Normally patient, she squirmed and gazed, from the cove across the large bay. To her right, a huge opal moon cleared the mountains, forcing her eyes along the crisp white breakers racing to the black north shore.

Bleep! The cell phone jolted, as she noticed movement above the white froth.

There, in the moonlight, stood Livia.

If her long bright hair had not fluttered, Cate may have turned away. She hit END quietly hissing, "Shit for service."

Her breaths came measured: "Four in, four out..." noticing Livia stare at Pu'uhonua.

Hopping over the running board, to the pavement, she puffed along. Again, the Speed Dial clicked — this time a call to Margaret, good friend and doctor in charge of Kona Hospital's Emergency Room.

Immediately connected, Cate quietly barked, "Margaret? It's me - down at Honaunau. No, no, not yet. I'm at the boat launch, and she's way across the bay. Yeah, she's on the north side. Hang on– I'm stumbling along trying to get up there. No, I'm not sure yet, but she seems fine. Soon as I get hold of her, we'll meet back at the inn. Oh? Herman's there to take your shift? Great– see you in a bit."

Three deaths in six years. She hit End and hurried along the rocky shore.

Livia's eyes searched the dark seascape. Deep draughts of salt air stung and brought visions of two little seniors. This morning brought sharp notice that she still grieved for her parents. She smirked and sighed, "Thanks, Aumakua," as if her mother nudged her shoulder to remind her: embrace the past but never dwell there.

She relived this morning's phone call from Indiana. Nurse Clara called, from Happy Hollow Full Care Center, after finding her aunt Pearl face-down in excrement. That detail Livia kept from Cate.

Though not realizing it early on, she sought this place all day. It proved strange refuge, even from across the bay. Lovely and powerful, the waves spewed beneath her - and beyond them lay the outer breakers and a barely discernible horizon. Early cartographers drew maps with loopy-tailed dragons out there. Sailors, plus fisherman, and an aviatrix with her navigator — all lost out there — but thank goodness not her father, Luke, back in WWII. Regarding both totems, Livia decided not to attend Pearl's funeral.

Her eyes glazed over, and as the warm rock pinched against her scuffed toes she wriggled them more forcefully and recalled this afternoon's drive across the Ka'u desert. Uplifting and yet, at the same time - it gave her the shivers. Nearly matching the stifling summers of her childhood, it stirred memories she both hated and craved. But now, in November, it could be colorful and cool along the Ohio River. Hopefully, both attributes soothed Pearl's last days; and if anyone did, that woman needed colorful days. Had Pearl noticed? Was she ever content?

She felt a twinge of sadness. Today's drive back from Hilo started out pleasant enough. Up through Puna, the highway climbed through lush pastures and cool Olaa Forest Reserve. That ended soon enough. Three miles further and the entrance to Volcanoes National Park also marked The Ka'u District's border.

Her mother's old red Cutlass Supreme purred along, between vast Pacific and high sloping desert; but in no time, the heat chased the car down the searing pavement. Like in that book: *A Walk Through Time*, where a man hiked the length of the Grand Canyon — while driving Annabelle's car, Livia felt time slipping away, and numbness soon turned to aloneness.

Then the car swayed but she dismissed it, as a none too rare tremor. Throttle nearly wide open, she whistled Sousa marches and drove on — one eye keen on Mauna Loa's distant horizon. It rose serenely to her right. Awesome steam vents clung to the tree line; and once, Livia mistook their wispy mists for low clouds. Hawaiians described this mountain, as *lilo* or *loa*, meaning long or distant — and it was.

Then Mauna Kea crept into her thoughts. Only thirty miles north, past Mauna Loa's distant horizon, slept the White Mountain. A good few feet taller than this one - it remained her first love. Her first glimpse, of the Big Island, was its snowy peak piercing the clouds. The very next night she and Cate got to the top of it and stood among its thirteen observatories watching the stars and Mauna Loa. Hardly a day passed she didn't think of the sunset, from up there - and hope her lost relatives, if they cared to, could see it through her eyes.

Both mountains filled the most gorgeous postcards, with their snowy peaks gleaming white above lush palm-lined beaches.

Sometime around 3:00, the heat and The Kau released her to Kona. Once again the highway wound through pastures and cool forest land. The few farm beasties and chatty birds made her feel closer to home and a great deal more peaceful. Although she planned to stop at the inn, she kept going — right on past Captain Cook down into Kailua town.

Her focus was on a couple tattoos. For years, she couldn't seem to shake the notion; and somehow, she knew today was the day. Parking near the King Kamehameha Hotel, she crossed the street at the Oceanview Tavern.

Deciding on a couple cold ones, she stepped in and chose a table near the ten-foot louvered windows. Kailua Bay's sultry breeze ruffled tourists' clothes, as they hustled off the pier and onto Ali`i Drive. Then, something caught her attention. There, opposite Hulihee Palace, pod people were yelling at something in the water. The orange tourist tender, en route to the mighty *Statendam*, reversed its engines, and its crowd of tourists rushed to its bow.

Livia stood for a better view, and sure enough, a lone swimmer pulled himself out of the water. On the bay's south tip of rock, he stood circling his fist in the air. She watched him scurry along the seawall to the harbor police hut. Minutes later, he stomped away shaking his head.

Another fifteen minutes and local boat traffic resumed, pulled up and docked appropriately, each having no problem with buoys or swim lanes. She hoped the no-boating rules were better enforced during the IRONMAN WORLD CHAMPIONSHIP triathalon, and many other swimming and canoeing races. Some outrigger canoes; although quite seaworthy, were hard to see if not brightly painted. What would happen when more cruise ships frequented this small port? Their diesel aroma was none too-friendly either.

Glancing down, she toyed with the tiny plastic pink monkey. Holding it to the light, she once again dropped it in the drink, sucking off liquor and nibbling pineapple from its front feet. Yes, indeedy — these frozen Mai Tais slid down way too easy.

Empty glass set down, Livia leaned back to watch the *Statendam* turn slowly toward Honolulu and the sunset, until four-long- **Pruuummmps!** nearly landed her on the floor.

This time, the offender was easy to spot. Enroute, to the *Paradise of Hawaii* - a diesel tender burst from the eyesore of Kialua's pier and crossed the *Statendam's* wake. Rules of operation governed the big ships, as they left port. So, why couldn't they have standard docking mechanisms? That way, each harbor could more effectively operate a small fleet of tourist tenders. Revenue and time schedules dictated most cruise ships fly foreign flags. Another Mai Tai and her thoughts flew to tall masts and pirate ships.

A shadow crossed the doorway as a fiery, petite red-head teetered in on four inch Spike-Me pumps. Drink in hand, she struck a pose against the bar and made eye contact. Livia made quick work of that. Glancing away, she tightened the black ribbon on her ponytail, slid a generous tip under the cocktail napkin, and made a beeline to the backdoor. She stood for a moment, exhaling sweet rum, before backtracking to the Big Island Tattoo parlor.

A couple pin-prickling hours later, plus a short hike to the parking lot, Livia headed uphill back toward Hōnaunau. Was it the cool breeze or green highlands? Oddly enough, her Greek and Polynesian fret tattoos pulsed with little pain. Halfway to the great bay, she stopped in Honalo, dashing into Shetima's for a box supper. No way would she end such a wild day without the island's best tempura and chocolate truffle pudding.

Ten miles further, she parked and walked along a short side street to Hōnaunau Bay. The waters glistened, and something about the Great Green Sea Turtles kept her to the front of the Great Wall. Behind it, back sat Hale o Keawehe on the platform of Puʻuhonua. She looked down again. The turtles were Cate's favorite. Many a delightful morning, she watched Honu feed. Livia often wondered which was more curious – turtle or people?

Whew! If Cate could have just seen that! One plump juvenille surfaced and stretched its neck, before quickly turning and flapping 100 yards to the wave-buffeted totems. How slow they were when beached; yet underwater they flew along – kinda like Cate on the ice. Her focus shifted. Long ranks of waves marched along side her to the north shore. From that more comfortable vantage point, she gazed past the totems at Puʻuhonua.

"Sunset and evening bell, and one clear call for me..." A bracing wind struck her, from behind, followed by two beams of light streaming into the water.

Oh Geez, she promised to be home by now.

The sea spray danced in the headlights. Not that searing blue halogen, but she still could not see past them till a warm hand found her shoulder.

"Thank God you're Okay," Cate whispered.

Livia dipped her chin and looked up. "Glad you're here."

Cate hugged her. "Me, too."

A few hard sighs and she leaned her shoulder into Livia's. "Do you have any idea – how worried we were? All afternoon, I drove up and down these damn coast roads looking for you."

The grasp on her wrist never loosened, as they climbed the rocks and cut past brush to the road. The first hundred steps, Livia's eyes never left Cate's denim patch pockets.

Once on the pavement, Cate turned and offered full condolences. "I am so sorry your Aunt Pearl died." Popping the Laredo's lift gate, she handed Livia a tiny bag. She reached in and gummed a few Hershey's Kisses, as Cate waited patiently and suggested they return for the Cutlass in the morning.

Gently poking the asphalt with the toe of her tennis shoe, Cate gasped and took Livia's hands in hers. Turning them in the headlights, she said, "Nice designs – didn't think you'd ever do it. You've wanted those for years. Are they what you expected? Good Heavens – your hands are freezing! Let's get you in the car."

Cate searched the backseat for Livia's red denim jacket, before draping it across her shoulders. "Aren't your tiny knit gloves there in the pockets?"

All she got was a shrug.

Livia didn't mean to be rude. She said, "Thanks for the candy. I did have a quick supper, from Shetima's. Guess it's been a few hours since I ate. Can't we sit here, for just a few more minutes?"

"No. Margaret is meeting us at the inn."

Engine started, Cate adjusted the mirror and caught sight of Hualalai in the moonlight. "Wow, almost what we saw from Mauna Kea." The breeze caught them again, and their eyes rose to the magnificent sky.

A quiet tap came on Cate's shoulder.

Cate said, "Yeah, I know. Glad you're here."

Livia grabbed her hair, from a harsh gust of wind. She grinned a little. "La'amaomao – the Wind Goddess. I read that she guides people on their journeys – guess it's time to scurry on home."

Cate snorted lightly and mumbled, "Yeah, some are harder to prod along than others." Flipping on the radio and hummed to the country music. Glancing over, and noticing Livia's wrinkled nose, she teased, "Okay, Miss Lilo - when we get home, you can lie on the floor and play your old Elvis 'Blue Hawaii' tunes."

That garnered no comment, and Cate kept driving.

Country music never had been Livia's taste, but she tolerated it when riding with Cate – well, except Bluegrass. She didn't mind ballads, except that last song – something about somebody left somebody in Kentucky - and her eyes glazed over. She favored rock; however, rap usually bothered her, if it reminded her of students interrupting with too chatty classmates. "Stop it," she told herself – attempting to contain her rambling thoughts.

"What?"

Livia countered, "Sorry. I'm just talking to myself. My brain's going full tilt."

Chapter 2: Caregiver

Pearl's passing came as a bare a blip, on the radar screen, of the recent past. Livia figured she had finished mourning her parents' deaths - till today.

First person she ever watched die was her father. Not quite eight years ago, she leaned across Luke's metal gurney – sad but honored to share his last thoughts. She started to remember his last smiles but Parkinson's disease had all but wiped clean his expressions - even ruder, every breath and bodily function demanded nearly all his attention. She could still see his brown eyes flit along the ER curtain divider, following shapes and shadows down the hall. Perpetually preoccupied with the weather, his last words came: "It's snowing. Can you and Mother get home Okay?"

She rubbed his shoulder and whispered, "Yes – it's melting..." and his eyes slid finally shut.

The nurse strode off, to the waiting room, and returned with her mother. For Annabelle's sake, Livia struggled to keep her wits about her, as they waited for the doctor. She couldn't help wonder if Pope John Paul received that new stem-cell therapy. His Parkinson's seemed harsher. How could he have survived without it? Various drug trials helped younger patients.

That evening, Cate did not let her out of sight. She phoned her mother with the news. Afterwards she set a couple beers on the table, and toasted, "Here's to Papa Piglet. A gentleman always knows when to leave the party."

And party they did. In Luke's honor, Livia and Annabelle spent ten magical days in Disney World. The next June, she and her mother toured Honolulu and Oahu, with Cate in tow — and so began their Hawaiian Odyssey.

Three years later came her mother's small strokes. The Saturday after Thanksgiving, Cate left town for a hockey tournament. Something told Livia to walk across the street once more, to check on Annabelle, after dinner. She found her mother slumped over, with her arms caught in her nightgown. Couple weeks later, like when Luke's illness worsened, Livia received another pink slip. Too odd for random occurrence, but she was thankful it allowed for her to care for Annabelle too. Livia kept sane by writing and constantly gardening. She sold her roses and fresh lavender to two fruit markets within walking distance on Monroe Avenue.

Fall came, and Annabelle had great fun with the Halloween trick-or-treaters. The next afternoon, she showed little interest in the Brave's double header with the Cubs. Once more something told Livia to check-in on her. No one answered the door, and she found her mumbling slightly and one eye a tad off-kilter. A hockey orphan once more – Livia phoned Cate's mother, Demi. From previous experience they knew EMS could not administer Heparin, so they drove Annabelle across Detroit to Thomas Fairmont Hospital. Its ER service was top notch, and they sat up all night.

Medication helped Annabelle rally, for a whole year, until she began rubbing her arms and no ointment soothed the itchy skin. Nor did any prescription ease it, so Livia's doctor ordered a quick CAT scan. Breast cancer had metastasized to her liver.

In and out of the hospital made for dreary days, as did driving Detroit's freeways in the snow. Armed with a cancer cocktail consisting of Reglan, Darvocet-N, Xanax, and occasionally a host of other drugs – plucky little Annabelle rallied a bit, came home, and held her own throughout the spring.

One month before her eighty-eighth birthday, they decided to invoke Annabelle's old Living Will that Luke had written in Indiana. Though Michigan rarely recognized such wills, Livia had little problem enforcing his legal handiwork. She may have to change an IV bag, or two, but Annabelle would not die in a hospital as Luke had. Hospice papers were signed, and almost daily Mother and Daughter jokingly planned their escape to Hawai`i.

Then came that first deer-in-the-headlights stare. Cate checked in before and after work and coached Livia through many a day and dreaded night. At sunset, Livia crept from room to room adjusting the lights. TV, medicine, then a few hours rest. That plaintive mew, from the adjoining bedroom, meant only one thing: their little two-step-to-the-bathroom and Annabelle's heady whisper: "Quit leading!"

At first, Livia wished it would end. Then she wished for anything: a snore, a cough, an IV bag to change – anything.

Those last few mornings, Livia stared at the ceiling till sunrise. Listening for sounds, which once would have brought aggravation, would now bring strange comfort. Nights passed as days, and days passed as years, but the old, tired teacher hung on. She had one more lesson to teach. Real courage meant getting up each morning to a battle you'd never win.

Annabelle's tiny heart faltered again, and Livia chose not to resuscitate. Hospice guaranteed no explanations to the police. After a day of nods and eye signals, Annabelle waited all night to see her last dawn.

Livia woke to a strange quiet. It took all her life force to peek through the bedroom door and see a soul lingering in a worn body.

She tiptoed across the carpet, to the porch door, opened it – and then followed the sunlight to the bed. Sitting in her mother's tiny sewing rocker, she kissed Annabelle on the forehead and murmured, "Go free." Immediately, a warm and peaceful June morning pervaded the tiny yellow bedroom - so unlike her that snowy day with her father.

The Laredo bumped over the cinder shoulder, as Cate turned north on the highway.

Livia exhaled. Sucking a huge breath she said, "Three deaths in ten years." She turned to Cate. "When I go, I want ashes. Pour 'em in an old purse, and shake 'em out, along the road at Pleasant Hill, Kentucky. Then, with your best softball arm, pitch the purse in the nearest trash container and go party. If you set me on the mantle, I will haunt you."

They chuckled. What really worried Livia was - what if Cate outlived her? Although eight years younger, she already had plenty of sick and dependent relatives; and once upon a time, their little princess depended on their good intentions. Not so much any more – Livia steeled Cate for that.

Hands dangled in front of her, she compared two sets of wide black tattoo lines. One set bordered a row of solid triangles, the other a row of Greek keys. "Kind of picky – but lots less painful than I anticipated. Do ya like 'em?"

Cate pulled left on the inn's lane and pointed. "See there - Margaret's already home."

Before Cate could answer, Livia's whipped her head around, sending her hair swirling behind her shoulders. Quickly braiding it, she snapped a clear band around the ends, before looking up.

Odd. Margaret left work this early, from her afternoon hospital shift. Six months ago, with renovations complete and the La 'Ohana Inn incorporated, she began attending her new position as head of Kealakekua Hospital's Emergency Services. After the recent hospital restructuring, she designed a critical care unit, to stabilize patients, and for transfer to Honolulu. In Metro Detroit, a much-loved pediatric oncology practice sapped her energy. Small town ER hours provided time for volunteer work and recreation.

Livia pressed the car door shut, and turned directly into Margaret's bear hug.

"Hey there, Kiddo - you Okay?" she asked.

Kiddo? That always struck her as funny, since she was fourteen years Margaret's senior, but she hugged back and said, "Yeah, pretty much. It's been quite the day." She chuckled. "Maybe now, I'm released from the past."

Margaret nodded with a hearty chuckle. "No answer is ever in a nutshell with you, is it, Livy?"

They walked to the inn's main lanai. Miss Lotus Blossom bounced alongside, before impatiently running past them and trotting up the wide steps between four, huge, koa wood pillars. The perky flop-eared Sharpei had become Cate's ward, since August, when The Ma (Cate's Granny Alexia) gave up her way too big lapdog. Lotus' cute little waddle and stumpy tail made Livia chirp, "Duck butt, duck butt"

Quickly turning, Lotus playfully nipped at Livia before nuzzling Cate's knee.

Scratching the dog's ear, Cate purred, "Aw – Lotus is a good girl! Good girl, Miss Lotus." Raising the dog's chin she measured her words. "Now settle down. It's Okay – we're home now."

Hawaii suited the young dog well, and with the daily hubbub of guests she grew more social and a bit calmer. Livia watched her snooze with paws in the air. Hard to believe this was the same bad girl who worried her squeaky toy and chewed furniture legs for Cate's grandparents. Still, there was a wee bit of pluck left in her. Yesterday, she made quick work of Margaret's clockwork mouse. They came three to a package, and the other two got delivered down the road to Mrs. Hathaway's cat.

With everyone home, Lotus slept hard and her mouth started working.

Livia looked down. "Aw, look - she's sucking on her ninny-bottle." She rubbed her weepy eyes and some dirt from her nose and mouth. "Miss Lola! You got a dirty puss - better not be digging again and tearing up my garden."

That brought the dog up, and Livia rubbed her stubby velvet ears. Cate jingled car keys, and Lotus pranced out the door and followed her to the car. Momentarily, a little head peered out the passenger window as her mistress pulled the SUV around to the carport.

Livia walked, to the more private side lanai, where she and the grand Polynesia stood eye to eye. The white-crested bird teetered on her perch chatting, in Margaret's mellow voice, "Hey there Kiddo. You Okay?"

Livia laid her little flat nose against the bars and piccolo puffed the bird's flight feathers. "I'm fine, Ms. Polynesia. Were you a good birdie today?"

The bird clucked and pranced back and forth - repeating, "No way! I'm a ba-ad bird…"

"Hey Livy," Margaret's smooth tenor caused the bird to stand still, as The Good Doctor rubbed Livia's shoulders saying, "Wait here. I'll be quick like a bunny and run upstairs to change my clothes."

Cate's head poked out the pantry door. "I still hear two silly cuckoos, no – make that three, clucking out here."

A noisy raspberry accompanied Margaret's throat clearing and a rare screech, as Polynesia cocked her head over-and-over, and eyed all three. Finally, after much pacing and head dipping, she climbed to her highest perch.

Cate leered over her tiny eyeglasses. "Livia, please– get in here, before I have to come out there. You — my dear — need to eat."

Livia followed and helped prepare dinner, then she noticed the light blinking on the private phone. Livia exchanged the phone, for a stack of dishes, and Cate returned the call from her mother.

Livia slipped out the door again, not anxious to overhear the litany of "You know you shoulds."

With the remote phone neatly tucked under her chin, Cate leaned out the screen door and waved Livia to the table. Another minute and she hung up. "Couldn't get my mom calmed down, from complaining about The Ma and Daddy. She still can't accept the fact that now– she's the Parent. Seems my grandparents put a hefty down payment on some horrid little house. Do you remember that eighty-year-old mess on Marconi Street? It's only two blocks over from Mom's; but she's so bossy, they refused to let her pack any of their stuff, to move back to the old house on Renee Street. Now, she thinks she's gotta move too, cuz they can't be that far way."

Cate sat hard and exhaled. "Finally – I got a word in edgewise and told her about your aunt. She piped down and said she's very sorry and will call back later. You know, they'll go to church tomorrow and probably light a candle."

Quite used to Mother Demi's ways, Livia nodded. Counting the moths, on the window, a slight motion near the two lanais' connecting corner post caught her attention. The porch swing wobbled matching the light flutter of newspaper, which a guest must have left on it. Its pup tent shape brought visions of Luke's rare Sunday nap. When she was a kid, he would read the paper; and usually, it fell across him as he snoozed. The summer hotter, the swing finer, and the porch taller where she grew up. Williamstown was quaint but all her high school buddies moved away – just like every other MEGA-MART towns back in the Midwest.

The cool breeze still rustled the paper, and she wondered if anyone checked the mailbox today. The old front desk phone clacked hard, in its cradle, as Livia called out, "Did anyone get the mail?"

Cate answered, "I don't think so, but dinner *is* nearly ready."

Already turning back, Livia yelled, "Be there in a second!"

A faint buzz followed her across the main lanai. One hand slid down the cool stair rail to the wide steps, and her vision tunneled. She gripped the rail in quiet desperation. Slowly, her fingers loosened, her legs buckled, and she tumbled forward.

From the upstairs hallway, Margaret flew down main staircase motioning for Cate to follow.

Livia's eyes fluttered, then she noticed she was sitting on the ground. *Oh - Shit – I'll never hear the last of this.*

Cate knelt, one knee at Livia's back. "Awe, Little Miss, what are we going to do with you?"

To Livia's front, Margaret hovered and worked herself around to the side. From the pocket of her old navy cardigan, she pulled out a Hershey Bar, carefully unwrapping it and placing a thin piece on Livia's tongue.

As her field of vision widened, Livia felt a burst of heat, and her well-meaning helpers seemed nearly in her lap. "Excuse me! I don't mean to fuss but give me some room to breathe."

Margaret stood. "She'll be fine. Let's go eat."

Cate nodded toward the ground, and Margaret stopped short. One under each shoulder, they steadied Livia, as Cate spat out, "You're damn lucky you didn't break your fool neck."

Livia's hand pulled at the seat of her shorts. Her nose wrinkled, and her other hand pulled free. With pinky raised, she gave the tip-up signal for a beer.

Cate laughed. "Yeah, right!" Slipping Livia into a kitchen chair, she chided, "Behave yourself, and eat some dinner. Whatta ya trying to do – beat The Ma's record for stumbling down the stairs?"

Ignored, for a minute, Livia gave no protest. Scooting up to the huge table, she piped up once more. "What's the deal? Do both of you follow me around with chocolate bars in your pockets? It gets a tad messy – doesn't it – in this heat?"

Cate cocked her head. "Yup, there's a stash upstairs and down, in the cars – no, actually, there are pudding cups under my car seat."

Soup simmered and Cate trotted out for the mail.

Facing Livia, Margaret sat smirking and sipping her tea.

Not in the mood to chat, Livia was hungry. Figuring it best to be sociable, she downed a small glass of iced water before exhaling into her coffee mug. The sweet waft of jasmine lingered till she finally poured it over a tall glass of ice. Snapping open a huge bag of Maui Sweet Potato Chips, she watched Margaret rise and climb the kitchen stairs, probably to change to cooler clothes.

Hand sliding down the banister, Margaret met Cate at the stove. Teapot quieted, they dipped out ladles of Livia's leftover vegetable soup. "Here, Little Miss. Start on this. Margaret will divvy up the turkey antipasto sandwich, and I want you to eat a good portion of it."

Listening to Cate hum, "After Midnight," Livia recalled Patsy Cline's calm unique voice and realized how many tea bags Cate dug through, to locate her Fujian Jasmine tea. True coffee lover, Livia brewed hearty diesel fuel, for breakfast only. Pulling herself tall, she relished each mouthful of the delicate pale tea, and fixated on Margaret's sandwich plate. It did not do her much justice to diet, with the sandwich plate's wide edges crammed full of ripe fruit, sweet gherkins, black olives and potatoe chips

Cate hunkered down to much of the same; whereas, Livia's stared up at her, as Lotus leaned hot and hard against her knee for food and an ear rub.

"Lola, Lola, Lola– Didn't Your Miss Catie Pat give you any treats?"

Lotus nibbled meat tidbits as Livia pecked at her chips. Eyes on Cate, she finished her sandwich and never flinched, while Margaret knelt, gingerly raised her blouse and fingered each and every rib along the red marks. Noticing that a bruise had begun to surface, she rose quickly and made an ice pack. A thick kitchen towel covered that, and she wedged it between chair arm and Livia's skin.

Now Livia winced. The searing cold made her realize the force her ribs must have hit the steps. Both women sat quietly till she said, "Yeah, I know. I'd best calm down, or I'll have my father's ulcers."

Cate grimaced then added, "Hate to tell you, but Miss Lotus dumped your little Kuan Yin statue. Only a small dent; good thing it was bronze and not glass."

Livia merely rolled her eyes and shrugged thinking that good old Kuan Yin would forgive Lola for a few hard lumps.

Cate selected a box from the cupboard. Livia barely heard her mutter, "Oh, Lotus – what would you do without your doggie cookies?" As if all three supper plates fell to the floor, Baby Girl high-stepped it for the postman-shaped treats. After doing the little pounce and bounce act, Lotus gummed her treats and rolled over for a tummy rub.

Cate cooed, "You are too much, you know that?" Glancing at with matching smirks, she added, "You got us all trained pretty good."

Livia picked out the peas and sipped another half-bowl of soup. As she reached for more chips, Polynesia chimed-in for her half-a-cookie.

Margaret answered. "Are you a ba-ad bird? Don't look away; I know you've been eavesdropping."

"Ye–es, Me, too," crooned Polynesia. Margaret slipped the pesky bird a cookie then hefted her briefcase with laptop to her thighs. Strong fingers ruffled her short sandy hair and she sighed, as the sweet mountain air rung Cate's tall bamboo wind chimes. Their deep woody notes lingered in the warm kitchen.

Livia was glad their property was free of those irritating little coqui frogs. By now, they could have covered this area. She wondered if the coffee farmers spread citric acid, hot water, or installed short PVC pipe to keep them at bay. Maybe there was some predator or lack of the coqui's favorite food. Tomorrow, she'd look it up on her bookmarked state website.

Cate hopped to her feet, for pickles and cookies. Once in the pantry, she motioned for Margaret to follow. Hanging up her car keys, Cate whispered, "For a while, keep an eye on her, Okay? You know depression runs in Luke's family." Margaret nodded heading back to the table with a bag of ginger snaps.

Grabbing kosher dills and double chocolate Cremeos she ran back and plunked the pickles in front of Livia. She grinned, "Crunchy for you, sweet for me."

Livia muttered, "Right. Thanks. Did you have a nice little talk with Margaret?" Knowing her friends, she stared at her plate not even wondering what she missed.

"Well, yeah – that too." Cate offered cookies. Turned down, she added, "Good choice, but you never eat sandwiches without pickles and chips."

"That's right — make light of your conniving at my expense. Livia worked it drawling, "Anyway, hup, hup! I want carrots, too –"

Cate bantered back. "Yas'am – Miss Livy! I'll just be a gettin'em! Now, don't you worry." Long arms reached back grabbing the refrigerator door handle. One grand swipe and she plunked baby carrots on the table.

Margaret sat hard. They munched and crunched until Livia broke the silence chomping ice.

Slowly, Cate reached across the table and gently lowered Livia's hand and iced tea glass. "Please, stop. You know how that bothers me. Shoulda stopped that a long time ago; one of these days, you're gonna crack all your teeth."

Margaret's pursed lips thinned as she swallowed. Tongue poked hard in her cheek, as her eyes tracked from Cate to Livia and back again.

Livia yanked back Cate's hand — hissed, "Stop that!" and kept chomping. Margaret's tongue clucked, but she covered her mouth after getting the melt-steel stare. Again Livia focused on Cate. "I've not broken any teeth, in forty some years, and I'm just fine. Just because your teeth are soft is no reason I can't enjoy some ice."

Margaret sniggered, and that made Livia review her choice of words. When she was little, her mother had coached her - not to drawl out "ice."

Cate bit her lips and kept playing with her fork. "Do you care to mean frozen water, drugs, or someone's derrière?"

Livia spit back, "Whatever!"

Quick came Cate's reply: "Whatever? That's my line!" She cleared the dishes and quietly stated, "You know; we are very concerned about you – Little Miss, so just deal with it."

That made Livia feel better. Cate's best traits surfaced when someone needed coddling, but, oh boy — could she turn edgy when prodded or pushed. Either way, she proved quite the mother hen.

A set of flat thuds near the base of the kitchen door broke the silence. Pinkie must have scooted down from his tall perch. That big whap of rough tail especially resounded on the screen door.

In a wink, all foot-and-a-half of Green Iguana cozied-up to Livia's leg. His hefty tail gently slapped the floor near her ankle. She trained him to do that when he wanted to be petted. It was that, or he might pounce on her lap. His hard claws gleamed razor-like. Only once had he accidentally sliced her flesh, and that was right through her cotton Aloha shorts.

She reached down and stroked his head. His great eyelids slowly slid shut - until she laid a turkey morsel before him. To no one's surprise, Lola sprang to attention. Pinkie's throat rippled as the turkey traveled south. Treats didn't come often, and turkey was his favorite; although, guests often commented that the house was nearly insect-free. Back and forth his tail swatted making sure Lotus kept her distance. Both pets merely tolerated each other. At a safer distance, she gingerly chewed another cookie.

Strangely enough, from their very first meeting, Pinkie tolerated Old Woofer (Livia's wiry Dachshund and Cairn Terrier mix). The dog had been Luke and Annabelle's best buddy, and at age sixteen, Livia got him through quarantine and flew him to Hawaii.

Though most house cats knocked Woofer for a loop, Luke deemed his little buddy "Tenacious Terrier," after receiving a nasty nip. The wily little poot was Annabelle's faithful sentry; and in the end – a stroke felled him one year after her death. Just like her, he survived another year. His last few days, Livia carried him around in his pet bed, till one morning, she woke — and he was curled, silently, at the side of her bed.

In Hawaii, the dog had another caretaker. The full-grown iguana, Pinkie, arrived via quite an unusual route. After Annabelle's death, Livia escaped for a couple weeks, backpacking on Maui's south side. She couldn't leave her precious pooch, so she toted him there too.

During a late morning stroll, she set him down and something triggered an unusual spark of energy. He dashed off, on what Livia assumed was a vermin hunt. Seconds later, his excellent sniffer located Pinkie.

The huge iguana glowed bright green in the midday sun, as he basked on a rare hot rock at the edge of North Hana's rain forest.

Iguanas not being indigenous to the islands, this one seemed quite content. Livia packed him off and spent her last few vacation days anguishing about returning her Pinkie to the wild.

Considering Hawaii's strict quarantine laws, her anguish was not misplaced. Obviously, she was someone's turned-out pet. The day before sailing for Kona, Livia overheard a couple Wailua fishermen planning their trip across the Alenuihana Channel to The Big Island's Kawaihae port. The lady with the cute old terrier sided up to them, and soon the men were bamboozled into carrying Miss Pinkie to the Big Island.

It worked. For a 100 dollars, they promised to stow the iguana, by tying her under scraps destined for fishmeal. Pinkie arrived safely. To Livia's surprise, she became Woofer's steadfast buddy. The nice young lady vet sent off a routine blood test and informed her that Pinkie was all male. Still yet, he mothered Old Woofer through every last infirmity.

The iguana somehow sensed the dog's dire predicament. When he lay hot and panting, Pinkie would waddle to the garden and slither into the inn's re-circulating pool. Temperature lowered, he returned and curled around Woofer soothing his feverish little body. Each time the tenacious terrier would rouse - poor Pinkie would be off to some rock, in the sun, to warm his bones.

"Hello? You still with us?" teased Cate.

Livia blushed. "Yeah, just having fond thoughts of Woofer and Pinkie. Too bad he and Lola don't get along so well."

Cate stretched. "There's really no need. Neither is out and about, at the same time of day. You must admit that Lotus Blossom pesters Pinkie a lot more than Woof ever did - especially at the end." Blinking a watery eye, she sighed. "It's not the same without Old Pooey Schnitz. I can still see our little Woofen Meister leading your dad – with his hand in the air, crossing the street 'Doing the Luke'."

She had not heard that phrase in a while, and squarely convinced Cate's German was slipping, Livia patted her shoulder and said, "What a mush! You'd love a bucket of mud if it had ears and a tail."

"Don't you call my baby girl – dirty!"

"Well, I'm not. We were talking about Woofer. Anyway, Your Miss Lotus gets never dirty - can't stay still long enough, for any dust to settle."

Lotus scampered off and silence prevailed.

Margaret licked her fingers purring, "Um-um! These Tropical Blonde Brownies sure are yummy." Leaning closer to Cate she added, "Be sure to add another batch in next week's baking schedule."

"I didn't even know I had one. Where'd you find it?"

Margaret grimaced, and then a half-assed grin surfaced. "Bottom of my briefcase." She chuckled sheepishly and continued, "One of my OR nurses – in Chicago – good person and a tiny dynamo, but, oh – what an Archie Bunker mouth she had. I found many a tasty mint cream cookie, because she packed the tasty little morsels in all her lunches. After munching two, she would lick each finger, lean her head back while exhaling a lusty, 'Ahh - almost organic.' Anyway, she was very good about sharing."

Livia and Cate's jaws slacked.

Reaching for another, Margaret glanced to the kitchen. "Oh, Livy, could you grace this tasty little morsel with one of your Mighty Mai Tais?" Eyebrows raised, she added, "Frozen ones would be nice."

That sparked Livia. Most Hoosiers, from way south of Indianapolis, spoke with a decidedly Kentucky twang - so she could appreciate Margaret's down eastern accent.

Drumming her fingers, she prodded, "'Organic?' After a few Chivas Regals, with Rector Ben, my St. Seaton's Principal winced and exhaled such cookies 'Almost Orgasmic'."

"Did your OR cohorts nickname you Doctor Lush? It's got to be nearly eight hours, till your next shift, or you wouldn't ask for another glass of my rocket fuel." Amused, with her own Kitchen Chemistry, she thought of her experiments with various fruity Margaritas with Triple Sec or Grand Marnier; in as much as, she always fell back her favorite one laced with Key Limes and Cointreau.

Cate sipped the last of brown goop and nodded at the cocktail glass.

"Fine; I'll make a batch of each. Anyway, both drinks freeze nicely."

Cate chuckled, "Sure shoulda with all you put in them."

Livia continued, "Do you remember Coach Guy finding Mina's first hockey recruitment poster? Said something like, 'Experience not required but must have good taste and a serious sense of humor?' She didn't drink, but quickly ordered those hot pink t-shirts with the logo: 'My drinking team has a hockey problem'."

Margaret gave her usual excuse: that it must have happened before her time.

Livia gave and open mouthed nod as Cate cleared the kitchen island and commented how much Coach hated their old pink jerseys and bought up nearly all those pink t-shirts.

Livia shook her head and set up her drink mixes. Handing Margaret a fresh Margarita, she split a Mai Tai with Cate. Captain Spice's Dark Rum, mixed with fresh pureed pineapple, lime juice, and a dash of Grenadine brought up both heads with lips smacking.

Refilling the glasses, she wiped down the blender and offered a toast: "To everyone we've loved, and to all those we will!"

"To the kitchen chemist," chirped Cate, with her drink held high.

Livia's ear met her shoulder. A long shrug and she purred "Just practicing. How about this one? 'A woman's gotta live in an atmosphere that crackles with sexual tension'."

"Oh, boy, sounds like another Daisy quote. I always preferred her – especially when she worried so and said, 'Oh– our Hyacinth wouldn't…'"

Margaret snorted, "What is that from – your British soaps?"

Livia tossed back a jigger of nearly frozen rum and continued sipping her fluffy drink. Licking the rim, she realized how much she appreciated their laughter. Holding another jigger high she said, "Feels good. Here's to the stuff– which just might have improved Pearl's humor. "

"Here's to Pearl," toasted Cate.

Livia tossed back the final icy jigger, and with a snort and hard wince barely swallowed the syrupy liquid. Smacking her lips, she watched Margaret glance to Cate and back. Privy to a few of Livia's problems, regarding Pearl's legal affairs, Margaret licked her lips too and matched Cate's toast.

Each merry clink brought sighs and hums.

Livia peered into her empty glass and asked if anyone wanted one more round.

Nodding no, Margaret leaned forward and patted Cate and Livia's knees, adding a slurred, "Love another sip, but better not." Munching cashews and almonds, she scratched Lotus under the chin and asked, "Aye, Livy– didn't you say you had a cat?"

"Yep– still do, in the attic. What for?"

"Oh, this ought to be good," Cate murmured as she sipped some water.

Margaret's head cocked to the side and her face was the picture of puzzlement, as Livia continued. "It was my Father's; very similar to the one that he slept on, on Tinian Island. He always used to say, 'Last year of The Great War – my back never felt better'."

Cate sat up, as Margaret's hands flew up. "Whoa! Nellies! Let's start again. What kind of cat was that?"

Searching for a meaningful answer Livia gestured, "Well – it's about yay-big and made of hardwood, with sturdy canvas stretched between…" Faced with two-sets of unrelenting eyes, her drawl slipped a bit. "You know. Take a hammer handle and slide it in, and the canvass tightens…"

Cate's eyes rolled to Margaret's. "I love it! A couple good drinks– and we've got another Miss Liza Doolittle here."

Undeterred, Livia explained. "I see. Well, most of your Bostonian accent got lost in Detroit."

Cate grit her teeth and hissed her worst feline, "'Kät," but got no response. "Livia thought you said 'cot'. Southern accent or Down Eastern – at first, I found it hard to understand either one of you." Another deep swig and she wrapped it up. "Actually, it's not so bad anymore; my brain translates everything automatically." She almost choked then blew her breath. "Good heavens, that's a mouthful."

Margaret chuckled, adding a tart and guttural, "Meow– `Kat!"

All three women made hissy noises, as they raked their fingernails in the air and laughed.

Livia had owned cats: eight in all. Lady ran off; Beast got feline leukemia but lasted pretty long; Tom Tinker got shot right after Little One ran off; the next two also died a slow death of leukemia, and the last two – Siamese litter mates – didn't survive the move to Michigan: Gung ran off, and Ho got run over. But after one roommate's deaf albino cat ruined her favorite love seat and matching antique chair, she said enough and only kept dogs.

It was her second cat that stole her heart. Neither Cate nor Margaret knew about him, so she explained, "My first Siamese owned me all through high school and the first year of college. Baast's Pharaoh was his registered name. I wanted 'Pyewacket' but Luke took him to the veterinarian, and he said they already had three named that. Well, Annabelle immediately dubbed him 'Beast' but I started calling him Beastie-Pye, and that's what stuck. I never saw my father so content, as with that cat in his lap. He followed me every trip to the corner meat market — then he'd sit there and wait, just like a dog.

"Yup, Beast even got free vacations. My high school band director borrowed him, so his family could get a little rest when their Sheherizad came in heat. Our neighbors called him the pride of the neighborhood pride. "

Margaret's fingers slowly stroked the couch arm, as she checked the details of tomorrow's surgeries in Honolulu. That finished, she was off to her nightly refrigerator raid. After she re-filled Polynesia's sippy cup, with cool filtered water, Margaret drained her cup of milk and said good night. "Tomorrow's a long day; I'm headed upstairs. Good thing Livy insisted I keep my long johns. They'll feel mighty good tonight."

Another half hour found Livia and Cate kibitzing about who'd throw Pinkie out. Matter resolved; Lola followed too. Gathering a few old hockey towels from the pantry, Livia climbed the lanai stairs and placed them in the reptile's flat wide perch. "He'll burrow into these and be out in no time."

Fond of anything high and green, Livia retained some of Annabelle's arty-fartiness and transformed the inside wall of the side porch into Pinkie's Paradise. Above an ethereal forest mural, she bolted a huge tree branch. It lined the back staircase all the way up to a good-sized ceiling perch. Good guess. Pinkie loved it.

After a few minutes of listening for Mr. Hooty, Polynesia's white owl suitor, Livia headed up. Cate always warned her that it was not always good, to sit in the night air, so she picked up the TV channel listings on her way to the great room. To her surprise, Cate peered over the top banister.

"Glad you came in. The evening air won't do your back any good."

Livia's insomnia kept the TV out of the bedroom. Televised sports might put her to sleep; but she had always preferred to play than watch them – except for lower bowl seats at the Red Wings. Damn, she meant to remind Cate about those Canuck tickets.

All winter, Cate signed onto Hockeytown.com. She and Margaret shared the expense of a bi-weekly care package of Red Wings videos, via their previous coach. Sometimes its shipment backlogged to three weeks to arrive; but whatever the time-frame, new videos spurred a beer and pizza or popcorn evening. Oh, well– anyway, that was for them not her.

Fifteen minutes later, Livia still gazed at the ceiling. From the sports homepage she caught an ad for a new theme park compared to Disney World. It was to have a military flair featuring parachuting and paintball-like weapon courses. Her stomach hurt, and she forced away visions of arsenals and bombs, till something rattled in her head about the article in last Sunday's Hilo *Hawaii Tribune Herald* – concerning the long awaited University Of Hawaii campus in Kona. There would be few boundaries, for Cate, had she finished college.

She heard Cate's house slippers softly padding across koa boards, down the hall to the bathroom. Stopping momentarily, she offered her own brand of good-night: "Now - Livia, don't you stay up too late." Glass of water in hand, Cate made off to bed, with Lotus close behind.

Livia waited a couple minutes and headed downstairs. She punched the remote up and down the major channels, searching for politics. Most the Mid East was a still a mess. She was saddened that she missed her chance to visit Egypt, right before President Nasser was shot. But her parents had asked her not to go. She was only a sophomore then; and now, she was pretty for sure there have to be trips, other than to pyramids. Never forgotten was the black and white photo she found as child – Grandmother Etter astride a camel near the Sphinx. In the summer 1978, Livia viewed King Tut's solid gold funeral mask, at Chicago's Field Museum - and suspected the British Museum might be the closest she would ever get, to the rest of Egypt's antiquities.

Way before Indiana Jones, archeology had been her passion. Enough of this daydreaming! Before any trip, they needed responsible help at the inn.

A weather advisory blipped across the TV screen. Dwarfed by the Honolulu forecast, the Big Island took only the last sentence. Today was Kona's coldest day in sixty-two years.

Her eyelids drooped, and she flicked off the news. Adjusting each night light, she crept through the service pantry. Hesitating on the stair landing, she noticed Margaret's bedroom light across the hall floor.

Livia always turned in last, got up first, and made a habit of checking everything. Cate slept cold after kicking off sheets, and quite often Margaret dozed off at her desk. Livia tucked them in, wondering if her habits bordered on the neurotic.

Paper cup in hand, she bared her teeth as she stared in the mirror. Not bad for forty-five. The warm washcloth soothed her face, as she roughly scrubbed her supple skin. Dabbing a dot of Vitamin E on a few fine wrinkles and age spots, she marveled at her wide brown eyes. Did they resemble the eyes of her Ani'Yun'wiga, her Cherokee great-great-great-grandmother, Barbara Burrell? She'd read stories about Laredo, or Real People, plus ones about Waikiki's fair-haired ehu, such as Leilehua who was gifted to Kamehameha I, but reclaimed by Oahu's Hakuole. She wondered - did she bear any resemblance to either?

Sliding open the linen closet door she set a wooden chest on the counter. Smoothing her long, braided hair Livia added another clear band, took scissors and cut it low on the nape. Hair loose about her shoulders, she wiped the marble vanity top, tossed the braid in an old purse, before replacing the chest and turning off the light.

Cate and Margaret slept easy, and Livia envied them for it. Cate slept hard with good reason. She grew up in a household with various work schedules. As for Margaret, quick sleep equaled survival for attendance to any medical practice.

Livia tiptoed to Margaret's study and flicked off the desk light. Continuing down the hall to Cate's room, she covered her with the quilt that had fallen to the floor. Good thing Cate was a solid sleeper, for Lotus lay snuggled across her chest. Cate often teased she laid so close she was making her into an Amazon.

In the big bedroom, she stretched and pulled on a hip-grazing linen nightshirt. Her shoulder to the doorframe, she looked toward the back stairs. Occasionally, she swung a leg over that rail and slid down to the kitchen. Crossing to the front windows, the heady breeze caressed her, as her strong fingers slid against her skull and lightly ruffled her hair.

Livia walked around the tall bed, rolling down the coverlet. Sighing, she thought of everyone who had shared the huge four-poster with her. Pulling her most recent journal, from the nightstand, she jotted 11/20 and a few thoughts, before marking her place, and setting it atop her laptop. Assured the computer was re-charging she downed half a Xanax before climbing into bed. Fine cool sheets soothed her elbows as her eyes roamed the ceiling. Satisfied that no geckos perched above, her eyes slid shut, and a thought popped up for one of her short stories.

Not finished jotting down a thought, her gel ink pen ran dry. Best not to leave it until the morning - she ripped open a blister packet, separating two ink cartridges. Pushing one into the pen barrel, of course, it got stuck. *Damn design engineers*, and she gave it a rougher poke. No luck – she yanked harder. Teeth sunk behind the metal nib, her head whipped back. Blue ink spewed everywhere, mostly in her mouth. Hopping off the bed, she almost gave a sigh of relief. It had missed the sheets and her antique quilt, only spattering the floor.

Trotting to the bathroom, she dampened her toothbrush with peroxide before adding baking soda. Tongue and teeth, which were grossly saturated in blackish blue, cleaned up quite nicely. She rinsed three more times and spotted her nightshirt with Fels-Naphtha Soap.

Nearly finished, she noticed a tapping of toenails followed by a light scratching at the door.

Somehow, Lotus brought another River Rat to mind. "Oh – what was it Mark Twain said? I think it went something like: 'If you pick up a starving dog and make him prosperous, he will not bite you; that is the principal difference between a dog and a man'."

The dog had to go out again. Dear God, would they ever get to bed? "My Little Toilet Flower - did you sit by the bowl while The Ma did her crossword puzzles?" Something about the dog doing her business brought to mind a little ditty from Mark Twain's Honolulu visit. That evening, he rented a horse to see Diamond Head. On the return trip, the old nag sat down in the Waikiki sand. Twain couldn't concoct fiction with that.

"Eww!" she snapped – vowing to limit those damn Doggie Cookies too close to bedtime. Livia clucked. "Oh, Lola, Lola, Lola – neither one of us needs any extra fiber." Skipping up the stairs she and the dog finally settled down, when she heard a moan and a wretch. "Geez O' Petes – now what!?"

The bathroom light shone across the hallway. Cate spat, "What the hell mess– is this? First, I go to bed with another lousy headache, and then I get up, throw up, and find this lousy ink spewed across the walls. I tried wiping it but got blue all over me." Clad only in a generous bath towel, her finger traced from wainscot to baseboard - as she moaned, "Only our Little Miss could do this." Kneeling at the bowl, she leaned against the lid. Not quite as green - she quietly closed it and wavered a moment before standing.

Livia handed her a fresh hot washcloth and a syringe. Cate's eyes widened at the sight of her hair. She said nothing – possibly because she had witnessed the ritual twice before. With a sheepish grin Livia whispered, "Pen exploded, then Lotus had to go out. Anyway, just relax, and take your headache injection."

Needle in hand, Cate's towel got away from her, leaving her dappled chest shining in the moonlight laced with blue ink. Quite a sight – as she grimaced laughed and injected herself simultaneously. But hurt as she may, Cate could not quit smirking. Both women sat on the tile floor, with Lotus licking their toes.

Two more hot washcloths – one for Cate's forehead and one for the ink – and they repeated the process. Now, the dog's tongue was only light blue. Cate finally gave up, admitting she could barely keep her eyes open. Livia held the pen cartridge packet to the light, and mouthed the words: "Permanent but non-toxic to children or animals."

Livia tucked them in and shuffled back to bed. Fresh nightshirt and she penciled their crazy experience in the margins of her journal. Shaking her head, she repeated, "Friends are stranger than fiction." Old sheets smoothed under her chin she drifted off to sleep.

The sunlight brought heady wafts of plumeria and wild ginger floating across the sheets. Savoring the lovely mix, Livia focused on the dark wardrobe's cabinet doors. Eyes soothingly refocused, on its interior, she pulled off her nightshirt and pulled on her clothes before reaching for her laptop PC. Checking her backside in the floor-length mirror, she headed downstairs.

The tall percolator bubbled, as the screen door slapped behind her. Two huge crinkly poinsettias plants flanked the driveway. She watched them sway, as she balanced coffee and indexed stitched notepad on her knee. Surveying barely legible notes, she copied key phrases onto the PC. 'Find .pdf illustrations for *The Teeny-Weeny People* and *The Barrowers* - Library of Congress website.'   She chuckled, hardly believing that her pen exploded on her notes.

Quarter till seven and the phone kept ringing. Livia wedged the remote receiver between ear and shoulder, and refilled her mug with coffee, wincing at Marion's voice. Heading back to the lanai, she figured it was nearly noon in Evanburgh.

Saturday's funeral plans were not yet complete. Livia listened politely and hoped Marion followed Pearl's plans. Reality was that Marion nudged people, especially if actions deemed lacking. She anointed herself Pearl's caretaker some forty years ago – soon after Grandmother Hinman's death.

Marion gave a detailed rendition, of her son driving her all the way to Badendale for a lengthy meeting with the funeral director. She reiterated, with hearty assurance, that all details were prepared to her best ability.

Livia gulped more coffee, and still listening she walked to the lanai - fully appreciative of Marion's attention to the arrangements. She pulled out her glasses and hit 'speakerphone'. From a safe distance, she sighed; as once again, Marion elaborately laid out her plans and eventually summed it up with, "Lord knows — I've helped out, as any good friend would have done."

Still she droned on, and Livia's thoughts drifted away. Born the year after Grandmother Hinman's death, she'd merely pieced together her father's family history from his copious notes. Last time she visited his family's grave plot, not twenty feet away stood a new tall obelisk, with the inscription: Revolutionary War Captain Asahel Hinman, marked "d.1825." Luke's notes included something about Asahel's great-great grandfather, Edward (a captain of the queen's guards, for Charles I), who fled from England to Connecticut in the 1650s.

Damn, that was some 120 years before Captain Cook landed down the hill. She recognized other names from the poster-sized family tree Luke had drawn. He got many details from a Mormon cousin, and she helped him find more on the Internet. He liked to joke about genealogy: "Look hard enough and you'll find presidents as well as horse thieves." She missed his smile.

How his words rang true. On Annabelle's side, they had a none too-popular Quaker president and a distant cousin who died in Andersonville Civil War Prison. She thought about how many later-day people she had turned from her door after she assured them – she was pretty much the same as her ancestors, who were listed in their book. As much as she tried to make light of the past – her eyes clouded over, as she saw the world's largest steam shovel in a coal field, and Christmas trees for sale on the courthouse square. She shook her head. It was her legacy now. Maybe she would write about it someday.

The high octane coffee cut in, and Livia began timing her responses thus allowing Marion to languish a bit in the glory of every comment. Friends told her she owed the woman nothing more than common courtesy; however, she did appreciate Marion. She was Pearl's good friend, though needlessly a meddlesome one. How often had Livia held her sharp tongue, always thanking Marion for her hard work? She poured another cup of coffee and listened

Marion's stoic, "Of course Pearl's wishes – to not be shown – are to be followed; however, it will be a glorious moment when our minister and sixteen parishioners walk up that red strip of carpet carefully rolled out by the sexton of Maple Grove Cemetery."

"Red? Definitely not!" Livia had not clamped her lips fast enough. She was Annabelle's daughter; and before he died, Luke deemed Livia tenacious too. She thought of young Woofer, in a fight, and took it as a rare compliment. Anyway, a tiny crowd would have pleased Pearl, but Livia wondered how many favors Marion called in to arrange such a funereal pilgrimage. In truth, Pearl paid-forward any such favors, by volunteering so much — exactly as Marion often described her dear friend: "Lord knows, she's quietly answered every call."

Livia kept no formalities except to order an old-fashioned headstone. Merely to be nice, she asked if Marion had any suggestions, about it, before spending the last $792 in Pearl's checking account. Adding another $60.00 Livia ordered it hand cut, in the slightly rounded 1920's style, to match those of her grandparents'. With them long gone, she attempted to cover any details that they or Luke may have provided. Marion's answers didn't really matter, for Livia was hell-bent on having that stone and was quite happy to spend every last cent on something Pearl may have denied herself.

Polynesia chirped and clucked mimicking a couple of Cardinals on the lanai railing. They always reminded Livia of her parents. Badendale was one of those quaint little heartland towns that many people left - then returned to be buried or bury their dead. Time and again she'd seen it happen. Nice place to visit but she was content not to have put Luke and Anna there. For that matter she'd skip the place too.

Margaret came and sat with Livia a few minutes before leaving for work. Quick hug and nothing mentioned about her hair, she crossed paths with neighbor Tom, who was pulling up the lane in his old pickup truck.

Livia nearly forgot: Cate mentioned that their guests: the Reverend and Mrs. Hensen reserved horseback rides, from the inn to Kealakekua Bay. Like Livia, Tom Smith had given up a junior high teaching position. Now, he gave snorkeling and diving lessons. She'd never met his partner, Tim Boki, but they ran Queens' Stables just down the highway. He said he was going to bring his partner by, and show him "their Kick Ice Bears team portraits, signed NHL posters, swords and scimitar that he noticed in the main hallway.

Finished with typing her news article, she watched Tom and the guests return in a larger truck. Cate greeted them at the door, handing them tickets to Captain Kona's cruise and dinner show.

Insisting Tom stay for lunch, the conversation quickly turned to plans for his new business project. He and Tim built a new pony circling mechanism, and wanted to know if they could set it up the inn's front lawn. Saturday mornings would be excellent for keiki rides. From his pocket, came a folded paper with details and a cute photo at the top. He brought extras for the front desk, noting that he and Tim would canvass the local bulletin boards.

Tied at the fence, the horses grazed quietly until Captain got a bit testy, pushing Hokulani aside and attempting to mount Princess.

Excusing himself, Tom calmed the horses and led them to the trailer. As he rolled down the cab's window, Livia and Cate reminded him the pony plans were fine; however, they always discussed any business plans with Margaret. If she agreed, then Livia would check with their lawyer and the insurance company. Always ready to try something new, Livia hoped the pony rides would be a success.

Less than a week and it was Thanksgiving Day. This year Tim and Tom helped Cate and Margaret plan the celebration, over which Livia usually presided. Holiday memories brought good days and bad.

The meal was elegantly simple – kappa cloth table runner filled with simple foods and sparkly bits of merriment. The men insisted on fussing about the kitchen, and reminded that they'd clean up afterward.

Margaret made hurried calls to her parents in Boston and brother in Florida. Cate's new webcam peered down from the kitchen's new twenty-one-inch monitor. Livia recently initialized its software and hoped it improved itself for mainland calls. They had the packing and crate, to send the old computer to Cate's grandparents.

Cate's call was next. Step-dad Heimi picked up the phone, and she kidded him about the Red Wing's hockey season. She teased him, "Really? The Piston's fans finally got that huge basketball jersey off the Spirit of Detroit." Obviously, he minced no words. He was ready for Hockeytown festivities.

As usual, Mother Demi stood beside him. Only a Chicago Bears and a Michigan State fan, she had heard enough of hockey. They waved at Livia in the background. Demi wished her happy holidays and made small talk about reading *Great Lakes Shipwrecks and Survivals*. Soon, Spartan and Wolverine announcers competed in the background, and they hung up.

For once, the phone call included everyone. Both ends got a good laugh when Livia nicknamed the three of them, The Witches of November. She glanced up. Above the parlor buffet, hung the stately T. P. Nagle lithograph of the *Edmund Fitzgerald* lashed by Superior's rough waters. Demi had designs on Livia's huge print until Cate packed it for Hawaii.

Margaret laughed, as Livia named the witch storms: Cincie, Eva, and Louisa. "You and your Ohio River Valley – that would make a nice print, for Wednesday's travel section."

Commitments fulfilled, all eyes turned to the turkey. Cate's wonderful wild rice and morel stuffing – complimented with Livia's cherry pie and persimmon pudding – had everyone drooling. The next trip to Michigan, they would replenish their freezer stash.

Tom slid open the patio door showing off his golden crusted mahi mahi fillets. The next half-hour, they ate, drank and generally made merry. After every dessert got topped with fun squirts of RediWhip, they formally opened the holiday season with an after-dinner toast. B&B chased by Annabelle's demitasse cups of coffee or tea, warmed their throats and hearts.

The women cleared the table and threatened their guests with bodily harm if they did not remain seated. Margaret covered Tim's barely sampled bowl, of curried raw ahi poke ringed with delicate Kawaihae lobster. On her way back to the sink, she held Livia's cake platter to the light. Thick rolls of sushi stuffed, with one Maine rock lobster tail, were history.

Their guests left early after hugs and nose rubs. Cate noted their manners - skipping any complaint of being miserably full.

By seven, all pots and pans were scrubbed and stored. Leaving the steady hum of the dishwasher, the women followed the makai path to the sea intent on a blazing sunset.

Chapter 3: **Kuhuna**

Livia stayed busy with the heaviest chores. Hard work proved mighty good therapy, so she planned more projects for the next two weeks. The following Monday would have been her twenty-fifth wedding anniversary. The next Friday was the sixth anniversary of her father's death. Not to dwell on either, she intended to stay busy.

A few gloomy thoughts stalked her, as a marvelous idea surfaced. With surprisingly little effort, she convinced Margaret to ride a white horse and play St. Nicholas during the pony rides.

All three sat quietly as the usual holiday grog marched across the TV screen. One cable channel cheerily offered a melting pot theme: "Our Holiday Traditions in the Making." Cate snapped that, to another channel - snipping, commenting, "Do I care – that this Saturday is the Orthodox Feast of St. Nicholas? All I wanna know is who's playing football, and can I get the Michigan vs. Michigan State hockey playoffs?"

Livia called Tom to ask if he would let Margaret ride his white Arabian, Kea Nani. She planned an hour of her handing out treats, but that would follow the pony rides. She asked him if he or Tim knew where they could get a large lush robe. They'd make a large bag and some semblance of a miter, to fit in the horse's stirrup.

Peering over the newspaper, Livia fixated on the country-style Christmas tree that did not quite fit the room's style, being only as tall as her antique ruby velvet wingback chairs that flanked it. Those chairs brought memories of a recent Christmas, which certainly did nothing for her mood.

The last dream jolted her awake squinting at a digital 5:30. A vision of their two fragile relatives: her Annabelle and Cate's stepfather, Heimi, perched atop the huge wingbacks. That morning had been uneventful. Cate started a fabulous dinner, till her sister's phone call.

Three marriages and Cate's sister, Ursula, had more problems than a wet cat on hot coals surrounded by dogs. Always digitally connected, she couldn't leave her manager mode at work. That ensured easy head butting with Cate and Mother Demi, by attempting to delegate holiday plans. Lately, even The Ma couldn't iron out the disagreements.

Not that Mother Demi helped matters. Most often she addressed Ursula as "Ms. Snippy." When the conversation progressed, she shucked it down to, "No! You call me; I'm not your secretary."

Just after the second, of three marriages, Cate's little sister held separate Christmas dinners. One was for her in-laws and the other for the Kievers. And that may have worked, if Cate's family's got their dinner invitation before the mid-January. The Kievers' counter attack was the cold shoulder, and things didn't get much warmer till way after Easter. Livia wondered how Ursula would top last year's gift certificates e-mailed to Heimi and the grandparents. The savvy computer couple noticed their gifts had not been accessed, and their query made up the bulk of Cate's text message birthday card.

Once, in an attempt to heal the rift, Cate and Livia asked Ursula's family on a trip to Maui. That met with a saccharine response: 'Sounds interesting, but I don't think so. It doesn't really fit in our Five Year Plan.' Livia's eyebrows raised as witty Cate slashed back, "Figures. It would have to be your idea. You know not everything in life is about you!"

Livia sighed, that was two Christmases ago. She'd rubbed Annabelle's shoulders and asked Heimi if he could smell the turkey Cate was basting.

The phone rang again. It was The Ma saying that she and Daddy couldn't make it because they had the flu. How many times had Mother Demi told them to buy the premium health care insurance, then they wouldn't be running all over town to doctors' offices and picking up every germ along the way!

Within the hour, Cate answered the phone again. It was Mother Demi. She'd been tending sniffles, all week – now she was sick. Livia heard Cate offer to run food to her mother and grandparents, and realized constant turmoil was taking its toll.

Secretly, Livia relished the quiet. Annabelle and Heimi were a handful but peaceful. She loved Cate's family – although, they seemed to thrive on bickering and rarely squelched any opinion.

An earlier holiday floated forward. Six years ago, the year after Luke's death, everyone rallied around overly concerned with their feelings. She'd escaped the seasonal formalities by escaping, with Annabelle, for ten wonderful days in Disney's Magic Kingdom and Epcot. She encouraged her mother to purchase her favorite souvenirs: tiny Mickey Mouse cardigan sweater and Figment plush dragon.

All cheerful they had flown home, and Cate picked them up from Detroit Metro Airport. She and Livia tucked in a weary little Annabelle before they finally crossed the rain-soaked street to the big house. Cate unlocked the front door and lifted Livia's suitcase into the dark vestibule.

The lights flashed on as everyone yelled "MERRY CHRISTMAS!" The huge tree and long dinner table sparkled through Livia's tears. Ten days later, Heimi had a stroke that left him unconscious for three months. She held down the home front as Cate —

A rush of colors yanked her back. A man stooped near the highway, attempting to support a massive woman slumped against the mailbox.

Livia yelled, "Catie Pat, Catie Pat! Come quick!" She flew down the steps and raced across the lawn to the old couple.

As she ran, she sighed 'thanks' that she anchored those twin posts in cement, for now they supported a good 300 pounds of woman. The stocky man braced himself and gently pushed from behind, as Livia clung to an arm the size of her own thigh. Slowly, the lady attempted to gain footing, only to exhale and swoon again.

Livia and Cate knelt beside the woman. "I'm Livia. We own the inn." She loosened her grip on the lovely red-and-white muumuu and pointed. "That's Cate. Please– let us get you to the lanai."

The woman grimaced a nod.

A brief powwow and they re-grouped their efforts. The man got a better hold from the backside. Cate and Livia each planted one foot between the woman's calves, counted to three and expertly pulled her to her feet.

Margaret caught the whole scene from an upstairs window. In an instant she pulled her car alongside them. A can of cola in one hand, and stethoscope in the other, she hovered as they gingerly lowered her patient into the Volvo's front. She listened carefully to her chest, as the lady sipped soda pop, and Cate drove them to the front lanai.

Settled in a double wide rocking chair, the woman lifted her head and exhaled a faint, "Mahalo. We greatly appreciate your help."

As Margaret knelt before her, the man introduced his companion.

"This is Chakra Kuhanamana. My name is Aye Noelani – her brother." He gulped. "We thought we could get a little further down the road. There was a man who pulled up. Quite fine he was dressed, in a khaki suit and cowboy hat, and he offered us a ride but she flatly denied him."

Livia's well-trained ear caught a subtle brogue before she answered, "Oh, it's no problem. You are quite welcome to stay here. Anyway - these days, it pays to be careful." Chakra released her fingers, as Livia continued. "Please excuse my manners. I'm Livia Hinman. This is Catherine Patrice Kievers and Dr. Margaret Anne Brown."

Cate squinted, "Yes - kind of unusual for her to be barking at someone." Her voice dropped a notch. "Her blood sugar's dropped. I'll run get some orange juice."

While taking the woman's pulse, Margaret looked up and said, "No, Coke is fine for now. If you would - please make her a sandwich."

The minutes crawled by. Aye repeatedly apologized for the inconvenience, as he knelt at Chakra's other knee.

Soon both seniors couldn't stop making their thanks. Aye added, "We live just down the road. We were headed home from a neighbor's house when our old Caprice stalled. Her niece's house is less than a mile. I suppose age is catching up with the Heavy Chevy and us." He nodded to Livia. "Chakra noticed you, on the porch, right before she collapsed."

Index finger to lips, Margaret touched her stethoscope under the white eyelet on the front of Chakra's massive red with white holomu. Listening carefully she glanced sideways — eyes blinking with her patient's every breath. Fingers tapping between shoulder blades, she slid the scope a couple times more and listened carefully.

"Did you have breakfast?"

Chakra shook her head no. Gasping for breath she answered, "Only tea, as we usually eat something upon arriving home."

Margaret helped her sip the soda pop, and then she glanced from Cate to Livia and said, "She'll have that sandwich now."

Cate had the drill down pat and was way ahead of the action. Livia's bouts with low blood sugar and Daddy Kiever's diabetes demanded that carefully measured serving of whole grain bread or cereal and tiny bit of protein every three or four hours.

Livia helped stack ham, smoked Pua'a, and bread on the serving tray. "Good thing Ruth was early and laid out the guests' breakfast buffet," thought Livia, as she exhaled. She gobbled small slices of ham, as smoked pork and sandwiches were anything but her favorites.

Cate piled napkins and plates on another tray, as Livia quickly built ham sandwiches. Both hurried to Chakra and back again; and after third trip for fruit and coffee, they joined their guests for a snack.

Aye teetered on his heels facing Chakra. She leaned a bit to one side straightening her hair. A little overcome by unwinding and rewinding it, Aye stepped to her side and helped her arrange it on the top of her head. Her face still ashen, he now seemed extremely bothered by the mishap.

Guarding against him slipping into shock, Margaret rubbed and patted his hand, saying that the food would help him too. She chatted and wrote Chakra a prescription for a five hour glucose tolerance test.

As they ate she stressed to both seniors, "Now, please remember - skip your morning walks until we learn more about this blood sugar problem. There are some promising new oral drugs that help many diabetic patients. Actually, it helps to eat slowly and chew everything to an extreme degree." She opened her hand and held it close above Chakra's knee. As the grand lady grasped it and smiled, Margaret turned to Aye. "After a late supper Chakra must eat nothing. If we can get you into the clinic first thing in the morning, then you won't have to wait very long. Cate will bring a cooler with nice snacks and pick you up at 6:30 sharp."

What followed was two intent nods; however, as soon as Chakra rallied she extended an eloquent and intense thanks. "Oh, you are such darlings to have cared for us whilst we ate your lovely food."

Cate and Livia cleared the trays. Margaret urged them to box plenty of leftovers, stating Aye must eat too, to care for Chakra before and after the test.

From the kitchen window, the circled lanai's chairs reminded Livia of a powwow. In no time, she and Cate joined their guests. Chakra's cheeks colored up, as she quickly became animated. Aye hovered about, as Margaret sat back, merely observing their interaction. She was in her glory, relishing private time with patients. Livia recalled how after Margaret's last hockey injury, she explained how the hospital and surgical partner welcomed her back.

The whole office partied, and afterward she found a legal-sized packet on her desk. It conveyed a big raise and promotion accompanied by a new contract stipulating she not participate in contact sports or dangerous activities such as downhill skiing and race car driving. She took it hard but signed it. Not a year passed before she mentioned "small town practice" or "bed and breakfast." Another year and Livia mentioned "huge inn in Kona." Although she kept tabs, on a few Midwest cancer patients, Margaret seemed satisfied with her progress at Kona's ER and her charity work.

Draining her tea, Margaret cleared her throat and leaned closer to the great woman. Eyes met, and she stated, with astute yet gentle bedside manner, "I propose that you two rest here most the day, so we can keep an eye on you. Eat the prescribed snack and supper, then no more food – only water till morning and your test. There'll be no charge. If I find any problems, I'll send some medicine and supplies to your house. Oh – and Aye, please do not rub her legs anymore – not until we run some additional tests."

Aye eyed Chakra. She nodded to him, softly patting Margaret's hand saying, "Of course dear, we'll follow all of your wishes. Mahalo and bless you. You are most kind."

Livia realized Cate was no nurse, but she missed her grandparents so much that she would dote all day on these seniors.

The kupuna got the royal treatment. In turn, they confided about living in a tiny beach cottage ten miles to the south. Chakra loved to quilt, and Aye fished for a living and was honored as a kahuna hoʻouli'ai – or agriculture expert.

Cate entertained them with Russian folk tales and recent stories about her family, which amazed Livia to see her warm to anyone so quickly.

Mid-afternoon, with a half-dozen low-carb lunches in tow, Cate and Livia drove the old couple home, before safely depositing them, in their tiny and dilapidated seaside shack.

Tom's spurs hit every step to the side lanai. Gently tapping the screen door, he wiggled the new orange and green pony saddles on his shoulder.

"Oh – they are so cute," said Livia, having never had seen anything like them. "So tiny and shiny, they'll soon be keiki favorites."

Tom nodded, blushing as he flashed an awesome grin. He took off for the second set of saddles.

With him busy, Livia phoned the local office supply store and placed an order for 200 matching orange handbills and 60 lime-green invitations. She thumbed through the Rolodex listing of all major businesses, from Kailua south to Kealakekua, plus the eight Gold Coast Resorts. What the heck? She was on a roll, and it was the holidays. Quite a few competitors returned her calls giving permission to post invitations in their lobbies. Three of them stated their high season guests constantly begged for children's activities.

The morning after, she tacked up more flyers and sadly turned down both local radio stations' requests to promote Margaret's Saint Nicholas visit. A little overwhelmed - Livia gave the standard "limited parking" excuse — really not wanting any news about keiki or pony rides common knowledge, from Waimea to Ka Lea, just yet.

The highlight of the week came, when the Kuhuna Slack String Ensemble volunteered music – and two drummers, who had hand-carved whole trunk coconut puka, would tap the background for an old-fashioned hula. They'd begin at 9:00 and stay till the families began to leave after lunch.

Livia added more candy and small treats to her shopping list, recalling how her father handed out "poke bags" at his Dogwood and Fall Foliage tours. She called these bags "ditty Bags" for poke was the name of a Hawaiian fish/salsa delicacy. Luke often said, "Any money from outside our county is new money." She chuckled, recalling how one cow – standing dead center – of a country road brought a 300-car foliage tour to a halt.

She mail-ordered a rubber stamp: La'Ohana Inn, and Tom bought another: Queen's Stable's Keiki Pony Rides. Red and black ink, in Courier Script, looked quite old-fashioned stamped across each brown paper bag. Tom, Tim, and Cate compared the donated items and their accompanying stories.

Tim's was the best. He bowed, as he portrayed the clerk at Mikura's Emporium. "Yeah, old Mr. Nagakawa kept dipping his head saying, 'fukubukuros...' His granddaughter's grin matched his, as she explained that in Japan, every store hands out a New Year's package to their honored customers."

The day-long canvass of businesses had turned up oodles of stuff plus 500 plastic grocery bags and forty cases of purified Big Blue Water, which was donated by ATA Market. The news hit the wind and more merchants dropped loads of stuff. The final count included sixty-three non-perishable treats plus advertisement pens, pencils, calendars, notepads and the like. It would not all fit, so Cate cataloged the non-perishables, and stored them for future handouts.

Margaret suggested they deliver goodies and poke bags full of goodies to the Trade Winds Retirement Center. After introducing Livia to the staff, the seniors busied themselves packing and stacking ditty bags. As they giggled and talked story, the women pushed the men aside for sticking candy in their pockets. The Good Doctor left orders for plenty of snacks for the seniors. Livia refilled plates of cookies, smug in the fact that most goodies fit better in purses than in pockets.

Her regular rounds done, Margaret helped Livia poke the bags full of goodies. Everyone had a fine time, and the last count had 620 bags. Tim scrounged huge boxes and promised to haul the bags to the inn the next afternoon, on his return trip from Waimea.

He arrived late that afternoon, finding Margaret exhausted after a double shift. She helped Livia stash the boxes at the nursing home curb before heading home. Tim and Livia hefted the bags in the truck bed and followed less than ten minutes later.

A cute group of seniors crowded around for hugs before waving them off with "God Rest Ye Merry Gentlemen." Livia overheard two old geezers joking, about giving Santa's elves a run for their money, as the nursing assistants herded them back indoors.

Nicely warmed up, the Laredo's diesel surprised Livia as it purred. Tim dialed the radio to the oldies station and crooned, "Grandma Got

Run Over By a Reindeer." Finished with that, he gave his own rendition of "Deck the Halls."

Livia snickered. Not one usually to pry, she searched for polite conversation. "So how long have you and Tom been together?"

"Oh, nearly eight years now. Not that I'm so easy to get along with - but once 9/11 happened, the day after my thirty-fourth birthday, I then and there realized how much I didn't know, and made every effort to tolerate other's differences; otherwise, we may not have stayed together. Just wish the perpetrators had a broader view of the world. Sorry; I didn't mean to—"

"No. The truth's the truth," said Livia. "It's like we've got the twelfth century and the twenty-first century butting heads." After rubbing his shoulder, she tugged her backpack off the backseat. Noticing the blue plastic light she asked, "What's the emergency flasher for?"

He cleared his throat and stated that volunteering as a fireman was the quickest way to enter a house.

Then he pulled the truck onto the shoulder, set the brake, and faced Livia. His hands grasped his knees, and his arms locked stiff as he hunched his shoulders and stared at her. "Margaret is seeing someone regularly."

Livia felt the pulse, in her throat, and stared back. "Okay. I take it – that is not good?"

His tone did not vary. "If it's the man we think it is, no– it's not good. That's why, on very rare occasions, we pretend to check for a fire and go into people's homes. We're chasing a seasoned pedophile."

Dumbfounded, Livia just shut up and listened. She had always been an excellent judge of character, and she realized Tim was not prone to exaggeration or petty gossip – so, what had she missed? She looked him in the eye and leaned closer. "...And?"

Exhaling, his perfect posture slumped. "He's a veterinarian, from Waimea, Dr. Richard Header. Way too familiar he gets with his animals, and it's impossible to pin down — mainly, because he's old family and has ties all over the island. His work is his cover. It takes him to all the islands, even little Niihau. We've also got thirteen affidavits, from eye-witnesses, that he's been way too familiar with quite a number of pre-adolescent children. To date, twenty-eight keiki have reported little fingernails having been clipped off."

A shudder ripped through her. She'd grown up with her father's grisly stories – that and his banter around the sheriff's poker table.

Tim rubbed the steering wheel and looked in the rearview mirror. "I can't say much more until we do a bit more detective work. There was a young woman who disappeared two years ago, in Puna, and Header was questioned but not held. Tom and a buddy are the ones who noticed him and Margaret keeping company following their shifts, at the Hilo Keiki Clinic." Tim asked that they keep an eye on Margaret, and discourage any overnight visits. He and Tom weren't as worried when Margaret was with her or Cate.

Livia knew that Margaret certainly was no puss. With Cate's goalie stick, and her own martial arts training, he dare not try anything stupid. She barely listened, as Tim's words got softer – saying something about how he helped Margaret buy a horse, from an Arabian horse farm owner near Volcano village. He asked that she accompany him, on his next couple blacksmithing trips, enticing her with some extra horseback lessons – gratis.

After a short ride home, they stacked poke bags at the back of the inn's carport. Piled high to the ceiling, it would be a good test for their new electrical insect deterrent system.

After downing a chilled glass of water, Tim balanced slices of cherry cake as she walked him back to the truck. All three nearly lost it when the paper plate gave way, and he came up grinning and sucking thumbs from a right-good save. Livia barely made out his hand waving above the cab as he turned south. Bag poking finished ahead of schedule; they could turn their attentions to the holidays.

Chapter 4: Mele Kalikimaka

English Holly draped Grandfather Kiever's grandfather clock. It hammered 9:30 AM as Cate recognized a low whine rising from the kitchen. Slapping open the breezeway door, sure enough, she saw 'Livia's Locomotive' — in full throttle.

This time of year and the kitchen chemist was hard at work – her gaze intent on Cate's KitchenAid mixer. Livia wiped her forehead; and on tiptoes, peered down past the bowls at Cate's dusty path to the oven.

Whoosh!

Cate jumped and slid, to the edge of the crease. "What the ever loving…? You damn near singed my eyebrows off!"

Livia cringed. "Sorry! I must of forgotten my grapefruit was broiling."

Cate grabbed baking soda, tossing it directly on the flaming mess. Flipping the oven off, she used her rattiest potholders to lay the singed fruit and broiling tray near the sink.

"Too late," drawled Livia. "Seventy-proof Stolichnaya, on brown sugared fruit, in an electric oven, is a worser fire hazard than your gas barbecue grill."

Cate leered.

Livia snapped, "Hey, I'm not the only one! Might be safer, if some people around here would ever clean the grease from the oven."

Cate shook her head and looked up to her raised hands. She dropped them hard and sighed. "You know, rarely does a Christmas season pass without you in the kitchen, and with flour in our underwear."

"Oh, pu-lease – don't play the martyr." She poked at the blackened fruit and muttered. "That takes the cake. So, you're the only one who's allowed to bake in *our* kitchen?"

"What?"

Fighting the urge to give Cate the fist above a high Italian elbow, she pursed her lips and stared at the kitchen island. Quick survey of the mess brought visions of guests fleeing a large kitchen explosion. This was not as bad as the time, back in Michigan, when Mother Demi's turkey exploded onto the ceiling. Livia had returned from her parents' house, to find tiny scraps of meat overhead; she never asked, and she never got the details on that one. Noticing Cate stuffing stuffing hot and sticky grapefruit down the disposal, Livia quietly began swiping the mess from the counter, oven and floor.

Following behind her with a towel, Cate said, "This is a bit stickier than I thought. I'm glad you're not throwing a hissy fit. I left the phone on Voice Mail and set the bell on the front desk but let's make short work of this."

Powdered sugar – not just flour – had drifted everywhere. Leaning hard on a couple of wet towels, Livia said, "I do not throw conniption fits," and took another swipe at the sticky *Springerle* mess. Nearly an hour later, she huffed, "Shall we paint the cookies, or the kitchen walls, after getting the Christmas lights from the attic?"

Cate shrugged. "How about sitting a minute? Margaret likes mixing sugar paints, and we can do that tonight after dinner." She glanced at the clock. "We've got time for an attic run. The cookies have to sit and harden. Anyway, in an hour, I need to be downstairs for check-ins."

Access to the attic came through an old linen closet in the rear upstairs hallway. Cate followed Livia up steep and creaky stairs to the Christmas decorations. Rare in Hawaii, this high space comforted her when she got homesick for her old house in Michigan.

"Miss Kringle! Where is your old tree?"

Livia flicked the light on and pointed to a pile in the northwest corner. After sorting, she had three neat piles. Repeating, "Lanai, parlor, kitchen," she sorted then tossed or scooted each box to Cate. Finally, she stood, lightly bumping her head into the rafters. Tears flooded down her cheeks.

Cate jumped to Livia's side, gently rubbing her scalp. "Settle down. There's no blood. Just your pride is hurt." As she kept hugging, Livia gulped for air, only sobbing more.

Stop it and breathe. Livia coached herself. Wiping her eyes, she forced back her shoulders and swallowed tightly.

Handing over a fresh tissue, Cate whispered, "Not gonna be quite the same – the first few Christmases with your family gone."

"I know."

Cate continued. "Do you remember the year after your father died, and for something different, you took your mother to Walt Disney World? Margaret and I will stick close this year. You know we'll find something different to do. How about this? I heard Mauna Kea has new snow. Maybe, we'll try snowboarding, or at least go and watch this first time. Something like that will be fun. Not to fret — Little Miss. We'll do the planning."

Livia sniffed, as she dabbed at her eyes. She managed a smile, which morphed in and out of a pout. Cate released her, and she grabbed for a huge box labeled "Lanai Lights," then staggered up to the stairs.

With measured huffs and puffs, they made six trips up and down three runs of stairs. Transferring piles of decorations to their respective places on the main floor, Livia worked quickly, knowing Cate was only good for two to three hours of strenuous chores. She called out, "Beer-thirty," with the last box set down in the parlor.

"Not a problem, as long as you have a snack too."

Livia dug out a pail of party mix, a present from Margaret's physician's assistant. She downed a few cashews and almonds, from a holiday bowl, before noticing Cate's stare. She swallowed. "Well, what? They're Margaret's, and she said to help ourselves."

By late afternoon, the tree was up, and so were Cate's feet. She sucked on another beer moaning, "I am so finished." Another gulp brought a sigh. "Well – for today at least..."

In unison, their heads turned to the "toot-toot-toot" from the driveway.

Cate rubbed her sore knees and peered over her glasses. "Will you hop up and see who's there?"

Already on her way, Livia wheeled around and gave Cate a small curtsy. "Why, I just be movin' – Miss Catie Pat." Her tune changed a bit when Livia noticed the big brown truck. With eyebrows arched she chirped, "It's UPS — must be my poinsettia tree!"

When the smartly attired driver slipped his loafer before padding up the steps and handing over two large packages, Livia thanked him "Mahalo," adding "Mele Kalikimaka." Wondering if she had mispronounced "Merry Christmas," she watched as his tires peeled dirt off the driveway.

Cate plopped down in an Adirondack recliner and watched Livia set out the tree's wire pieces. "That's a nice tree frame. Where are you going to set the contraption?"

Livia pointed across the main steps. "That way, everyone will see it; hopefully, it won't block the flow of traffic. One box contains fifty-six five-inch pots plus a larger one for the top. The catalog featured fancier one, with lights on the frame, but I figure our garden spotlights would be fine enough to make the flowers look even brighter at night."

"What poinsettias?" asked Cate.

"The ones I ordered from Misty Waters Nursery, up at Holualoa." Noticing Cate's eyes glaze, she said, "You know, on Mamalahoa Highway, just before Palani Road? They ordered sixty plants, in four-inch pre-moistened soil pellets, and they threw in two bags of bags of potting medium."

Stepping back, she surveyed her tree assembly. Assembled, the five tiers seemed taller than nine feet. That accomplished, it took less than ten minutes to fill pots, arrange them, and add weak fertilizer water.

Cate rubbed her knees. "Well, that kept you out of trouble for a little while. And the flowers after the holidays?" She stared blankly, as Livia pointed to the lawn's side borders. Then Cate mellowed and mentioned that the perky little flowers reminded her of Mama and Papa Hinman, which made Livia snuffle against the back of her hand.

They finished decorating and got all the boxes to the attic. The late sun reflected off the long parlor wall, and Livia took a fine picture of Cate and Margaret beside the lush red poinsettia tree, with the excuse that it would make lovely Christmas cards next year.

The festive mood stayed steady all season. One morning, Livia hovered over *The Honolulu Advertiser* NHL Scorecard. Inspired by various Kona in-line hockey teams, she outlined a Los Angeles Kings and Detroit Red Wings article for a *West Hawai`i Today* sport special. Picking Cate's brain for old hockey trivia added depth to the story.

Cate turned from the stove. "Know what? That's something we can do. Let's go see an NHL game – or even more than one."

"Maybe - Vancouver, Seattle, or L.A.?" added Livia. No immediate answer, but she never pleaded her case for a sports trip with Cate or Margaret. Margaret could not accompany them due to her work schedule and recent fervor for horseback riding. She accompanied Tim, to a farm near Volcano village three times, but had not purchased a horse.

The NHL season began, and Cate fussed. "You know me and hockey. We've not been to a Red Wings game, in over two years. Damn strange, how they've not made the playoffs since then."

Livia nodded, as Cate added, "You've always said Vancouver is beautiful." Her eyes followed Lotus pacing around Polynesia's cage. "I'd pick Vancouver, Calgary or Edmonton. I checked, and last year their exhibition tickets were easier to buy. Actually, I wouldn't mind seeing Anaheim either."

Livia smirked. It must have been years ago that she mentioned that Seattle ferry ride past Vancouver to Victoria's wharf. She had only been twelve when her parents took her on that train ride from Portland, along the coastal mountains, to Seattle. "Well– I've never seen California, except for twice from L.A.'s airport, but I realize you're not a Duck or King's fan. It's your decision, but you know I'd enjoy anything Canadian. Pretty soon we'll need a passport."

She blinked, re-considering her choice of words, and thought of her favorite north-of-the-border haunts. Actually, she could go for anything big city about now – restaurants especially. Spago was cool in Chicago and Maui. Toronto's Peter Pan was good if you had a hankering for vegetarian, and she'd never forget her friend's little Serious Moonlight Café in Windsor. Her thoughts turned to closer nightlife. Dancing, at Waikiki's The Wave, would be awesome. Especially, since rumor was — that it might close soon.

Both were quiet, until she added. "You know - I'd kinda like to go night clubbing in Honolulu or Waikiki before taking a hockey trip. Kaneohe is gorgeous, and I never got to see the Buddhist gardens over there. Five years ago, you and Mother waited as I trotted around Foster Botanical Gardens. You liked the Kuan-Shi-Yin Temple at its gate, and changed your tune pretty quick once you spotted that Zippy's deli across the street." She chuckled. "Good thing we don't live near Honolulu, or we'd each tip in at 300 pounds."

Cate said she could do Oahu again; maybe, for Livia's birthday. "You always say January's the best to see Pipeline surfing. Wasn't that *North Shore* TV series filmed up at Turtle Bay Hilton? And *Lost* is filming on Oahu too! Margaret mentioned something about having to use two vacation days before April 1st. Mind if I ask her? Herman probably wouldn't mind taking one of her hospital rotations. Sure would be a hoot, if she could come with us."

Before Livia could nod, Margaret bounded down the stairs. Remarkably agile, she broke stride by skidding to the table. "You're not going to believe what I just found on the Internet. Pleasant

Holidays has the best Honolulu packages offered - after the first of the year."

Cate said, "Oh, yeah?" as Livia said, "And?" Over the next hour, they planned a three-day weekend for her forty-fifth birthday. Afterwards, they wrapped presents singing "Mele Kalikimaka" and a few other carols, until their guests arrived.

Four presents were opened with care. Margaret gave Cate and Livia a huge bottle of champagne wrapped with a note 'Dinner and an evening at Volcano House'. Livia tore tissue paper, from a heart-shaped locket, then unwound it from a quarter size rare pale koa wood Pueo, her aumakua. After setting it in her lap, she handed Cate her present. Cate raised and lowered a hefty box wrapped in red ti leaves. Sliding off the plain white shell lei, she found an ironwood sea turtle nestled in moss-green silk velvet. After a few winsome smiles, and they handed over Margaret's gift. Having pooled their finances, they were not disappointed - when she gushed 'thank yous' and 'you shouldn't haves' after opening their gift certificate, for a horse bridle custom made by Tim. Group hug and the inn felt like home for the very first time.

Tim and Tom arrived and were disappointed that the women put the cabash on their plans to throw Livia a birthday party; although, they did not skip a beat in suggesting the women be their guests at The Establishment night club's New Year's Eve Gala. Livia took little convincing — and once Cate and Margaret learned they could wear formal, or Aloha Wear, they hopped on board by asking the men to a candle light supper en route to the festivities.

It made Livia's day to wear her Christmas present from Margaret. Running upstairs, she returned, modeling her crisp white shorts topped with her Red Wing's Aloha Shirt. She intended to glow, on the dance floor, decked out in Christmas red and sparkling white.

The week passed in a whirlwind. Tim and Tom came for New Year's dinner. Everyone played charades and board games till nearly ten. The breeze felt lovely as they motored down to Kailua.

Kailua's palm-lined Kopiko Street was nothing like the neon nightlife of Miami's South Beach, as white fairy lights were strewn everywhere, illuminating the patron's faces as they posed on the sidewalk. Once past the entrance, they found themselves in a gauntlet of poinsettia plants dripping with white Pua Male flowers along the wide hall to the ballroom. The scents mingled and wafted making the air soft but intoxicating. The maître d's Jasmine-spiked wristbands topped it all. With a flourish, he removed his own scentless lei, of dried cranberries and crown flowers, and wound it around Livia's head. The waiters wore huge collars of purple orchid leis, and each gave a breathy, "Aloha," as he gingerly lifted off one lei and placed it about his guest's shoulders.

Tim whisked Livia to the dance floor where they jammed to "It's Raining Men." Each refrain brought the crowd's hearty "Hallelujah!" A few more songs were just as rousing — and in less than twenty minutes, it was time for a breather and a refreshing drink.

Hearing "Let's Give Them Something To Talk About," Tom couldn't refrain from grabbing Cate. After the tall angular couple repeatedly circled the dance floor, to a waltz, and polished off a line dance. Tim cooled things down, by drawing everyone into a snaking Conga line, to the beat of "Hot, Hot, Hot."

The band took a break, and half the patrons crowded round the bar.

Livia hated small talk.

Rimming her tongue around the salty Margarita, she tried to keep up with the liquor and loose lips. Finding a break in the conversation, she said, "I heard a cute jingle on the radio today. Does anyone know - how many *fa*, *la*, *la*, *la-la's* there are in 'Deck the Halls'?" Covering her mouth she leaned sideways and stage-whispered to her buddies, "594? — but a lot less, the more one drinks." With a wink, she flicked salt at Cate.

Sensing a cat fight, Tim yelled, "Oh, those oldies but goodies!" Hands high in the air, he twirled around. This time, he grabbed Margaret by the waist, gently pulling her away from a licentious old fart at the bar. They giggled, fell in line, and wiggled their way with the rest of the crew to "Do the Locomotion." Then all the couples elegantly paced the dance floor to the lovely Bette Middler's, "Wind Beneath My Wings."

As the DJ spun a line dance, Livia skipped over to the nearest waiter and lifted a soda from his tray. Still thirsty, she sucked the ice and watched Cate step and turn in line with her buddies. Afterwards, a bit of silence preceded the DJ stepping down and the dimming of lights. A tenor sax and familiar drum roll brought Livia's head up. Her mouth fell open as Vince Vance and the Valiants took the stage. His trembling low falsetto filled the ballroom, with "All I Want For Christmas Is You." It gave her the shivers. Gentle people packed the dance floor, and there was barely a dry eye in the house.

She moved to the bar and backed up to a dark wall adjacent the loading dock. Staring into the starry Kona sky, she dabbed at her eyes. She had a vision of her parents: Christmas, and she videotaped them laughing and hugging beneath the chandelier, in the vestibule of her Camp Fortson home. Dashing to the street, she drew up her collar and panned for a better angle. Through night's silent flurry, they glowed in a spot of light. Radiant, they waved back at her. Cate came up beside them for one perfect moment. Luke shivered, and Cate rubbed his shoulders as Annabelle adjusted his cardigan. The scene faded as the music ended.

The bouncer had propped open the east side door, and drawn to the cool air Livia moved to that door. Her brain clicked up and down the kitschy melody of "Take a Chance On Me". She knew it would drive her nuts, for days, so she concentrated on the tall palms swaying along Henry Street. Her eyes and nose wrinkled as she squinted to see them, and her incredible sense of smell failed to discern the lavender- and clove-scented smoke that curled from a tiny red glow in the night.

At the end of the loading dock and lightly puffing, on a golden cigarette holder, stood a tall and remarkably handsome woman. Her flat eyelids never blinked as she watched Livia, who barely noticed and pocketed a damp linen handkerchief before heading back to the dance floor.

Joining the crowd, no one seemed to have missed a beat. Cate gave Livia the last sip of her deliciously dry Volcano Symphony white wine. Livia grinned, sending Cate trotting off for more. They raised chilled glasses to their new friends. How lovely. If next year was anything like this wonderful evening, they were in for some heady times.

Half past 11:00 — the stage lights came up, and the seasonal merriment began its finale. Sporting a creamy white tux and tails - a huge, tan, and dreadlocked gentleman arrived center stage gently ringing a silver bell.

A hush filled the ballroom as he flashed a glowing smile and seductively drew the mike to his ruby lips. Clicking his heels, he turned sharply and gave half a bow. He drew back the curtains bellowing perfectly, "Greetings to all!" He paused to wink saying, "And before your good night, I present The Establishment's Fifteenth Holiday Review."

The crowd cheered, as the Kona Cuties opened with a rousing number, "Merry Stripmas," which was followed by one jolly Santa Claus and his sleigh pulled by nine prancing and gorgeously decked-out reindeer. Next, the upbeat Windward Womyn's Choir sang, and the whole entourage stopped occasionally to "Ho, Ho, Ho," wave, and greet the crowd.

Each time the procession halted, Santa's nimble reindeer took every opportunity to nibble at each other's flanks. A young man sang John Denver with a twist: "Take Me Home– Mauna Loa" and you could have heard a pin drop. A few minutes before midnight, a stately Miss Botoxia led the Grand Finale. She blew kisses from one sparkling gloved hand and tossed pastel condoms from the other, as the platinum-quaffed transvestite frequently repositioned her gown, for an every grander pose, and Santa's elves joined to help. Finally, everyone subtly cheered, "*'Ohana! 'Ohana!*" between chorus lines, of "We Are Family."

Filling the stage, the entire review bowed to shrill cat whistles and roars of applause. Once again, the master of ceremonies took center stage, flashing his sparkling ebony eyelashes. He bowed fully in every direction nodding and repeating, *"Mahalo Nui Loa…"*

Someone nudged Livia and pointed to the ceiling, as an old mirrored globe began to turn. Three laser spotlights hit the large orb and threw a million sparkles across the room, as waiters charged among the crowd with trays of highly polished champagne flutes.

Firmly, he began the countdown: "Ten!"

The crowd echoed: "Nine, eight, seven, six, five, four…" as four gorgeously coiffed fairies, dressed in silver lamé elf suits, skipped spryly to his coat tails. The crowd roared, "Happy New Year!" as his elves popped corks from grand magnums of non-alcoholic bubbly before handing them to the waiters. Each accepted the bubbly. Holding it aloft, each flashed a smile and in unison gave a cheeky, "And a many happy more!" Everyone followed their lead, rubbing noses and giving generous pecks on the cheek.

Spontaneously, *"Aloha `Oe"* ensued until every verse was turned over twice and the curtain swags rippled down. A gentle but noisy crowd dispersed from the bar area and dance floor.

The Kawaihae Canoe Club was lined up outside. For a mere $20.00 charity donation, one could run their gauntlet of outrigger paddles and a member would provide a local ride home. Distant rides were charged accordingly. Tim handed over a crisp $50 bill before escorting the women and Tom to an old Mercedes Woody Surfmobile, which often sat on Ali`i Drive near Quinn's.

It was a brief but lively ride home. The old station wagon hit a small chunk of construction debris, and Livia gave up a hearty "Arrp! Everyone turned, as she gave a silly-ass grin and a meek apology. "Sorry. It bounced a burp right out of me."

Laying out the breakfast place mats, Livia shook her hips and boogied around the kitchen table. Holding a slotted serving-spoon to her lips, she quietly crooned "Beyoncé Be With You" then straddled the back of a kitchen chair and purred a breathy Elvis' "A Little Less Talk."

Margaret rolled her eyes as Livia held the spoon to Cate to echo the "a lot more action." Quiet again - no one was too-worse-the-wear from not getting all the lyrics perfectly right. Fortunately, they hosted very few guests during the holidays.

For billing and staffing purposes, Cate kept the breakfast buffet scheduled. All three helped themselves to the goodies as an off-season treat. Following her afternoon errands in Kailua, Cate took any leftovers to the seniors at Trade Winds Retirement Center.

Much to Livia's surprise, more women attended the gala than she expected. Maybe on an island this size, it was easier to share one nice nightclub than patronize separate lesser ones. Watching Tim dance all evening assured her that he was the one she noticed on the dance floor during her first visit to Kona.

She jumped when the phone rang and answered, "That's strange; I was just thinking of you. Yes, that happens to me too. We're fine, and you? Good." She listened. "Um hum – Sure; we can do that. Right back at ya. Bye."

Then she lied. Although she told Cate and Margaret that Tim called - asking them to look, for a lost section of pony bridle; in reality, he confirmed Margaret's gentleman friend (the previous night) was indeed Richard Header, veterinarian and convicted beastialist. She would tell Cate the details later.

Mugs splashed full with coffee and tea, the quiet banter ended quickly.

Livia and Cate's head bobbed up, as Margaret compared The Establishment to The Colony Club in Provincetown. Divulging little about her past, she did say she went with dorm buddies as an undergraduate at Dartmouth. With that revelation, Cate settled down, and all three re-hashed last night's festivities.

Livia's eyes glazed. Overhearing a portion of yesterday's strange phone message, she quickly visualized the gorgeous gardens and beaches of old Honolulu. She looked up at the sudden quiet. Not one to pry, she changed subjects by asking, "By the way, who was that man at the bar last night?"

Abruptly, Margaret got up and moved to the sink. She rinsed her mug, saying, "Oh, he's the veterinarian, from Waimea, who volunteers at the Hilo Clinic." She headed for the door, pointing her finger toward the lane. "Be right back – gonna get the mail."

Cate and Livia quickly cleared the buffet and stacked the dishes, arguing the whole time Margaret was gone. Neither agreed who'd ask Margaret more about Richard. Neither cared for the added chores but they doubled their efforts, so Tina and Ruth had extra personal time during the holidays.

Tina was a gem and came highly recommended by the Merthermans. As the inn's caterer, for twenty-two years, they found her baked delicacies to-die-for. By blood or by marriage, she was related to probably half the people in South Kona. Husband Nuggy, got laid-off after twenty-five years as a longshoreman; then a month ago, he lost his part-time job with the local propane supplier.

Tina said that Nuggy sulked all night when she accepted a dinner invitation with Eugene. She shook her head. "All he said was, 'Fine — but it's a small town and people see everything.' I gave it my best shot, explaining that Eugene was married and we're just friends."

Still Nuggy grilled her. Finally she hissed, "We're friends! You know? It's poor people's only therapy!" She calmed down and said, "It's been a rough few months, and Eugene's point of view really helps me. Nuggy got real quiet before storming out for a drink with his work buddies." Tina gave Livia and Cate big hugs and told them how much she appreciated her personal days. Then she asked if they knew anyone who could use a little red 1999 Jeep — real cheap.

Livia just about died. For years Cate had listened to her prattle on and point to, *Consumer Reports*, noting the '99 was the best Wrangler in the past eight years. Nuggy bought it new but Island Motors demanded he take a six year lease. The odometer had 45,000, and it was kept tip-top by his brother. If Livia could cough up $3,000 plus his last four payments, it was hers. She'd keep the Cutlass. With Margaret's job and all, it never hurt them to have a backup if one of the cars was in the shop. She'd give her mother's little red buggy a good coat of wax. It would sit in the carport protected from the sea air.

On Saturday, Tina and Nuggy delivered the jeep. Life at home must have mellowed, for all their grandchildren attended the next two pony rides. Crowds came more regularly, and merchants advertised with complimentary dollar tickets, leaving Tim and Tom with less cash to handle.

The second Saturday in March a smartly dressed man in a Stetson hat, and khaki vest and shorts suit helped Livia set out food. The pony line thinned and food line filled out and curved, through the front lawn, she reminded their few employees that pop, hot dogs, and chips were free to family and friends. Something about his eyes struck her as odd, or possibly too overzealous with a washcloth; however, she looked right past him at Cate waving her to the lanai.

She excused herself and joined her friends who were giving Tina's older grandkids three pairs, of their old but perfectly good in-line skates. Good call - each pair fit. Livia hurried back, to the food table, in hopes of introducing the stylish man to Cate but he was gone.

The twins, Mike and Mickey, immediately got their sea legs under them, and they zipped by on the pavement along the tall hibiscus hedges. It was good to see Tina laugh as the twins made a game of who could tap the most yellow blossoms in one run. Younger sister, Clara, fell close in behind after removing the insoles from Livia's old skates. With Lotus showing off with the skaters, and the ponies plodding along with their new keiki baskets, everyone relaxed for an enjoyable few hours.

Tina thanked Cate for fine-tuning the kids' skates. She also said the Hawaiian Homeland's Keiki Patrol was considering adding in-line skaters to their sting-ray bike club – it was Mickey's idea. Later, Livia overheard Tina say, "Dr. Brown — my daughter Ailiana said, 'Ya, ya, that's great!' Oh, they'll have loads of fun skating after school when she's at work, and Tim can show them a few tricks with an excuse to keep an eye on them. Oh, by the way, how did you like that fresh ahi Great-uncle Aye sent at New Year's?"

Margaret face went stone blank. "Oh– you mean that spicy raw salmon? Hope you don't mind but Livia ate most all of it. Ailiana – such a lovely name. Did you choose it to match Tatiana?"

Tina pulled her long ponytail through one of Livia's hand-crocheted hair bands. "Not really. Nuggy fashioned her name first, and I picked 'Mildred' as the other name but good thing an auntie suggested 'Tatiana'." Tina's broad forehead nodded toward the children. "You know, Livia's old Mickey Mouse short set fits Clara nicely. It's her very favorite, and I cannot help say that I find it refreshing not to see a nine year old's midriff."

Overhearing them, Cate laughed. "You should have seen the old photo we found in her college yearbook. Some of Livia's get-ups were high 1960's fashion, like those dyed seed love beads draped over her Peter Max mini-skirt and top. I saw a picture of her wearing it, in her old college yearbook. She stood next to her friend Cherise, in the front of a group's dorm picture. They looked like Peggy Lipton and Janice Joplin. Evidently, the last time she had worn it was at an 80's Halloween party, and some of the younger guests thought she dressed up as a hooker. She said she lost track of it after her parents' auction, and some thrift store probably made a few bucks off it. I haven't told her yet – I recently noticed eBay listed a similar outfit for $499."

Margaret waved her fingers slightly and asked, "Who's Peter Max?"

"Oh, sorry; you were barely born then. He's a marvelous Op Artist — even at five or so, I remember his colorful Seven-up commercials, with people, rainbows and butterflies morphing into other images. Anyway, that cool gray top and skirt, with yellow stars strewn across orange and planets, sure would be worth a chunk of change now - these kids would go nuts for it."

She watched Tina's eyes dart to her grandkids, saying, "Will you look at what they're wearing? We aren't all missionaries out here, but I sure could do with seeing a bit less of their moms showing bare tummies and cleavage. Little Clara's friends are always parading around hiking their swimsuits up, in the back, like their big sister's thong bikinis. On school registration day I counted three mothers sporting navel rings; one was even pierced into an eight month tight belly. I mean - if that is so pretty, why not snap one through a guy's hoo-hoo and stick that out for everyone to see?"

Their eyes crossed - as Tina swigged bottled water, placed her hand over her heart, and said, "So proud I was when Ailiana mustered up. She had a heart-to-heart with little Clara. Afterwards, I found her sobbing. That was no fun explaining to a second grader that skimpy clothes suggest the wrong things to a few perverted adults."

Margaret watched the grandchildren before excusing herself - soon to return with a bag of old helmets. With a few quick pointers, she adjusted screws and chinstraps before Cate explained a low-speed snowplow stop. Most agile was Mickey — except for his hockey stop, as he flew from asphalt to grass.

Everyone applauded, as Margaret yelled, "Only on the ice!"

He rubbed his knees saying, "My friends and I are gonna build a rink someday!"

Margaret added. "Maybe sooner than that. You are lucky having hit the grass. Usually the pavement hits harder than on the ice." She helped him up. "Anyway, you work hard. Maybe we can make this the first island with a municipal or private ice rink. Maybe a location near Saddle Road and Mamalahoa Highway would work, or down on Highway-19 near old Kona airport. How about calling it the Solar Skate Club? Maybe a federal grant could cool the inside, and fans could sit outside the boards. We all love to skate. Anyway, it might be a few years off - but I'm pretty determined."

Livia and Cate's eyes met, as did a few others in earshot. Heads nodded as Margaret concluded, "Wonderful idea; we could brainstorm on it."

The kids jumped up and down, and Mickey yelled, "Wonderful? Ice skating is awesome!"

Livia's suspected that Margaret could float the ice rink herself; especially, if she got the tax write offs and some state funds. A parcel in the high country would be perfect at 40°F, in the winter, and midway between Hilo and Kona. Hauling more cookies from the kitchen, she envisioned a Zamboni crossing the Pacific on a Matson ship. In the late 1980s, her teammates teased her for snapping pictures as it skirted the rink. She giggled, "We don't have these where I came from. It's for my parents."

The holidays outpaced Margaret's infatuation with Richard. That off the table for a while gave Livia a bit more time to figure what was familiar about Tim. Finally, a detail jolted loose from memory. Yes, he was the hunk on the dance floor; she'd seen him on her first trip to Kona. It was Halloween and everyone was either painted or masked. Now it fell together. That was about the same time Tom's teaching career ended. She knew full-well what could happen when parents figured the Gay Bug was catching.

She pulled her cart down the garden path to a circle of sunlight. Lotus hopped off and sat quietly, as she uncovered a hole in the harsh rocky soil. She took four items — Pearl's box-style hearing aid, Luke's envelope with antique hair combs, a broken china vase painted with Annabelle's pink roses, and her own too-often resoled walking shoes — and set them in the good earth. Cutting loose a small cedar's burlap root ball, she lifted it gently and patted it in the soil. Gloves off, she watered everything - before stepping back to admire her work.

Cate's saying came to mind: "That will do nicely, Little Miss." Yes, every year she would line the high mound with wide patches of orange and purple annuals, such as marigolds and impatiens. Back on the lanai, she petted Lotus and considered transplanting Luke's orange Day-Glo Rose in front of the cedar. Memories vanished, as footsteps resounded on kitchen stairs. The rose was fine for now – actually, it never stopped blooming – ever since Cate arrived and constantly tossed tea dregs on it.

On the way back to the inn, Livia whooshed her new machete through the air snapping off a few plumeria blossoms along the way. In the garden Lotus cowered, as she fell a foot-wide banana tree in three strikes. It worked using Tim's method: first - an undercut, then - chip out a neat wedge, pull it over - and deliver one final blow. Soon, Livia and Lotus shared three tiny apple bananas. Loading the rest in the cart, they made off to the carport.

Winter business took off. Eight long-term guests occupied the three rooms over the inn's northwest corner; and with the wide upstairs hall, the women's physical activities did little to disturb their privacy.

Margaret warmed up for her Tuesday morning workout, as Livia scrutinized Cate's pallor. "You look a bit peaked. Did you stay up too late last night, watching hockey? Did Edmonton win?"

Margaret whispered to Livia, "No more iron tablets," as Cate grumbled her complaints: "No, not yet. I shut off the mindless odyssey. Commercials repeated and I heard enough of *Don Cherry's Pro-Talk* yesterday afternoon. Anyway, today should be our first direct broadcast from the NHA Western Division."

Livia toweled off and pointed to the kitchen where Tom sat quietly. From the buffet, she filled a coffee carafe and placed it on a tray with a bagel and sweet rolls, dropping it in front of him on her way upstairs to change clothes.

On her return, she noticed Tom had done serious damage to the breakfast goodies. She set a stack of pony ride handbills near his mug and filled him in on yesterday's advertising blitz. "Yesterday went well – we hit nearly every bulleting board in Kailua town. Don't know if they'll show up too good on MEGA-MART's and Sack 'n Save's — since they're quite loaded. The day before, I snagged most the Mom and Pop stores in Honalo and Kainaliu. If you can catch the ones in between Kmart and Safeway, then I'll post ones at the other KTA and the Keauhou Shopping Center this afternoon. I'll take Lotus - she loves her walks there, and those merchants are dog-friendly. Tim's probably right – tourists and boat people will show up, if it's free. By the way, how's the coffee? Need any more?"

He nodded yes, thanking her for the inn's help. A pensive look preceded him jotting some notes and asking if she could share La'Ohana's coffee flavor secret.

"Very little to it." She gently turned his list over and jotted down the ingredients, reading them to him. "One large container Kirkland Signature Dark or Tim Horton's coffee, plus two tablespoons cinnamon, three tablespoons vanilla, and one tablespoon almond extract. The only trick is to mix, mix, mix in a big bowl – because POOF, and it's all over the place – and the flavorings can get kind of sticky."

He grimaced.

Her eyes rolled, as her mouth scrunched a dimple. "Sorry. Anyway, I try to mix the mess when Cate isn't around. Oh, and it's a rounded half-cup coffee per pot."

Tom gently swallowed. "No offense taken. You know, Livy – this endeavor has already proved kinda fun. Tim and I've seen lots of folks, and a few faces that we'd hoped not to see again." He reached for her mug. "May I try yours?" He swallowed. "Umm, hmm." His moustache thinned against his teeth. "Yes, well– piquant but not quite refined. So, you really don't care for Kona Coffee?"

She patted the coffee pot. "No, I just can't appreciate its subtlety. Actually, my diesel fuel's secret is my father's steel percolator. Only thing I add is filtered water. Tom flinched, and she added, "Oh - I should have given fair warning, in case you're allergic to any of the flavorings. Are you?"

"Nah! Only feta cheese and lamb set me off – and they only bring a good case of the vapors. Not to change the subject, but I've gotta check on the ponies and circling mechanism." Stepping into a John Wayne stance he played Quickdraw and shot off two air pistols. Puffing air from each barrel and twirling them into their holsters he said, "Sure as shootin' someone will have keiki down to the corral before startin' time."

Livia helped clear the table and walked him to the barn, as he confided, "You know, Tim was quiet taken with Cate's Amish quilts. He slept under one, of his Uncle Rocky's AIDS Quilts, since late high school. Nearly wore it out; so for Christmas, I'd like to buy him an extra-long lap quilt. I'll pay Cate hourly, as well as for materials — if she'll sew it."

"That's a lovely idea. She is pretty busy, but you know what might spur her interest? Give her some competition, like a quilting bee. We'll get a photo of a design that he likes, and there are scads of stitch patterns. Do you like swirly ones stitched through every piece, or a stitch-in-the-ditch style? Cate's been practicing Hawaiian rainbow quilting, though on only a couple sample squares; however, since those quilts usually aren't built in pieces, she's not attempted a whole quilt. Most styles can be hand- or machine-quilted. I prefer hand stitches. The simpler stitch-in-the-ditch doesn't interrupt the view of appliqué details."

"The who?" He starred. "No. It's fine if she machine stitches it, but I think we need more time for you to explain the craft's terminology."

"Sorry. I get going with way too many details. Tell ya what. How about she shows you some samples?"

His dimple deepened. "Succinctly said. Sounds good."

"I'd like to barter for my services," clucked Livia. "If I give you quilt suggestions, will Tim critique my tattoo designs?"

"No, way. Just ask him. He knows plenty of artists. They all talk story. Early morning is best. He plays smithy at the forge. If you can stand the heat, he will be glad to gab."

"Well, my mother got so upset when my father gave away free legal advice. So, I just didn't want to impose."

"Aw — you gotta remember; this is Aloha Land. Beside that, the inn gives us excellent business. We're makamakas." She blushed, and he leaned closer. His eyes mirrored her squint. "The word means we are good friends who give and share."

With a few quick shoulder nudges, she teased him about getting all teachery. A quick hug and she headed out the door. Noticing yesterday's mail still in the box, she walked it back to him. Once again at the highway, she turned to wave and saw him rip the envelope in half with a look of disgust.

Her imagination ran from bad credit to hate mail. Kind of scary, in this lightly populated area. She empathized, having learned from her father's profession and from living in Canada, that human nature was much the same everywhere. Her gut told her it was something other than junk mail.

Climbing the side lanai's steps her pace quickened as she noticed Pinkie's perch ajar. *Such a noodle!* She couldn't recall checking his food or water this morning. Luckily, he sat at the screen door slapping his tail and rolling his eyelids at her. With him settled below his newly-leveled perched, she noticed Cate at the kitchen table – with hands cradling her head.

Livia grabbed a fresh teabag and whispering, "Headache still there? Let me freshen your mug."

Mug to nose, Cate leaned against Livia who whispered, "Just rest, now; Tom's coming."

Ten minutes of silence and she handed Cate another mug of hot water and plain toast. "Well at least it's not one of your migraines. Eat your breakfast. Tea's cool enough; take your medicine. Snooze a bit. I'll come wake you for my potty break."

Eyelids fluttering, Cate's finger touched her lips. With a strained smile and a nod she fumbled with the Imitrex blister packet and mumbled, "Sounds fine."

Less than two hours later, with a soothing flax seed bag draped over her shoulders, Cate hurried Livia along. Big strides and they returned from the carport with more paper napkins and plates. Food table arranged, they waved as Margaret left for quick trip to the hospital.

The smaller Shetland ponies, Oho and Una, fascinated both adults and keiki. At least thirty-five had ridden by noon, and the lawn buzzed with another twenty waiting with family and friends.

More tourists arrived than were planned. Most didn't ride but stayed to watch and quickly cleaned out food and the inn's brochure rack. Good guess on buying extra hot dogs and buns. Any extra packs could always be frozen, for later. Livia was glad she reserved the donated Lez Beans specialty coffees for another day, as many guests brought coffee and slushy drinks from the nearby Gas 'n Go.

Lehua whinnied but let Livia adjust stirrups and halter. However, she struggled against the other large pony, Pōkā. She watched Tim side-up to him cupping a handful of Maui sugar so the bad boy had to work for it.

He laughed. "Tom mentioned you wanna talk-story. Kinda nice when a blond malihini gets interested in our culture." Pointing to the back of her hands, he rubbed his chin and smiled. "Nice tats. Looks like Aunty Nani inked these."

"Yes, seemed like a nice lady – actually, the only artist interested in my Greek key and circular weapon designs. The other artists tried to sell me their own, and they could have — till she interceded. Cuz I'd had a wee bit too much to drink."

After the crowd thinned out, Tim and Tom stabled the horses and returned to clean up and visit. Tim herded all three women across the lawn to a regally seated woman. Slowly she turned to face them. Her lovely white ruffled muumuu, with pink yoked bodice took Livia by surprise. Fine cotton lawn was hard to come by. She and Cate stitched on voile and tulle but didn't prefer either. Livia tried not to stare.

Bending down, Tim bestowed a hearty hug on the sweet old lady who seemed greatly pleased before releasing him. Finally, she focused on Livia's gracious smile. The breeze wafted the scent of plumeria from the hala weaver's soft shoulders.

"Livia and Cate, this is Auntie E. Lee. She wants to donate four wonderful 'Keiki Ekes', or baby baskets for our pony rides." He pursed his lips. "Wait till you seem them. They are woven with ribbons and are too cute."

Livia extended her hand and was surprised at the elderly lady's strong grip. "I'm honored to meet you. How often do you make riding baskets for tiny keiki?"

Tim and Auntie's eyes widened, as Livia quoted a basket weaving article from last September's *Hawaii Magazine.*

Auntie Lee explained how she designed strong baskets for car seats and bicycles - and would weave more - if parents would only use them. She described her shop at the base of Mauna Hualalai. Her hats and finer woven items commanded a good price these days, and her students asked to strip their lau hala leaves a little wider so they could quickly weave four nice and strong keiki baskets. They wanted safe pony rides, plus it never hurt to advertise.

Tim was to tie a pillow in each basket, before cinching each pair to the larger Pintos. So pleased he was, when Auntie told him that all her students wanted, in exchange for their baskets, was to sign the insides. She nodded, when he and Livia assured her that an adult would accompany each keiki.

Two more Saturdays and the pony ride lines backed up, to the highway. The Monday after, everyone met over dinner to discuss whether or not they should add a second pony circling mechanism. The plans proved no problem, except Livia suggested they might contact their insurance company for a basic service contract.

Tim and Tom agreed to always be on site, one at each mechanism, and they signed a guarantee that no one would service or run the rides for them. If one should be absent, they would post a "One Ride Only" sign, at the road, and set up only one circling mechanism. The plans were toasted, for good luck, with a bottle of Cate's best Beaujolais.

The more she saw of Tim. the more familiar he seemed to Livia. She noticed that she and Cate were not the only ones having a fine time on Saturdays. Cate noted that Margaret cut down her business hours and broadened her flex-work hours at the Keiki Clinics. Yes, after playing St. Nicholas, she seemed most at ease mingling with the parents and children. Livia nodded at the prescription pad twice the last hour.

Only recently, Livia admitted that most of Margaret's activities escaped her attention – well, except for one of them. She had only seen Margaret speak with Tim and one other guy. Glancing around, she pointed out a neatly groomed man. "Catie Pat, I'm sure that's him - the one with the big gray cowboy hat and the way-too crisply starched khaki pants and vest."

They teased that Tim and Margaret were the "Will and Grace" of Kealakekua. As for the dude, in the hat - his mannerisms seemed local, but his face not familiar.

Livia squinted; the teacher in her was ever alert. "I've not seen Great White Hunter before; however, this one's mannerisms are definitely professional. I wonder — do Tim or Tom know him? Now that I think of it — he's kept his distance from both of them. You know me: I'm not nosy but concerned — and to err on the side of prudence, well — I'll find out."

Chapter 5: Old News and New

After twenty-eight years of living in the same home in Michigan, Livia learned nice neighbors meant a lot. The past few months, she visited Queens' Stables two or three mornings a week. Most days, with Lotus by her side, she only called out a quick "How-do?" On occasion, she accepted a friendly invitation to come in. One day, she and Tom learned they had more in common than teaching school. Tim slid by in his socks. Broom in hand, he gave a little hip action and crooned a Hawaiian version of the "We are Family". Was not long and they mastered each other mannerisms - talking lots of story.

One Friday, she stood near the stable's entrance sketching lipstick red hibiscus towering over gold-edged red cannas. She sighed and soaked up the raw tropical sun, as Lotus sniffed along the row of newly painted fence posts. Merely contemplating how much richer the hues were than in Michigan, and it came to her — where she had first seen Tim.

Ages ago when she attended The University Of Michigan graduate school – she found Ann Arbor's dance clubs less crowded than those such as Menjo's or The Backstreet during the summer. Detroit's heat had Livia and roommates: Tillie, Susan, and Ralph so restless that they carpooled thirty miles and cruised the college town's less mean streets. After sharing Cottage Inn pizza they would head up State Street and zigzag over to Main Street sampling a few brews in between.

One evening, fresh drafts of Bass Ale sent them ambling down a row of tall windowed storefronts. Livia skipped up and down the curb, to a nimble bass player's progressive rendition of UofM's fight song. Like Detroit's Back Street and Five West, though smaller in scale, these dance clubs had the meanest DJ's.

She stretched, in her chair, and watched Tim sweep and croon to the broom. Licking her lips, she fondly remembered Ann Arbor's all-night vegan delis and restaurants. None of them matched the glitzy yet cozy atmosphere of Woodward Avenue's Back Stage restaurant, piano bar and small jazz club theater just south of 8-Mile. Oh how she missed every one of them.

Ann Arbor's gem back then was The Rubaiyat, and its dance floor fielded the most diverse patrons. Many came only to dance, and she always wondered how the minimum cover kept the place open. Time answered that question. Probably its last year open was when she first saw Tim.

The next time she visited with him, she found the opportune moment. "Were you ever in Michigan - say in the mid-80s?"

He reminisced about blacksmithing before saying he had demonstrated the craft one summer in Camp Fortson. That was close enough, and with a few more questions, she learned it had been the same summer. She mentioned a couple dance bars, and when his eyes twinkled, she knew he and Tom were definitely `Ohana.

The crash grabbed even the guests' attention, and everyone within earshot of the private lanai had their noses glued to the kitchen door.

From the hubbub, Livia caught Cate's comment.

Parting a row of guests, she said "Kitchen Chemist – at it again." Towering over Livia she knelt beside her and tersely whispered, "May I make a suggestion? Just, for today? Let me help. Yesterday, you flipped three pounds of powdery sugar mess off the counter." She swiped at the mess. "I must say your painted Springerles were so gorgeous and tasted supreme but I'm glad you took my suggestion before picking today's fare."

Looking down, at the pile of No-bake Beaumont Inn Bourbon Balls, they gave a stereo sigh of relief.

Livia shrugged. "The pan was more noisy than messy. Tomorrow will be quieter. I bought ground almonds for my Zimmet Sternes, and that's my last Christmas cookie project."

Cate rolled her eyes. "Somehow, I find that hard to believe. The last two couples I checked in — you know what they said? 'We only had to follow the flour, to find the place'."

Livia's tongue flashed between her teeth, and she moaned, "Ha – ha – ha." Feigning deafness, she heaved the mixer to the shelf and scooted it to the back of the cabinet.

Tina tiptoed in from the pantry, as Livia spun around and shoved a bottle near her face. Tina batted one back and exhaled. "Hoo-ee! They're tasty but pack quite a wallop."

Livia grinned. "Yes, Ma'am. Old Grand-Dad is 100-proof bourbon. It's bonded and one of the best, if you can abide it. Another sip?"

"Hmmm, I don't think so – but I'd love the recipe. Bet you don't know, but your booze locker is one of the island's best. Sure tops most the bars around here."

"Really — you don't say?" Livia downed a half-sip. "Well, I'd never turn a profit bar tending out here. The small quantity of really good stuff would have to be specially shipped. You know how that goes in the islands."

Handing Tina a recipe card and pen, Livia said, "I'll name the ingredients. You jot them down. My hands are way too sticky from bourbon balls."

She handed Tina a small split oak basket. "Take some wax paper and fill it to the handle. The bourbon will keep them for years, if you keep them in your fridge."

They heard Husband Nuggy drive up the lane, and Tina reminded Cate that her daughter, Ailiana, would deliver the inn's bake goods for the next few mornings. She chuckled. "Ruth's Emma may pick up cookies too. Where'd Miss Livy go? Oh – forgot what time it was. Good thing she's got that TiVo, cuz no way would she miss watching her Odetta show. I remember when I first started here; even during check-in, she had that little TV set up on the front desk. Oh, well - most of the guests used to watch it with her, anyway."

Cate agreed. "Years ago my mom would give her two VHS tapes every Friday. Livia would exchange the previous week's tapes of late night 'Are You Being Served' with my mom, and this went on for four years."

Tina chuckled and confided, "Families — just gotta love 'em. Just like Little Denny, my other grandson. He stole Mike and Mickey's skates. His mom, Kenike, made him write the twins an apology, and she told him – 'No sports for two weeks'."

"He was hard at writing when he slipped up and said that he hated her.

"Kenike played the martyr and said, "Well, then, my work is done."

"I am so proud of her, but it was everything I could do not to laugh in front of all three my grandkids. Well, Little Denny sniggered all right - but he kept on writing. Finally, he stood, handed over the apologies and hugged his mom. Emma took the twins out for burgers. Kenike stayed home with Little Denny and grounded him a third week from softball and soccer. Later she confided that she was getting him some skates for his birthday."

Livia walked in - just in time to hear Cate reassure Tina that another pair of old in-line skates could probably be found. Cate asked Livia to watch the front desk, for a few minutes, and that was when she learned that Tina had been raised 'hanai.' An old auntie raised her, after the tsunami washed Tina's parents, Alani and Kip, out to sea.

Tina collected her things, and Livia moved quickly and waved bye, from the main steps, before trotting in and tossing Cate a few bits and pieces of their conversation. "There is a custom, which is still common in the island, much like adoption. Tina's adopted. I read about the practice of giving a child away, as hanai, to be raised by friends or family, but I never realized it was still practiced."

What Livia could not quite fathom was why Ruth and Tina were so efficient but could barely tolerate each other." The stove timer's familiar ding sent her scurrying. "Anyway, I'd best get my cookies or they'll be up in smoke, and we'll have a mess all over again."

Cate followed her, halfway to the kitchen, remarking that Ruth handled the books and reservations with great skill. "How about going out for some Japanese food tonight?"

Livia nodded, knowing that meant supper at Mrs. Shetima's restaurant.

Day after New Year's, and Livia set out nine huge ring binders–one for each Big Island District. They contained maps and brochures describing activities and accommodations, with the exception of their competitors in Kona. All year, she watched as guests and friends added their tidbits among the pages.

Livia flipped the last binder shut. It once had surprised her that there was a North Hilo District. She sighed, "November again." For almost a year, she religiously filled the binders adding them to the huge resource cabinet, which made the great room's corner nearly into a library

There were video and audio tapes, along with logs of visitors' excursions. One family promised to return for the next three years, if they could store their spelunking records at the inn.

The Puna District was least familiar to Livia and her guests, and its small binder had been updated most frequently. The others' records were now quite extensive, and their maps continually sat open on the parlor's library table. The papers dried her fingers, so every morning she soothed them with quick absorbing *Oils of Aloha* Kukui Cream. With the last of it rubbed in, her gaze shifted to the front lawn as she relished her coffee.

A seductively cool breeze ruffled Polynesia's feathers, as the great bird preened in the corner of her cage. She fluffed her tail, and Livia's imagination drifted to long-ago patrons. She wondered: did they glide about the grand lanai that once encompassed the inn?

The women renovated the grand lanai, separating the front from the north section, thus opening it to the kitchen and for their private use as a service entry. They covered this direct route to the carport, with a spacious upper lanai that gave guests a grand view of the ocean.

She tipped her mug back and toyed with the ideas of replacing the inn's sign and mailbox. Peering over her glasses, she noticed the pre-dawn shadows did not limit her view. The inn's front lawn spanned a good 1000 feet of the highway. She decided to stretch her legs and let Lotus lead the way.

Back on the lanai, Livia balanced her laptop and bagel, aiming for the huge oak bench. Before she could turn and sit, Lotus hopped into her space.

"Scoot over!" she hissed. She and dog faced off, nose-to-nose. All she got from that was tiny dog licks.

A terse "Thank you" and she wriggled her derrière on the bench with Lotus squirming against her. Taking time to cuddle the dog, she watched Pinkie's tail hit the floor. She stayed in her perch three days following the inn's last termite treatment. Usually, the day after treatment someone took Pinkie to the seashore. She basked on the black rocks and often came home even more reclusive. Livia figured Pinkie's purpose had ended with Old Woofer. Tables turned; now, the Green Goddess spent her days any way she pleased.

Having had enough of her belly rub, Lotus flipped over and scampered to her food dish. Sitting at attention, her stubby tail slapped the floor as she kept moaning for a breakfast treat. A firm "No" brought her muzzle to the floor between her front paws.

Thoughts drifted to Detroit, where dawn and work came at a dreary and often raw time of day. Since her boss got sick, most of Livia's work mates had transferred to different buildings. Engineer buddy, Sharlene, came to Hawaii for what she called her 'two most wonderful weeks in paradise'. Joanne visited but mainly golfed. Livia missed working with them as a technical writer. Stifling as it was, with supervisors constantly jockeyed around, and the yearly November layoffs - Livia's old work had proved satisfying. It did not surprise her one bit when the national news magazines reiterated the same type story these past five years.

She shook her head and arranged her laptop and notes. Mornings at the inn generally gave her writing that added boost. Was it the six-hour time difference or South Kona's colorful palate?

She recalled their first visit to Kailua-Kona. Cate thanked a shopkeeper for her purchase, adding that it was too nice of a day to be at work. He flashed that grand Hawaiian smile and said, "Work in Hawai`i is like a vacation anywhere else." So far, the saying rang true.

Half the time, Livia met the newspaper carrier at the mailbox. That short stroll and her strong coffee pumped blood to her head. Recalling Professor Menlo's brief statement, "Truly original ideas are rare," Livia scanned the daily paper. She needed more information about *Newsweek's* story on discrimination. It compared today's racial differences with those of the Rosa Parks and Martin L. King era.

Luke took her and Annabelle on a vacation to the Deep South. At dawn, they plowed across the Ohio River on a diesel ferry, and drove through mountains and cotton country to Charleston. He wanted to see Fort Sumter. Odd things to a nine year old: there were cannons, shadowy mansions, boiled goobers and creepy Spanish moss. She stood between two drinking fountains and stared at a parade of marchers in heavy layers of clothes. Tugging at her mother's sleeve she asked, "Aren't they hot?"

Annabelle whispered, "It's in case the police might hit them or if they get put in jail."

As a kid, she missed the importance of those clothes and the separate drinking fountains. Barely a toddler, she stood next to the bus driver and pointed to sit upstairs but her mother tapped her hand twice, for "No, ask later." An old Whippet Lines Segicruiser it was, and she stood for most of that four-hour trip down gut-wrenching old State 37 from Indianapolis to Badendale. Weird what you recall from such a tender age. Later that year, they moved to the little town. She hopped down from their old gray Hudson with her big dog, Pal King. As the only girl in the neighborhood wearing denim overalls, she played Huck Finn and Zoro, and left food for Jiminy Cricket under a huge shaggy maple tree. Her father surprised her saying, "It's so big because there's a dead Indian buried under there." Grandmother Etter and Uncle Peter B. lived next door. She traveled lots, was strict, and smelled like old skin and Youth-Dew parfum. Livia knew he always carried his black bag home for supper before returning to the office; likewise, before first grade Livia learned to tell time, and she was nowhere to be found each evening at four. Other than fearing his free polio shots, she enjoyed a carefree childhood.

By 1990, Livia had taught in rural Indiana and downtown Detroit. Times had not changed much. One of two reasons she and Cate left Camp Fortson — other than the sewers were a mess, was that the old suburb had stayed absurdly segregated. No separate drinking fountains but that invisible thin blue line kept Detroiters at bay – especially after dark.

Anywhere money was involved, most people behaved the same. On this island, she observed disgruntled malihinis who often wrote to the daily papers. They did not much appreciate that their children counted second-in-line to attend the Kamehameha Schools. Queen Emma's Trust had chartered its educational institutions. Its resources were top-notch. Livia smirked. Queen Emma — as well as Princess Ruth and Queen Liliuokalani — had been pretty astute ladies. For way over 100 years, their philanthropic assets had been kept from sticky fingered kanaka 'ē.

Livia watched distant Hualalai. Her 8000-foot silhouettes emerge slowly from her sister's mists. Squinting, she recalled the lower peak's name. Book 'Em Danno – what a name for a mountain. Collecting her thoughts, she sketched before writing. She recently had read an astronomer's story citing that lightning between those peaks meant snow on distant Mauna Kea. She had good intentions about keeping a file with local lore.

Sniffing the air, she looked for the source of that heavenly hyacinth scent. The only flowers were tiny white clumps, on a boxwood bush, that were twenty feet past the sago palms. Why would their scent be carried further in this silent air? She could use a breeze right now. Come to think of it — what morning was free of bird chatter? Her eyes followed from dozing bird to dog. Having made haste to the garden, Little Miss Priss, dewy paws and all, hopped back to the bench.

Hair released, from a short ponytail, it fell lightly against her shoulders, as morbid memories marched forward. She shuddered. All those months she could not write – as Annabelle lay dying.

Forcing away the painful scenes, Livia found the next hour unproductive. Lately, she refused to peck away at her laptop after 6:00 PM most evenings. Even so, last night's flashbacks kept her flailing the mattress until nearly 2:00 in the morning. Non-prescription sleep aids were of little use, so she gave in and wrote for another hour. Finally, she fell asleep after outlining one of her bi-annual features, for the editorial page of the *Michigan Daily*.

After a few moments of sketching new garden paths and listing plants she would purchase at the next Pua Plantasia sale, she re-opened her editorial file and reviewed last night's notes.

First, she listed topics for her bi-monthly auto industry articles, which often headed the *West Hawaii Today* editorials – even a full page in last Sunday's feature section. She finished a good rough draft about nepotism and age discrimination still reigning supreme in the Motor City.

Secondly, she jotted another few highlights: top management and corporate attorneys earned premium pay, stock options, and premium health care; whereas workers with degrees like hers often hit a plastic ceiling. Receiving little premium training their career wages fell below the average blue-collar union wage – and its buying power had fallen the past decade.

She couldn't forget that last SAKO annual meeting. Upon witnessing a room full of professionals being goaded into signing papers thus reducing their wages and benefits, one disgruntled coworker stood and yelled at their contract house CEO, "You're pimping us! First, you outsource us to an automotive customer who found a way for you to take part of our wages. On top of that insult, you now pay less benefits and keep us dispensable with your one-year contracts. Decisions like that make us no more than cheap one-night hookers. We know the company is tightening your bottom line but doesn't quality work stand for something?"

She jotted notes about her automotive work. It had two profitable spikes: one from 1994-95 and the last one from 1998-99. In March, the regular employees' and share holders' bonus checks came. The following day, one coworker had the guts to hand a $20 bill to every contractor who worked on his programs — 62 in all. Even so, he apologized, saying that he once was a contractor (although, in those days, if you worked hard, you got trained and eventually hired).

Livia motioned him inside her cubicle and told him about a news story she read, on the Internet: that Washington's State Supreme Court ruled against a big company that did not hire temporary workers that were sitting right next to and doing the same work as their regular employees - exactly what Southfield had done. Then she complimented him on breaking with the brainwashed sheep and following his convictions.

A grin spread across his red face, as he stood raking his shoe across the stained carpet. Needless to say - that poor gentleman became no favorite with his fellow employees at Southfield Engine Company.

She sat quietly with a sigh of relief that she and her partners managed to buy the inn outright. With ten surrounding acres there was room for expansion, though they would never subdivide. She outlined a few more examples for her article. Two described how a tart second-rate supervisor bartered for her, on loan, to cover for a regular employee taking maternity leave. For a year, she gave Livia additional work, in addition to her regular job, for no extra pay. Such a nice, nasty guy in that he belittled her Master's Degree because it wasn't recently earned; and in the very next breath, he said she did such good work, and he was sure each duty was well within her job description. She leaned closer and told him that she heard recent grad-students say their local coursework, paid for by this company, lacked real meat. She added, just for the record, that her unpaid duties of Xeroxing and stapling his weekly records was not part of her contract work, which was engineering modification release technical writing. Worst part was: she knew he knew it.

She jotted a few more insider stories and outlined the conclusion: Big industry can more easily control and profit from a naïve and narrowly educated workforce; although, this practice rarely produces a superior fleet of cars.

She chuckled and pet Lotus. Did all that education keep her sane or make her neurotic? Cate and her friends were quick to note her agitation, and rarely talked shop around her. Occasionally, they slipped up and got an earful. Like the time Livia asked a supervisor why most colleges charged the same tuition, for BS and BA degrees, and how most companies paid way less for the later. That drew a dumb look from him. Nowadays, she wrote instead of unloading on someone – well, at least she tried.

She felt a bit better and realized that to do any justice in her editorial, she must compare the bad days to good ones. Doodling along the margin, she quickly reviewed her two careers and tallied the best. She listed the work she'd done for Biff Melton's section; another couple years with an auto supplier's IT managers; as well as, working with two great principals out of the six she worked for. Oddly enough — most of her good managers were relatively new to their jobs. The most successful ones treated her like she had a brain, asked for her input, and only hired dedicated workers in the first place (not Southfield legacies). Oh - and most possessed a better than average sense of humor, would try a new idea, and could admit a mistake. Oh pooh, her list grew too long – well, she would edit later.

Then auto work turned sour. Her last supervisor's diabetes worsened. His loyal crew circled the wagons and worked harder than ever — till 9/11 hit. Profits fell, and he turned stoic, knowing the company was about to split up his section, by siphoning off regular employees and foreign contractors to other departments. As one of her school principals had done, he counseled each employee on career choices; however, he could do little for his non-green card contractors - they, Livia, and two other women over fifty just plain got canned.

On top of all else, came Annabelle's cancer. That is when Livia threw in the towel and plotted her escape: to move them to Hawaii.

They would sip coffee, eat custard and discuss light stories from the morning newspaper. One morning Annabelle pointed to a quote from Katherine Hepburn. Livia stuck it to the refrigerator after reading it aloud: "You just need enough money to say no."

Her eyes grew heavy, with visions of warm afternoons and clinking Margarita glasses. She saw herself lift a tiny Hallmark poem book and quote, "And what is so rare as a day in June?" Like Grandmother Etter, Annabelle could recite the whole damn thing. Comforted, Livia drifted to sleep.

Two steaming stacks of Cate's Fabulous French Toast quickly disappeared. Quiet and satisfied, Livia and Margaret read the paper, as Cate whisked together a water-based version for herself. She chattered about how she liked adding a pinch of cardamom, instead of the usual nutmeg. Livia liked it, but Margaret murmured that she could not really tell the difference.

Still peeking beneath the seared doughy edges, Cate relished a few mouthfuls - until the topic of gasoline prices came up.

Livia knew Cate always filled the Laredo at the cheapest gas station. Hawaii's gas cap let petro prices go up twice last month; however, the national newscasts no longer chided the president's failure to open the oil reserves. How much would prices rise, so the party-in-power could conveniently fix them right before the next election? Nevertheless, the lowly cartoonists kept drawing ever-larger ears, on the man, with the Texas and Iraq oil management MBA. He still spoke, as though choking, on that silver foot, which Governor Ann Richards said was stuck in his father's mouth. Livia chuckled. Even if he meant well – he just plain looked better, in his baseball-style jacket, than in the clothes his advisors dressed him. All that was sad comic diversion for the $70 billion tax cut, for corporations – what a debt load for the war in Iraq. Yesterday's newspaper headlines explained - since the late 1999, lobbyists gained a giant foothold between taxpayer and representation. With workers so busy, it worked so well, for now.

She could not forget her father's word: "Whomever is elected – always support that person in office. Her head reeled, as she considered how nations fell slowly before the big war in Europe. The elections of late were screwy, to say the least. The first one's deciding electoral vote got cast in his brother's state. And the last election – went off even better in Ohio. Who would get the nod this time? If communications were tapped, why not the e-polls? If Castro's right hand man was his brother, then why not–

Warm hands, on her shoulders and a confident "Breathe–," from Margaret, and Livia set her notes down and got busy shaking kibbles into the dog's bowl, as Margaret tossed together salad fixings and packed a half-dozen of Cate's leftover Featherbed Pirogues. The dishwasher hummed, and they moved to the massive kitchen island.

Stifling a yawn, Margaret unlocked the drawer to her prescription pad. Writing two for Chakra, she encouraged Livia to lecture their ample friend about blood sugar and diet, and then muttered, "Oh, forget it. She is an adult."

Just like today at breakfast — Margaret had encouraged Livia to dip bites of pancakes in light syrup saying, "You used to get quite snookered on sugary Wood Cabin."

Livia blew her off - but she fully appreciated the concern. Hugging Lotus, and batting her big brown eyes she crooned, "Well, Lola loves me."

As Margaret teased about Lotus' tongue sticking to the plate, Livia considered what and what not to eat. Grazing on protein all day was one a big pain in the posterior. Although, she found pride, in maintaining what she called her 'fighting weight', while constantly reminding herself - so much of the world went hungry.

Cate interrupted with a toast: "To The Good Doctor – so nice of you to help our friends and relations."

"Oh bother – I came here for same reasons as did you two. Not to change the subject - but Livia, what do you think of *in vitro* and gene splicing? I do not mean the medical techniques, but you read current opinion, and I value your opinion. As you know, we're both from the sort of families that drug all their Victorian values into the 20th Century."

"Whoa! Wasn't that the doctor's line from *The Haunting*?"

"Oh, by golly, you caught me," Margaret laughed. "I do my best to keep it light."

Too late. Livia thoughts flew to Margaret's veterinarian friend and back. That aside, she promised herself to stick to the KISS Principal and keep any answer hypothetical and short.

"Well, my only problem with in vitro fertilization is that additional egg extractions might be required, to avoid multiple births and waste of embryos. Of course, not to worry about that: we — like the poorer women — may be wearing red robes and lose any choice, if we don't stand up, for rights of others to speak for themselves."

Noting Margaret's silence, Livia continued. "As for gene splicing – I support it. Twenty years ago, I attended ISNA meetings. Back then, it was a bunch of gals, called Womyn, who met at The Michigan Union.

One cold Sunday night we'd heard plenty from a clinical biology student dominating the discussion, so I baited her with the idea of splicing two women's genes. To this day, I wonder if she ran with my idea. I hear the Koreans beat us to combining two XX genes in an embryo. I figured - why not? If our carbon is merely a resting place for our souls, is it not possible that any two people might provide the next portal?"

Margaret sat down hard and fingered her necklace. "Hoo-lordy! Glad I asked." Fingers still busy, she asked, "What about the church? Your denomination sent the first missionaries here. So, did that have anything to do with your move here?"

Livia winced, "No – ma'am!" and she left it at that.

Cate took a big step back, as Margaret's next statement hit the fan: "I've been thinking of offering myself as a test subject."

Livia got the stare as Margaret asked, "Since you have no close blood relatives, can I count on you for one of my tests?"

Abhorrent to needles, Livia gulped. "I guess, maybe. What's to do? Do I teedle in a cup, give a swab of my mouth, or what?"

"I don't know yet. You can read the procedure later. Okay?"

Livia winced again and followed Margaret to the pantry. There she unplugged her laptop, and replaced it with Livia's. She fiddled with the wires and quietly said, "Cate mentioned Pearl's funeral."

Livia shook her head, and Margaret gave her a big hug. Livia exhaled. Finally, she pulled free and said. "Ten years ago, she planned her own funeral service and burial arrangements. My work, with her power of attorney, is done."

"Lord knows you've done enough. Whatever you decide is fine."

They walked to the kitchen. Livia pulled down the front of her old oak secretary. Miss Lotus snoozed, head on the chair roller, as she wrote personal checks. That finished, she unlocked the center drawer and removed the inn's three-tiered checkbook. All accounting remained Cate's domain; Livia merely slipped a few receipts in the front cover.

Closing the desk, she grinned. "Margaret..." she snickered. " I can sure think more fun ways to get cell samples."

"What?" Margaret looked up from the kitchen's rocking chair.

"Nothing, just thinking out loud." Livia swiveled around, shredded a few papers and quickly snapped, "Ow! Lola! – that's my toe – not your chewy treat." Heel to dog's head, she pushed, and said, "What? We don't give you enough to eat around here?"

She opened Annabelle's file box. A large gray envelop held her mother's final tax documents - submitted twice, following the sale of her home. A young Southfield engineer and his wife bought Annabelle's yellow bungalow, and a professional woman took Livia's huge old house.

Still, the life changes were hard to fathom. When Annabelle laid dying, Camp Fortson's Building and Safety Department officials drug out roof inspections over two snowy months. So nit-picky – the city left them with $1,500 of unexpected bills, and Michigan refused any income tax credit for it.

Margaret's shadow fell across her. Strong hands gently massaged Livia's weary shoulders. Her thumbs pressed and rippled down her spine as her fingertips plied their way, to her waist, and rising in tandem along each outer rib.

She stiffened.

Margaret moved back. "I'm sorry. Was there bad news?"

"No; nothing recent."

Margaret pulled up a chair offering a fistful of tissues.

Mirroring her Grandmother Etter's impeccable posture, Livia stated, "My mother promised to help me — if I'd only hang onto that darn house. Actually, I held onto two of 'em. Big as my home was, I cashed in most every asset for the inn's down payment." Tears swelled. *Finally, all on my own now.* Cate and Margaret's faces came to view. *Well, not really.*

"We are here for you. You do know she'll always be in your heart," said Margaret, kissing her on the cheek.

Livia nodded. Shoulders squared and eyelids lowered, she said, "Guess so, but they sure did end an awesome century."

Margaret slipped the paperwork from under her hands, and pressed her thumb to Livia's palm as she placed it in her lap.

Livia barely noticed. "Thanks, Aumakua." As she reached for the newspaper, she figured some how - her mother kept watch over them.

She wrinkled her nose, at the classifieds, and set them aside. The inn's small expenses were adding up, and she could not shake the crazy notion: it was honorable to protect what her parents had worked so hard for. Confident in the fact that she had written the last letter to creditors, she pushed her worn ledgers aside.

Siding up close - Margaret ruffled Livia's hair and said, "You know better than anyone that I came out here to help."

"Help me?" Livia turned sideways. "Coincidentally, I got the idea to buy an inn from a comment of yours. After answering your pager twice during a hockey game, you said, 'Maybe someday – I'll own a bed and breakfast.' Yep, only a few years later - you quit your job at that prestigious hospital."

Margaret glanced away. "True, but I never figured anyone heard me."

Nose in the air, Livia chirped, "That would be me. Warming the bench those two half-seasons, believe me - I heard plenty."

Margaret said, "Yeah? As I recall, when you did play goal, you patrolled the top of the crease and got pretty scrappy. What was it? Oh, yeah – one team called you 'Livid Livia'. I always thought it a bit strange - how most players could not tell you and Cate apart, though your equipment did match."

Livia smiled. "I heard that a lot. Actually, Cate towered over me, and we played very different styles. I always idolized Bad Eddie, and she was more a mix of Andy Moog" she gulped, "and Patrick Roy." Funny, how she once admitted - if I were younger than she was, I would have had more ice time than she had. I'm just happy that I saved us a few tournaments. That first year we played against you and The Blades; I finished the season after you reeled off that slap-shot that bounced off her knee."

Margaret winced, adding, "Never knew that. Cate was the best. I can't remember how many times her puny shoulders got us to the finals."

Tears welled. Livia reached for the small puck trophy that always sat atop the secretary. "My only most valuable player award. Cate had that awful migraine, at The Golden Blades Tournament when we played my alma mater. You're right – I got us to the finals, and she won it. Sponsors got us mixed up and awarded her the MVP trophy. I was never so touched, as on the ride home, when she handed me her trophy. Can't toot my horn too much - those Canucks handed my ass to me quite a few times. All-in-all, Cate was the better goalie."

Margaret looked down pensively. "Damn, I forgot that I hurt her knee. That was the only season that I played for the Berkley Bruisers. We won nearly all the time, but I hated playing with them. Guess I do not remember too much except my pager going-off all the time - until my residency was complete. Such great fun. Never minded working all those hours, but all that changed when I became a fellow plus injured my shoulder. With me not able to perform surgery for six months, my partner gave me an ultimatum: 'Hockey or him'."

"Yeah. You, Cate and I were just plain lucky to have played as long as we did. It's just that — I needed to play a couple more years."

"I hear you there. I do miss hockey, plus my teaching and research at Charles Montgomery; however, it grew too big, and with all that red tape and too many hands in the pot – that practice had to go. Not only that - it became way too exclusive, morphing into other businesses, and transferring too many patients with too little insurance to other hospitals downtown."

Livia thought, *Yeah, like how that HMO messed with Cate's Granddaddy Nick after his knee surgery.* She stood and said, "Not to change the subject, but I've got to run to town and be back here by 10:30 for the upholsterer's delivery. You realize that's a big reason - I wanted this inn. Everyone kept teasing me that I needed a big place for all my furniture."

"No way? The love seats are finally finished? I cannot wait to see that gorgeous burgundy brocade embroidered with gold pineapples. Sure took you long enough to find that damn fabric. We must have a sit on them this evening and give a toast to our hockey years with my best Rhine wine."

They enjoyed a little peace and quiet — until Margaret glanced at her watch. "Anyway, about Chakra's prescriptions, let me show you the inserts."

That complete, Livia placed the inserts in a cubbyhole and the medicines in the fridge. She finished the bills by retracing her steps, by reviewing each check number in the inn's register then marking them off her calendar. Then as Cate taught her, she neatly placed each bill and its check in a previously stamped envelops – pencil-marking each flap before sealing it.

Cate breezed in, tossing car keys on the pantry counter. She peeked around the doorframe announcing, "Here I am! Glad to be home!" After quick hugs, she scooted past them saying she had a couple things to finish before they left to meet Aye. Still in work mode, she barked, "Livia! Are you ready? Got the prescriptions? Is there anything else we need to take?"

Five minutes later, they were on the lanai. Cate looked over Livia's notes and the prescriptions, as Margaret stood at attention with briefcases and lunch. They waited politely, as Livia scooted out the door with a grocery bag, a jar of Falafel Chili and a Ziplock of neatly packed beef jerky.

Cate was the first to bite. "And what's in the bag?"

Livia kept walking.

"Oh, just a little show and tell. You know, some quilts: two yours, one mine"

Cate glanced to Margaret, and lip-synced to Livia's words: "Just relax and humor the school teacher."

Fastening her seatbelt, Livia watched Cate boost Lotus to the back seat then wave to Margaret.

A slow pendulum, Margaret's chin swung side to side. "Please — try to stay out of trouble."

They followed her car to the highway. Margaret turned north and Cate the other way. Livia watched Lotus stare out the back window, then hop down and lick Cate's ear.

Was it the newly paved highway or the Laredo's newly oiled suspension? It seemed today - this hilly and curvy section of road no longer sent Livia's stomach reeling. The trees bending over the road reminded her of old State 66 skirting along Southern Indiana's river bottoms. Here – Kona's seasons ebbed and waned a warm polonaise. Back there – The Ohio's flood plains flooded and oozed rhapsodies and requiems. Its dogwood and redbud dappled spring forests. Golden and crimson leaves layered its musty fall paths. Snow sparkled briefly on its dark winter branches, and its Cottonwoods breathed you up in the summer air. Cate choose Hawaii first, and Livia chose The Big Island for its variety.

A gentle tug on her shoulder interrupted them, as Cate said, "Hey there? You still with me?"

"Yeah. Memories – never been so vivid."

Cate squeezed her knee and said, "Seems pretty normal – considering." She slowed the car, and they enjoyed the early morning sky. "Would you rather not remember them or rather not had 'em?"

Comparing people and memories in general, Livia said, "Always the Russian soothsayer," then finished quickly, "But, you're right." She popped open the console and yanked out her favorite map. "By the way, where is this place, anyway?"

Cate pointed down the road. "It's on the right just before Ho'okena Beach, maybe two or three miles from here.

Livia asked, "Wonder how Lola will get along with Aye and Chakra's little snorter? Sure was nice of them asking us to bring her. She's not been out much. The only animals she's ever been with were The Ma's cats, and that's been almost a year ago. The only way to know is to bring her. If need be, we can always put Lola back in the car."

Cate turned. "See? It's cool, and she's sound asleep. The Ma had Baby Girl all upset and skitterish. "Now, she's calmed down – and we still worry."

The car tires bumped from asphalt to cinders. Cate got excited. "Chakra told me that she'd explain all about her quilt designs. Traditional patterns are cut like huge intricate snowflakes. I'm curious if her ideas are different from those in our quilty books."

"Maybe," said Livia. "Look! There's Aye. That must be a bag of greens for the table. He told me it's good to gather herbs and stuff in the morning after the dew dries." *Curious,* she thought. *Rarely had she seen dew in Kona.*

Lotus hopped down, as very small pot-bellied pig cleared the woods and ran full tilt for her passing Aye and nearly bowling him over.

He teetered, and with balance regained - he once again started to his guests. Warmly greeting them, he introduced his pretty porker, Tallulah. She ambled alongside, as they passed through a small and oddly placed arbor and gate – both fronting a rickety lanai, which matched the beach shack's weathered gray clapboards. Though not that old, this humble abode seemed to belong to another era, like that of Thoreau's at Walden Pond. It definitely brought back fond memories of Livia's first house in the country.

She glanced from the statue to the conch shell-lined path, and back to Aye leaning against the porch rail. With his weight, she figured it would give way at any moment.

He walked to his herb garden. After gathering a few blossoms and leaves, he poked his head through the window, and he gently announced their guests' arrival. Before he could reach to help her, Chakra opened the plain and planked door - quite modest except for the two weathered kahili flanking it. She mirrored their grimaces and waved their guests inside.

Aye solemnly said, "Komo-mai, and welcome to our humble home." He followed Livia and Cate after slipping off his old zoris.

Cate said, "Entré-vous."

Livia's eyes followed Cate's hand gesture, noticing an ancient Glengarry, of the Douglas Clan tartan plaid, hanging on a wall hook just inside. The sun glared off the polished koa wood floor, as her toes kneaded something soft. She squinted, nudged Cate and pointed to the rare *lau hala* woven mat that soothed her feet, before glancing up again. Centered on the wall, separating the living room from the kitchen, was a huge old black-and-white photograph of the inn.

They both stood transfixed until Cate nudged Livia, and ever so politely pointed at a lovely red-and-white snowflake quilt.

Aye cleared his throat and quietly guided them to the kitchen where Chakra sat at a round huge table, her ample fingers smoothing its cloth.

It was impossible not to notice how dilapidated the cottage was. Except for a lovely handcrafted bay window, which held dozens of potted orchids and tropical plants, everything seemed loved to death.

After seating them, Aye took his place at the stove, and quickly quieted the teakettle. Setting it on the counter, he lifted a handsome French Haviland Limoge teapot from the cupboard, and set it on the old porcelain drain-board. After adding loose tea, he filled the pot with steaming water. As the tea steeped, he placed a matching cup and saucer before each woman. He covered the pot with a bright calico cozy, and set it to Chakra's right.

Cate seemed a tad overwhelmed, until Livia interrupted the silence. "Cate and I brought some sample quilts: her Amish Purple and Blue one, my mother's Sunbonnet Sue, and an old version of the tipsy Log Cabin." She glanced up at Chakra, adding, "I've always been curious about Amish quilts and how they compare with Hawaiian color schemes. There was a Polynesian pattern, which I've often dreamed about – not a brightly colored quilt such as your traditional red on white one — but one with angular tappa designs. It was very similar to some bookmarks we bought." Getting the eye from Cate, Livia concluded, "Your quilt in the living room – well, the handwork is exquisite."

Chakra smiled and said, "Thank you. My mother and aunties taught me well." Noticing Lotus' pounce and bounce act, she pulled the dog closer and introduced her to Miep the cat.

The animals calmed right down. Livia glanced around then looked up to see dozens of orchids plus a few tropical plants hanging above the window. The sun warmed her bare feet on the smooth floor. If sold, its gorgeous koa and that in the cupboards could finance a new cottage. So calming to sit here, until a sinking feeling moved to the pit of her stomach. Her skin flashed hot and moist, and her shirt felt glued to her back. By the time the sensation had passed, so had thoughts of standing naked in between the refrigerator doors.

"Tea is served," said Aye. "Afterward, I'll give Livia a tour of these orchids' baby brothers and sisters. Beneath this window is their nursery," wagging his finger near the window's baseboard.

Chakra offered a plate of pineapple macadamia nut shortbreads. After eating a couple, she talked story - how many years ago, in a poker game, the inn's acreage was deeded from her family to Mr. Mertherman. "He and my father were such good friends. After winning the property, he employed Aye and me at various times following World War II. Poor thing, he nearly wasted away after that first heart attack. At that time, I began tending the front desk. Aye kept the place spiffy when not fishing here or in Hilo. Oh my – let me ramble on so – you are so polite to listen. Now, did you bring some goodies to show me?" She smiled contentedly, as she nibbled another wedge of cookie.

After a few quiet and tense seconds, Aye chirped, "Let Chakra know how you want more tea. I prefer mine, in a beaker, still steeping, whilst you get started on your next cup."

Livia rubbed a tiny craze in the rim of her cup. She figured he was making his last. They probably had a short supply of good tea, as well as teacups.

Chakra added, "Yes, I do hope our calamities rest in the past. All our kupuna would wish us happy lives. This wonderful day, we must honor our ancestors and share with our new friends." She turned to Aye. "Maybe after tea, Livia would like to see your orchid nursery? Cate's eyes have not left my quilts. When we are finished you might share your gardening secrets; and possibly, Cate would be so good - as to inform me about Mainland quilting."

Aye leaned closer to Livia. "My orchid babies sit outside but are nicely protected." He pointed just beneath the window.

Cate watched Livia fixate on the plants. After a few minutes, she politely attempted small talk. "What a gorgeous view. Except for a few seaside restaurants, such as Hang Loose, I've never been indoors and so close to the ocean. Did you design this lovely window casing?"

"That we did not build," Aye answered. "Friends of ours wanted to make something nice for us, so they helped renovate this house on our kuleana."

Chakra's clear alto phrases hung in the air. "The view and the orchid nursery make our home. Come closer. See, next, to this wall?" She pointed outside. "Those stones are remnants of the big house's foundation. The storm that followed the 1960 tsunami destroyed the main portion of our home. In those days, our Ohana lived in Hilo - most of the year." Folding her hands, Chakra's eyes glistened. "That horrible kupua killed many family and friends."

Tapping his foot Aye pursed his lips and nodded in agreement.

Livia sat as straight as she could, and raised an eyebrow. *Who speaks this way? Damn, he must have read my expression.* Scooting her chair nearer the window, she looked past Cate's shoulder. Sure enough, there were the black remnants of the foundation.

Cate commented that Aye had fashioned a wonderful cottage garden among the ruins.

To Livia it was huge - more than twice the size of this cottage's foundation.

Then it hit her. Their manners were British. However, that history preceded them, by almost 250 years. She sat rock solid, as they chatted on.

Eventually she asked, "Wasn't most of this coastline Hawaiian Homelands? Looks like your previous home was triple the size of this cottage."

Chakra nodded and said that there were long strips of land here. "Since our children are grown, the cottage has become the perfect size for us; although, these days it seems to require continual repair. A permanent residence is difficult to keep so close to the sea, and it seems that the tide level and wave heights have risen a few inches."

Livia looked around. The thirty-year-old cottage looked way beyond its age – more like a shack than a cottage. In her opinion, the gorgeous kitchen window was its only redeeming feature. The inn's storage shed had to be a few square feet larger, and its timbers and flooring seemed much less worn.

"Just like us, things age." Chakra smiled.

Aye politely piped up, "Did you know? For a while, I was the caretaker of the inn. Also, Chakra is Pa`a`āina, or a landholder. She owns our family's property wedges that run mauka downhill makai." He pointed from the mountains to the sea.

Livia's jaw dropped. "No way! The Merthermans never mentioned anything about you and the inn, or about your properties."

Cate added. "No. They never mentioned you took care of the place."

Friendly banter ensued, and Livia quoted a magazine article, noting the wonderful Kona fishing villages from Captain Cook almost to South Point.

Aye beamed. "Yes, and most are still here – hidden away a bit."

Chakra passed around the last few pieces of shortbread. Still fixated on Cate's bag she asked, "Oh, how nice - did you bring goodies to show me?"

"Yes. If Livia will help, we'll hold up our quilts, so you can see." Cate opened her bag after carefully wiping the buttery cookie crumbs from her fingers. "These shortbreads are delicious with the Earl Grey; I'd sure like to have the recipe."

It was not long until everyone could barely get a word in edgewise. Polite banter came easy to Cate, and she talked mostly about nine patch quilt patterns and Livia's experimental cooking.

Livia smiled, as she petted Miep and looked out to sea. Aye was too politely quiet, and she forced herself to be sociable. Attempting a trick that her father used often, she lifted the cat and spoke to her. "I bet you love to roll in the flowers when you get outside. Don't you?" Miep merely purred; however, Aye took her hand, led her to the massive window, and pointed below.

He asked, "Would you care to see the orchids now?"

Enough of quilts, she thought. She thanked the gods for giving a good reason to get outside. "Never had any luck growing orchids or African violets, but I would love to see them."

Aye escorted her outside and politely asked, "And your specialty is?"

She blushed, her thumb tracing the flowers on her Aloha ring. Her mouth pulled to one side, as her eye lit up. "Roses."

He seemed interested, so she described her old roses and miniatures, plus a few hedge roses and good climbers, adding that she had planted over 100 of them, in her backyard and at her parents' house. Hybrids were not her favorite, but she coddled a few now and then. The fragrant Lady Banks Rose, a prolific and tall yellow climber, had always intrigued her. Delicate and suited only for tropical winters - she planned to purchase a specimen for the inn.

"Count me in; we'll have to mail-order a couple. Lady Banks — you say? I wonder if its namesake is any relation of Sir Joseph Banks, the botanist aboard the *HMS Endeavor*. You know that ship anchored right near here over 200 years ago? I have read that a yellow rose symbolizes friendship. I am not familiar with growing roses but a grand climber will be a good place to start."

Both watched Tallulah as she rooted in the dirt. Dislodging a gecko, she lightly stomped at it. Finally, its tail fell off, and the lizard scurried for safety. Aye broke the pleasant silence. "I'd be honored to teach you, if you'd like to learn about orchids."

Livia nodded. "Oh, I would, very much."

Spread across two mossy cedar shelves, Aye's nursery held at least 200 baby plants. Dipping a small pump sprayer into a barrel of rainwater, he quietly misted his fantastic assortment. "See there?" Aye pointed to the back of the lot. "In the surrounding trees and underlying stonewalls, these babies have big brothers and sisters. I may sell them at Kailua's World Marketplace when it opens. Right now I take orchids to Hilo, and sometimes a few choice ones make their way to Waikiki and Kaneohe."

As they walked for a closer look, he held up two stubby fingers. "Never gather orchid plants wider than this big. A.B.H. Greenwell knew that when she gathered native specimens for her ten acres, up in Captain Cook. Not like that elevated botanical garden, it is much drier here. Later this month, if you like, we will hike to a lovely orchid cove. It is quite protected, and the misty cliffs are dripping with flowers. Only two thing do I ask – keep the place a secret and use the boot brushes that I keep at the trail head."

Fist touching her heart Livia stood at attention and promised, "No one will learn its location from me. Just let me know when you want to go." She squinted and asked, "Do you think I could make some sketches of just the flowers – not the location?"

Aye skipped flat piece of coral in the surf. "That would be fine." He suggested some close-ups, reminding her that his photos never came up to his expectations. He got one, with a neat water effect on the lens. An awesome rare ginger - right pretty it was, all waxy in red with little droplets sprinkled across its huge petals.

Once they were back in the kitchen, Livia noticed all the shortbreads were gone and wondered if Chakra ate all seven from the nearly full tray.

For years, Livia had watched Cate follow the strict Waist Watchers diet – no exceptions, except on weekends. She always said, "If ya don't eat the brownie – you'll eat everything on the way to the brownie." Having planned her calorie laden treat two days in advance, she would enjoy it today. After briefly explaining the program to Chakra, Cate was presented with a neatly tied box of shortbreads. She thanked their gracious hostess, and Livia counted prescription bottles stacked high near the sink.

Chakra turned to Livia.

"Cate mentioned that you finished your mother's fifty-year-old Sunbonnet Sue quilt the Christmas before she died." After discussed its white-on-white background and antique aqua-colored pieces, she breathed deeply and confessed, "I feel so weary. You must stop by anytime. Another day - and you may see my British-inspired red-and-white quilts. If you glance in our bedroom, I am certain you will recognize the Hawaiian flag pattern of my mother's handiwork. Pieced with kapa hae – it has been over our bed since we moved here. As of late, I prefer machine appliqué for my intricate designs."

Aye nodded, as if to remind Chakra of something else.

She pulled herself up straighter. "Oh yes, our surprise plan: we both would feel honored if you and our Good Doctor Brown would be our special guests, at our luau on Mololi Beach this Saturday."

Cate's nose wrinkled. "I'm not familiar with that one."

Livia added, "It's a neighborhood fish-netting luau – isn't it?" She snickered. "Mololi is kinda off the beaten path for us haoles."

"Hukilau!" chimed Aye and Chakra.

Cate accepted accepted the invitation to the fishing luau, noting that she liked mahi mahi and ahi, and it was Margaret's first Saturday off in almost two months. She laughed. "By twisting her arm, she might be persuaded to come. If that doesn't work, I'll add that chunk of Kona chocolate that Livia bought yesterday to my party brownies. Hook, line, and sinker, Margaret likes nothing better than fresh fish and brownies."

Livia moaned, "Eww!" as Chakra and Aye covered their grins.

"Not together!" Cate jabbed Livia in the ribs.

"Just teasing. I'll mince the chocolate - if you'll bake two batches – one with walnuts. Just like Chakra's shortbread, everyone gets a taste."

Goodies in hand, they received hearty hugs and touched noses on their way out the door. *Different,* thought Livia - but she was no less respectful than when Aye had asked to feel her hair. Both he and Chakra were kinda touchy-feely. Yet, there was something aloof but charmingly warm about them.

Once at the highway, Livia and Cate waved at their new friends. "Look at those holes in the roof." Cate got no response, so she repeated it adding, "I know how your mind works. Is there something loose up there?"

Pleuueth! Livia gave her a noisy raspberry. Nose in the air she scoffed, "Yes, it's almost like gables have been removed. Anyway - I have an idea!"

"Oh boy, what else is new?" sighed Cate.

The tires hummed, and Livia mulled over a bad situation.

On vacation three years ago, she and Cate got chummy with a Hawaiian vendor and his wife. Benny and Irene tended a kukui nut stand in the mall between King's Shops at the Hilton. The first year Livia lived in Kona, her Michigan house had not sold - so her big weekly outing was visiting with the two kupuna before grocery shopping on Friday morning.

She had her heart set, on one Benny's lovely Gray Francolin feathered leis, after noticing the piercing *titur-titur* as a pair, of the large quail-like birds, ran along the inn's lane. The darker lei matched her eyes, and it would sit nicely on her old cowboy hat. For five months, she scrimped and saved. Patting the $75.00 in her pocket, she reached for the lei, and the handsome old Hawaiian locked eyes with her. Irene took note, blinked hard, and leaned back. Mincing no words - he told her that she was way too much, of a distraction, for their customers. Like a rooster, his forehead dipped rhythmically, as he told her repeatedly - she was not welcome, to visit them, as they worked.

Striking a Cold Kung Fu stance, she bristled nearly spitting out, *You—!* Thoughts of her parents clamped her lips shut - leaving Benny's heritage to history. Merely thanking him for his honesty, she walked off.

All the way home, she cursed various drivers and fumed at herself, for having protected various men's frail egos. Somehow, Benny's tirade unleashed memories of her ex-husband, so sweet yet so patronizing. Fortunately, thoughts of Jonathan did not last long. She paced the house. It plain hurt, and she coached herself: *Feel it and let it go.* She phoned Cate and whined, "I thought I was being nice…" Cate's silence was deafening, as she continued complaining about saving, for the lei, and missing Irene's cynical wit. "Maybe, I'm too conceited – but I just cannot make up and be nice."

"Whoa! Get a little perspective! It's hard being alone. Anyway – I'll be there soon, and you have plenty to do. When will you learn? What's meant to be is meant to be?" She chuckled. "Remember what Annabelle always said? 'Old men go through menopause too'."

They laughed, and Livia felt better. She hung up quite smug. Years of politics, work, and sports – and she should have realized that liquor laced with hormones made for quite a toxic cocktail. One good thing came of Benny's confrontation - the old fart got her writing again.

The Laredo's weight shifted as Cate turned down the inn's lane. She cleared her throat and patted Livia's knee.

"How about that old storage shed?" She lightly punched Cate. "Hey, I have some good plans that I want to pass by you and Margaret. They may add some value to the property."

"You're not making sense. What about the shed?"

"Oh - I meant we could renovate it. It was a caretaker's cottage. The roof and foundation are sound. With a little paint inside and out and if we finished the three sided lanai, I thought, Chakra and Aye could live there – maybe just for utilities, if they kept an eye on the inn once in a while."

"Oh, boy. Nothing's ever simple – huh?"

Livia let the idea rest; and sure enough, as they pulled up the lane, Cate suggested it might be a good night to ask Margaret. She answered, "No problem."

Ten minutes later, a delivery van pulled up. Another five minutes and Livia's old love seats set neatly placed flanking the parlor's bay window. The main doors fastened top and bottom, and Cate signed the delivery sheet. Livia noticed her waving when she and Lotus were halfway to the storage shed.

Chapter 6: **Hukilau and Barbecue**

Margaret sat quietly in the back seat, as Livia called out the 101-mile marker. Cate smoothly turned down the county road that wound down to Hookena Beach. Soon, not one of them could keep quiet about the hukilau, and what to expect at a neighborhood net fishing luau.

"Look!" Livia jabbed her finger past Cate's nose.

Whipping in the wind was a long line of brilliant orange, red, and green flags. Hanging out the passenger window, she watched two men pack wet banana leaves over an imu. With the fire pit smoldering deep in the coarse salt-and-pepper sand, the wind shifted and blasted the car with the scent of spicy sweet pork. Margaret suggested parking downwind.

The sun felt so good. They kicked off their sandals and heard "Nani Wahines!"

Aye followed the keiki, grinning and pointing to three tide pools south of the beach. Stripping down to their suits, the women grabbed reef shoes and snorkel gear. Perched on a huge rock Aye watched the women paddle around the warm surf, until someone called out, "Volleyball game!"

Honoring their hosts, Cate and Margaret threw the game and lost by two points. Livia noticed Aye join five old gents sitting on the upturned hull of a boat. She watched them talk until her eyes roamed the small crowd and found Chakra presiding over a group, at the back of the picnic shelter. Six kupuna women sat around a large table quilting. A few onlookers set out food, and plenty more keiki played games at the shelter's other tables.

Cate joined the women, and Livia ran back to the car to retrieve her journals. She sat with her feet in the calm surf and sketched. Not sure if the old gents were mending or detangling a huge net, she drew them anyway. "Oh bother." She wrote in her journal that she had never seen Aye so content.

A burly young man and a woman tightened the flag line and strung up a second line. From 200 feet away, she could barely see some something written on them. She examined them closer: sure enough, each had a note of thanks or a short petition.

Aye touched her shoulder and offered her a Dixie cup of iced water.

Livia asked. "Are they prayer flags? They're so bright but so translucent."

"Yes, they're called Wind Horses." He chuckled. "Actually, we call them Seawind Horses. Thanks and wishes are inscribed on those delicate rice papers. Tomorrow, the fishermen will take them, far from shore, and slip them off the lines – tossing them across the waves. They will drift a while, then dissolve, some eaten by the fish. I will be down here in the morning. Would you like to join us? I shall ask the men, if you like, and they will take you out."

Livia backed up. "Oh– no, no, no, no. Deep water makes me nervous. As a kid, I saw this man dragged out of the Ohio River. Good swimmer but he got caught in an undertow and died. Me, I stay where I can see the bottom." A scene passed before her: she, as a six year old, perched on the muddy bank watching a draped gurney loaded into the ambulance on the steep boat ramp.

Aye watched her eyes and sighed.

She refocused, as the Wind Horses suddenly flapped harder. "What a lovely tradition. Who'd have thought it: Wishes in the wind?"

"My mother, after reading a few of my grandfather's Far Eastern texts, cut her died her kappa cloth bright colors, cut it into triangles, and hung them near the shore."

"East Indian. Is that how Chakra got her name?"

"Yes, and she had a twin, Dharma, who died at birth. We were quite inundated with the missionaries' well-meaning intentions, but our mother stayed quite enamored with Eastern and Hawaiian traditions. Grandfather encouraged her to read about various customs, myths, and religions. He was a missionary but so different from his contemporaries.

Well, that is the past now. I am so pleased our glorious customs are once again celebrated. A couple of ne'er-do-wells sold some gold-lettered flags but I nipped that in the bud, by requesting they indulge their enterprises elsewhere. That metal might harm the wildlife. My opinion: "Plain gaudy."

Lightly bouncing his shoulder against hers, he nodded at The Good Doctor. "See. She figured it out. It's pretty rare around her for a physician to be so down-to-earth." They watched as Margaret helped a keiki secure his flag to the lines whipping in the wind.

They watched, as three young women strung up a second line with violet, ultramarine, and teal triangles - and a few bright pink ones for contrast. Livia considered helping them. That way she could read their sentiments, but she decided to leave them with their private hopes. She told Aye, "Thank you for sharing your mother's story. There were pictures of prayer flags, in my *Smithsonian* and my *National Geographic* magazines. Don't Tibetans believe the flags link us closer to nature? Oh, please tell Cate. She loves bright colors and stories. If you'd like, she may share a Russian folk-story or two."

"Yes - I believe they do, and I would be pleased to tell Cate." His eyes glowed, as he pulled a flag from his pocket. He unfolded a golden yellow triangle adding, "Chakra inscribed this one similar to a two-century-old royal edict: 'Kanawai Mamalahoa'."

Livia touched it. "A nice thought for us all. I suppose we are still in the presence of great philosophers."

Aye gave her a gentle jab over the heart.

As they nibbled Kailua Pig and freshly marinated salmon, Livia and Cate traded volleyball and wind horse stories. Then Livia mentioned, "Yeah – seems that I'm going fishing in the morning," to which Cate merely grimaced.

Livia squirmed as they stacked their plates and set them on the sand. Cate watched the tide rush in and finally confessed, "Tomorrow, you must go."

Livia gave an incredulous look before stammering, "You know how I hate deep water. All I've ever done, since I've been in Hawaii, is paddle around – and I'm still not sure that I want to go."

"I know. It makes you very nervous. But you'll be fine; you have taught swimming and lifesaving, and all."

"Not in the surf!" Livia hissed.

Scooting the paper plates back and forth with her toes, she figured Cate knew something.

"Nope, no specific thoughts - merely a feeling," added Cate. "Here, hand me the plates. I'll dump them, and you go get Aye. He must taste my brownies."

She caught sight of him under the only tall palm tree. As he licked the last bite from his fork, the flags stilled to a mere flutter. He looked up and smiled. "They fascinate you, don't they?"

She nodded yes. "I have reconsidered, and I want to go when they toss the flags in the water tomorrow." Pointing to Cate, who carried a covered pan to the nearest table, she added, "See there. You do not want to miss this dessert. She's divvying up her chocolate chip party brownies. I added the thin glaze of white frosting, which shows up her pastel sprinkles. We added red this time." Grabbing his wrist, she pulled him along with very little resistance. "Come on. Let's get some, before they're all gone."

The fun only began with the brownies. Livia found that the fermented sweet and slimy poi slid down a bit less easy, than did the other desserts. A bit too full, they sat for some time watching the tourists dangle, from two parasails, and soar the thermals from Kealakekua Bay.

Margaret joined them. "Tim says both the long and the short UFO parasail rides are great fun. I'd like to try them sometime."

Livia shuddered. "Not me. I'm a big wuss when it comes to heights or deep dark water. For nearly fourteen-years, I've considered taking a helicopter ride around the islands. Till now, I've settled for hiking and horseback riding." Cate smiled. Livia read her thought teasing: *That in itself is quite something!*

At sunset, nine women lined up and strummed guitars, as a woman in a long flowing holomu directed four younger women dancing an old-fashioned hula. Livia sketched the dancers and penciled in shorts beneath their ti-leaf skirts. She could not quite make out what lay beneath their huge multi-layered orchid leis, but she doubted any coconut shells graced the women's breasts.

The evening air might have been a bit stifling, if not for the early mauka breezes rustling down through the scrubby palms and fleshy nuapaka. A one-man-band stood near the road lightly strumming his guitar. Livia marveled how he played harmonica and kept time with his foot stuck through a tambourine. Suddenly, the sea breeze won out sending everyone scurrying to replace stones that held down Lauhala mats covering the food.

After dinner, Aye spoke a mo'olelo, building on the men's talk story.

Cate's cell phone sharply tweeted and interrupted the lulling waves. She answered with a general apology about testing new ring tones. "Sure; we can take Aye and Chakra home on our way back to the inn." She snapped it shut and explained that it was Ruth in Waimea. Her youngest son, Randy, may have snapped his ankle at a roller hockey game. "Says she's 'following the ambulance to North Hawaii Community Hospital.' Isn't that near Hawi?"

After a mighty short night, they drove back to the beach before dawn. The fishing boat was big enough, for a bathroom, and Livia was thankful to finish her coffee. She woke extra early in order to gulp down a few Dramamine. Twenty years ago, sailing the gulf coast of Florida, she learned the hard way - one motion sickness tablet did not keep her from turning green.

Cate laid out reef shoes and goggles before helping take inventory of Livia's backpack. Momentarily, Aye arrived with five fishermen. He kept Cate company, as the others loaded the boat with tackle boxes, their nets, and Livia.

Livia watched Cate sit on the dock listening intently to Aye. She overheard him say that he hung up his nets the day of his seventieth birthday - had an experience similar to *The Old Man and the Sea*. Nowadays, he mended the nets and hunted crab and octopus, along low tide shorelines, but he still dreamed of his old outrigger slicing the breakwater. She wondered if rumors were true: that the drinking buddies who Hemmingway immortalized really stayed angry with him.

Aye motioned for her to lean closer. "Remember, whatever you catch always belongs to the captain of the boat. Etiquette states not to ask for any of the take. If they catch lots, he'll probably give you a line of small grilling fish." He licked his lips. "That's the choice stuff, anyway."

Livia drained the last of her coffee, handing Cate her insulated mug. They hugged, and the young men waved her onboard. She swung her backpack over her shoulder, adding an "Aye – Matey!" and gave Aye a big hug. He squared his shoulders, giving her his best Old Salt's squint and a nod.

Soon the engines gurgled, and she watched Cate and Aye wave. The captain introduced himself as Samuel and asked her to come below as they crossed the breakers. He excused himself and climbed topside, to ply the helm, grumbling, "It was easier to cross 'em in the old koa outriggers."

Stomach rolling, she dug her nails into the vinyl cushions, feeling the boat lurch as he forced the down the throttles and headed north into open waters. She tapped hard, on the inside of her left wrist, then tapped and pushed harder hoping to keep down breakfast.

Not long and they coasted to a stop. She choked down another Dramamine and hoped for the best, as the forty-footer hawed and rolled. Called topside, she watched the men tend big hand-lines and unfurl a few weighted nets.

The youngest fisherman, Adonis Pedro, explained that this boat was not large enough to tend heavy drift nets. They abided the seasonal fishing grounds and never dumped chum to lure larger fish. Hand-sorting live fish and cleaning their take, well away from the shoreline, was more humane and attracted fewer sharks.

Andy led her to a bench, and she found it quite comfortable to lean against the outer cabin wall. Not long, and she found the stern's shady bench. Paper on her laptop, she began sketching the fishermen. They trolled another good hour before icing down fish. In good time, each man climbed the narrow wood plank, of the bowsprit, and turned his back to her and sprinkled the sea.

They offered her a drink and mid-morning snack before wandering in various directions with tackle boxes in tow. Long fishing pole tips whipped skyward; their handgrips anchored in tie-down wells. That type of fishing seemed a giant version of childhood sinker bobber fishing – fond memories of her and Luke spending Sundays on silty banks, of the Mighty Ohio, or above deep stripper pits until the coal companies closed them.

The sun beat down on the boat's wide deck, and she slathered on another coat of 50-SPF lotion on her nose, cheeks and back.

They plowed further north. Not long and the big inboards slowed and churned. As the foam settled, they drifted seaward and rode the swells.

Last night, she signed onto the Internet and researched the depth of these waters. They bobbed like a cork; for right below - this coastline's drop-off was deepest except for fifteen miles north, offshore the Natural

Energy Lab near Old Kona Airport. Last August, Kanaka'e began caged fish farming along the drop-off between there and Honokohau Harbor. A newspaper editorial mentioned more shark sightiings in the adjacent surfing areas.

She shuddered to think what lay beneath this boat. A shadow fell across her computer screen, and she tilted her head back to a huge wall of a man.

Bending forward with a smile, he introduced himself as Big Rafe (short for Raphael). He asked if she would like to fish. He suggested attaching his spare lanyard to her sunglasses, or she could store them.

She agreed, and he most graciously showed her to his fishing chair and poles. Once they selected and cast-off a lure, it kept her attention and seemed quite fun. The men began reeling in catches and throwing back any endangered fish or anything deemed too small.

Everyone roared with delight, as an arching shower of silver flying fish sparkled across them. She shielded her face before looking up through wet sunglasses as a few landed on the deck. A few minutes later, she snagged something, and Rafe helped her haul in and release a footlong octopus into his bucket. His mates cheered, "Tako, Tako, Tako!" as she recalled an *Animal Channel* documentary showing the tentacled ones. Rating them, in a list of top-10 smartest animals, at least they did not eat them alive as on some shows.

The men fished as a team, congenially comparing their catches. She had some odd inkling: they all had laid small wagers – probably not caring who would fish the best, as long as they covered the restaurant orders.

The small ship's bell rang right after lunch. Rafe told her they had a half hour to go before they moved to their last fishery. They were just reeling-in when something jacked her line. It pulled so hard and steady that Rafe tied his line off and put his hands on her shoulders.

They fought for over ten minutes, until a sailfish cleared the waters. She was stunned when Rafe yelled, "Bet it's eighty pounds if any!" *Wow* – and she had guessed it weighed only fifty to sixty pounds.

He whispered. "The sail and flared fins make it look much larger." Livia considered the creature's great form and the way it fought. It was greater than anything she wanted to see hauled on the deck. Suddenly, she compared this great fish to other fish stories.

After three long sets of pulling, Rafe had it almost to the boat when the men circled him. They reached for a net, which Livia could fit in, to scoop it to the deck.

Livia scrambled for her shoes. Goalie reflexes, she turtled beneath a huge arc of khaki pants soaring over her. Her head bobbed up, at two heavy splashes near side of the bow.

The captain's words hit her like ice. "He can't swim!"

Damn! Captain Cook could not swim either, so it was possible. She wheeled around following the men's fingers: in the nearest swell where Rafe flailed, gasped, and sank.

Releasing her grip on the rail, she jumped in. Slamming her arms hard together in front of her chest, her head still went under but she popped up spitting very little salt water and slashed to him – well aware that most men were dense and sank quickly.

After thirty years of teaching Lifesaving, Livia had no trouble keeping her distance, or Rafe would drag her down. A sharp surge of adrenaline, and she breaststroked the last five feet.

Seawater and adipose tissue kept her buoyant. In these swells, her last choice was to dive under him, so she breathed out and hung dead vertical, sunk face to face with him, and drove her fist into his massive chest.

Instinctively, he grabbed her wrist. He clamped down, and she swung her shoulders forcefully, to the left, spinning him away from her. Still clinging but shortly stunned, she forced her free hand across his scalp and grabbed a fistful of hair before yanking back.

A few hard kicks and they were up. Her right foot found the small of his back, as she simultaneously pushed her heel and pulled his head, popping him to the surface.

Everyone cheered, as the ship's dingy plopped the water beside them.

Pedro yelled, "Fin!"

Oh shit! Sharp chills raced down her spine. She wrapped her arms around his chest, locked wrists, and scissor-kicked for their lives.

Arms, then a foot extended, she pushed Rafe hard tight against the boat. Releasing Rafe, just as his shipmates grabbed hold of his clothes, her hands found the gunwale. She pushed herself underwater, popped up, and the men caught her under the shoulders - gingerly lifting her from the waves.

A huge fin and slid by followed by two more. Rafe was so big that his legs still dangled in the water.

Livia yelled at the men. "Dig your nails into his shirt and push him under - then yank him up!"

Down he went, and up he came. One man pinned Rafe's shoulders, as Livia and Pedro rolled his legs in.

She sat down hard and puffed, "And that's why I prefer swimming in pools."

Pedro whispered, "Yeah. We need practice, at getting 280 pounds into a boat." He kept rubbing her shoulders.

The captain threw down some towels, adding, "Here – Aye made sure I carried this Hershey Bar for you. Pedro, make sure she eats every last bite."

"Thanks," she muttered, as Pedro broke off a thin piece and slipped it under her tongue. A moment later, she leaned back shaking and spluttered, "Way — too — close."

The captain answered, "Indeed."

Livia finished the candy after they pulled her into the boat. "I wouldn't know a sailfish from a swordfish, let alone one fin from another." Then, she blubbered, "Can we get back to land please?"

They got Rafe settled and threw ice on the catch. Not soon enough – and she was wrapped in Aye's warm dry arms. Her new shipmates expounded her gallantry, as she tried to forget the whole situation.

"See," Aye reminded, "Humility does come before heroics. I bet you never noticed the second two dorsal fins slicing the water - a wee bit differently than the one chasing Rafe. They were sister porpoise, my aumakua, chasing Old Brother Nuihi. It is not the shark's fault - that he likes to eat.

"See here?" He pointed to a couple wavy v-shaped tattoos, one above each of his ankles. "Bottlenose Dolphins are very powerful swimmers. You saw their smaller spinner cousins in Kealakekua Bay. Old Whitey could kill a Nai'ʻa, but it would be hard. Those two big sisters are expert shark rushers. Their pod, of ten or more, could not be far away. Anyway, you are fine after trying to land that grand sailfish. Now, you have a fine chapter to add to my moʻolelo - and maybe, someday Rafe will land my old pal, Sparky."

"Sparky?" Livia chuckled. "That's your pet name for that gorgeous sailfish?"

Aye squinted. "Oh yes, and I hope he gives me a ride to the Evening Star someday."

"No way! You wish! And you think he is big enough to give you a ride?"

Aye remained quiet, as she gazed westward and sighed. "Wow, what a way to go." Her chin came up as she stretched it above his shoulder where his cooler sat. "Did you catch something?"

"Sure, I did!" I yelled, and "I am going to the woods! That's what my daddy taught me, so the fish would stay put." He drew closer and whispered, "Never say, 'I'm going fishing.' That alone will tip them off."

"Right after you left, I poked a long stick along my old watery haunts to find Brother Heʻe. I was lucky today and had two twenty-inchers grab on. I got my hands around their eight legs, and then I bit them between the eyes, to kill them. They're smart – the hardest of all shore creatures for me to kill – when they get mad and let out their plaintive cries." He held up the limp octopus. "I'd buy these at the supermarket but Chakra likes them better than crab or lobster; and somehow, she knows if they are fresh caught." A silly-ass grin came across his face, and he licked his lips. "That woman does bake the best dish of; well – you might as well call it octopus casserole, on this island. She combines the best morsels with chopped taro tops and coconut milk."

Livia grimaced.

"Oh, it tastes so wonderful, quite a lovely delicacy. Actually, these past few years, we do not eat it often — too rich, you know."

Livia watched his elfin eyes as his toes grabbed the rough sand. She realized he was giving her time to digest the vision of the hot bubbly octopus.

"I used to wade and float out a bit and throw an old handkerchief of bait in my net. Made my first one, at fourteen, and pulled in a dozen or so eighteen-inch Opelus that very first day. Most the young Hawaiians do not make or sell nets any more. They find the waiting game no sport, so net fishing has nearly become a lost art."

He finished explaining his catch. "I was lucky to have nabbed some nice fish." He held up a nice Mu'u and a baby Papio. "I packed them loose, for supper. Pried loose a couple dozen 'opihi (limpets). Glad I kept fishing; the last I caught were my favorites." He opened the cooler pointing out the delicacies packed in a row and sitting on top of ice and a bag of seaweed.

He pointed to the furthest tide pool. "Once, way out there, a little squid attached itself to my net. Took it to a lady in Hilo. She's still got it as a pet."

"Not to change the subject but speaking of fish…" Livia patted Aye's shoulder, "You know Percy? Well, he was minding the wheel, and had not made it far offshore when he cut the motors, right up near a Coast Guard Cutter, the *Horatio*. He throttled back and yelled over, 'Would you like to buy some mahi mahi?'

The cutter's scowling captain strode across deck and answered, 'You stopped this boat to ask if we want fish?'

Percy yelled, 'Yeah! At $30 a fish – that's a great price!'

The captain turned to his men, who were shaking their heads, and crossing his arms he said sharply, "Now, that is a big fish, and I guess as long as we're here then we'll take a couple.'

Percy laughed, "Well, we don't have any yet; I just wanted to know - if you wanted some.' The men roared — and with that, the captain flipped his hand and the cutter's massive twin diesels churned hard carrying them off swiftly."

Aye raked the sand with his toes. "Yes, indeedy, that Uncle Percy – what a great fisherman. He spins some great yarns – but not the sharpest tack in the box."

They sat a little longer as the men loaded the last of their catch in an old pickup. Soon its oversize tires scattered dust, leaving the youngest men to chat and clean up.

Young Pedro was quite beside himself, when Aye called him over and asked him to drive Livia back to the inn.

Chapter 7: Orchid Cove

Saturday morning, Livia and Cate hiked down to Kealakekua Bay and found Tom packing his scuba gear. Not a big fan of moustaches, Livia noticed his looked quite fine.

"Well, ladies, I notice you're taking your walk a bit earlier than usual. What brings you two - way down here?"

Livia explained they got an earlier start on Saturdays, to be back in time for the pony rides. Her voice faltered as she noticed Cate's eyes wandered up and down every inch of his torso. It cut a fine figure, in addition to his thick, unruly russet hair.

He stepped closer. "They start this Saturday." His bottom lip met his mustache. "Been so damn busy – pony rides skipped my mind."

His gear sparkled in the sun. He rinsed it with his water bottle and shook sand off a few small plastic bags. Removing mesh bags from his weight belt, he offered them to Livia. "Here are the orchid blossoms I promised you. Pick out the one that you like and give them to Tim. He'll dry-finish those epoxy key chains for the inn in a couple days."

He removed his weight belt and stashed it in a mesh bag. Drying his hair, he stared up at the cliffs. "If those 1,000-foot pali weren't so damn hard to climb, I'd have brought you more orchids. Hundreds of varieties perched up there, but only experienced divers can swim in the other way. Even so - the currents and tides are downright treacherous, and they have killed two experts since I moved here. Doesn't matter, if I could swim it, the salt water would probably kill most the plants. Pacific is calmer in summer, and a year ago, I managed to carry a few. They were dead once I made shore."

Livia held the flowers up to the sun. "Thanks. These are perfect."

Not really a flower person, Cate said she had never seen anything like them - especially the bi-colored ones that were simply awesome.

Livia hopped along, in each sandy footprint, as Cate's barked, "Scurry along! We're running late and gotta set up for the keiki rides." The trail was so steep even she breathed hard, as she lip-synced Livia's retort. "Well, wait up! You know my legs are five inches shorter than yours."

Both kept going, to catch up with Tom, who had paddled across the bay. Half a mile opposite the small parcel, of Great Britain and thirty-foot white obelisk to Captain Cook, Tom loaded his truck and hightailed it to meet them at the trailhead near the highway.

Halfway up the steep 1,300-foot trail, Livia and Cate stopped to drink in the scenery. Wide Kealakekua Bay lay between them and the far horizon of sea. Livia recalled Miss Lotus' first trip to the rocky shore, near Holualoa Bay's Living Stones Church, and her muzzle jerking back at first taste the water. Peering past the rocks she said, "Prime snorkeling down there - but what's to dive for?"

Cate squinted, as Livia answered her own question, with a scene from their last snorkeling adventure. A rogue wave flipped her over, and she pawed to the surface catching her chin in Cate's tankini briefs. She wondered if Captain Cook's sailors swam this bay in the buff.

They continued on, and reaching the meadow at the trailhead she noticed Tom waving from the truck. He hopped onto the tailgate and busily packed Blue Ice under the orchids in a cooler. "I'll change clothes and be at the inn in half-an-hour."

They waved as he drove off. A shortcut through the woods got them to the inn's back lot within minutes. Cate stored the orchid bags in the refrigerator, as Livia sat at the kitchen island jotting down a few notes for her book. Cate was deep in thought; when the phone rang, she handed it to Livia.

It was Aye and he inviting her on an orchid hike. Yes, she could meet him at 2:30. A wide grin spread across her face.

Cate stood still, giving her that look: *Are you going to tell me, or do I have to guess?*

"Yeah, they're moving back to the caretaker's cottage. They agreed that we'd all sit down and figure out how to renovate the place."

Livia examined the orchids through two clear bags. Awestruck by one huge lavender blossom sporting a frilly white trumpet rimmed in ruddy coral, she said, "If Tim could accent its design with cloisonné on pewter, it would make a stunning keychain fob or charm." She twisted the blossom in the sunlight. "What do you think? I could see it carved and painted, on a nice sign, near the inn's mailbox."

"Very– nice. Now show him exactly what you want." Moving the bags — Cate felt Lotus' hot little body, and she put the orchids right back against the ice until Livia repacked them for the refrigerator.

Another Saturday and it was picture perfect. For the second week running, the pony ride patrons increased. As the keiki laughed and played on the lawn, a growing sense of 'Ohana settled about the inn.

One man asked if he could set up a volleyball net. The game drew a small crowd - as a varied group of women gathered around Chakra and stitched quilts. Livia worked the pony rides but she could not help noticing how Cate kept circling Chakra's group before hurrying to the inn and returning with a quilt on each arm. Heads popped up, and the women reached for Cate's quilts and stretched them on top of their own.

Livia walked closer, and setting out hot dogs and pop, she noticed a young woman point to Cate's quilt with the big tree. Said it reminded her of the center of her grandmother's Hawaiian Flag Quilt.

Cate said that it was a Shaker Tree of Life design." That got inquisitive looks, so she explained how they lived communally and that their nineteenth century lifestyle provided a bit more money and free time for larger and more intricate quilt projects. She traced details on Chakra's Hawaii quilt, with the Union Jack design, and compared them to the Shakers' – most of whom fled England.

The woman smiled and teased Cate about running a quilt store. Chakra laughed and nodded her head, as she fingered the other quilt's cool Amish colors. Its plain pieces had been stitched onto black backing, and she noted how it reminded her of the cool sea at night. "Reminds me of Shinto gardens and kappa cloth designs. We believe that these muted colors are those that wahine were allowed to wear."

"Allowed? Does that happen nowadays?" asked Cate.

"No, well, rarely. Most do as they please for many years now." Her forehead wrinkled. "Do Amish still have kapu?"

Cate nodded. "In a way, they do. There are different German religious orders. Livia says Old Order Amish are the most strict, of their orders. In their quilts, the same as here, it usually goes against the rules to mix a set pattern or combine plant types or nature designs. I could study their work forever, but I sure wouldn't want to be an Amish woman."

Chakra smirked. "I've read they still use horse and buggy."

"Pretty much so; although, in Northern Indiana we never saw Amish ride in the saddle."

Livia handed over the concessions to Ruth. She walked to the circle of quilters and said, "We would be so pleased if you would come again on a weekday. Bring a guest – and keiki too."

Cate turned to Livia and back to the ladies. "This is my partner, Livia. I am still working on her, as a quilter. Her handwork is lovely, but she still claims to have other irons in the fire. She has designs on china painting."

Livia nudged Cate. "Aye expects me for a nature walk. I'd best run and grab my sturdy shoes and some insect repellent."

Back in the kitchen, Cate phoned Margaret, getting only her answering service. By the time, they ate lunch and Livia packed a hiking snack, Margaret returned the call.

"Yes, the seniors are moving in. Now comes the Waikiki weekend, for Livia's birthday."

Livia's eyes lit up. "Really - all of us?"

"Excuse me?" taunted Cate. "You're not supposed to be in on the planning stage.

Late Monday afternoon, Margaret's head popped around the pantry door and caught Cate wagging her finger, at Livia. "What are we going to do with you?" With no answer, she glanced to Margaret. "Yes? What's up?"

Answers cut short they looked to the window, as Livia said, "Looks like Pedro and his Aunt Selma."

Car parked at the front lanai, Pedro ran up the steps handing over a large bag of tomatoes. He gave hugs, Selma pulled a U-turn and they drove off calling out, "Aloha, Aunties!"

They hurried to the kitchen, where Livia peeled and sliced a few of the ruby red fruits, Cate scrambled eggs, and Margaret set the breakfast table.

Not privy to any more Waikiki plans, a couple weeks later, Livia helped plan Margaret's barbecue. Extremely impressed by Aye and Chakra's luau, Margaret wanted to treat everyone and her ER staff to a clambake but Livia convinced her to serve barbecued turkey and pork instead.

She built the menu around the inn's famous barbecued pork spareribs, Cate's Rooskie Red Potato, her own fruity Schnapps Salad and southern pecan pie. Noticing she was all alone – she shouted up the stairs, "Everyone loves cookouts, and I can't figure why we've not had one since moving here!"

Eighteen adults accepted the invitation. Cate had earned the title of Grill Master. She preferred a real charcoal fire; however, due to the scarcity of wood, she decided to soak the last of Livia's apple wood chips and scatter them on the gas grill's white-hot ceramic brickets.

As Livia laundered and stretched a gingham tablecloth and its matching napkins, she began to wonder if she had lost her good sense. Who was she trying to impress? Simple place settings and a kappa cloth table runner would have done nicely – but, no — she had to make more work for herself. With one less custom to be homesick for, she vowed to save the formal settings only for weddings or funerals – and then, only if requested.

In the process of hosing off both lanais, she noticed a commotion just past the south property line. It was Cate dragging home a small old outrigger canoe. She ran down and helped boost it over the fence from the neighbor's pasture. Mentioning the damn thing was no longer seaworthy, Cate assured her it would hold a shipload of ice and cold drinks.

By mid-afternoon, the women had concocted a delightful assortment of appetizers. Livia stirred up a couple of tangy cocktail sauces for Cate's boiled crayfish and lobster bits neatly skewered between chunks of fresh pineapple, celery and red bell pepper, which would be arranged with spinach dip, rye bread, pita pockets and toasty corn chips. Six small tables were scattered about, so when the guests arrived, they could select their munchies and drinks then sit or move-on to the horseshoe pit, croquet court, or volleyball court.

Most of the guests arrived a bit after 4:00. Cate came in huffing after picking up a few last essentials, since Livia had not figured on feeding all of Ruth and Tina's families. Margaret chirped, "The more the merrier - we'll just seat them on the side lanai and at the kitchen table."

Someone found an old badminton set and some Bocce Balls. Cate was the only one who knew how to roll them. Margaret commented that they sounded like old Nine Pins but there were to be no Rip Van Winkles tonight.

Becoming quite adept at the game, Tim and Tom set their drinks down and invited Cate to Kailua's bowling alley for gentle Anuenue members' late evening Light Fantastic Night. The guys in the group bowled their best under the mirrored disco balls, which threw rainbows across darkened lanes. She agreed after asking Livia whether 'Light' referred to wrists or beer. All she got was a shrug, with one diva commenting, "Don't worry – darling. We're always light and lively, and you're guaranteed to have a ball."

They received various compliments on the barbecue. With way too much food, most guests took home containers of goodies. The next morning, Margaret finished her oatmeal, filled the dishwasher, and nearly made it to the parlor with her copy of the *West Hawaii Sun*, when Cate caught her by the elbow.

"Are you feeling lucky? Do you *really* want to go in there? Thank God, no guests are up yet."

Livia's eyelids fluttered at the 'feeling lucky' comment, yet Cate continued. "She's found an article in Hilo's *Hawaii Tribune Herald* about some Canadian citizen that our government deported to Syria. So, I did a quick on-line run through of *The Honolulu Star-Advertiser*, and yes sirree, there's a similar article. Hear that? Just listen, how she's ranting about some politician – and that's been going on, for some time now."

Peeking past the door jam, Margaret noticed the computer screen loaded with news harshly glaring in the morning sun. Livia quietly chattered, switching topics, from soda pops' sodium benzoate combining with citric acid to the shrinking ice caps. The web pages flashed wildly until she snapped it off after muttering a few choice expletives.

"What does the emperor expect?" Livia spat, snapping her middle finger against the blank screen. Yanking another newspaper to her lap, she jostled the front page muttering something about multiple shootings in Detroit's Hart Plaza: "Whatta they mean by 'Argument Escalates Into Altercation Wounding Nine People'? I am shocked that this fodder makes the headlines clear out here, and 'Hundreds of Somalians Killed' is relegated to page 14B." To Cate's comment, of what the rantings were about, in the background – Livia snapped, "Oh that's just Ben Glack."

She clicked off the radio, saying, "He just comes on after the news; I wasn't even listening to it."

Glancing back to the headlines, she expounded, "What the hell does he expect? Bad enough we've got another Vietnam. Now France wants in on the moneymaking deals, after they've prejudiced most the U.N. against our involvement in the Middle East." She remembered her Grandmother Etter's tart comments about France: 'We pulled their arses out of two world wars, and they can't even be civil when we buy food or visit their museums'." Livia never forgot about complaining, to one college roommate, about being detained at the Canadian border for attempting to cross with a carton of cigarettes – only to be chided with an early 1980's story about East Germany borders and machine gun-toting guards. Well, Cate and Margaret's generation knew little of that – they barely remembered Desert Storm.

Unlike Grandmother Etter, Annabelle never traveled abroad. She did not state too many reasons, but she did speak fondly of her father. One of her mother's stories had him sitting on the steps, of the big Main Street house - naming clan members, as they marched in white robes. He would yell, "I'd know those bare feet anywhere!" Quite ballsy back then, for the clan had a death grip on Indiana's state government before WWII - but they rarely retaliated - for he delivered their babies and gave free medicine to the miners with black lung. Grandpapa Etter worked himself to death, of a heart attack, right before Christmas of 1938. It amazed her - how people survived - some did not. Her parents' families never went without food, during the Great Depression. Luckily, Annabelle and Luke survived the influenza and polio epidemics. Only Pearl had caught Scarlet Fever, losing most of her hearing and all. Boy – what all had Livia's college textbooks negated to included? She hoped PBS was reputable about filling in the gaps.

Anger not satiated, she let fly, "Bad enough we've got another Vietnam." The faces of two high school friends, who died there, floated forward, as she said, "At least they didn't label this one as 'a police action'!"

Margaret's gray eyes got wider shifting from Livia to Cate. A few seconds of silence and she whispered, "Holy Goodness, what's set her off?"

Livia said, "Oh– that is just great! Some fool engineer answered an editorial about handgun restrictions. Small town prosecutor my father was - and with no deputies to boot - still he carried no gun. Why is this numb-nuts yapping about his right to show his ten year old how to handle a special .38?"

Calm for a moment, her expression gave the impression an attitude adjustment was evolving. Although embarrassed by her tax dollars supporting such lunacy, Livia appreciated the blessing of living in this great country. Her eyes grew darker considering how half the women and children of the world lived. Could the USA once again lead by setting good example? She tried to do her part by purchasing the inn. She realized all three possessed the skills and might grab a bit more freedom and fun as they had playing hockey.

Retreating to the pantry, Cate shelved cereal boxes and told Margaret, "Whew! When I think she's nearly finished, off she goes again - shucking it down to the cob. I read somewhere that anger is a normal stage of grief. Keep an eye on her, will ya? At least until I get Aye on the phone." She hesitated. "Second thought, I'll take her down there. Please get her ready. She will pay attention to you. Oh, and find out how much sugar and that rot-gut diesel fuel she ingested since breakfast."

The walls felt too quiet. Livia's mind wandered to her parents. They had good long lives. Thank goodness - Margaret's family was young yet. For now, all they had to worry about was Cate's family. The numbness crept in again. Since cutting back on the meds, she kept waking up all night. By the time she got to the kitchen, she shuddered. Knowing it was not fair - venting on Cate again, she began coaching herself: *breathe in, and out...*

Cate walked downstairs and very patiently said, "I spoke to Aye on the phone." Garnering little attention, she took it up a notch. "Livia!

Aye would like you to help sort through some orchids." She walked closer. "Excuse me– but I'd like Chakra to have some of my old quilt magazines. So if you'd like, you can come down there with me — that is, if you want to help him."

Livia nodded. "I'll get my things." It would take her only a few minutes to change clothes and throw some gardening gloves in her backpack. Visit and help Aye – any real activity had to be better than sitting and stewing.

A minute later Margaret poked her head around Livia's bedroom door and buffered Cate's orders. "Maybe you want to get a move on. Cate will probably get gabby about quilting, so she'll need any extra time you can give her to finish her errands."

Peering over the banister Margaret cocked her head at Cate saying, "Hey — did you hear about Livy's fine new breakfast: leftover bean and meat burrito, with a dollop of spinach dip?" She cringed. "She says: 'It slides down right fine with a small pot of coffee.' You know - if I ate like that, I'd probably tip-in at 250 pounds." Glancing back - she noticed her audience and said, "Hey, Livy — did you share any breakfast with the pets?"

Livia shook her head 'no' but remembered how fast Lotus licked the plate. Polynesia would have liked it too.

Margaret looked at Cate. "When I get a free minute, I'll find out when Tom wants to take us scuba diving. Oh– and that tour company, Park and Trails, left a message concerning their Mauna Kea Summit Adventure. It was something to the effect of: 'Sorry, but we're full up through January'." Tapping her foot, she continued. "You know — Tim invited me to check out those Arabians down by Volcano Village. On the way back, he is taking me to watch the 10K Rim Run at the National Park. It starts at 6:00 PM on Friday and loops twice around the old caldera. They used to run down and back on Chain of Craters Road, but with its recent instability, they cannot use that route. Would you like to go – Livia?"

"I get the idea, but no thanks," Livia opened her scrapbook. Fingering a few hockey pictures - she flipped it shut and swung her backpack across her shoulder and trotted across the parlor. Heading down the hall, with Margaret tight on her shoulder, she asked, "Remember three years ago, when I asked Cate to call and wish you a Happy New Year? —Boy, did that story snowball."

Margaret glanced at her watch. "No. I must admit; I have not heard that one. Would you care too fill me in?"

Livia continued. "Yeah. I called Gracie, my old teaching buddy, with the intention of spurring our Miss Procrastination to call you. Oh, Cate overheard me all right. Problem was that she misunderstood me, and thought I was speaking to you."

Margaret's head came up.

Livia continued about gullible Cate. "Well, you were in Florida visiting your family. As I'd planned, Cate overheard me on the phone. I asked Gracie about her son's condominium in Florida, and then I watched Cate nonchalantly edge a bit closer. Gracie's Voice mail interrupted us, and she cut our call short."

A few minutes afterwards, Cate yelled from the shower, "Where did she stay in Florida?"

Livia peeked through the steamy door speaking clearly, "At Bruce's condo."

The shower nozzle got hung with a ka-thunk. "Oh that's nice. I didn't know her brother's name until now."

Livia shook her head "No, Bruce is her son."

Cate dropped the soap. "A son?"

"Yes. Actually, she has two sons." Blonde hair scattered water everywhere, as she stifled a chuckle.

Cate whipped open the shower curtain. Eyes wide open and nipples to the wind she gasped, "You're kidding! I didn't know she had any kids."

Margaret roared.

Livia wiped back the tears and wound it up. "Yeah, I hesitated a moment and said, 'Cate! Gracie's oldest son, William, is my age. I've told you that before. You're such a noodle!' Well, our Ms. Catie Pat nearly yanked that curtain down whipping it shut and yelling, 'You've got to be kidding. That was Gracie on the phone — not Margaret!?' I must admit: I nearly bust a gusset - laughing and slipping and sliding outta there - as she hosed me down with the showerhead."

Margaret busily composed herself, with both arms wrapped around her waist —as a long shadow spilled from the pantry door to Livia's feet.

Cate squinted and said, "I see. Having fun again, at my expense?"

"Not quite," jabbed Livia, "You're the one who sent Margaret upstairs to keep an eye on me. Paybacks are hell. I figured: the longer Margaret stayed, the more curious you'd get."

Margaret stepped between them adding, "And– to please get a move on; I need to get to work. I called Ruth, and she will come over and watch the front desk. Now - can you ladies get down the road to Aye and Chakra's without killing each other?"

Both women eyed at each other, as Margaret quickly collected her briefcase and computer. Cate fell in step behind Margaret leading Livia down the hall. Safely installed in the Laredo, Livia sat patiently.

About a mile down the highway, Cate sniggered, "That idiotic story was pretty funny. You had me going for twenty minutes of phone conversation. Even half an hour afterward, I thought you'd been on the phone with Margaret – couldn't figure out how you knew her phone number even though you'd just asked if I could write it down for you. You little snot!"

Livia said quietly, "But you never wrote it down for me. I figured - if I just called one of my buddies - you'd follow suit and call Margaret." She looked down at the side of the road. At the great risk of Cate slamming on the brakes, she added, "For an extremely smart person, you are so– gullible."

Cate patted Livia's knee adding, "Um– hum. Well– that's what I have you for. Now– why don't you straighten-up, for our visit?"

Livia followed the path along the tall row of crimson cannas, as Cate hefted her quilt bags from the back seat. Both yelled, "Aloha!" to Aye, as he waved from behind a red-and-white quilt draped over his rickety lanai railing.

Carefully he hopped down from the small lanai and joined them halfway down the path. Helping Cate tote her bags, Aye explained Chakra's progress. As he escorted them to the cottage, Tallulah ran beside them bouncing and nuzzling their knees.

With Cate and Chakra soon busy, Aye led Livia out the door and across the rough sandy beach. She quickly matched his stories, with Cate's Eastern-European folktales and some histories about the Sandwich Islands.

He listened politely then stopped and yanked out a small can of bug spray. As he doused their clothes, Livia glanced back at the cottage. Behind it, the tall travelers palms clapped in the mauka wind, making her wonder if today would be good to ask him and Chakra about moving to the inn.

A few hundred feet down the trail and suddenly he wiped his shoes and ducked makai between two thick fan palms. She followed close behind, as once again they headed further south. They tamped down brush and carved a path, through hard panax thickets - then it emptied them onto a lower path that she realized, from her geological-survey maps, should be off the coastline.

Another 200 feet and he stopped on the right. Stocky arms outstretched, he ran widened fingers through whip-like canes laden with inch-long pickers. Carefully, he spread the dense Bougainvilleas that hid rough black rock. Wiping his brow, he pointed into the brambles. "See there? This tunnel was formed by the Honukua lava flow, and it leads to a ledge that trails along 200-foot pali facing the sea. Stay close to me. It is the only access."

Livia gulped and stiffened. Her vertigo ran a close second to her motion sickness. It mattered little if open air was over land or water, and she mouthed direct petite prayers for rough old grapevines on the other side.

Patting her shoulder, he said, "Not to worry; you'll be fine." His eyes got bigger, and he lightly shook Livia's shoulders. "Hey, as my grandchildren would say, 'Theese– is gonna be so– sweet–'."

The puka was black, damp and it smelled sweet of trickling water. Her eyes never left Aye, as she followed him toward the pinpoint of light.

She blinked at a rush of sea air that announced a myriad of brilliant reverse waterfalls, which occasionally loosened to plummet to the misty cove. Halfway to the rough horizon, rough blue and white swells lashed a dark crescent reef leaving its watery keep well hidden and perfectly serene.

For lack of words, she drank in the moment before realizing she never dreamed this existed in Kona.

"You're right, and we did our best to keep it secret." A few deep breaths and he said, "Nearly impossible to see this from a boat – most planes and helicopters loop way too far offshore or scoot inland hell-bent for the big sweeping valleys. Pointing out whales and waterfalls makes the money, and most flights leave from Hilo, where you get more airtime flying over the volcanoes.

"Long ago a few guides helped draw all the maps and etchings. You know your sketches remind me of John Webber's, who sailed with Captain Cook. Except for a few, who have been charged with cultivating these orchids, this place has always been kapu. So, you won't tell anyone — will you?"

"Oh, no– I wouldn't dream of it — really, I promise." She wanted to thank him for sharing this treasure, but the words were not necessary. "I've read natives hid their ancestor's bones from Kealakekua to Keauhou. Great honor it was to hide Ali`i remains in caves high in the pali. Are the legends true, of the slaves falling to their deaths after priests cut the access ropes?"

"Some were, but most who gave their lives were priests. Not like most legends – it was very rarely a slave. Anyway, I am one of the few Hawaiians that think bones are merely bones. This area has proven excessively moist for that. Come now, we'll pick orchids before taking tea with Chakra and Cate."

She shadowed him down the steep trail. Annabelle's "Stick Tight" rang in her head. Nervously, she hummed, like warding off Monkey Mind when her team pelted the other team's goalie for a good long time.

She hoped Cate got good quilty ideas from Chakra. Ruth learned the front office duties quickly, but most likely, Cate would stay up late sorting December's bookkeeping accounts for their mainland accountant. Livia realized Cate played chaperone today because she and Margaret are worried. Cate pulled plenty of that duty with her puny relatives. Such a private person, she thought, I hope that Chakra's quilting —

"Wikiwiki," she heard – then a scream – her own. Foot mid-air, knee slipping, eyes soared skyward until Aye grabbed her wrist.

"Breathe!" he demanded and yanked her up.

She sat hard.

Stunned and rubbing her elbow and shoulder, it sure was quiet. It all happened too fast for her heart to pound. She counted her blessings, and slowly the waves, the waterfalls and peculiar birdcalls came into focus.

Aye stopped. Brushing off dirt and cinders, he kept an eye on her. Unsnapping the leather pouch from his waist, he dabbed his wide smooth finger in a small pot. He tapped dots of the goo, on her sunburned face. "My special `awa mixture absorbs quickly. It is fermented from a special type of kava plant and ginger."

Her nose wrinkled and she swallowed hard. "Pew– it's kinda like the egg and castor oil mix my ex-mother-in-law smeared on her kids with the flu."

"Yes, a bit similar; in as much as, this has a bit of egg and castor oil too. Livia's eyes crossed, until he said. "She must have been a wise old Appalachian healer – hum?"

Minutes later, she stood. The potion's heady ginger took over, wafted up her blouse, and brought her around nearly giving her a headache — so they continued edging down the ledge again. A bit of a trail appeared but Aye halted at a narrow switchback. "I'll tiptoe around this point, and I'll call back when you can follow." While he made ready, she noticed Monkey Mind was long gone.

Aye called, "Come along," and once again, they faced the sea.

The mists parted and the sun danced on a thousand dewy orchids. Farsighted, Livia was drawn to the myriad of specimens above the path. Fairy flowers - some shot hot with pink and others with lavender trumpets edged with ruffly white - perched atop craggy drab roots clinging to moist cinders. Leaning behind them, sat a pert row of waxy yellow mushrooms - so round and clear they seemed to float - on a rivulet as shimmering and silvery as freshly oozed dragon's saliva.

Livia sat mesmerized, with Hi'laka's work, as Aye pointed out tiny brachen and lichen. As politely as she could, she asked, "So, how did your family come to live here?

His response: "Mine were of Kapeliela, a noble seaman, who returned to Bora-Bora for his wife, Mahina. They landed huge double-hulled canoes, at what is now called South Point – later they moved up the coast. My more recent relatives descended from the British botanist, Joseph Banks.

Livia almost spit up her gum. "The– Sir Joseph Banks? He was in my *National Geographic*. The famous botanist who traveled with Captain James Cook aboard the *Endeavor*?"

A humble smile and nod were Aye's only answers.

The sun lit his furrowed brow, as Livia regarded a face from the past. Suddenly hungry, she unwrapped her few snacks, asking Aye to share them. Gnawing homemade beef-jerky between sips of water, they savored mango oat bars, until she quipped. "Somehow, your misty coastline reminds me of 'The Witches of November'."

"Oh - that's the 'Rang 29 times...' and the Mariners' Church in Gordon Lightfoot's ballad. My seafaring rovers once said they would rather sail the high seas — any season — rather than navigate the Great Lakes during late fall or winter. Can you tell me more about the old lady?"

"Well, the song says the winds of November came early in 1975 for the *Edmund Fitzgerald*. Not named by Mr. Lightfoot were three witch sisters. Like many witch storms, those three spawned in the Gulf of Mexico's shimmering waters before running the Mississippi River's gauntlet into the Heartland."

Her eyes sparkled. "From the Chippewa on down, to the Ottawa and Potowatami, The Three Fires sit many a lakeshore vigil and tell many tales. The Wyandotte first named the storms: Cincie, Louisa, and Eva. The morning after the front passed, a tall zephyr of oak leaves caught Cincie's stormy eye. Weary from battling Pittsburgh's smokestacks, she slowly turned and noticed Louisa and Eva, preening in the warm Indian Summer mists.

"Soon, they grew petulant and lashed the Ohio River lowlands snapping lightning at each other. Enticed, Cincie turned and refreshed herself in the great river. Cool and sassy, all three raced north, sucking more witch water from Lake Michigan.

"November 10[th,] I believe it was. The Chippewa said that it was barely past sunset when those witches careened down, on the big lake they call Gitche Gumee. They say that earlier that day, the airways filled with numerous warnings. At barely two miles per hour, the huge straight-decker *Fitzgerald* and two other massive iron-ore freighters, loaded with taconite, labored along the last nine miles of invisible Lake Superior shoreline to safe haven, just past Whitefish Point.

"Cold and homesick, Cincie cried buckets of rain then spat ice and snow on the ships' decks. Louisa joined in and wailed 70-knot southwest winds, which whipped up twenty-foot waves closing the

Mackinac Bridge. However, it was silent Eva who slithered off Corbeil Point – and slicing deep between Superior's ice water mansions, she shot up through the *Fitz* snapping her 730-foot hull. 'Superior, they said never gives up her dead.'

"After two foreign ships refused the Coast Guard's plea to turn back to the Fitz's last sonar sounding, the *Arthur M. Anderson* finally arrived and sat the dangerous death vigil 530 feet above the *Edmund Fitzgerald*.

"One legend says that Eva, weak from battling the sailors' ghosts, climbed onto Caribou Island. As Cincie winced back tears, and Louisa took a deep breath — Eva caught sight of a raven's silhouette winging its way across the Northern Lights. Enticed by the lovely cold cousin of rainbows, she chased Aurora far past the Canadian horizon. Cincie and Louisa finally followed Eva, and all three met the dawn as shimmering icebergs."

Livia sighed, smug that she added the Canadian part. As a survivor of twisters and a jetliner that had fallen near her home, as a kid, she still wondered why this particular wreck caught her fancy.

Aye kept quiet. Then he said that she had some imagination.

She agreed. "Anyway, the closest Cate and I got to Whitefish point, was driving over the Mighty Mack Bridge in late January — in a Geo Tracker nonetheless, and right after that Yugo got blown over its low railings. Eww– at 10°F those dry winds sliced through that 150-foot high nearly mile-long suspension, and believe me – there's a whole lot of creaking and popping going on up there.

"Most people see such storms as only destruction, but their floods do replenish surrounding farmland. Anyway, you heard right – any sailor, in his or her right mind, would prefer the oceans to the Great Lakes come November."

Aye smirked. "You ever consider writing kid's stories?"

"Pardon me?" said Livia.

"Oh, merely making note how alike our legends are." He gazed out to sea, for a while. Soon, he looked back, gingerly lifting each orchid and gently filling his mesh bags. "Remember the two-finger rule. Their beauty is so tempting that I marked my snips. Go ahead. Your bag is half full."

Five minutes later, Livia contemplated picking a few more rare beauties. A very slight tremor jostled them - prompting Livia's recollections of how spooked Cate got when that 6.7 quake shook their hotel's sixth floor.

Aye pointed the way home.

Something made her glance back, as the sea spray kicked-up. Aye noticed and followed close behind until they made their way through the puka opening. An early-afternoon cool breeze stirred about and dried their clothes. True, to his word, the trip home was more pleasant.

Dropping their shoes on the lanai, Livia and Aye looked up to see Cate in the doorway. She nudged Livia asking if she had a good time and reminded her to wash up before tea. Aye arranged the mesh bags on the drain board. After dousing them with cool rainwater stored under the sink, he joined the women in the kitchen.

Cate talked quilts, as Livia talked flowers; and in no time, everyone sipped tepid tea and munched more cookies. Chakra relished hers and noted the finer texture. "From now on, I shall bake only small batches with butter-flavored Crispo and raw Maui sugar."

Noting the lull, Cate squinted at Livia. Her teeth rested hard in her bottom lip and an infamous "Well?" popped out.

Livia knew. Glancing from Chakra to Aye she said, "Truth or Dare?"

Aye hesitated a bit – then he said, "I'm game."

Chakra nodded, and he blurt out, "Dare."

Livia sucked air. "Well, we thought, since the inn's storage shed is a tad larger than your cottage and has an excellent foundation — we could wrap a lanai around it; and if you choose to, you could live there, gratis, of course. We dare you to move there."

Too many details? Did they miss the question?

Watching Livia waver, Cate came to her defense. "You must know Livia to get her weird sense of humor. Her game was to bait you. We would appreciate your help – anytime. Besides remodeling our storage shed into a cottage, I've been thinking of fixing up a quilt shop, on the inn's south lanai."

Livia snickered. "Oh, please say yes — you'd add atmosphere. Sorry; just teasing about the last part. You'd have privacy, and we are good people."

She held her tongue until Chakra nodded.

Aye spoke. "We will definitely consider it and let you know. Let's say in a week's time." He looked at Chakra, hung his head a bit, and said, "I'd miss this old window. But, true, this place might not last through another good storm."

Livia swallowed her tea and baited Aye. "Back in Michigan, I supervised many a fix 'em up project - on our house and on my parents.' If you can command some extra muscle, we can move that nice window of yours."

"Excellent ideas," stated Chakra. Her expression smoothened. "Quilt store. I would be so honored."

Cate jumped. "Yes. It is definitely a place to start. A little inventory, a few consignments - what about sharing our expertise? We could meet, say on Wednesday evenings, and brainstorm with any quilters who care to join in."

Everyone nodded, and Aye said he would do what he could.

"Great place to start," added Livia. With the last of her tea gone, she craved strong coffee, possibly with a shot of Bailey's.

With errands pending, Livia and Cate excused themselves as politely as possible.

With Chakra settled on the lanai, she waved and Aye called out, "Kipa Mai!" and watched Cate and Livia head down the lane.

It was a pleasant ride home, and Livia's mood brightened. Intrigued by the few details Aye pointed out in the 1920s photo of the inn, brought to mind a similar era photo of a steam-powered tractor in front her Camp Fortson home, she never realized the La'Ohana Inn had been two dwellings that were later connected by a center entrance and wide upper hallways. Finally, the cooking got too hot for white folk, so they added a summer kitchen. Aye once helped remodel the structure, forming the present kitchen and necessaries.

Passing Queens' Stables Livia sighed, "South Kona is still one of Hawaii's best-kept secrets." Little response and she said, "Quilt marathon?"

Cate's head popped up. "Sounds good to me - but, wouldn't that be a bunch of quilting bees? By the way - Aye mentioned 'Necessaries'. What the heck are necessaries?"

They discussed sponsoring quilting bees; that he meant 'privy' like in colonial times, and Livia broke the record for spitting gum out the window.

"Anyway, I found out a couple things. You know that chirpy banter he and she speak – like what we heard on hockey trips, back in Windsor. Sounds sorta British; 'eh—?' And wait till I tell you about their family."

"What about? The fact that he and Chakra are brother and sister?"

"Oh? How did I miss that one?" answered Livia. "That means that Chakra could be related to Joseph Banks."

"Who's that?" Cate asked.

Livia figured they both were in for a shock, and gossip usually meant little or nothing to Margaret - but wait until she heard this.

"Oh, yeah, wasn't he one of Captain Cook's men? You know, I bet Margaret's privy to a lot she cannot repeat. Damn. Not to change the subject, but Chakra slipped and called me Katarina, then she asked me if it was Okay. I said sure. It's the first time anyone called me that - since Great-granny Tattie."

Livia patted Cate's knee. "I'm glad Chakra's so taken with you."

Home again – they unloaded the car. Cate pushed open the front door, and Livia nearly ran into her backside. There sat Margaret, knee to knee, on the loveseat facing Ruth's Emma. Then Margaret leaned forward and applied an icy blister pack, to the young woman's brow and cheeks

"What's up?" politely barked Cate.

Evidently, for months, Margaret had been coaching Emma about the importance of taking the second pill. Twelve hours apart: a never broken rule.

With the details spilled, Cate quickly escorted Livia to the kitchen explaining she overheard Ruth asking her daughter to call Margaret. "I didn't think much of it — until later, after Ruth asked Emma to deliver the inn's baked goods and pick up a package, from Margaret." Meeting Livia's stare, Cate quipped, "If Emma doesn't get her doses right, the cookies and brownies may not be the only baked goods she delivers."

Livia chuckled. "Oh, yeah, right — and we're not the gossipy types."

"Ssh!" Cate glared, as she nodded toward footsteps and the front door's hard click. Slowly- she and Livia peeked, through the pass-through, and followed The Good Doctor up the main stairs.

Half an hour later, Margaret plopped down at the kitchen table. Bottle of hard lemonade in hand - she glanced, to her watch and the calendar, and looked up at Cate. "Your mother called, twice. She wants to come for a visit."

Cate said, "That's fine. I'll call her back."

More hard lemonade and silence — and Margaret folded her hands on the table and finally said, "What is with you two?

Both shrugged and nodded.

Margaret gulped, "You were eavesdropping!"

Livia fingered her mug. "I saw orchids and quilts. They were great."

Undeterred, Margaret gave a flat "Uh – Huh–" and switched to Cate.

Cate said quickly, "How was your morning? Any new prescriptions?"

Margaret leaned back, eyes squinted and jaw set. "Was I that obvious? That did a whole lot of good: Ruth asking me to meet Emma here." Her jaw slackened, as her fingers quietly drummed the table.

Livia and Cate crossed their hearts, held their fingers to their lips, and leaned closer - until Margaret spat out, "Ooh– I forgot. Tom called. He wants to take both of you scuba diving."

As Livia sat, with her face all pruned up, Cate timed-off a perfectly edgy sigh and answered with a coolly rehearsed complaint: "Well, with the audits and all, I can't go. It sure is too bad — I hate to disappoint him." She glanced from Margaret to Livia, saying, "How about you?" Shaking her head Cate said, "Yeah– too bad, because it sounds like fun, doesn't it?"

Livia decided not to let Cate stew in her own stuff. She agreed to go and acted quite excited.

The next day they unloaded the car after another shopping trip. Livia stood brooding at Cate's shoulder while she pitched the newspapers, under the reception desk. She feigned interest, as Cate flipped through business cards. By trimming vendor and guest cards, she kept them handy by indexing them, in separate Rolodex boxes. "See? Here it is!" Cate waved the card in front of Ruth, to remind her that Mr. Lumbrowski settled for a lomi-lomi massage. "If you call this number..." She pointed out the name, Chiquita LaRue.

"Oh, I nearly forgot." Ruth gasped. Have you heard what happened to The Good Doctor?" She hesitated, "I mean — did you hear what she did?"

Both women's jaws dropped at learning Margaret had laid a mugger low, right there in the hospital parking lot.

Ruth said it was of the Mainland Boys who worked on Livia's old Cutlass engine. "Evidently, Margaret dropped you off then went on to work. The police radio dispatcher overheard her say that she bent over, for her black bag, and someone shoved her. She noticed Livia's socket wrench, under the seat, and came up swinging."

Ruth set down her baked goods and said, "The police were shocked at how neatly the perpetrator was laid out. They said he came to, just as Margaret was escorting him to the emergency room. Needless to say, she checked his injuries and taped him up good before giving her statement."

To Cate's "Did they restrain him?" - Ruth said a quick, "Of course!"

Livia sighed and said, "Well, we're just glad she's Okay."

Nervously snapping both plastic file boxes shut, Cate smoothly said, "It comes as no surprise. Margaret worked at Detroit Receiving and at Chicago Grace. She may be a saving angel – but I'd not cross her in a dark alley."

They arranged Ruth's goodies, and Livia poured three bourbons slammers. Collecting three empty shot glasses she said, "Back to the massage specialist appointment - our Chiquita person handed me one of his, I mean her, cards, down at The Establishment. She towers over me. I sure wouldn't wanna get past her, in a doorway. Anyway, she was a marine specialist, over in Kaneohe – and now she's hell bent, on staying in paradise. Claims she learned lomi-lomi, from some French speaking Hawaiian. I'd bet she's our person. Least ways, she can handle herself, if a guest decides to get out of line."

Opening Chiquita's folded pink business card, Livia ran her finger down the list of services. "See here, at the bottom, 'Have table; will travel.' I checked some references, and her clients seem quite satisfied. Oh– and Tim said, "No one's reported anything kinky going on."

Ruth leaned closer. "How do we know if Mr. Lumbrowski likes them kinky?"

Cate cocked her head. "Not our concern. If he does, he'll have to find it elsewhere. He's only getting lomi-lomi here."

She wheeled around, forefinger to Livia's nose. "And you, Missy - Get your backpack and outdoor shoes put away."

Whipping back to Ruth, she asked, "Can you see if this Chicky Person can be here after lunch - say, between 1:00 and 3:00 tomorrow? Then, please page Mr. Lum's room with the details."

Livia headed to the kitchen stairs. Only five weeks, and she wondered how Cate ever got along without Ruth's help. She kept climbing but noticed Cate stationed, at the kitchen landing, reviewing Ruth's shopping list.

At her bedroom door, Livia stopped short when she barely made out Ruth's plea: "Ms. Kievers? You know much mana follows Ms. Livia? Our Chakra says so. You see it, too. Don't you, Ms. Kievers?"

Livia strained to hear, Cate's quick, "I guess." That sent her scurrying to drop pack and shoes.

She trotted downstairs, as the house phone bleeped. Five seconds and she heard the receiver click. She jotted a post office and vendor supply list and set them on the front desk.

Cate looked up and scanning the list said, "Tomorrow, I'll swing back to Kailua for stamps, paper for flyers and envelopes." She followed Livia to the pantry and whispered, "Sorry, Little Miss. We're sorry. We didn't mean to keep pushing you today. We're just concerned about you missing your family."

Chapter 8: The Good Doctor's Doctor

Muffled noises roused Livia. Her feet touched soft dog lounged on her house slippers. As long eyelet curtains fluttered across orange and pink bougainvillea blossoms, she sucked in the cool breeze with no heady scent. Dressing quickly, she headed downstairs and wrote a quick note: "At Tim's. Been invited for breakfast and a tour of his workshop and forge."

Blacksmithing was not new to Livia. She was a member of the Marconi Institute, in Michigan, and she attended nearly every Christmas Festival at Evergreen Village. It stayed open every evening, from Thanksgiving until the middle of January, so she'd drive home from work, change her clothes, then drive another six blocks to the institute's front gates. A frosty mile hike and she would smell the smoke and hear the distinct ping and clang of the smithy.

She laid the note under Cate's teacup and walked to Queens' Stables, not believing her good fortune – or so she thought.

With the patience of Vulcan, Tim draped a red-hot snaffle bit across the huge anvil's horn. He paused as Livia said, "Horses sweat, men perspire, and women glow. Ever hear that one?" He nodded as she mopped her brow and tightened her ponytail. The bit glowed hot orange, sparking yellow each time heavy tongs rotated it between clangs. So hard was the impact that the anvil's support block was loosening from the barn floor.

Mesmerized, Livia sat quietly. Thank goodness, this forge was gas-fired. Two huge fans whirred close by making the heat barely sufferable. On rare occasions she missed Michigan's chill air - this being one of them.

They discussed Tom's teaching career. Livia mentioned having read *The Golden Cloak*. Tim gave insights, about the last few monarchs, and noted legends about three high glowing ānuenue following the death, of King Kamehameha III in 1854. She asked about the Kamehameha Schools. Not making light, of any recent problems, she made it known that she considered Queen Emma and Princess Ruth quite a savvy ladies having provided for the schools' trust fund.

Tim agreed, and he thought both women and Queen Liliuokalani were as wise, as the kapu breaking queens of King Kamehameha I. Emma invested her inheritance from Princess Ruth's estates. Even now, people found it a privilege to marry Hawaiians in order to get spaces reserved in our private schools. Like many other states, the money is there but administrators rise to their level of incompetence. Then he changed the subject and asked Livia - why she was carrying buckets down the highway to Mrs. Hathaway's house.

"Well, she called and asked that I bring them and help her shut off the main water valve near the road. There was a leak, and water department was taking its sweet time to get there. I filled my buckets and hers for the toilet tanks. How in the world do people find out about my handy woman experience?" With a shrug, she said, "I don't mind helping. She even gave me three pounds of this year's coffee reserve, for my time and effort."

Fingering a chunk of wood, she watched him put curly-cues on the bit. She could not help ask, "Why do they use a snaffle bit? Where did you learn to do this? How come you trained as a blacksmith and a farrier?"

Without missing a beat, he answered. "Depending, on the job a horse must do, the snaffle bit may keep its mouth in better condition. My granddad first taught me smithing in Hilo, and then there was that time spent in Michigan. Tom teases me that our horses' shoes are better than our own. You know the story about the cobbler's kids having the worst shoes? Well, I like driving around the county and seeing my customers, horses and people alike."

Her fingers ran across a chunk of rough heavy wood. Aye helped her select the old piece of Koa. She had only carved pine to repair on of Cate's colorful Russian Wibbly-Wobbly Dolls. This chunk felt too hard to pencil her bracelet pattern on it, so she gently scraped her knife outlining each link.

Not having carved a bracelet before, she chose this project because none of the local stores sold linked wood jewelry. She took her time, and it seemed the perfect portable craft project. Daddy Kiever's had given her one of his Henckel's pocketknives. She gouged away at the wood rough edges, until her wrists twinged with beginnings of arthritis.

Chatting with Tim felt right comfortable. She pictured Will and Grace chatting at the breakfast table. Setting the Koa aside, she noticed the sweat trickling into his eyes. His chest hair glistened as it dripped to his mahogany washboard abs, so generously framed by his bulging biceps.

Raising the glowing steel above his magnificent torso, he examined his work. Moving it ever so slightly against the sunlight, he surveyed its glow, from every angle.

Livia jerked her head back, as the red-hot bit flew past her eyes and hissed into the bucket of water at her feet. "What the...?"

Tim cautiously handed her a clean towel and said, "I thought so. You startled and merely twisted at the waist. What martial arts did you study?"

"I played goalie, but kicked the ice hockey habit by studying Kung Fu. My mother got sick, and after earning a gray belt, I quit that, too.

Actually, I would not accept my Arabic classmates refusing to practice with me. I told the instructor I'd read that skin contact with a woman was akin to touching snot, sweat, or feces; although, these golems twisted the truth, and told the instructor that 'out of respect' they didn't touch women. I pointed overhead to the sign that read: 'Leave all your differences and shoes at the door.' Then I asked him why he thought Abbas, Zach, and Elie ran to wash their hands after practicing with the women. That brought little response, other than 'I guess they'll be washing their hands a lot.' To that, I asked if would be acceptable for me not to spar with the black or the oriental students. He looked down and said that they also refused to shake hands with his wife. He told me he understood my concerns and promised to talk to the men. Another week and nothing changed. Obviously, three tuitions totaled more than one. When Abbas showed up with an instructor's belt, I bowed out – permanently."

Tim stroked her shoulder and gave her a big, sweaty hug. He banked the coals and removed his leather apron before stretching in the bright barn door. Motioning her beside him, they leaned on each other. Possum and Army (Armadillo) waggled their tails and padded up close. They rolled upside down, as Livia took turns scratching their bellies. Offering Livia a piece of Dentyne, Tim asked, "Do you know the Kung Fu Sifu and his wife who moved here a couple years ago?"

"Not really. He's my instructor's instructor. I raised an eyebrow, when the man explained that his wife was the only one who ever beat him at sticky-hands. Twice, he visited our school but I wouldn't pay extra for his concentration seminars. We had a potluck dinner, and he mentioned giving a seminar to the NHL Mariners. I figured that made, for good small talk, and mentioned I played hockey. Boy– did he cut me short, with some sort of comment about it being a brutal sport.

"I laughed at the time but it hit a raw nerve. I mean he started out, as a boxer, and sparred with Bruce Lee – talk about brutal. A few more visits and I noticed he mainly kept company with students in the instructors' classes. Why not? I mean, they paid a higher tuition. I sent him an e-mail before I moved here. He wrote back, 'I'll be out of town. Call me later.' So, I left it at that."

Tim confided that a couple of his Martial arts friends trained some Arabic CIA agents. Supposedly, it was for some Middle East ground rescue missions. That made Livia feel better. She hoped her instructor pooh-poohed her complaints for a similar reason.

Tim hopped up. "I'm afraid I've not been the perfect host. Would you like to sample some freshly smoked salmon poke while I do the fun chores?"

Returning with her fish snack, he first handed over a huge glass of milky iced chai tea before polishing the snaffle-bit and hanging it on a peg. After scooping out the barn entrance, he stood tall and stretched a bit.

The fans were between them, but she heard him say, "Not a bad morning, combining work with a workout."

She licked her lips and finished the tangy fish and side of corn chips, then patted the chocolate-covered protein bar in her pocket. It would taste good later.

Tim pointed from newly gated paddock gate to highway. "Tom says we must spiff-up, to modernize key aspects of the business. It has grown nicely since he moved here. We met five years ago but he didn't move in till that summer he stopped teaching."

Then he laughed and mentioned that hammering was hard work but he would take it any day, over cleaning out stalls — referring to the stables as the Yin and Yang of home business. Selecting two pairs of huge horseshoes, he set one on top and one below the anvil. Both pair would keep until tomorrow, so having turned the gas supply to a mere flutter he walked to the door. Pacing a bit, he finally sat on the stoop with his knees touching hers.

His demeanor changed, and she pulled back.

Softly, he took her hands and asked, "Did you mention anything to Tom – you know, about Margaret seeing Richard again?"

Livia swallowed hard. "Well, a few weeks back, I think she said something about a picnic. Yes, Margaret did say Richard took her somewhere – uh, I think it was Mau'umae Beach. Did I say that right? Anyway, I found a piece of paper with some directions drawn along Ala Kahakai Road. That must have been the time she said they were all alone - and that 'Ricky got quite frisky' but each time he got amorous – the trade winds whipped up. They re-anchored the cabana, and the waves swamped their beach mat - so they left."

She smirked. "Guess that took Dicky down a notch." Her fingers smoothed her shorts, as she continued. "He called, yesterday. Got her all excited. She mentioned something about a weekend in the Koa Tree House at Waipio Valley. Evidently, he doctors mules for the wagon rides down there.

"We've never stayed overnight there but I warned her about the Wayside B&B; you know how allergic to cats she is. She talked some more before setting the phone down and flipping through her pocket calendar. Guess it is three of four weekends before she can get away. This morning, I found my Big Island map laid open to the Hamakua District — with a tiny red-x on Mauna Kea's eastern side. Pretty remote but not that far from Hilo or Waimea.

"Evidently, he does mares, and other animals, at his ranch up there. He promised her a long Sunday drive home down the back way to Saddle Road."

She paused, watching Tim's face reflect the glowing coals.

"Yeah, I bet he 'does' their mares." Sucking a deep breath through thinned lips, he turned away and swatted at pair of valves.

Wheeling around on the heels of his boots, he grabbed a poker from the forge and struck the white-hot coals as the gas surged to a hard hiss. Flames jumped to a steady roar, and Livia envisioned him forcing them higher with his stare.

As he hammered a piece of old slag iron, she chomped ice and cringed at the incessant pounding. Her iced tea glass emptied, she set it on the windowsill and faced him.

Prattling on, Livia tested the waters. "She certainly deserves a gentleman friend who provides for her emotional needs and complements her interests as well as medicine." Sighing romantically Livia pressed further. Toying with her pocketknife she said, "Oh— what was it she said? I think it was: 'Sure is nice having someone, to appreciate me, for more than just sex'."

The hammer crashed down, and she grabbed for the tea glass, yelling "Shit! What was that for?"

He leaned on the hammer then flipped it hard, in its slot on the wall. "Fine! We'll see if you can keep a secret – well, except for Cate."

A good five minutes and Livia got all the poop on 'Slick Dick'. Tim filled her in about how, over three years ago, things started to go wrong just about the same time Richard returned from some Texas veterinary school and set up shop. When he made his usual blacksmithing rounds, most every rancher talked horses and kids (not the four-legged variety). They always asked him - had he heard any other weird stories from parents along his route?

"Before Tom left teaching, our virulent vet became an M.D. and that summer, he began his pediatric residency over at Hilo. Not a month later, his name popped up, on the Kiper Ranch Middle School Sports Medicine Volunteer List. Tom was not yet privy to that fact, but he was asked for every student athlete's address and phone number. The principal authorized handing over the lists, so he thought nothing of it until the volunteer list surfaced later.

"That week our wily doctor/vet attended two junior high softball practices. Afterward, he walked Tom to the parking lot, bragging how he penned a web site conducive for sports trainers, and asking if Tom could supply the boys' e-mail addresses.

"No gay radar needed for that! Figuring he had the least to lose, Tom sacrificed himself for his students' welfare. He made his excuses believable, by raising his limp wrist and taunting softly, 'Oh – no, no, no– I never share.' Yes, sirree, in that one grand denial — Tom extinguished his teaching career.

"It's possible that Tricky Dicky figured he could access Tom's whole e-mail cache, if he got him fired. That evening, we set up our Big Isle Surveillance Group. Nailing Header became Tom's crusade. He hacked into Header's website, and he was appalled. No – disgusting was what it was. The skank's main page stated 'Students Only,' only accessible via their school ID numbers. Damn thing even promised free Mickey D. chicken salad coupons for filling out questionnaires.

"What really put the icing on the cake was when, after one soccer practice, Tom noticed Richard handing out cheap little web cams to the best looking sixth grade boys and girls. Earlier in October, kids began bragging they could bop off any parental controls from their browsers. They trade how-to-dos, in their chat rooms under 'Dislykes.' I hope we're closer to nabbing him; but in the process, Tom risked his career by lying."

Livia could not help throwing in her opinion: "Oh, well, it's all for the kids. I too was a dedicated teacher. Back then I'd say, 'Stand your ground and stick it out.' Now, I'd probably salute them with, 'Shove it'."

Tim grinned. "Hopefully, we are passed all that now. Tom's the best, and he needs to stay around those who appreciate him. I know it sounds like a *CSI* story but armed with his information, I asked a good IT buddy to cull the Header's hard-drive during a routine service call. Hits to all kinds of kids' web sites, such as myspace.com, popped up all over but nothing matched any return links to Header's PC. My friend did find that his personal screen name, johnnycyber, embedded in many customers' files. It had been bouncing around since 1990, as Header had copied it from his previous computers.

"You should have seen the ungodly amount of pet names listed in the instant response cookies. An adult must have suggested those names for the pack. Some of the special ones were Bongo, Strider, Meow Meow, Mound Hound, Pee Wee, and worse. Well, you get the picture.

"A week before summer vacation, the school board notified Tom that his teaching contract would not be renewed. Joe also confided that the school hired new soccer coaches too. In the school board's minutes were recommendations by Dr. Header, as well as his nice donations to the uniform budget fund.

"Another clue came from another teaching buddy, Leon. He joined our group after hearing we lead the group, which this time connected Dr. Dick's – oh, sorry – Richard's escapades to three promiscuous students' stories. Leon overheard them brag about favors they got, after being extra nice to someone they called the 'Nice Vet'. Leon added his sources to Joe's list, and they reported Richard to the police department. Their leads went down in flames. Dick's nephew worked there, and the papers got lost in a trash fire.

"Since we've had no spectators, in our bedroom, a few parents must have received some assistance in guessing Tom's sexual preferences. Nothing but excellent annual reviews, but it got him sacked.

"One evening, a keiki went missing north of Honaunau. I had the trailer hitched when I got the call. Boy, what a joy ride that was. Flew down that old seaside roller coaster and turned up nothing. Heading back home was the first time I ever saw Cate. She pulled right up behind my truck when I yanked the emergency flasher off the roof. Never forgot her, cuz she looks like no one from around here.

"That's about it. Tom taught his last class and came home utterly dejected. Wasn't much to do, but divert him with some late night nookie." Tim ran his crisp bandana over Livia's sweaty ice tea glass and then dabbed below his ears. Yes, our big guy seemed quite consoled, and he set up the Slick Dick Database the very next morning. Ever since, he's made it his mission to update its records daily. Every web page, in our database, is only accessible to our surveillance group." He chuckled. "Wouldn't you know it? By chance, it was awarded the Ho'onani Website Award last month."

Tim doubled over and spit. He wiped his neck and turned toward the sun. "The point is we are concerned for Margaret; please watch her. Sixteen months ago, a young tourist went missing over in Puna. She was never found. As a teacher, you know the helping professions must report any possibility of child abuse. That's been done. It's the next step that's difficult. We know Margaret is not going to mention case names but, if she even alludes to something improper, please tip us off, Okay?"

"Yeah, I know," was all Livia could manage.

A tiny sucker punch to her arm brought a nod.

"I'll tell Cate and find a way to insert some abuse tips at dinner tonight. Believe me — I'm familiar enough with the stories my father used to tell. Once in a while, he'd bare it all at the supper table. Some stories were funny but occasionally Mother would let him mix another stiff cocktail then cut him off, by giving him the nod."

Noticing his inquisitive stare, Livia said, "Well, I'll tell you just one. In the late 1960s, my father phoned one night, and said he would be a little late for supper. When he did come in, he washed his hands, poured a stiff bourbon and water, and we all sat down to a nice beef stew. Then he piped up and said, 'Mother you might appreciate this one: A woman limped into my office and said, 'I need you to arrest somebody.'

"After helping her sit down, he said, 'Yes, ma'am, what makes you think so'?"

"The lady sat, with her arms on her purse, and said, 'It was last Friday night, and me and my girlfriend was dancing over to Junie's Bar — when presently, I felt this stinging in my side. It keeps up till near closing time; and you know they don't have no ladies' room at Junie's, so she walks me across the street to the Glo Room that does. Well, we get situated and she pulls my blouse up, and to my horror– Mr. Hinman, I had been shot'!"

Livia blinked and swallowed back a smile. "I'll never forget him turning three shades of purple. I just roared. Mother pretended to have choked on her stew, and then she nodded to the pantry. As he poured another bourbon, she snickered to me: 'That's as bad as the time he accidentally walked in on his tenant (Mrs. Earl), as she was cleaning — in nothing but her boots.' Taking a second hefty swig, he sat and completed the story. 'Well, you know — I couldn't smirk, or let on, or anything. I assured that poor woman not to worry. The crime scene would be properly investigated, and justice would be served. She seemed satisfied, signed some papers - and I quickly led her to the door. After spraying my office, for fear that clients would think I tippled the bottle during work hours, I had to sit down and write in order to compose myself.'

"We had a good laugh before he finished his stew; although, as a child, I didn't appreciate that poor woman's plight." Tears welled, in her eyes, as her trembling hand covered her mouth. Wiping her eyes against each sleeve, she sniffed out the words, "I miss him. Oh– how I miss that grand smile. The Parkinson's took it. Sometimes — I fear I'll get it too. Why can't the feds allow funds for stem cell research? Give the doctors and scientists some good guidelines and let it go at that? They can do it; other countries paved the way."

Tim offered her a Kleenex and moved in closer, wrapping his hot arms around her small wide shoulders. She snickered nervously. "You know, my mother kept her snarky humor till the very end." She blew her nose, and they had a good laugh.

Tim said, "I'm sure she knew – a good chuckle or two is just what the doctor ordered."

For a minute or two, you could hear the fly buzzing the windowpane.

Eyes dried, Livia said, "Anyway, if I were you – I would want to know why the county officials have not questioned this Richard person."

Tim scraped his heel across the old koa flooring. "Same as anywhere else, I guess. Dick is pretty slick, and he is among this island's primo 'Ohana — well, all except his dad being some rear end that moved out here from Illinois in the early 1960s. I've heard he found another man, some Sons of the Revolution member, and married his daughter."

Livia said, "That's S.A.R. My father joined that, and my mother was in something similar too, but neither membership guarantees anything, as to one's character."

He agreed and motioned her to sit, on the barn bench, and he soon came back with fresh glasses of plain iced tea.

Considerably cooled off, he continued. "Let me tell you about that young tourist and her dog. She was biking in the Hamakua foothills and went missing. The deputies found the dog's collar, down in Puna, and the DNA on it matched Header's. Our prosecutor worked so hard and convicted him on the bestiality charge; however, Header's cousin, Judge Cindy Edwards, pulled some *habeas corpus* thing. For a while, all the records were sealed. Now ask me - how that happens? Finally, both our newspapers printed the authorities' lame excuse: it had something to do with Header being the main vet, for the tourist industry, over on the windward side.

"There's been nothing more about the woman's whereabouts. Without a body, there's no evidence to indict anyone. Oh! And get this one: the judge who issued that writ has been disbarred. Seems she had a husband, in Vermont, when she married some fellow out here. She was docked a year's salary and was to pay extradition expenses; but a couple months later, all that was rescinded by someone in the statehouse.

"The state attorney general's office eventually dropped the case, so she's finishing the rest of her term, with only a tether on her ankle. From what I've heard, there's little chance of her re-election – well, that is, if the good citizens don't forget. The election is three years off."

The tea had a nice flowery aroma, so she rolled it around, on her tongue, a while and watched the horses. "You know, come to think of it, Cate did mention something about one of Margaret's volunteers at the Hilo Keiki Clinic. He's a veterinarian - the same patient who complained his hips hurt. Said he sustained the injuries two days prior. Margaret snapped some photos of small double-D shaped bruises on his pelvis."

Tim winced. "Sounds like goat hooves. Damn donkey or mule hooves would have laid him up for weeks. When did all this happen?"

Livia blinked hard. "This was early last fall. Let me figure the day. Yes, it was a Monday or Tuesday, because Margaret volunteers, once every two weeks, and that's usually on Thursdays. Don't worry - I'll find out."

Tim brushed the dust off his boots. He nodded, as considering a thought, but looked up and forced a smile.

Livia relaxed a bit, and something jogged a long dead memory. *Header's related to officials – huh?* Boy, she had heard that one before. This island was no different from counties where her father practiced law. The last one, so sparsely populated, that he had no deputy. He gave twelve years to the job, and became president of the State Prosecutor's Association. That group saw a hard worker coming. Even so, her father's constituency often would not put his election signs, in their yards, and The Good Old Boys imported a lawyer from a neighboring county thus winning away her father's job.

Two years later, the new prosecutor had a stroke and Luke took care of his business, from the nursing home, with Annabelle shaking her head the whole time. Same in Michigan. Nepotism and payoffs ran rampant in the auto industry - leaving Livia wondering how most cars made it down the road.

Livia's lip quivered as she gently bit it. "Sorry. Can't turn my brain off.

"One more thing and I'll hush up. Cate's usually right in her predictions. One Thursday night - we were driving to hockey practice, and I was talking-shop, about a nasty week at work. She told me, to stop harping about office politics, and said, 'Anyway — you may get laid off again. I have a feeling you are never going back to work, for that building down the street.' The next afternoon they came through and chopped three of our jobs.

"Three times, I got rehired for the same temp job. The last time, they paid me a lower hourly wage for the same work. Reality was if a contractor was forty or over, he had little chance of getting a permanent hire. Human resources told regular-hire employees 'If you're fifty or over, then you'll most likely not get another promotion. Last I heard – the company got sued over that one. I mean — who can do good work, when you're worried if you have a job or not? Their old slogan was best: 'Intellect and respect get the job done'."

Tim's nose touched her nose. He held her back and gazed deep into her eyes. "You don't care about all that. You miss your parents – it's always that way, with the gems of our lives. Cate knows. Living here is better for your physical and mental health."

He spoke, of his Auntie Lena, and how he missed her. "She was Aye's wife. Not much mentioned of her now, but right after the tsunami, my uncle hugged me and said, 'You know, Kid — the dead hear our thoughts.' Even lately, an auntie will say something the way Lena did. I try so hard, to be respectful and listen, hoping she knows I remember her – so witty, so warm.

"She was teaching her second grade class that day. I was only four when the tsunami hit Hilo. Some days I can still feel that horrible sadness right after my relatives." He stopped briefly. "I mean – Lena, Emanuella, Keawe and Kimo were washed out to sea."

Tears welled up, and they snuffled a bit. After walking around the front yard a bit, Livia blew her nose again and said, "Beer-thirty?"

That brought a twinkle to his eye. "Sure. Actually – I'd better not. Promised to take Margaret to Volcano village. I'm not finished with a little work down at Arabesque's Arabian Farm. She saw the farm's homepage, on the Internet, and she asked me to introduce her to the new owner. He's already warned her - his horses don't come cheap. Anyway– she still wants to go."

The next day, Tim took Livia on a stakeout. Actually, she took him. He promised he'd do the inn's grocery shopping, for a week, if she'd drive. She figured she couldn't barter better, in heaven, plus Richard would never recognize her little Jeep.

The front seat cramped Tim's six-foot-four-inch frame, so he jostled for positions all the way there. Leaning closer he bragged. "Yesterday, I found the date of Header's injuries. Tom says he's got an eyewitness too.

It was September 16th." After popping a few aspirins, and gumming beef jerky, he washed both back, with double-stiff Kona coffee – as they sat watching the veterinarian complex across the road.

His research proved worthy, in that the Header's schedule matched Margaret's dates. Livia had not realized Tim kept a notebook but it should not have surprised her.

As if he read her thoughts, he pointed to his notes. "I give credit to Tom for suggesting these four little sections: Animal, Minor, Adult, and Other. We file each occurrence, with M for misdemeanor or F for felony. If it happens to be hearsay, then it is M-H or F-H. So far, there've been no eyewitnesses to a felony. At the pace he's moving recently, he's bound to slip up." Tim shook a fistful of notes at her. "When he does, the prosecutor gets copies of these."

Livia shuddered and looked over her shoulder. She leaned closer and whispered, "Good, but keep your set of papers well hidden."

Fifteen minutes of silence paid off when Header's Land Rover skirted the curve and headed up the lane. Margaret's Volvo was not far behind. Livia sighed. "She can handle herself, if she's not too flipped-out over him."

Tim shook his head, "She may be streetwise, but who can guess how smart, or strange, he is."

The house lights came on, at the complex. In less than a minute, a figure came out the front door. Margaret backed the car out, before pulling past them, and heading toward Kona.

Figuring the evening uneventful, they followed her home.

The next morning, Tim passed Margaret in the doorway. Pleasantries exchanged, she left for the hospital. Cate and Livia fixed a nice tray, of fresh star fruit and bagels, and joined him at the table.

He explained, "My IT buddy phoned me from the San Francisco Airport. He found a drawing, on his nightstand - a crude but graphic sketch of him, in his work van, leaned forward on the steering wheel. His eyes dangled on ligaments to his chest. Above the van was a crude sun with long rays beating down. There were no captions; however, he knew who laid the sketch in his bedroom and left the sliding glass doors wide open. He hung up after saying, 'Hope I was able to help, but this scares the bejeebees out of me. I'm done. I can't help you anymore'."

Chapter 9: **Caretaker's Cottage**

Mid-morning, on the Wednesday before Halloween, Tim and Tom headed down the old dirt tracks leading to the Caretaker's Cottage. Cate and Livia followed behind them, bumping along to pick up the first load of Aye and Chakra's household goods.

Tina covered check-ins, at the front desk, so Cate could help pack the last of kitchenware and bedding. Chakra shared stories, and soon Cate learned that 'Tina' was short for Tatiana. Similar to Livia - she gave up smoking after a terrible bout, of bronchitis – ten years ago, and she read tarot cards.

Chakra and Aye finished their other packing early, and by midday, both rested. With four extra pairs, of helping hands, unloading the truck was a snap. Soon, Aye helped Livia set up the bed frame. He found it easier to unpack and arrange the essentials, in Chakra's absence.

The last loads filled the car and truck. Tim and Tom ate sandwiches in the truck, waiting to escort Cate who was chauffeuring Chakra. At the last moment Livia decided to ride the Laredo's hump, and Cate sent the guys on ahead to check on Aye's progress.

The door shut tight behind her, Livia watched Chakra's eyes mist over. Cate purposefully carried nothing, so she could wrap her long arms around the grand old lady's shoulders. Livia walked ahead noting that familiar tone, as Cate said, "Lean on me, now. You know you're not alone."

A wide smile, matching her cheery red and yellow muumuu, saturated her previously solemn face. "Oh, my angel – so comforting you are. Now, I know why my Maui ancestors talked story about the 19th century Russian American Company's Dr. Scheffer caring for them so wonderfully."

Livia quietly cleared her throat. "Angel? I wouldn't go that far."

Cate shushed her. Livia rolled her eyes saying, "Okay, Russia's a big country. There's probably lots of nice people from there."

Cate adjusted the front seat then gathered Chakra's long palekoki, as the she grabbed skirts and hefted one foot to the running board. Like a graceful surfer, she set elbow to knee and swiveled herself high onto the passenger seat.

Back at the inn, she found everything unloaded. In no time, the two seniors were left to themselves for a while.

Livia and Cate sat a while, on the lanai, sipping iced tea, and tending the pets. Aye waved after tying back the living room curtains.

Livia refilled Cate's glass, stared out the, and said, "I had my doubts where at the cottage colors were concerned, but I must give you credit. It was all your idea - to paint the outside walls geranium pink with maroon and green accents. It came out kinda cute."

The white-on-white aloha print curtains gave the color scheme sparkle. After Chakra mentioned it looked quite wonderful, Aye added, "Didn't think I'd like it, but it somewhat reminds me of a gingerbread cottage."

The next morning, Livia plunked herself on the side lanai's bench and surveyed the property. The cottage's porch light brought back fond memories of her parents' little yellow house. Back then, she sat on her big brick porch and watched until their porch light came on, before snapping Old Woofer's leash. They would trail, along the main sidewalk. She let him sniff along the low and pickery barberry hedge until he chose to trot across the street.

Luke would be sipping coffee and have sectioned grapefruit ready for Livia's lunch. Already privy to a good hour of Annabelle's early morning banter, he made a production of saying, "Oh dear, it looks like Woof is ready for his walk. It wouldn't do, to disappoint him." Leash still attached — off they'd go, leaving Livia to peck her mother on the cheek and head on to work.

Livia kept her eye on that porch light. After Luke died, Annabelle kept his habit of turning it on. Every morning she would sip coffee and rub Woofer's ears. Emphasizing to Livia that she was not a real pet lover, she added, "But you know – he is a good boy and he never gets into things." When Livia collected him after work, Annabelle would once again note that Woof had been a very good boy.

As her parents had done, Aye snapped off the porch light at 8:30 PM.

Early Monday evening, the women gathered for a cocktail and discussed how their kupuna spent a goodly portion the day on the cottage's lanai. Chakra and Aye stayed on the east side most the morning. When the sun got too hot, they moved to the west side. Mid-afternoon the pattern repeated itself. Finally, Cate no longer could contain herself and said it was time for her house-warming gift.

Noticing that Cate and Livia were up to something, Margaret quickly asked, "What's up?"

Cate grinned and set two neatly folded stacks of material, on the kitchen table. As she unfolded them, Livia explained that Cate made a couple of nice lap quilts. After their first trip to Kilauea Kreations quilt store - they ordered a couple quilt books. Cate pieced both kupuna matching pineapple designs, for hospitality, until she noticed they already had one.

"Get to the point," hissed Cate.

"Alright, already – Geez! We were up on Mauna Kea, and I saw a rare Silversword plant. Inspired, we returned to the quilt store and Cate found the sword pattern as well as a breadfruit one. I helped by choosing off-white materials for the backgrounds, plus sky and earth colors respectively."

Margaret chuckled. "Oh, how nice. Well, I am sure they'll love them."

They stretched out the quilts, and Cate's fingers traced the rainbow stitching around each intricate design. I sewed the whitish gray plant on top of Livia's silvery blue and gray Cicely Mary Barker Fairy Fabric scraps. The breadfruit quilt matches, except in drab tans and muted yellows." Her hands smoothed both quilts.

Livia interrupted Cate. "Go on, go on now. Go watch Chakra snip her snowflake appliqués. I'll fold your quilts and bring them down in a minute."

Margaret asked, "Which one's for Chakra?"

Cate grinned from the door. "It doesn't really matter who gets what but I bet she chooses the Silversword quilt."

Moreover, Chakra did choose it. Aye beamed as he grabbed the Breadfruit one.

The very next Friday, Livia watched the sunrise and thought of her New Year's resolutions. Making them was not usually her habit. This year she listed six. Completing twenty sit-ups, she collected Lotus and tiptoed downstairs. Sipping coffee and scribing, as Cate often called it, she outlined an entire story, until she noticed the Volvo's directional signal, as Margaret headed out to work. Quickly packing a bagel sandwich, Livia pocketed her three resolutions: isometrics, walk, eat better, and took the less worn footpath, which led past the cottage up to the highway and Kalukalu.

For six years, and one before that, she walked to work. So she walked, clutching the Kona Historical Society's booklet *A Guide to OLD KONA*. She soon faced an old one-story stone building and knocked on the door. Supposedly, this place housed a small library.

From the steps, Livia could see over the wall, to the adjacent cemetery, where a woman was pinching back weeds and flowers. She stood, replaced her zoris, and took the long way around from the highway.

Smiling, she nodded once and said, "You, the lady who called earlier?"

"Yes, Ma'am. I'm Livia Hinman."

She gasped. Her words — their tone, their cadence — mirrored her father's. Gave her the willies, it did, and she shivered as if Luke touched her shoulder.

The woman touched her elbow gently. "I'm Bobbie, Mrs. Roberta Miyazaki. You all right? Too much sun? Come with me."

The woman got Livia re-focused. "Yes. Mahalo. I'd appreciate it very much, if I could review some historical papers."

Mrs. Miyazaki's muumuu brushed her ankles as she walked. Livia figured that Roberta walked and weeded on "Aloha Time" but that was fine.

The woman pressed down on the big brass door handle, set her hip against the old door then faced Livia with one of those wide island smiles. Gesturing for Livia's entry, she announced. "Please, make yourself comfortable. If you need any help, I'll be in the cemetery."

The woman turned to leave, then turned back and paused before replacing her sunglasses. "Aren't you the one from Old Mertherman Inn? Oh, I mean La'Ohana Inn. 'Sunny Family' – Nice name. Kind of rolls off the tongue. Doesn't it?"

"Yes, it does. Dr. Brown thought it up."

Mrs. Miyazaki nodded and lifted the door handle. "Oh, we think highly of the doctor. Well, take your time." She floated out, as gracefully as she came in.

The door came ajar and Livia jostled the handle until it clicked noticing how warm the sun must have heated it. The woman continued her grave keeping. Livia kept her in sight, until she left the front room and the intense morning light. The other room faced north, was soothingly cool, and lined with tall bookshelves, all of which formed a perfect backdrop for two massive tables. Gliding through the archway, she noticed very few artifacts scattered throughout the room. That seemed to be the extent of it, so she began combing the bookcases. Fingering each book's spine, she found them perfectly arranged according to handwritten Dewey Decimal labels.

Many selections were a half-century old, or older. She sighed – well, so much for her afternoon plans to also visit Captain Cook's new bookstore: Kona Stories. Selecting five books, she sat at the table and made her notes and replaced them with five more and so forth — soon realizing quite a few selections had Bernice P. Bishop Museum labels affixed, as well as the State Foundation for Arts and Culture labels and various Greenwell or Shipman family members' names. A few had inscriptions, as to when they were donated.

Fingering each inscription, she wondered about the individuals who donated the books. Then she lost herself, in her selections. Mid-afternoon, her hands ached, and she set everything as it had been before shutting the door. Stomach gnawing her backbone, she chided herself for having packed too litle lunch. Retracing her footsteps, she cut across the inn's grounds. To save a few minutes, she pushed palms fronds aside and skipped over to a path edging the caretaker's cottage.

Lotus' head popped up from digging, and she was quickly on Livia's heels. "Hurry, Lola. Time for your supper and medicine." Granny Alexia gave Lotus up after she nearly died of Addison's Disease. Noses to the path, they focused on kitchen and food. Not quite past the cottage, Lotus veered off the path, intent on joining Tallulah. The pretty porker sported a dirty pink ribbon and intently rooted in the leaves near the cottage lanai.

"Lola come here. You can play later," she hissed. Ignored, she raised her voice. "Lola! Come on! You need your medicine, and I need to eat!" Oh bother - she had forgotten her third and most important resolution.

Mindful of Aye and Chakra's privacy, she bent over and crept up on dog and hog. Right under the window she latched onto Lotus' collar as a hard thump and Chakra's moans froze Livia, dead in her tracks.

Oh shit -she's fallen! Livia stood erect.

Then came more thumps and Aye's voice, "Ohh, yes. Mmm, mmm…" As Livia crouched down, the wall resounded - followed by euphoric inhaling.

She quietly placed her hand across the dog's mouth and crept backward. The sweet old couple never skipped a beat.

Tighter and tighter, she held Lotus, but she squirmed, sending Livia's index cards fluttering to the ground. Snatching up cards and dog, she scurried down the path to the kitchen lanai.

For a moment, she stood. Plenty of books told of Hawaiian brother and sister living as husband and wife. Her gut sense said no problem. She understood prejudice full well. *Yeah. Get it on! Wish I got as much.* Anyway, they were too old to have children - so what was the problem?

Then it hit her - why she never met either set of surviving children. From the corner of her eye, she noticed the cottage curtains part, and she stumbled up the second step. Aye released them the moment she looked up. She ushered Lotus into the kitchen, as the door slammed at her heels. Topping off the dog's water bowl and kibbles, Livia looked around, for something to eat, and wondered. Boy, could it be any more quiet around here? Cate not in sight, she administered Lotus' Percortin herself. She watched Lotus chomp her food and pulled index cards from her pockets, with one hand, and pulled leftovers from the refrigerator with the other. The adrenalin wore off, and she stood all jittery, cheek against the cool doorframe, munching rolled up lunchmeat. Numb, to hunger, she stared into space wolfing down whatever she could grab. Zoned-out, she stood staring for a while.

Cate found her stuffing her face, and said, "Maybe you should pack a picnic lunch next time."

With a half-ass smirk, Livia swallowed hard.

Cate looked down – only for a second. She quit toying with Lotus and shot Livia an angry squint. "Thanks, for remembering to call from the library before you started back."

Livia's lip curled against her teeth — but she said nothing.

Aware of her condition, Cate kept talking the talk. "Find anything new or interesting over there, or on the way back?"

Livia nearly choked. She held back the shaved ham long enough to describe the library. "Well, there were some old historical romances that you and Margaret might enjoy."

Cate's tongue flattened. "Ha, ha– You know; that's almost funny."

Livia added sweetly, "No, really. There's scads of paperbacks. I'll find out if you can borrow them. I'm sure Kona residents can sign out books."

Cate said, "You don't give a rat's patootee about any romance novels. I can still hear you tease me: 'Catie Pat, you got a brain. Catie Pat, don't turn those pages too fast – you might melt those little Ice Princess fingers'."

Seconds of silence ended with her adding, "I saw you stop, down by the cottage, then scurry on home, like your tail was on fire. Anything down there - that I should know about?"

Livia nodded and swallowed. "Damn dog! Can't keep her nose, or your nose, outta anything."

Cate drew a breath. She composed herself and said, "Please, Sweetie — you know, I'm not nosy. Sit and eat your food, and if I need to know – plain tell me what's going on."

Livia kept shaking her head, no, until Cate made an icy retreat to the front desk.

Later that night, Livia explained what she heard and had seen. Cate hugged her hard, and said, she wasn't surprised. Then she shook her head slightly and said, "But they are our friends and good people…" And in stereo, they finished each other's sentences, with "…and we still love them dearly."

Livia inhaled and thought how often they said that concerning each other's family.

Cate gave her a rare compliment. "I'm way closer to you than I am to my sister."

Livia patted Cate's knee. "Thanks, but I've never been your sister."

They gazed out Cate's bedroom window, neither noticing Margaret quietly climbing the back stairs.

Chapter 10: **Birthday In Waikiki**

The pony rides got to be quite the thing in Kona. They even gave the local luaus a run for their money. The weekly planning required so much of Livia and Cate's attention that the women agreed to hire-out the laundry chores. Reservations increased; but as planned for the first three years, the women did not increase prices. With Livia's assistance, Aye's nursery stock doubled. Cate quilted, and Margaret bought a fined-boned Arabian filly.

With no slack in business, or hustle and bustle, it was fall again.

Margaret plied her case. "You know I'm not merely altruistic; and I know it is high season - but we need a brief vacation. The second weekend in January is free. If Aye, Chakra and Ruth watched the inn, we could plan a weekend away.

Cate got her cue by Margaret saying, "It's perfect timing – don't you think? We have worked so hard, and come February, the tourists start again. Aw— look there; Livia's dark circles make her nose look like a tiny packhorse. I think a few days and nights, in the big city, might be fun."

That was it. In less than a week before Livia's forty-ninth birthday, an old 727 whisked them away, on the early morning commuter flight to Honolulu. Flight smooth, as usual, a continental breakfast lay before them. Livia glanced around - before slipping out a mouthwash bottle, and spiking all three juices with smooth sweet Stoli. Before 9/11, she would have packed her monogrammed flask. Couple of drops of food coloring, in her hooch, worked just fine. In a couple of years – would toothpaste, and other toiletries, be banned on board?

Cate and Margaret nodded their approval with plastic cups upheld. Promptly, Livia produced a plastic bag of lightly salted cashews. Batting her eyelashes, she chirped. "Coffee, tea, or fly me, and you won't miss first class."

The engines droned as Livia noticed Margaret chatting up the man in her window seat. Minutes later, she visited the bathroom, as he took the opportunity to stroll aft to first class. A quick wink and a swat, with his *Waimea Gazette*, got him a nudge and a fistful of toasted almond packets.

Margaret picked up the nuts before swinging herself into the seat. Their eyes met. He stacked trays and topped off her drink.

Livia turned and grimaced. His silly little giggle reminded her of ex-husband John. The stewards sashayed forward, commanding her attention. She had to smirk at the same little dance: trays balanced high - exchanging glances and bumping shoulders, on each pass down the aisle.

She could not help overhear Margaret and Richard comparing prescriptions and dosages. He topped it all off comparing the steep prices of inter-island charter flights. Livia sat up when he whispered something about landing his twin-engine Aztec at Kahului and Keanae on Maui.

Livia considered covering her ears. Instead, she shoved tiny banana chip packets in Cate's lap. A bit too hard – she latched her fold down tray to its seatback, before hunching forward, and fiddling with her earrings. Hand cupped to her ear, she still could not understand every detail, of the doctors' conversation.

Her goalie reflexes sat her bolt upright, with hands to knees. Peripheral vision slowly trailed to Margaret, as his sticky-sweet voice followed another silly giggle. "Aw– Doctor Brown — I am sure; it will be fine."

What the hell - could he assure Margaret about? High, on imagination, Livia cleared her throat hard.

Sure enough - Margaret reacted, with hockey and physician coolness, and placed his hand in his lap.

Livia's fingers shot straight out. *Not his lap - on his knee!*

Undeterred, he said. "Actually, my nuts are quite tasty. Want to try them? On Pacific Wings Charters, you would get a hot and steamy towel. Today, I missed my regular Waimea flight, to Honolulu, via Kahului. Last minute plans - and they were overbooked. Have you ever flown them?"

Livia felt an elbow in her ribs. Cate pointed out the window to Molokai and told Livia how much she regretted them missing that trip to the ranch and taking the trail ride to Ili'ili'ope Heiau and the old leper's colony.

How could she remember all those long names? Livia feigned a pout and patted Cate's hand. Cate yanked it free and leaned back to the window. Livia pulled her backpack to her lap. Intent on the center compartment, she zipped it open producing fresh Bing Cherries and lime slices.

"Mm – mmm..." Licking her lips, she placed fruit in their plastic cups.

Drinks garnished and Cate's edginess soothed, they privately toasted her birthday week. The cool liquid slipped down so easy that they sat quietly, for a bit, before chasing a couple more fruit cocktails with vodka.

The plane began its descent, and once more Cate leaned to the window. Majestic Diamond Head rose past the right jet engine. Soon, the engines slowed, and Livia pointed across the aisle to the airport below. Touching Margaret's shoulder she cheerfully called out, "O-aa-huu!" Landing gear crunched down and the spoilers slid out. Lower and lower - it seemed the tires had skimmed the water's steel blue sparkle, before they touched down.

"Loud braking roar and Cate cheered, "All righty! We are Fun and Free in Waikiki!"

Margaret leaned closer cheering "Here - here! Happy Birthday, and many more - for us all!" The surrounding passengers tossed leftover pretzel mix, in the air, as Livia's cheeks flushed pink.

Too tall to stand, Cate waited, hugging her backpack. "Yeah – I'll never forget our first trip. Remember how you bribed me to come with you, your Wing Chung Fu buddies, and your mom?"

Livia chomped her last bite of lime and smirked. She said, "Yeah." As she imagined Cate saying, *'Glad it's lime, and not that crappy gum.'*

Margaret stood, arched her back, and rubbed her legs a bit. Livia offered her their extra Danish cherry pastry. Cate closed her eyes, leaving Livia a few minutes to glance at travel brochures. No longer able to contain herself, Livia jostled Cate's arm, asking, "What kind of car did Margaret rent? If you'd have let me add some money, maybe we could have rented a convertible."

"Such a wiggle wart," Cate exhaled. "Anyway, I'm sure she got something nice and full-sized. You know, a sedan sporting a plush rear seat for your delicate tush and bad back." She glanced sideways. "Oh, that reminds me. Did you bring plenty of motion sickness tablets? What if we go whale watching?"

Livia could feel her questions being ignored, so she answered 'yes' and zipped open Cate's backpack to store the brochure. As Cate checked a phone message, she pulled open the corner of their itinerary. Hopes confirmed, it listed the Hilton Hawaiian Village and what a shocker: four days of Five-O Limousine service. Usually the one to plan their travel, she covered her mouth.

The regular air travelers' hubbub pushed the women through the open air terminal to the curb and Ewa Forest's cool trade winds. Livia soaked in the atmosphere and watched passengers receive the standard purple orchid lei greeting. Her first and only one came nearly fifteen years ago. Much to her surprise, she heard a familiar 'pop' behind her.

Margaret and Cate held a Mylar flower box from Emma's Flowers. In it, lay curled the most gorgeous red lei. Cate put it on and stepped closer. Smoothly she lifted it off and breathed out a warm 'Aloha' as she placed it on Livia's shoulders. The sun wafted a heavenly scent from the folded Red Plumerias. Livia gathered the flowers to her face, as she fingered tiny bunches of golden Niihau shells. A lei greeter approached them and gently pulled Livia's hair loose commenting about its fine texture. She explained that this lei would dry superbly, in a week or so, before demonstrating how to slide the flowers and shells tight together, to form a smaller hat lei.

Livia babbled all the way to the hotel, noting the time she found the same Hilo red plumeria blossoms by the old bookstore on Ali`i Drive.

The fine sea air and Waikiki shopping made for an early night after a fine rib dinner at Tony Roma's.

Saturday passed quickly. Early morning, they lolled on Hanauma Bay's glorious beach. On the way back, they tailed Cate through the Waikiki's shadowy shops before washing up and catching Da Bus through Chinatown, for a leisurely stroll through Foster Botanical Garden. Livia loved seeing Cate enjoy herself. Suggesting she and Margaret light some incense at Quan Yin Temple, she took off for one last tour of the gardens. Ten minutes later, she found them staring across the street at Zippy's. It was Cate's favorite deli, and she suggested a good lunch would hold them until their dinner cruise.

Margaret explained about the *Honolulu Star* and the fun, for the night. The ship's food and show commanded a four-star rating, and its seating had to be more comfortable than a luau's — plus they would be back to the Hilton by eight. Afterwards, their evening plans included the Waikiki arcades, a few dance bars, and drinks or dessert at the Hard Rock Café.

The *Star's* shuttle had them to the dock by 6:00, and on the return trip, from Diamond Head, the rowdies gathered on the upper deck after the Tahitian floorshow while the older guests mellowed out at Ye Ole Salt Bar. Cate took pictures, as they laughed and danced along the ship's starboard rail.

Livia considered this evening sweet prelude to tomorrow's separate activities. She asked about Sunday's plans. Margaret planned parasailing at Waikiki Beach then take surfing lessons after lunch. Cate had a round trip bus pass to see the *USS Arizona Memorial*. She had seen Pearl Harbor once but had missed touring the battleship *USS Missouri*; and on the way back, if time permitted, she would stop off at Ala Moana shopping mall. Livia appreciated both of them entertaining themselves so that she could take the limousine, through the H-3 tunnel, to see the gardens near Kaneohe. Truth be known, another afternoon of botanicals might leave Cate and Margaret brain dead. Fifteen years ago, Livia stayed a whole week near Kaneohe's marine base; however, she barely saw the gardens except from the roadside. If luck would have it, tomorrow she would be alone in their splendor.

Cate slept in, during Margaret's early morning parasail lesson. When she changed swimsuits for her surfing lesson, Cate left for Pearl Harbor on the 9:30 bus. They would meet Livia, in the hotel lobby, at five.

Traffic backed up, on Highway 3, but once through the tunnel the driver hugged the curves that skirted Nu'uanu Pali. Her largest tour book estimated 800 local warriors escaped Kamehameha's warriors by jumping to their deaths in 1795. Soon, the limo crossed onto state roads and cruised through the peaceful surroundings near Haiku Valley and the Valley of the Temples.

After a late morning walk through Ho'omaluhia Botanical Gardens, Livia kicked off her shoes and selected a bottle of water from the limo's refrigerator. They headed south from Kaneohe toward Kailua, and she asked the driver to turn southeast on Kalanianaole Highway.

Attempting, to find Haiku Gardens, he made a wrong turn taking Highway 83 south.

Livia decided they were near enough to Kailua Bay, and they might as well see Kalama Beach County Park. The driver agreed with her, noting this quiet beach was the most secluded from tourists.

En route, she watched Kawainui Swamp pass to her right. Livia had read about Ulupo Heiau State Monument and the temple that overlooked the marsh. She pointed out the sign and said, "Supposedly this temple was dedicated to the Ulu Ali`i." The driver shrugged, as they passed the sign for Enchanted Lake.

Livia heard a low hoo-hoo, hoo-hoo and glanced to the left. Just as they had looked that first winter, the deeply folded emerald mountains rose behind the valley floor. Same as then, the green velvet astounded her.

Wishing Cate and Margaret could see it, she said. "Excuse me, would you mind pulling over? No, I think up there by that sign would be good – then turn on the road to the left."

The tour book had a good sketch of Kawainui Marsh. Yes, she planned to hike around the trail encompassing the ponds of Hoomaluhia Gardens. Sightseeing always pumped up her newspaper articles, and she was planning a nice one, about Waimanalo Bay and its gardens.

The driver turned on the park road and headed north, and she lowered the power divider window. Sticking her head opposite him made for easier conversation, as well as turning to see through the rear window.

The unexpected caught her eye. Not so much a pond, but a small cerulean lake mirrored the sky. Both contrasted the stark elegance of temple and garden. To the east sat two smaller lakes adrift in the noonday heat. A slight movement caught her attention. She could force nothing to view, by scanning the far lake's shore, to the swamp. She shifted her gaze slightly. There, at the far right, was the backside of an old mossy Buddha. Odd, it was so close that its heels were in the lily pond. "This area seems to be a flood plain. Surely the waters here rise and fall with the storms and seasons." The driver shook his head in agreement. Livia shrugged. She figured, possibly a group of kids moved it there, as a prank or a dare.

Overhead, an owl glided on the afternoon thermals. Many mistook Pueo for hawks but Livia always recognized owls, in the upcountry and during early evening in Kona. After a moment's consideration, she decided the reason it flew early, in the afternoon, was because this coast's cliffs grew shadowy earlier. She watched it swoop, then take flight, with a hawk, due north to the cliffs. That seemed odd. At the very least, she had never observed it before. Both raptors usually hunted separately.

She stepped out, and once again, she scanned the swamp's lily pads and noticed some figure in its far grassy shore.

Probably an old statue - it looked nice here. She would sketch it and make plenty of notes, on the drive back. Looking uphill at the Hawaiian temple, Livia recalled that it was called Ulupo Heiau — and she wondered why her brain latched onto such trivia.

She noticed the trees rustle. Facing them, the sea stilled her. A warm breeze floated up through her Aloha Shirt, and a movement near the swamp made Livia wonder who placed the low statue at its edge.

The figure rose. Startled – she never considered a man had been kneeling in the lily pads. No, not a man, but a very tall woman with ebony hair smoothed back against her neck. This woman approached, with such a refined manner, that Livia stepped back, in a ready stance. The embodiment of elegant Ali`i, except for her long green silk-shantung coat, the woman floated up the path nearly camouflaged by the garden's shadows.

Confirming her own presence - Livia asked the driver, for the second time, "Wasn't this a temple built by royalty?"

"Possibly; yes, I think so. Legend says it was the Menehune." Checking, if there was anything she needed, he excused himself to air-conditioned limo and replaced his headset.

In no time, the stately woman stood before her and smiled. She extended her hand and took Livia's. "Welcome. My name is Ma Loa

– Ma Loa Hakkalani." Her chin lowered ever so slightly as she focused intently.

Livia tried hard not to stare. There was no escape - so she shook the hand, saying, "Livia, Livia Hinman!" Then she yanked up - loose of the grasp.

Ma never skipped a beat: "Aloha too. Are you enjoying the park?"

"Oh, yes– yes Ma'am. It's as awesome as the first January I visited Kaneohe – years ago." Livia blinked swallowing hard. *Why did I say all that? Probably just nerves.* Hearing a light snort, she forced herself to look calmly over her shoulder. The driver, visor down and head back, was snoring.

Ma never released Livia's hand and began guiding her across the path along the bank adding. "I come every time I visit Kaneohe. Let me show you a few highlights of the gardens. They are at their best this time of year." Pointing, to the 30 by 140 foot stone landmark, she said, "and that structure, the Ulupo Hawaiian Temple, was dedicated to the Ulu Ali`i, and it is a state monument."

An hour passed as a minute, and Livia soaked up the cool evening breezes as the sun disappeared into the sea. Her eyes followed Ma, on the trail below, until she remembered Waikiki and dinner.

Ma smoothed her slacks and leaned closer. "I'm sorry. It took a little longer than I promised. Here, let me help you down from there."

Unnerved, Livia politely declined. "I'm fine. I'll just hop to that little ledge." From conversation alone, she judged Ma to be her age, or possibly older. Crouching down, she grabbed a small boulder, before whipping out her left arm for balance, and vaulting far out as possible. Sticking a solid 9.0 landing, she stood tall as possible.

"Yahoo, Little Indian!" Ma flashed ten fingers and a smile that rivaled Aye's smile.

They continued around the trail to the park's entrance, and stood a few moments at the limo. The driver must have seen them, for the engine already had the car cool.

Ma stood tall. "Well, I assume it must be Aloha – for now."

Her long, strong fingers grasped the nape of Livia's neck. The old Hawaiian greeting came with sweet breath and deliberate nose rubs.

Struggling to keep her feet beneath her, Livia had not noticed that the exotic woman had moved before deftly opening the limo door. She managed a halfway decent, "Aloha and to you, too," as the door was pressed shut. Waving in silence, she found curious solace in Ma's tropical scent. Sandals kicked off, she glanced back to nothing more than a valley of fading light.

As the limo wound its way over the mountains, Livia noticed an intense sense of hunger. Digging through her backpack, she snatched up a Solar Bar and devoured it before they crossed the canal on Kalakaua Avenue. She was late. Hopefully, there was plenty to occupy her best buddies. She could hear Cate say, "Time for a brewskie." How to make her excuses? Cate could spot a lie at twenty-paces; whereas, Margaret would merely listen and tuck away all the details, for later.

An idea: her success would depend on the quality of the drinks. If lucky, the King Kamehameha Hotel's bartender had a cousin at the Hilton. Just like customs, in Canada, Livia would answer only what they asked.

Thanking and tipping the driver, with a finger covering her lips, Livia gave him instructions to be on call in an hour and a half, time enough for diner and a tank of fuel. His chin snapped down, and she was off. When she slid him her room key, the concierge handed her a note stamped 609 - 5:20 PM. Clearly printed was "Freshen up and join us at the Shell Bar." She slid him $5.00, and he mentioned the women ordered a second drink, served poolside. Riding the elevator, to the fourth floor, she was back in the lobby in less than ten minutes.

The stylized piano and ukulele melodies drifted across the open lobby. The sea was golden and calm. She tiptoed across the trail stones, as Cate waved her to the poolside bar.

"Did you lose track of time in the gardens? How you get along with your plants and you're scribing."

"I guess so. The gardens were great, and I scribbled a few new ideas." Livia giggled, and with thumb wide from little finger, she wiggled a shaka at the bartender. When they visited Waikiki four years ago, the waitress explained how to order a Mai Tai Supreme. All that washed down fine, with a cold draught of Kona Light Ale. That quenched her thirst, and the wonderfully flaky fresh mahi mahi, on grilled French bread, proved lighter fare than last night's rib feast. Of course, the macadamia crunch and custard pie, smothered in a cloud of coconut cream topping, decimated their calorie count.

Cate asked how her day was, before answering, "Magnificent!" And you're never gonna believe my day. I forgot I needed to buy my *SS Missouri* ticket by early morning."

"Oh! So, you did get to see it?"

Cate chuckled and said, "Yes, by the skin of my choppers."

"You're kidding; the last one on?" chuckled Livia. Pointing to the empty glasses, she motioned to the waiter. "Lushes! You had these two – plus a couple foo-foo drinks too?" She focused, on discussing their day, but was cut short by the sunset. Pink stretched across the horizon to their –oohs and –ahhs.

"See." She pointed to Venus then to its left. "Awe, Cate – just look at your moon. Here's a toast: 'To many more wonderful evenings such as this'!" They clinked glasses and sat for a good while just watching the floorshow.

Soon they were on another shopping excursion at the far end of the Waikiki Strip. Livia burned off her liquor, which limbered her legs for hours of dancing. So wonderful it was, with the ocean breeze purging any second-hand smoke from the open-air bars. They sampled the bartenders' and DJs' fare, finally giving it up to the younger crowd. For half the way back, they cut to the boardwalk. Near the last call, Cate suggested they walk along the open-air shops and eateries.

Livia stopped on the next street corner and asked. "Right here. Isn't this where we caught the 5:00 AM bus, to the airport, for that day trip to Kauai?"

"Oh, yeah – go ahead and rub it in."

"What's going on?" said Margaret.

Cate chuckled. "Oh, Annabelle and I were sitting up front, on the bus, and I pointed out all the women standing on the corner going to work. She patted my hand and said, 'No dear: take a closer look at how they are dressed. I think they're coming home from work'."

Margaret rolled her eyes, as Livia sniggered.

She followed Cate into a vendor's stall. When they came out Margaret gave Livia's shoulder a good nudge, and she unrolled her purchase.

On a good-sized poster was a nicely detailed caricature of two female statues posed, in a post-WWII embrace. "I heard about this on an IPR interview. The political cartoonist explained his 'Lady Liberty Kissing the Statue of Justice' had been commissioned, for the cover of *The Village Voice*. Instead, it went to press, as page-two, facing the story it previewed. Later, I noticed the image, on the Internet – not realizing he fashioned his two ladies in the style of that famous *Life* cover splash. You know the WWII New York street photo of that young woman swooning under a sailor's kiss."

Cate gave the poster a quick once over. Proudly displayed was a sword and scale-laden bronze Goddess of Justice swooning under a teal Ms. Liberty's definite lip-lock.

"I like it! Two dignified figures taking a little liberty," said Livia. "I first heard about it on public radio, but I only found a sketch and never realized how nice it was, in full color."

Margaret shook her head and stuffed the poster's tube under her arm, and they strolled back to the hotel.

Skipping the commuter flight to Kona, Cate bought breakfast on the beach. Most mainland to Oahu flights did not land until mid-afternoon, so they strolled along the boardwalk, with plenty of time to catch the Monday noon flight. Mid-morning, they made a quick dash to the airport, and jetting up and down to Kona they ran to the parking lot and were on the road home by 1:30.

Aye seemed glad to see them before 3:00 check-in. His tan cheeks a bit more drawn, he gave quick hugs before hurrying up the path to Chakra.

Chapter 11: Work Hard. Play Hard.

With the winter trade winds, came the high tourist season. Work hard, play hard, not much different than in Michigan. The women made time for their hobbies. Livia hung loose with Aye and Tim. Cate quilted with Chakra only when shooed away from her never-ending duties. Whereas, Margaret bought a horse rather than fawn over Richard.

And such a horse Gladys was. Her pedigree papers named her 'Gladiatrix Princess'. Margaret's Palomino Arabian's namesake had ridden the horse's Grandmare Tillie, a television stunt horse. Margaret rushed all the way home to tell Livia, who chuckled. Cate said they read on the Internet - that the Kiwi actress thought it was mighty cute when a critic compared her character and Raphaelle to Pooh and Piglet.

The first two weeks of 2004 brought the normal progression of guests and chores.

Livia brewed a fresh pot of coffee while jotting notes for Halloween treats for Saturday's pony rides. Cate and Margaret grabbed their mugs and joined her. One by one, they gazed at out to sea for that ever elusive tiny morning rainbow. Between 6:00 and 6:30, very little was said, as the three women watched for that ever-elusive rainbow.

None rose from the mists today. The waves became more distinct, and Livia glanced over her newspaper at Margaret whose eyes flit through Monique DelaRue's *Liaison of Lust*. Speed reading to the max, that woman could turn pages; whereas, Cate savored novels and sports sections, touching her pen to each passage or team and memorizing each character's traits or point spreads.

The quiet nearly choked Livia. Reading glasses in hand, she turned to Margaret. "I'm glad to see someone entertained by an outstanding romance novel." Then she turned on Cate. "Satisfied with the stats? Damn! We could be at the beach!" "

Margaret choked down her tea. "Watch it, Toots! This little book is my foothold on romance. With my sad lack of practice, it's the least I can do to keep well abreast of theory."

Ignoring her, Livia read from the sports section, about the Liliuokalani Outrigger Canoe Races and snorted her coffee, "Really, you mean it's a recent romance not a historical one?"

"That too..."

Margaret was cut short by Cate's referee-like whistle followed by "Enough! Wanna tell me how you really feel?"

The bickering recommenced, and Cate touched their shoulders. "Nice! Guess I might as well hop in the water with the real sharks."

Livia complained, "Well, I mentioned the beach sometime ago. Sooner than you two, I won't be able to haul my lame body down there."

Cate rolled her eyes to the ceiling. "Oh, here it comes." She dredged up her most dejected look and whined, "Oh, Margaret - she'll probably outlive both of us. Hardly a year will pass, and we may have to build a water tower and convert this place into The Shady — I mean — Sunny Rest. I'd better rustle up some more tea, while I can still lift this dern pot and not spill it. Now, Miss Livy, you let me know if you need something. Hold on– just give me a minute. Margaret - be a dear and give my rocking chair a start, so I can get out of it."

Livia looked, at Margaret who shut her book, and said, "Actually, I wouldn't mind soaking up some rays. Let's pack a picnic lunch, with some cold diet cola, frozen Stoli and rum. I can call in most of my work orders. Didn't we get all our new fangled cell phones at the business rate?"

Livia took exception. "I don't know how we switched subjects but I called the service center and was told an update to our owner's manual —"

Cate grabbed Livia and her old split oak basket and insisted they begin packing leftovers and lunchmeat. Then she pressed her luck with Margaret. "Anyway, I thought you were seeing Dr. Header on Friday and Saturday in Waipio next weekend?"

Margaret shrugged and excused herself to check her answering service and fill her tote bag. She returned to a very quiet kitchen, as Livia cleared the table and sorted items for the trash compactor. Standing well out of the way, she pretended to scan newspaper sections, as Cate finished.

Clearing her throat she said, "I know you and Cate were only looking out for me." She walked to the window dusting the wide louvers with her fingers. Moving to the table, she sat. For a few seconds only, her chest moved, in and out.

"Too much to believe – he's so nice. But I must admit – Tim might be right."

Livia stood guard over Margaret. *Might and Right.* She wondered if those days existed, or had they merely balanced serfdom and slavery. Gingerly, she rubbed Margaret's soft shoulders saying, "This whole thing is a mess. I've not heard such stories since Detroit and a few of my Father's gruesome tales. Just plain disgusting - but I've never known Tim Boki to lie."

Cate added, "And Tricky Dicky does get around, not only to the big ranches but the smaller ones too."

Margaret's breath came labored. "Yeah, they're the best. Tom's such a sweetie, and I've followed Tim around enough to know he's well respected." She straightened her back. "I can't hold it against them that they asked you to watch out for me."

Cate rinsed a small towel and handed it to her.

Margaret wiped her face and ran it across the back of her neck. "We'll go into the details later. Right now, can we have a nice picnic? Livy – did you know that Tom has a Kachina doll collection that his dad gave him? I guess his father was an archaeologist, and a few dolls were quite old when he found them. Now, they're all wrapped in acid-free tissue paper - sort of like your foreign doll collection. Maybe, he'd like to show you his and see yours."

Livia snickered and pounced on a lighter subject. "I knew he fed a pet roadrunner named Beep but he said nothing about dolls. Love to see them - I saw hundreds of Kachina, in the Phoenix Goldwater Museum. The next time I go to the stables, I'll take mine. Maybe we can do a show and tell."

Cate and Margaret agreed choosing Arched Rock Bay for the picnic. Livia got excited. "Cool! That's where Aye told me the octopussies crawl ashore at night." All she got was wrinkled noses and forced swallows.

All in all, the afternoon turned into a pretty good picnic. Over next few months they repeated the fun at various beach sites.

A warm southern shower fell on his face as the young man watched for sharks and smoothed the wooden ornamental fishhook. Nearby, Tim finished snorkeling along the shallow ledges. Earlier that morning, he taught Livia to snorkel the drop-offs of Kipahoehoe Bay. Content with her achievement, she tended her bobber 200 feet to the north, hoping the myriad of brightly colored fish would nibble her old-fashioned Mud Creek bait. She bragged about her picnic near Arched Rock then snickered nervously, quoting Cate and Margaret's recommendations for skinny-dipping in a cove past Paakai Point. She realized Tim and Tom preferred moonlight swims somewhere closer to home, usually at Kaopapa or Mokuakae Bay.

"Did you see an octopus?" asked Tim's fishing buddy.

"Sometimes, if the tide is right and the moon is full, the big ones chase smaller ones across the tide pools. Have you been following former President Reagan's funeral? Almost over the top, in pomp and circumstance, but you know, being an election year and all…"

Tom joked, "Pomp and Circumstance has been the best-produced footage since the summer re-runs began."

She agreed. What touched her most was his daughter's recitation of Tennyson's 'Crossing The Bar,' – well that, and the elder George Bush quoting something biblical, such as 'humility goes before honor.' Sounded more like something the great Ghandi might have said.

She adjusted the bobber and sinker and eventually caught a Parrot Fish. Releasing she asked, "Didn't there used to be a nude beach near the Old Kona Airport? I read about one near Opihikao, on the Hilo side, too."

"Yeah. Some private ones in Puna are good. Not Opihikao, but another one was nicknamed Puna Tuna Cove. The owner got ticked-off and penned an editorial, to Hilo's *Hawaii Tribune-Herald*. A Honolulu paper picked up, on it. Eventually the state put a cabash on it, by buying the property and developing a wildlife reserve. Quirky groups are down there; you probably want to stay on the Kona side. Even up in Hilo, well — it can still get pretty racy."

Feeling for a good finger-hold, he pressed-up out of the water and slid across the smooth rock to sit beside her. Slowly, he raised her chin near his. "What did you hear?"

Shaking her head, she looked down. "It's hearsay. You will have to ask Margaret. I feel bad for her. Give her until your riding lesson tomorrow; she is so enjoying the calm today."

He looked south, and eyed Cate and Margaret, about a quarter mile down the shore, then smiled graciously and drew back, shaking his head in agreement. "You're right. We must give her all of our support; there may be more of this, to come later."

Livia grinned tilting her head, so her hair touched halfway to her elbow, until Tim met her gaze and extended his arm - waving a shaka near her heart.

The Wednesday afternoon before Labor Day, Margaret blustered in, fuming something about lunch and the fruit not agreeing with her. As she blew through the kitchen, she pointed to Cate, who was sewing a nametag, on her Teddy Bear that sported a very nifty Aloha Shirt. "That's too cute. How long did it take to make it?" Not stopping, she garnered "Too long!" from Cate's expression, and stepped right along to the bathroom.

Much more composed upon her return, Margaret said, "It is so nice down in town. All along Ali`i Drive, everyone's all a twitter about the outrigger canoe races, and the food service must have delivered some tainted fruit. I wonder - had Queen Liliuokalani ever paddled their route from Kailua to Honaunau?" Switching to all seriousness, she inquired if Cate could deliver Chakra's supplies. "Tomorrow morning is your regular quilt date, right? I'll have the pack of Epiquill syringes and the insulin cooler ready."

Overhearing Margaret, Livia mouthed, "One-thousand and one, One-thousand and —"

Cate lip-synced then said, "No problem." She mentioned Aye's promise of ricotta cheese omelets with white pineapple, and that he sautéed mushrooms and turkey for hers. She grinned, as Margaret pinched the tip of her nose.

Margaret wrinkled her nose. Cate said, "Well, I wish I could eat mozzarella and pineapple. Chakra invited us to see her quilt collection. She's piecing three, one of which she and her friends sew on regularly; you know, sort of like a quilting bee. Livia talks of white pineapple; I want to taste it."

Livia's cheek dimpled, as she looked at the floor.

"You knew; didn't you? You little shit!"

"Supposedly, it was imported to Kauai plantations - finely textured and spicy sweet. He regularly adds a bit of iron sulfate to the soil. Wish

I could go too. Maybe you could bring us some of Chakra's purple stuff."

Margaret held up a time-out hand signal before removing her contacts and saying, "Umm-mm, pineapple sounds yummy. But, I cannot abide that slimy poi. I know; you keep informing me that Chakra's poi has a much different texture than that slimy luau stuff. Suppose I best give you the benefit of the doubt. Who knows? Maybe, everyone saves their best batch for home."

Cate explained to Livia - not to forget - she needed to watch the front desk first thing in the morning. Noticing Aye and Chakra amble down the walk, she grabbed the remote phone on her way to the lanai. A hearty hug and she reminded them to be ready, at nine in the morning, for their drive to town.

With all reserved rooms filled, Livia wiped her face, and sniffed something delicious wafting in from the grill. Early evening and she handed an icy one to Cate. Margaret joined them, and they made short work of chicken kabobs and grilled corn on the cob. The dishwasher hummed, as Livia set the blender in motion and crooned, "It *h-ain't* Margaritaville - without *h-our* Mai Tais." No matter - the second verse came out, just a tad outta whack and off key, "It *ain't* Konatown - *without* Labatt's *too*."

They winced at her tone but howled at the lyrics.

She took a bow, as Cate nursed her beer quietly. Livia offered Margaret a tall glass of papaya juice with a hint of spicy rum. To her surprise, she pounded it back.

Offered a bit more libation - Margaret wagged her finger at Livia. "No— I don't think so. Your bar tendering is fine, but I have had plenty enough of your spicy lime juice. Humor me, and add another ounce to this one."

Cate let Miss Lotus out and stopped on the lanai. Peeking back through the window, she pointed at Margaret and asked, "You Okay?"

"Well — I met someone."

Cate asked, "When? Weren't you in Waimea yesterday?"

"Yes - and again this morning. I assisted Dr. Macey with surgery, on a little girl's hand. We finished around 1:00 and after lunch I stopped at the supermarket to get vinegar and fresh dill weed, for Livy's pickles. I dropped my keys, in the check out lane. Guess who picked them up?"

Both women shrugged.

"That guy I sat next to, on the plane to Waikiki. He walked me out. Oh — those dreamy gray eyes and fine tumescence." Sighing, she sucked her lime-laced papaya right down to the skin. "Impeccable manners — we ended up around the corner behind the food court. Such a crisp evening, and the views, from up there. From the parking lot, he pointed down past tiny Puako Bay - where stars twinkled above the horizon. For the love of Mary, if I was one to take chances, I'd have pulled him to that empty pasture, pushed him down, and had my way with him." She gave her prim church-going stare.

Not long, and an insipid smirk gave way to a sigh, and she licked her lips. "Seems he is a veterinarian, with an office and home northwest of Waimea. Kinda crazy - but I followed him there, and he showed me his pets and horses. The extraordinary part is that he volunteers at the Hilo Keiki Clinic – finishing up internship. Can't say I ever have known a double doctor."

Cate snapped. "You followed him home – and you waited to tell us? Was a phone call possible from up there? I mean, we all carry cell phones?"

Margaret pulled herself up, dipped her chin, and said. "Sorry. I guess I forgot." Rarely a complainer, she started in on the local cell-phone service provider. "You know their ads say that you can use them like walkie talkies. However, in two months of use, I have never been able to connect them that way. For your information – Richard and I have a date planned, for next Wednesday, when we volunteer in Hilo."

Again, that half-assed smirk surfaced. "Couldn't miss how nicely his tailored slacks fit. Bit of a clotheshorse he is. Somehow, I could not put it out of my mind, as we strolled around the shopping center, that we'd make nice babies." She blushed. "Doesn't hurt to keep an eye on any prospects, you know, especially with my work schedule."

Noticing the absolute quiet, she said, "Actually, he asked me to the Kiper Ranch Grill, for lunch on Sunday. Says his family always sponsors at least two scholarships - through the Kiper Ranch School Rodeo. "

Livia tried not to, but a dissenting, "Oh, shit–" slipped out.

Both women pointed to the counter, so Livia stifled herself and dropped a quarter in the Curse Jar. Words had to be used in a derogatory context to count. On this account, she had no ground to stand on. Still fuming, she quietly traced the edges of her place mat until she effectively diverted to, "Well, I wanted to see that rodeo - haven't seen one, since Colorado when I was twelve. The grill has elegant decor and great service. My tour books say that it's run by the same owners, as Kailua's SAMMO's on the Rocks."

Cate's eyes flashed daggers.

Livia snapped, "What? Can I help it if the wait staff was excellent?"

"More like her sunny smile and trim body in that white shirt and bow-tie." Cate wheeled around to Margaret. "Besides that, I'm not really comfortable with you tracking around with some strange guy, on the far side of the island, and I don't care how many qualifications he has."

Livia knew how protective Cate could be but this was a first time it surfaced concerning their Good Doctor.

Margaret pushed back from the table. "That's silly; I will be fine. I am sorry not to have kept you abreast. There is simply no reason to turn down his rodeo invitation. It will only be for a couple hours on Sunday. Beginning that afternoon, I will take Simone's half-day weekend shifts, until the end of April. If it makes you feel better, my work can be an excuse for an early exit."

She hesitated, reading both their expressions. "All right; I'll see if we can't get four lunch reservations, for say — 12:30?" Noting their nods, she began rinsing dishes. Swigging her last gulp of tea she muttered, "You're like a couple of old hens - though, I do appreciate your concern."

They meekly nodded, and Cate mentioned a guest's request. "Mr. Rumkowski dropped a note, in the suggestion box. It asked we remove the piped-in music to his bathroom or add a station selector."

That got three sets of rolled eyes. Along with his note was another page-long diatribe. Cate summarized. "His words included 'captive on the commode to the local station's Viagra commercials.' Also, he described the various problems created, for him, after Mrs. Rumkowski showered to *Do You Think I'm Sexy* and then again to *Let's Break the Rules Tonight*'."

They smirked, and Margaret cleared her throat, expounding, "Just turn off the music — for now." She busied herself packing work items, as Livia scooted across the floor humming the Rod Stewart and Kim Carnes songs.

She stopped at Margaret's timeout signal. Cate said, "I'd better get to the front desk. If those books don't get updated, I shudder to think of you guys messing with them tomorrow." She handed them each their shopping lists and recited her usual details about some of the items.

Margaret nodded, and Cate squinted - watching Livia's nostrils flare as she held her tongue flat between her teeth.

"You're a shrewd woman but a nice one," said Livia as she stomped off.

Margaret followed Cate into the main hallway. "You just have to keep bouncing the ball back in her court."

Cate ducked her chin. "I know; Livia can be a bit acidic when she's upset. We're used to each other's responses, so I try not to feed into it."

"Well, yeah–!" taunted Margaret. "That ought to bring on the warm feelings. Ever think of trying some big hugs?"

Cate shrugged it off. "That's just not me. Well — maybe, a little at first. You know, every time I've gotten too involved, it's all turned out the same – so, I just don't know."

"Excuse me for asking, but how long of a time?"

Cate remained quiet. Then she said. "Maybe, ten or more years."

Margaret sat down and stared up at her. "I've known you two for that long. Livia once confided, that your mother moved back home in 1966 and filed for divorce. You were only two at the time but you remembered many 'hard happenings'."

"Yes, it comes from way back. Some parts of me must still find it too scary, and I go along just so far, and then I get numb."

"Lola!" Livia passed them - chasing Lotus from pantry to front door. Well aware that she interrupted their conversation, she faced them and said, "Sorry!" She corralled the dog and yelled back, from down the long hallway, "I don't know; she's got something stuck in the roof of her mouth." With dog pinned in the corner, she waited for Cate's assistance.

Margaret watched Cate stand by Livia, and she sighed. "Well, anyway, I must leave for work." Slight nod to Cate, she added, "I'll be home tomorrow afternoon, if you want to talk."

"We'll see," said Cate.

Margaret grabbed her things. "Hope so. Anyway, I'm almost late." Heading to the door, she brushed Cate's shoulder and she whispered, "You're lucky; she's worth it. Better take care of her. It gets more fun with practice."

Cate blinked hard, giving a tiny nod. Margaret left, and she knelt next to Livia helping her pry Lotus' mouth open. Cate stroked the dog crooning, "Awe, Let Miss Cate see. What did she do to you? Well, whatever it was – she must have fixed it. There's nothing there, and you'll be fine."

Sheepish grin and Livia said, "I heard your conversation, and I decided to give you an out, in case you were too uncomfortable." The term 'enabler' stuck her mind. Yep, that psychology minor got her in trouble.

She yelled back, "Sorry to leave you with both the cleaning and front desk. If the elephant ears and begonias are not planted today - we'll get busy, and I'll be watering flower crates all week." Noticing Cate's quizzical stare, she stopped to explain. "Kalo means taro - you know the Elephant Ear plants you like, the plants for poi?" Lotus yapped and bumped the front door. Livia followed. Maybe Margaret would offer Cate a blood test and some hormone therapy. Hand at her waist, her intuition told her even a placebo might work.

Cate stood, at the front desk, sorting bills for Livia. She finally booted the inn's computer. She scrolled through the e-mail. Topping the list was a message from Hulda Schimmelfiney, office manager at her last job. It contained two attachments: '2003 W-2 Tax Form' and 'Guy - HI Trip.' Filing the tax message, she opened the later. It was a note from her previous boss and coach, Guy Rosetta.

His address began. "Ho - Bear and Hockey Gals!" Briefly, it stated he and wife, Mina Chahine (their hockey captain) would fly into Honolulu, the day after Christmas to watch the 30th Honolulu Marathon and possibly attend Kona's Rough Water Swim. That would depend if Kate could guarantee a suite at La`Ohana.

Most often Livia did not type after dinner; however, noticing the exquisite sunset and the high rustling palms she patted her pocket holding paper and tiny pencil. She doodled until the breeze changed directions, and began wafting fresh sage to her. Cate's kitchen concoction drew her to supper. Chicken and dressing was well worth the wait, and not a morsel went to waste.

Margaret had showered and powdered off, after her late afternoon run/walk. She finished her plate adding that supper was quite satisfying, and she was very pleased that Guy's visit prompted her to begin some serious training. Participating in the run/walk marathon was a high point, during the past five years, and she meant to keep up with it, as long as her knees held out.

All evening, everyone chatted about plans for their visitors. Funny how things had turned around — but no one could ever say, "Good Coach Guy didn't know how to have fun." Livia began taking notes and started a second sheet, of her infamous lists including plans for tomorrow through early January. Cate would keep the master itinerary beginning the last week of December. In no time, it was eleven-thirty. Dead tired, they called it a night.

The next morning, Livia first heard Margaret stump down the hall - no matter, for Cate beat her out the door and up the highway.

Livia took Lotus to the lanai. Handing over a fresh mug of coffee, Margaret dipped her teabag and engaged Livia in a rare post-breakfast chat. Pointing to a couple Cardinals, she glanced down at the dog and pointing to scraps of hair on the back steps. "What the —? Did Miss Lotus thrash a mongoose?" She lightly knuckled the dog's head, as she watched Livia rush to the carport and return, with broom in hand, and attack tufts of hair, all the while mentioning something about trimming Cate's hair the night before. Margaret chuckled, "Only you would take on a project like that right before bath time. That reminds me. How is tomorrow after dinner? Mine needs a bit of shaping over the ears." She sipped the last of her tea. Setting teacup aside, she exhaled. "This is nice to relax. Rarely do I take a few minutes, in the morning sun, and enjoy your peaceful garden." She rubbed her forehead with the back of her wrist. "You know, it's been nearly two years, and I've never taken the time to thank you. We do appreciate your keeping up, with all these small chores for us."

That garnered little response. Margaret paused, with a glance across the inn's well-kept front lawn, and prodded. "So, tell me — how are you?"

Rarely nosy – more likely than not, her innmates figured that she had not properly mourned Pearl's death. She sat and took a hefty swig of coffee. "Not too bad. Well, I sort of mourned my family ahead of time. Loved 'em dearly, and it is probably awful to say - but I am more focused at writing since they died. My parents always said, 'We don't live in the past'."

They were quiet again then Margaret chuckled. "Oh, Livy, if I know you — you have a couple projects. If you can, write as quickly as possible."

"Hard to force being arty-farty," muttered Livia. "Kind of Zen: when I putter around here; ideas come. I don't know – how I ever got anything done back in Michigan. Like going to work, tending parents and running around to various sports - plus the fact: I caught every little snot and sniffle. I do miss friends and our teammates; only thing is, living here seems so natural – well, that is unless you need a face-lift or some cutting-edge medical treatment."

Margaret's eyebrows arched a bit.

Livia said, "Bad choice of procedures. I meant, you know, like brain surgery or bone marrow treatments. Anyway, back to good living; such as yesterday, when Tom kept me plenty busy helping him add that new barrier to the paddock. Later on, I saw Aye for a few minutes and took a couple low sugar treats to Chakra. Here's the deal: as long as I have a little money in the bank, what else do I want? More of our friends come here to visit than we saw at home. Oh, damn — I forgot to tell you." She dug in her pocket for a quarter, and noticed Margaret hold up her hand. "They're planning a hukilau for us. Next week, Aye's showing me orchids he transplanted from his kitchen."

Margaret sat wide-eyed leaning on her hand. She smiled and drank in Livia's excitement about the hukilau. Finding a pause, she sat straight and feigned a clinical assessment. "Okay– I see you are in no need of hobbies."

Livia giggled. "Nope! Don't think so! Not in Hawaii. So far, work and hobbies are one and the same."

Cate was not long. She hurried Livia down the path.

Even with the turnaround delay, they still got to the cottage right on the mark. Cate grabbed her quilt bags, as something hard yet soft rammed her in the knees from behind. A quick gasp and she snapped to attention. Composure regained, she bent down and timidly scratched a cute potbelly porker's ear, crooning, "Oh my! You're mighty rough and tough, for such a pretty little thing."

Soon she began rooting Cate's ankles and nuzzling her knees before herding Cate and Livia, duck fashion, to the cottage.

"I see you've met our Tallulah," Chakra called out, from the lanai. "She is really a good girl but has the bad habit of surprising people."

Aye stood at her side, as the grand lady rocked herself back-and-forth and managed to rise from the chair. By the time Livia and Cate climbed the steps, stately Chakra stood ready and bestowed a big hug. "Aloha Nui Loa, and welcome to our humble home."

"Mahalo," Cate returned with a shy grin.

Chakra whispered to Aye. "Please mind to practice with Tallulah's manners. We want no heart attacks here."

As Livia sunk into a warm hug saying, "Much Mahalo. Cate has a big heart. You know— bears can be quite friendly with pigs. I searched for 'Tallulah' on the Internet. It's the Indian name of a gorge and waterfalls, in Tallulah Gorge State Park, somewhere in Northern Georgia. Besides Hollywood, there's not much else about the name. Don't think it's Seminole – I'd have to guess Laredo."

Invited inside, Livia watched Cate's eyes widen. She gasped, "These are works of art," as her hands hovered at the quilt racks along the living room wall. Careful not to touch the fabric, she ogled three quilts from up close. As she traced and named the various quilt patterns, Livia lightly elbowed her ribs, thus forcing her to glance through the bedroom door. In awe, Cate asked. "Is that the Union Jack? I've never seen appliqués stitched so evenly."

Chakra assured her, "You're welcome to touch them but let's eat breakfast first. The flag of England is the basis for the Hawaiian state flag. We brought it into our bedrooms after 1959, when outside displays were dissuaded."

Five minutes of Cate's undivided attention, and Chakra prodded her further, "You are most welcome to look at all of them for the rest of the day; however, Aye will be sorely disappointed if his fancy omelets get cold. We'll talk patterns whilst we eat."

"I'm very sorry. I get totally overwhelmed when I see beautiful quilts." Cate added that her family taught her manners but somehow they got worse since she played hockey.

Chakra engulfed the largest kitchen chair and politely offered them fresh pineapple or orange juice. Waiting for them to choose, she passed a plate of warm homemade Hawaiian sweet bread. "Take all you want; there's another loaf in the oven for Our Good Doctor."

Cate apologized, citing her allergies. "Oh, it does smell wonderful but store brands often list milk as an ingredient." Assured the dough was mixed with only water, she heaped three golden slices on her plate.

Livia licked fresh pineapple juice off the glass rim, gave a five-year-old's grin, then put her hands in her lap and said, "Oh - that reminds me; Margaret sent your packet of insulin syringes."

Excusing herself, Cate hoped up. "If I don't get them now, I'll probably forget them. You know me - and my quilts. Anyone's for that matter."

Livia passed Chakra more sweet bread. She examined a slice and remarked, "I might usually build a fine sandwich with layers of brown sugar and fresh butter, and dip it in a bowl of pala poi – however, I'm limiting my caloric intake." Turning slightly, toward the stove, she held out her hand. "Aye is a fine cook. I come to the table early and test my sugar levels whilst I wait."

He offered the blood test kit then returned to his omelets, garnishing one with pineapple, chives, and low fat ricotta. Spooning sautéed turkey and mushrooms, on the other, he proudly announced, "This sticking and pricking Chakra must master for herself, in case I am not here." A proud smile engulfed his brown face, as Chakra demonstrated her skill with the glucose monitor.

Their speech patterns made Livia consider her hosts' near perfect grammar and dialect (or lack of it). For more than twenty years, her ear had become a bit ragged, bombarded by Detroit banter and engineers' clipped speech. Since childhood Annabelle teased her, "Your speech suffered severely – ever since you started school." Five years after college,

Livia brought her pleasant Louisville drawl, laced with Appalachian Scots-Irish, to Michigan. There she added a little as she could, of pidgin and junior high 'Valpseak', to her repertoire. Later, she caught a good ribbing every time she corrected the Kiever's verbs. Of all of that, she missed the exhilarating Scots-Irish.

Nary a scrap o' hit, or pidgin, spoken here. Near Canadian their speech was; she could not put a finger on it. Then it hit her - the Brit automotive engineers' sharp *whilst*.

The six egg plus four egg whites made two tasty light omelets. The normal chitchat took a turn when Aye called off seven names of their children, proudly mentioning that the five that attended and four that graduated college.

Both of their previous marriages seemed long and satisfying – thus giving reason for the ramshackle place. Offering help with the dishes received a firm "No," so Livia nursed her second cup and settled back to enjoy Chakra's fine historical banter.

Chapter 12: **Poliahu**

They decided on an over night trip to a couple quilt stores. It was early morning and Volcanoes National Park lay barely twenty miles ahead. As Cate flipped off the radio, Livia ran her hand across the dashboard noticing the simple beauty of Kau's Pahala Stretch. The highway cut a stripe between Mauna Loa's southern slope and the sea, and the Laredo hummed along, above the 1949 lava flow.

Cate pointed at the black fields. "Wow, you told me about South Kona's Honokua Flow but these rocks steam all day. You say the seamount off this shore will make another island? Remember how close we got to Pu'u Loa's lava that day we hiked to the end of Chain of Craters Road?"

"Yeah, April of 2002 it was – kind of gives ya the shivers, huh?"

Cate was intent on hitting tomorrow's fabric sale in Hilo. Today, they agreed to stop at the Jaggar Museum, so Livia could see the artwork, then hit the winery and Kilauea Kreations before checking into their room. Either today or tomorrow, if they had time, they planned a drive up Kipuka Kulalio Pass' 6,000-foot lookout, almost halfway up Mauna Loa's east side.

Livia prattled on about horseback rides in the park. On their last trip, the desk clerk, at Volcano House, did not know about any horses, in the park, and her story matched that of the rangers. From the conservation standpoint, it rather made sense but she realized she had read it somewhere.

Cate rolled down all four windows and stretched, soaking in the warm morning air, as the highway grew steeper. Lulled by the tire hum, Livia sat bolt upright and pointed to something way down the pavement. Squinting, she blinked again. Pointing to the far left she said, "Catie Pat, look there. Way out here in nowhere, and someone's sitting by the road?"

Always the cautious one, Cate even stopped for squirrels. She slowed down, crossed lanes and pulled onto shoulder before leaning out the window staring down at the old woman.

"Ma'am?" She leaned a bit further and gentled her voice. "Hello there? Ma'am? May we give you a ride?"

The old woman sat quietly, in a long rusty red muumuu. She seemed to be admiring some sort of low shrub as she fondled its few smooth leaves then patted the small white blossoms circling her hair.

When she finally chose to recognize them, she snapped off a branch and shook it at them. A few red berries cascaded to her lightly clad feet. It took Cate back a second or two, when the woman stared right past her at Livia. Quite aware of her habits, Cate did not rush the senior and quietly repeated her offer. This time the woman lost no time quietly rising to her feet while starring out to sea and shaking her head no.

Cate turned and stared up the road. She spoke softly and evenly, to Livia, but recalling that whispers were rude, she continued in a normal tone. "Obviously, the woman does not want a ride but we're a good ten miles from anywhere. Have you seen a driveway or crossroads?"

"I haven't, for quite a long time," said Livia. She peered past the steering wheel adding, "Seems strange that a woman of her age goes anywhere without her purse, and she has no water either."

Finally, Cate closed the door. "I'm going over there. She's ancient and can't stay out here alone."

Soon, Cate helped the woman around the car. Livia jumped out. She had barely touched the old woman's elbow and was stunned when the woman stiffened and jerked it back. Solemnly, Livia backed up, as Cate continued helping their guest onto the running board and into the passenger seat. All this left Livia standing in the dirt.

Cate shrugged and returned to the driver's side, Livia followed and hopped in the backseat. Doors shut and seatbelts buckled, they were off.

Sighing, Livia dug through her backpack. Laptop and baseball cap retrieved, she looked over the folds of her *Visiting Volcanoes* map. Scanning the National Parks Service map, her finger followed the smooth, straight road past the Great Crack and some cliffs near the visitors' center – over eighty-five square miles in all.

Good thing it was not rough or curvy pavement, or she would need medication. She remembered hurling on her Luke's suit. And the time she did manage to get out of the car, he stooped to help her and lost his car keys. Yes, relief from motion sickness gave her the reason to drive – at a very early age.

"How you doin' back there, Missy?" called out Cate.

"No problem – so far,"   answered Livia.

And, for the moment, the ride was not too bad; in as much as Livia could read her travel brochure – well, that was, until the old lady turned slightly and leered at her. As it continued every other minute, the ride became increasingly uncomfortable. Livia scrunched against the door frame, a little further out of sight.

Cate broke the silence saying they were on the way to the Jaggar Museum and had no problem taking their passenger to the west rim visitor's center. A bit of silence passed and she said, "You say your niece works there?"

The woman nodded yes. Once in the parking lot, Cate helped her step onto the running board and down to pavement. Remarkably agile, she kept up with Cate's long legs, and soon, they talked a bit alongside the building. Livia stretched her legs then slipped back to the passenger seat. Most kupuna got quite chatty; strange how this one had not said a word to her. It seemed that a good ten minutes passed until Cate returned.

"Well?" Asked Livia.

"We went inside and she pointed to the restroom. I waited by the door giving her a few minutes of peace, and when I went in to check on her - not a soul was there. I asked the men, at the desk, and they said that they'd seen no one. Then I asked about her niece and learned that no woman had worked there for over two years.

"Damn well gave me the shivers – like someone watching me. She and I were the only ones in the lobby. Both men exchanged glances, as if I wasn't privy to something. They were pleasant enough – asking if there was anything else, they could do for me, and where we were lodging. If I wanted, they would call ahead for us.

She hopped in the driver's seat adding, "Oh, and they said that, since we found the Kilauea Lodge Restaurant a bit too upscale, we might try the Lava Rock Café. It's just next door to the quilt store."

Livia shook her head. "Let's go to the quilt store. You can nose around while I run in the general store. We'll ice-down some hooch and get lunch before we head back to Volcano House." She started the car and patted Livia's knee. "It'll be Okay now. We'll have time, and we can go to the winery afterwards."

Cate cut out the side drive, to the highway, and headed east to Volcano village. Passing the main park entrance, she said, "I still think those museum men were way over the top with Aloha spirit."

Livia mentioned she could get a better idea of it, if she had witnessed what happened in the visitors lobby. Ten more minutes and they stopped for gas, before parking in front of the quilt store. Feet dangling out the car door, she ran her finger down the map in the bright sunlight. Cate finished her first run through the quilt store – and loaded with bags, she stacked them neatly to Livia's side. Watching patiently, she thought her stomach would nearly gnaw through to her backbone by the time they headed next door for lunch.

The café skylights provided an unexpected treat. Between them and the openly fake floral décor, the whole meal was very satisfying but sort of funky and surreal. Cate talked quilts as Livia recalled the side street from the map.

This time, she followed Cate back to the quilt store. Ten minutes and she had enough, of quilts, so she decided to explore Alanui Street on the northwest edge of town. A couple blocks over, the golf course bordered the last street and could provide a nice view of Pu'u Oo Trail and maybe even a glimpse of the winery. She left the parking lot and followed Volcano Road, west past Haunani Road. Three private drives further a sign said Alanui Street.

From there, she could see down to Maie Avenue's little soccer field and two young boys tripping along passing a ball. Opposite them was a long ditch. She noticed a movement in the bushes bordering the woods. The hot early evening breeze ruffled a young woman's skirt as she stepped to the pavement. She glared at Livia, who immediately recognized her features. Before Livia could back up, the woman crossed the road to the golf course. Both boys never took their eyes off her, and with a swift kick they chased after the soccer ball. One boy turned and looked at Livia and back to woman again, as the other boy scooped up the ball and ran ahead backwards grumbling, "Dang — it's hot. Come on! Let's split a shave ice." Both ran off between the houses toward the center of the village.

For twelve years, Livia taught junior high, and something about the boys struck her as odd. Cate expected her back in half an hour, so she followed them. Once last glance, toward the golf course, and the woman was gone. Two women, too much like the Madame Pele stories - but why did they glare at her so? Shaking her head, she kept her feet moving.

Not a jogger - Livia leaned over and breathed hard before climbing into the Laredo. A bit more composed, she kicked off her shoes and ran her toes across the ribbed running board. She cleared her throat, to get Cate's nose out of her purchases. Always worked; Cate was at the car in two minutes. Livia huffed, "I'm pooped. Mind if we skip the museum winery today? We can go to Volcano House, a bit early, and sit in the bar till check-in time."

Cate shrugged and tossed her bags in the back. "That's fine. You know me; cold beer is as fine, as wine. You sure – you are Okay? Looks like you have a touch of heat stroke – that, or have seen a ghost."

Livia just shook her head. "Yeah – I'm just hot. Let's get going. Buy you a beer and fill you in when we get there." Not at all surprised by Cate's careful attention, after a few drinks, she described the women; however, it did come as a surprise when Cate quickly switched subjects.

"You know, I'm glad we skipped the heat and the wine. Cold beer will taste good with chili on hot dogs. If you like, we can get our sweaters, eat on the bar's patio later, and watch the sunset. Remember that first trip up here — when everyone sat in here all evening, with the windows boarded up, and watched KHNL's Stormwatch as that tropical storm passed by."

Livia in was no mood for small talk. "Yes, let's get our sweaters."

A few cool hours later, they toasted their day and Pele. Locals huddled, as before, watching the evening news, as meteorologist Lester Miagi mentioned today's steady low quakes on Mauna Loa's usually quiet east side. Cate raised an eyebrow and a finger for beers noticing that Livia drained her mug first.

The next afternoon, the Laredo zipped up the long haul from Hilo. Cate mastered the urge, to stop and shop, and drove right on past Kilauea Kreations.

Margaret waved from the lanai and listened to every detail. After a light supper and a bit of television, all three agreed on early to bed and early to rise.

The next morning the banter was light, and Livia calmly said, "Nothing compares to sleeping in one's own bed." She finished her scrabbled eggs and headed to the store, before Cate picked up the phone.

She watched Livia leave before phoning Aye and Chakra. Familiar with Tallulah's pattern of rooting, in the weeds near the garden gate, she hopped the rock wall and got to the door first.

Aye hugged her. Peering over his shoulder, she noticed a lovely tea service set on Quaker Lace. He accompanied her to the table and asked. "How was your trip up the big mountain?"

"Oh, perfect for me but hard on Livia. That's why I'm here."

"I see," Chakra hesitated. "You relax and sip your tea, whilst you tell us what happened."

Cate leaned hard on the table. As the chain of events came bubbling out, Aye busied himself re-organizing the spices and emptying last night's groceries in sturdy containers. Chakra topped off their teacups. Presented with a small plate of shortbreads, Cate selected two cookies and complimented their slight hint of lavender. Chakra nodded. "About your trip, our legends say that Halema'uma'u Crater at the southwest bottom of Kilauea Crater is Pele's fire-lake home."

"That's not far across the rim, from the Jaggar Museum, where I took the old woman."

"Yes, you are correct. She must have liked you; however, she may have noticed something about Livia that reminded her of Poliahu. Some even say like pueo – she has wings of an owl."

"Polyhu-hu-u?" quipped Cate?

"She was Pele's nemesis, and pueo kept chosen warriors under their protection," explained Chakra. "You've see that lovely painting with Poliahu sleeping in the snow, on the mountain - and her eyes are awake - like the painting of Pele. Many people, even scientists, think she is active. Some believe she and Pele are sisters. I take most of it, as glorified pish tosh; although, it never hurts to keep an open mind. Legend says that Pele visited the area that is now North Hilo District.

There, the age-old archrivals had a major confrontation. Poliahu floated down the eastern slope of Mauna Kea extending her best welcome. However, Pele's fire climbed too far uphill, blowing the top off Mauna Lilinoe.

"Poliahu retreated back to her home, an icy peak west of the main summit. Pele figured the island would be hers, if only she pushed the silver-haired goddess a bit further. Poliahu's sisters cheered her on, to drive Pele south confirming their reign was supreme. Refreshed by the cold, she told them she cared nothing about being all-powerful. But the next rumble of flame and steam scorched Pu'u Kalepeamoa, near today's visitor's center, and Poliahu hit Pele with such force that she never crossed the high gulch lands again. Later, they briefly battled a while over a lover, Laie, the chief of Kauai; but eventually, they left him and returned to their respective summits. Most are thankful the trio did not continue battling. Most islanders agree Mauna Kea sleeps peacefully, affording the great scientists a fine place to study the stars. Others say that whenever Pele sleeps, she often roams the islands and the sea in many guises. Such may explain Livia's encounters as well as your old woman. Livia's light hair may have provoked some disfavor; whereas, you seem to have found her approval."

"I see," Cate said matter-of-factly. "I would never give that story a bit of credit, except for the fact that my grandmother told some pretty tall tales that over the years, which later I came to respect. Doesn't much matter what we believe. As The Ma always said, 'What's meant to be is meant to be.' Anyway, with Livia and Lotus - we should see few Menehune around the inn."

Chakra swallowed. "I wouldn't worry about them. Instead, be wary of those few humans who wield a serious amount of mana – good or bad."

"Well, it should prove interesting. Wonder what sets it all, in motion?"

Chakra winked. "I cannot say that anyone knows with certainty. As you like to quote: 'What will be, will be'." To that, Cate tried not to nod.

Chakra smiled and warned, "Yes. Your grandmother sounds like a wise woman." She pointed near Cate's elbow. "By the way, those branches of little red berries are called `ōhelo, and they're Pele's favorite, to wear and to eat. Never pick or eat any without offering some to her first." She whispered, "Katarina - that day, when Livia's aunt died, and you searched for her after she drove back along the Kau - no wonder she stopped off for a couple potent drinks." Patting her knee, she said, "It is quite clear, dear; we all have those days when we need a really good stiffener."

That raised her eyebrows. Obviously, this grand old lady was more than a mere tea totaler. For her next visit, she planned to have Livia mix a saucy Old-Fashion for Chakra. Cate meant to learn all she could. She sat a while and quilted, until Chakra quietly said, "You know – Pele's noticing something about Poliahu, in Livia, is not all to worry about." Setting needle and thread aside – she took Cate's hand, patted it lightly, and said, "That morning when Pearl died – you were very fortunate after seeing six of the ka huakai o ka po 'Marchers of the Night'." Cate tried to pull free of the large woman's gentle grip; but instead, she caught a whiff of The Ma's sweet Windsong and kept her mouth shut. Chakra gently pulled her closer. "What you saw before that dawn was the Ali`i Marchers – and since you left the window and lay quietly, they spared your life."

"But I didn't know Pearl died. I did sense someone passing. I feared it was Livia since she was away, in Hilo. Only when she called me, did I know."

Chapter 13: **Hockey Visitors**

It was two days after Halloween - that Cate noticed another e-mail, from Hulda Schimmelfinney, stating that Guy and Mina accepted her offering of suites. They would attend the Honolulu Marathon, late in December, and fly to Kona on January 3rd. Cate quickly scrolled down, to the personal attachment, as she relished news from former office buddies and teammates.

Below Hulda's message was one from Priscilla (previous teammate and member of Cate's golf league). She and her husband, Mark, were planning a week to participate in this, their seventh Honolulu run. Good thing they had not requested room reservations. Things would not go smoothly with them at the inn, with Guy and Mina — because Prissy, as they called her, did not leave the Kick Ice Bears of her own accord.

Everyone knew that Guy hated to fly, so Cate quickly phoned Hulda's office. Once connected, Hulda put her on conference call, brightly chirping, "Thanks for calling us back, so soon; you know how Guy hates to wait – especially before an airplane trip."

The Guy-Mel employees sounded, all atwitter, until Hulda brightly announced, "Oh, hold on a minute, he's coming in the main door. Let me flag him down for you. Believe me — he's glad to get back from the print shop." Once again, she spoke privately and whispered, "I believe he's having some special red-and-white Aloha Shirts made, with various logos."

Cate and Hulda reminisced about Guy. His family came from Eastern Italy, via Sault Ste. Marie, and he bought into a fine apparel store, which was located on Detroit's Woodward Avenue. He soon located a partner (Melvin) and they quickly branched out to two suburbs. Their business expanded to include producing appliquéd sports jerseys. In the late 50s, they landed a military contract for outerwear and sold even more flap jackets during the Vietnam conflict. They kept the slim twelve-story flagship store, from which they ran their small empire, until it was bought-up, to complete the new Tigers Stadium parking.

Guy latched onto all the original hockey players (except Margaret and Livia) at a golf outing that Mina organized for their businesses. He built them into The Kick Ice Bears and decked them out in Red Wings style uniforms. A year later he helped them organize a women's league before helping to build three ice rinks, one of which was located between his cottage and the Big Mac Bridge in Cheboygan.

There was no mistaking Guy's upbeat voice. "It's great to hear from you. What's up with my favorite goalie?" He asked about Livia and Margaret, saying he missed taking them for rides, from Cheboygan to Harbor Springs, in his Mustang. He punched the Hands Free button speaking louder, "Just let me get my coat off. How's the sun out there? I bet it's beating down on you and all of Hawaii."

Cate confirmed that it was – adding that it could not be a better golf day, in Kona or Kohala, and they still had plenty of rooms available all through January. She could hear him rustling papers, so she made small talk - mentioning how Livia often compared him driving his sports car to her father's tooling along Indiana's back roads in her old Firebird. That got a chuckle, and Cate skipped on to business matters by asking, "By the way, how long do you and Mina plan to stay? I suppose you'd like a tee time for the big golf course."

He teased back, "…and which one might that be?"

"Well, let me check my list," said Cate, well knowing which one, since they had sparred, for years - about his ignoring her suggestions to play the Mauna Kea Resort's grand courses.

"You know - the one with the views of the ocean, Mauna Kea and the Kohala Mountains."

"Well, let's see." She played along. "I believe there are at least three or more excellent courses up there."

"It's your phone call," he continued.

She had had her fun, so she promised to call the Mauna Kea starter as soon as they hung up.

The phone went dead.

That's Guy, thought Cate - shaking her head. He called again within fifteen minutes, for the details. This call, they talked for twenty minutes, as he wanted to catch up about all three women. It was a hard shot when he lost her to paradise, and she wanted him to have a fine visit to make up for it. No sooner than he hung up, she had run to the front lanai and yelling to Livia and Aye, who were on their weekly weed patrol of the front lawn, "You cannot guess who I just got off the phone with!"

"Guy?" Livia calmly answered, as she helped Aye to his feet.

"How do you know these things?" Cate asked.

"Well, there's only one thing that gets you all that excited: Hockey. The sport can't dial our number – so, I figured it must be Guy. What was it he had to say?"

"They're coming for a visit after Christmas and stay into January, right after they watch Priscilla bike and Mark run in the marathon. You know the one that Margaret completed the run-walk. He and Mina can't wait to see us."

"Oh, yeah," interrupted Livia.

"Be nice," taunted Cate.

Livia was quick to add, "Well, she does like to golf, plus there's shopping and horse riding and all." Aye stared, at Livia, then shifted his weight from leg to leg. That got Tallulah's attention, and she ran right up– nearly bowling him over. Lotus Blossom was quick on her heels– veering off stopping against Cate. Their tiny tails wagged, as they got their ears scratched.

With that - Polynesia sounded off, and Margaret pulled up the driveway. Her car door slammed shut, with her saying, "Hey there, what's up? Is this a meeting or a convention?"

Aye left, and the women got cozy on the side lanai. Cate filled Margaret in, as Livia chattered away. "Anyone else coming? It would be nice to see Priscilla and Mark." She knew, after every competition, the couple headed home the very next day, and she continued, "You know that Priscilla starts riding in January, for her Bluegrass Cycle competition." Cate noted that Prissy would get some great practice, by riding the Honolulu course the day before the Marathon. Since they'd not follow with a Kona trip, this year, and Cate missed seeing Prissy - she'd damn-near have to convince Mark he could compete in the Kona Ironman that October. She mentioned it to him once, as they stood outside Joe Louis Arena - after the Red Wings played —"

Lotus repeatedly nosed Cate's index finger. Cate interrupted herself calmly saying, "I know; you want some yellow stuff." Livia and Margaret rolled their eyes – as if the dog did not recognize the words.

Margaret agreed, with Cate's plans, and patted Livia on the back, saying, "Well, Livy – Cate has a fine idea, to ask Miss Priss and Mark to stop by. Why – you can invite them, to stay a couple days – either after the Ironman, or after the next Marathon. Convince Prissy, and she will convince Mark."

The women completed a few chores, and Lotus gulped her cheese. Livia found them once again installed on the lanai. Cate looked up. "I got hold of Mark. Priscilla was not in. He declined this year; however, this is her cycling club's last Bluegrass race - so they will definitely consider coming here after the next marathon. Well, I tried. So, now– we'll just have to wait."

Margaret nodded as Cate solemnly put her arms around Livia's shoulders, leading her to the couch. She knew the holidays would be rough for Livia. "You know I enjoy visiting with her, and your heart is always in the right place. We will get them here. You'll see — even if it's not this year."

Without hesitation, Margaret looked at Cate and said, "Yes, it will give us time to plan, on a special visit, focusing on them. Will that not be nicer? That way, Mina won't have to spar with anyone for attention."

It was Livia's idea to drive to Kailua, for a Scandinavian Shave Ice. She offered to buy. Cate and Margaret always shared a large raspberry/cranberry yogurt smoothie called The Alaskan Punch. Livia brought a tiny bottle of citrus Stoli to add, to her favorite: Cherry/lime Kick.

Walking down Ali`i Drive she knew Margaret read her expression. Livia ran next door, to the ABC Store, for another tiny vodka and some Cointreau for the Hula-Hula Coconut Surprise that she and Cate would share.

As Margaret motioned the hula, on the way to the store and back, as Cate leaned close to Livia, and said, "Humor her; it's not often she lets her hair down. She's actually getting excited about Guy's visit. She missed the race last year, with her bad knee and all. I think she'll get to walk it this year."

Livia kept quiet. In fact, she planned to keep in good humor for the remainder of the evening; although, she was onto her buddies running interference between her and her emotions. They often forgot that she was the eldest and most experienced.

They had a glorious evening along the Kailua-Kona seawall. Livia loved it down there, only avoiding it in the afternoon heat. It sparked her to watch the tourists and locals alike. They wandered a couple blocks down the boardwalk and watched the usual awe-inspiring sunset. Occasionally, her eyes followed someone wandering into the nearby tattoo parlor.

Margaret's cell phone rang. She answered and clasped it shut, muttering that she couldn't believe she paged herself earlier, in order to get home to review some nursing schedules. Cate and Livia knew the work schedules were posted every two weeks and tomorrow was the day. "Figures — just when we could have a nice evening's walk," Margaret added.

Livia moaned, "Couldn't we just do a short one?"

Cate glowered and Margaret conceded. "Okay. It won't hurt me. Just for tonight, we can try to match Livy's pace. She is eleven years my senior."

Livia bristled at the remark and strode out, in front of them, reproaching Margaret and doing the David Waddle with her hips. "Yeah, fine, and I've got the shortest legs too. So, see if you two don't have to keep up!"

To Livia's surprise, Cate poked Margaret and chided, "Boy, you don't play it, to win, halfway — do ya? Just remember that she walked to work for eight years; be careful what you wish for."

Livia turned just in time to see Margaret's eyes widened and a bit of bottom lip protrude, as she countered, "Who? Me? I am only funning with you; she may not look like it – she is a tough little bird."

Cate just winked and shrugged her shoulders. A flash of silliness and she pretended to stagger, then tipped her thumb to her lips, and enunciated, "A bit much Cointreau," then she wiggled a shaka and grinned - as Margaret chimed in saying, "A good stiff walk always does us, noble citizens, good."

Livia let them pass her, and taking her own sweet time she returned, to the car, and twisted up her hair before noticing she forgot a barrette. Windows wide open; she leaned back and breathed-in the night air. On the way home, Cate suggested they sing along, with the country station, or have Livia tell them about Poliahu and explain which peak was the snow goddess' home.

Livia chalked it up, as another diversion tactic. Their questions still surprised her – so why not play along?

Margaret continued. "My last roomie at university was an anthropology major — totally hooked me with some of her research. She fully explained, about Maui and Pele. However, isn't this Poliahu a sister of Pele? A couple patients have asked me about your blonde hair – especially how it seems even whiter in the moonlight."

Livia tried to turn a deaf ear, to the compliment, as Margaret continued.

"No – really, Livy, it is quite nice, and I'm sure the color is quite unusual to this island."

Cate's eyes narrowed. "Actually, her hair is quite white-gray now; whereas, it used to totally come from a bottle."

"That's enough!" said Livia. "And what's your shoe size? Must be quite big since you added it to the dimensions of your mouth? One more word - and I'll dye my hair chartreuse first thing in the morning."

There was silence, until Margaret said timidly, "I really did want to know about the snow goddess."

Livia sniffed and finally replied, "Well, from what I've read, she wasn't Pele-honua-mea's sister. Pele did have sisters but Poliahu was not among them. A younger sister accompanied Pele to this island and an older sister of the sea plagued Pele many times."

"And, what about the snow goddess?" carefully prodded Cate.

Trying her best to be congenial, Livia continued, "…and it seems that Pele picked her fights pretty carefully. After leaving Maui, she carried her little sister, Hi'iaka, to this island, in an egg. There was a lesser fire god residing here — I can't remember his name – but she ran him off with her fire stick. Later, Poliahu rushed down the slopes, in an avalanche, to greet Pele. Usually slow moving, Pele took offense to the chill that she shook what is now North Hilo so hard - that in shock, Poliahu blew herself back to the snowy peaks with her sisters.

"Finally recovering her wits, she gathered her defenses and froze Pele's fire, thus forcing her to retreat all the way to Mauna Loa. There's been a shaky standoff since that day. Aye told me many a time that Pele's older sister, the sea goddess, Namaka-o-kaha'i, still tempers a few secluded areas of this coastline, from cold winds or fiery lava."

"Amazing– I've heard tales of the Menehune and Night Walkers but never this story," admitted Margaret.

Cate added, "Oh, yes; Livia inherited being a history nut, from her father, and those little ears take in way more than most of us realize. Guy often called her Rose — you know, like in the *Golden Girls*. But, I'll tell you what: as doofey as that character was, she was one smart cookie. That gray matter was constantly churning up there." Hugging Livia she added, "It's probably what keeps you from sleeping most the time."

"Brain scientists," Livia answered curtly.

"Put your claws away," nudged Cate.

Livia shut the car door. Twirling around, she wanted to get the last word in. Instead, she grabbed her hair flipped it over her shoulder and made a beeline past Polynesia's cage and in the kitchen door.

Margaret held open one of the huge front doors, for Cate, and said, "Can't ever say it's not real."

Cate shrugged and did not move, until Lotus ran by and nearly toppled them en route to the kitchen.

Margaret leaned against the door to shut it, and asked how they first came to live in Hawaii.

"Actually, Livia used to tease that I stepped off the plane, and I seemed to melt in the Honolulu morning rain. We stood there, soaking in the warmth, and the passengers behind us nearly pushed us off the platform. You've heard the saying about rain."

Margaret shook her head, no, as she sat down on the front hall settee.

"No? Well, the first time I heard about it was the first time we visited Annabelle's friend, Mrs. Mulligan, back in Badendale. She mentioned in the 1950's it rained when she got off the plane in Honolulu. A muumuu-clad lady greeted her, with a lei, and said, 'Aloha 'oe. It rains– and you must return'."

Margaret smirked and squinted between two fingers. "Glad you're here now. You were a tad icy back in Michigan – if only just a little."

Cate squinted and shrugged. "Yeah, I guess I was. I sure got bit, by the Aloha bug — really bad. Back to Livia - you know there's nothing she wouldn't ever do, for either one of us. Remember how long she sat the bench, for me, when I played goalie. She'd have been on the ice more often than I was, if she were younger. You left, after your last knee injury, and her hockey career ended; although, she still played fill-in coach and door-jerk supreme."

Margaret sighed. "Yeah, too bad she had to start and end hockey, as your greatest fan." She rose, rubbed her knee, and ambled off toward her office. A few steps and she turned with a smile. "Still Teammates?"

Barely audible - Cate mouthed, "Yeah," as Livia leaned behind the pantry door and smiled.

Chapter 14: Accident At Captain Cook

Today was the trail ride to Captain Cook Monument. The sun shone brightly, and the gangly red poinsettia bushes danced in the January breeze. Lotus sat at the base of the kitchen stairs. Her tiny tail beat the wood floor, as Livia's sock feet skidded to a halt alongside the kitchen counter. "Ah–" sighed Guy as he cracked open a fresh can of coffee.

He caught sight of Livia, as her eyes danced from dog to coffee. His fingers tapped the counter in time to his words: "Hair looks nice. Have you been up long enough to fix it all wavy?"

Livia flicked the screen door open, answering with a definite, "No." Watching Lotus hop off the lanai and joining Guy at the kitchen island she smoothed back her unruly locks. Quickly braiding it she quickly added, "Well, I used to straighten the crap out of it when I worked at Southfield Engine. Nowadays, I rarely even blow it dry."

Both stared at the coffee pot. She glanced down to her mug. It still stung her ego – counting herself part of the Rust Belt's mass exodus. Never a quitter - she slogged through major career changes, three times. Politely conversing, she decided against reiterating the weather report. She almost explained how quickly her hair dried, but was saved by Margaret at the screen door. Grabbing groceries and an armload of flowers, she set them on the drain board, before turning back and catching another bunch of flowers.

Margaret hunched her shoulders, as the screen door slammed shut. Watching Livia rush back and forth, she said, "Good catch!"

"Guess so. Maybe we should fix that door." She filled vases - arranging one with clear yellow hibiscus, and the other with five flaming red- and-yellow torch gingers. She was the first to admit she was always a little spastic before her first cup of coffee.

"Door slam probably woke everyone," Guy quipped as he adjusted his watch, "Half past five – guess Mina's awake – kind of grouchy when she doesn't get her six hour fix. I called work, before realizing it was nearly 10:30 in Michigan. Hulda said they waited three-hours, in that conference room."

"Yeah, and in the summer, there's a six hour difference." Livia turned to Margaret and teased, "Good thing you already brought your briefcase and thermos inside. I'd have smacked them in the door too." Inhaling more coffee, her thoughts bounced around. She mulled over their Supreme Morning People: Mina, Guy, and her Annabelle. Until Hawaii, winter mornings were torture. With a long line of morning people preceding her, she must have inherited being a night owl from Grandmother Etter.

Margaret moved her briefcase and paraphernalia from inside the pantry door. Returning to the kitchen, she shook her head and sported a wide grin, as he patted her on the back. "Still my best defense man." She nodded, as he added, "I guess it's better to have a sore foot here than dropping something in the operating emergency room."

Margaret plopped down. "I am exhausted - small wonder I even made it home. Guess thirty-hour emergency room shifts are for residents only." She poured tea and turned to Guy. "Just like our travel hockey days…you're up pretty early."

He glanced to his watch again. "Big time change, and I just don't sleep so much anymore. To top it off, I forgot my Sonora tablets."

He pleasantly chattered and gestured, as Margaret blew steam from her mug and hazily stared at him. Livia wondered, "How would she analyze him? For his age, he was extremely spry."

Margaret finally volleyed back an offer, "Yeah, well, Livia usually has something in her stash. I will write you a script, to fill later. You know, if you are hungry – Tina should have already prepped the buffet with goodies. Umm, usually, there are fresh muffins and bagels and sausage, plus milk, juice, and a variety of fruit. Come on, with me. We will fix our plates together."

He sniffed the air and spun around, poking the air with his finger. "Great, as soon as I grab some more coffee. Delicious this Kona stuff!" He spun back, to Livia - then he spun around again. Popping open a cabinet door, he barked, "Good girl! You still keep the mugs, to the left of the pot." Filling his fancy one, to the brim, and with a wide grin, he snapped, "Want some?"

Livia's head slowly stopped wobbling. "No thanks."

"What? You don't want your own coffee?"

"No, I meant - this kitchen coffee is not Kona coffee. You're in luck. Today, we have Kona Peaberry, Koa Decaf, and Lez Beans Extra Dark in the dining room urns. You're welcome to try them - but my brew packs more of a wallop. Cate's Mother sends boxes of Tim Horton's; it's delicious. I brew it strong enough - a spoon stands up. I call it Java Jolt or plain old Diesel Fuel."

"Then that's what I want! You can save the light premium stuff, for the rest of the guests." He savored his mouthful, of the Canadian brew, and tipped his mug to Livia - before requesting decaf for that evening, and asking if it was Swiss water processed. As soon as Margaret returned, his free hand gestured like Caesar, at her, as he said, "Not to change the subject — but isn't your blacksmith friend taking you and Mina horseback riding, to do some snorkeling down by Captain Cook Monument? Oh– she has her heart set on getting her picture taken down there, after reading so much about it. Seems, someone told her the monument sits, on British soil that was donated by —"

Margaret interrupted. "Yes — he is, and it was. Livia is coming too. She and Cate rode with him, four years ago, and they convinced Mina it's the place to see."

Although, she only was half listening, Livia nodded thinking about their friends and hockey. How funny – during all fifteen years she had known them — Mina, nearly twenty years his junior, got up every day and exercised at what Livia coined 'the crap of dawn.' Whenever they traveled, the Bear's first hockey couple was always the perfect hosts, except that they left everyone early evening - with a well-stocked bar, of course. He did request that everyone meet two hours before games, for his treat: breakfast, lunch or dinner, as it may be. Some Canadian tournaments began at 7:00 AM – rude awakening for most of the spoiled party goers.

Margaret scraped her plate, rinsed her thermos, and had sipped part of a leftover smoothie - as Guy ambled back from the dining room. Chewing on a large chunk of strawberry papaya, he glowed. He pulled off a chunk, of Parmesan bagel, and chased it with Livia's Diesel Fuel. Gnawing it and waving the other half, he whispered slyly, "All you think of is hockey – eh?"

Livia repeated his "Hockey – eh?" recalling how his catchy Canadian phrase peppered the team's banter, within weeks of their first practice.

"Um-hum, hockey," dropped from Margaret's lips, as she turned noticing Guy and Livia quietly focused, on the blazing pink peeking over the high horizon. A fine sunrise soon crowned Hualalai's peaks.

Presently, the smell of fresh coffee reclaimed Margaret's attention. Offered a small cupful - she declined and shaking her head said, "Yeah, and I'd give my two little fingers for another five good years of play." With a deep sigh, she excused herself, "Nap time. See everyone for dinner."

With a mouthful of bagel, Guy nodded to Margaret, and raising his mug to her said, "Wouldn't we all?" Watching her tread upstairs he sipped more coffee, leaned toward Livia, and whispered, "Only two fingers – huh? From a surgeon's standpoint, that was no small price. Sorry you and Margaret had to quit playing hockey before Cate. Your goalie reflexes wore pretty thin, and I guess the knee operations greatly compromised her surgery schedule."

Livia said, "Yes" but knew half of Margaret's problem was Mina – a great slap-shot forward who, when relegated to defense, constantly butt heads with new coach: Michaelene, for more ice time. If Mina got it, Margaret sat.

Every fall, for the next few years, Guy thanked Cate for constantly asking Margaret to return to the Bears. The whole team teased her about being 'Old Green Pants' — from her Dartmouth days, but they missed her severely. From outside the blue line she could reel-off a crucifying slap shot; which, if correctly angled, could whiz through any goalie's sweet spot. Livia and Cate often reminisced how those first few months, her green pants really clashed with the Bear's red jerseys. Guy said, "She's gonna look like a Christmas tree." He rush-ordered a pair, of custom women's pants, from his nephew's Soo Locks Sports Shop. They finally got the right fit, which was no small order back in 1995. By Thanksgiving and Fraser's Friendship Tournament, Margaret was decked-out, like Konstantinov, and terminated many an opponent's breakaway aimed right at Cate. Boy, how Livia missed those glory days.

She looked up as Margaret came downstairs. Glancing to the lanai, she told Guy, "Oh – I see Miss Polynesia has a new stretching buddy." Waving, as Mina jogged away, Livia figured she had time for a quick couple of miles, before they headed out, to ride, at 10:30. "I asked Richard to join us, but he's tending two dehydrated nanny goats — so, it'll just be the three of us, unless you'd like to join us. I'll be out of your way in a few minutes. I must grab a quick nap before we head out. Mina seems excited to try out Tim's new filly, Hokulani. Evidently - she has a short mane, sparkly eyes, and is a real sweety."

Quickly, she jotted his prescription on the pad. "You know Cate goes to town most every Wednesday. She will not mind stopping by the pharmacy tomorrow. I still have a hard time understanding - how patients have so much trouble sleeping. I barely put my head down, and I'm out like a light."

Guy nodded but he said, "Me on a horse?" His swift reply came, as he waved pinched fingertips, from her face to Livia's, and said. "It's enough for me to fly to my relatives in Piza. Now that I'm here, my feet stay firmly on the ground. This is my day to repeat my hole-in-one. –Oh! And I want to go back to the Prince Resort's gift shop and get Mina that Fernando Botero. You know, a print, to hang alongside our *Bath* one — you've seen it hanging in the foyer of our Northville house." He glanced down and tapped his ROLEX. "Not to change the subject but it's admirable how Cate reserved another marvelous tee time on the Mauna Kea's front 18-holes. She must know someone up there."

Livia surmised that Cate bribed the starter again. Usually it was with a free night at the inn. Brent and his congenial wife, Sherry, were becoming regulars, in the seldom-rented handicap suite, on the first floor. She smirked as she glanced at his shiny back golf bag, which sat grandly on the front lanai. "I see you're on a mission." Looking over her left shoulder, she trotted upstairs.

He grinned a big thanks, waved his prescription in front Livia, as they followed The Good Doctor upstairs.

"Bliss," Livia heard, as she peeped in Margaret's bedroom door. She watched, as her head sank into the stack of pillows, then she wheeled around on her way to her own room, and caught sight of Mina at the head of the stairs. Livia asked to see her videotape and the scrapbook, of The Bear's last season. Viewing them should keep them busy, while Margaret got a bit of shut-eye. It worked, but not for the whole two hours that she planned.

"It's already 9:50?" moaned Margaret. Looking at Livia and Mina she stretched and said, "Guess I got a good snooze. Let me grab a peanut butter sandwich, and I'll meet you at the car."

Livia headed downstairs but she could still hear Mina chirping to Margaret. "It's so quaint – our Rose mowing that little grassy strip with that little reel mower. Everything else is neat and tidy ground cover. She must enjoy it — or something. I don't do any of that. Guy hires a lawn service; and what they miss — I have Steve or Timmy clean up. Let's see if she's almost–"

"Great!" Margaret cut her short. "See you in the kitchen in a few. You have to know Livia; she's been ready, but puttering around, ever since I told her that you were driving – guess she doesn't like to ride with me. You do know where State Road 12 connects, with the highway out there, don't you?"

Mina was already heading downstairs, so Margaret called out, "Can't imagine why. Tell Livia to give me ten minutes, and I'll drive you out there."

Livia knew Margaret checked-in with the hospital's answering service every morning, and would do so before leaving. She looked across the hood and hoped Mina chose to be pleasant today. Bossy on the bench and damn dangerous on the ice, their blustery hockey captain had taken the Kick Ice Bear's jersey #7, after her idol: Terrible Ted - Detroit's Treasure, who was quite nice – off the ice.

Livia felt a bit edgy and scooted across the car seat to lean out the car window. Morose thoughts hovered and tad of nausea nagged. Opening her collar, she fumed at how hormones, or lack of them, still caught her off guard. She busied herself filing her nails until she notice Lotus had left something for the guests. Sheathing the file, she placed it in the front console and hopped out. Quickly traversing the lawn she grabbed a plastic grocery bag, from the well-disguised trash container. After depositing the offending turd, she noticed Mina cross the lawn and slide into the passenger seat. She followed suit and plopped down on the back seat. Both shared pleasantries, until Mina held a map up to read, and Livia once again scooted to the opposite window and drank in the cool breeze.

Heading south, they managed to catch the lull in traffic, and they arrived at the trailhead in less than ten minutes. Margaret made her calls in record time, as another heady breeze banished any humidity, which often plagued the low country. They all minded their manners waiting for Tim.

He pulled off the shoulder and soon the truck and trailer sat, at the edge of a small meadow that fronted the half-mile of high cliffs rimming Kealakekua Bay. Tim mentioned Tom had called the inn, and he was enroute to drop off the other two horses near the mile marker at the trailhead.

Soon, all four horses were saddled and chewing grass. Adjusting his spurs, Tim smiled as Margaret sided up to him. Their jovialness was short-lived as soon as Mina glanced from the shady trailhead to Tim, and with her usual bravado she shouted, "Is it Okay to leave the cars anywhere along here?" In a quieter tone, she purred, "Ooh – we're almost 'The Misfits,' Mr. Gable here's got on his spurs." She walked along back of the hitching post. Running her hand up and down the smooth wood, she surveyed the horses, from underneath, and seemed impressed that Tim's lead mount was all horse.

The only non-equestrian of the group, Livia piped up and said, "Hercules is half draft horse." She looked from Mina to Tim. "I forget. What was it Tom said? — Is Herc part Perchon or Belgian?"

Tim glanced back at car and truck, and he answered with his usual baritone calmness. "Car's fine up there. Yep, Herc's mama, Lakanani, fine broodmare she is, got loose with a Belgian when I took her to the vet at Kiper Ranch. Mostly, Herc's a big pussycat." He tipped his hat to the far fence. "But those ladies over there — this guy shows no mercy if rider, or any other horse, mistreats them — hence the spurs." They walked across the small field. Running his hand down the filly's flank, Tim flicked off a tick and continued. "This one here, little Hokulani, is for Livia. Margaret gets Princess, and you should be able to handle mighty ole Captain, down there on the end." He handed Mina Captain's reins and left her alone to preen at his compliment. Jangling over to Livia, he boosted her up. "Now, circle her around a bit while I get your friends attended to."

He stroked each horse, and murmuring to each, he re-cinched each waist strap then re-examined every piece of tack. "Livia, you're up first, come here, and I'll give you a hand with our lunch and emergency packs. Since you're the lightest, Miss Hokulani can carry them strapped behind your saddle."

All the while, Tim's Border Collies, Possum and Army, were getting their full due of scratching from Margaret. She's been good pals with Tim, ever since she tagged accompanied him to Puna looking for an Arabian mare. Being nearly fourteen, Army got stationed in shady truck, with water and kibbles. Possum got the signal, hopped down, and waited by the horses.

Continuing his instructions, Tim assured Margaret, "Just keep a tight rein and parade Princess around a bit. You will begin to notice how a fine a ride your Arabian is. She sure is small, even for a mare, but you'll find not an ounce goes to waste when you need her." He lowered his voice, adding, "Not as Captain over there."

Noticing Army's nose stuck to the truck bed between his front paws, Livia rubbed his head and listened in careful appreciation that Tim did not make light of her last few ordeals with Captain. She soon had Hokulani going round and round, as she watched the more experienced riders warm up their mounts.

The one who captured her attention the most was Mina. She made some flourishing gesture, and with all eyes upon her, she deftly swung up onto Captain's back. Livia wished her luck with the ornery old cuss.

"Little Livia! You doing Okay back there?" bellowed Tim. "Hokulani won't give you a bit of trouble." Locking eyes with her, he flashed that fabulous grin. They both wrinkled noses, recognizing what a time of it she'd had — getting Captain down the hill last time. "Miss Starry Eyes is exceptionally gentle and keeps her head to her business." He grinned again before nodding to Margaret. "She helped me get a very good deal on Princess. This little Palomino filly came at an excellent price — with a bit of smithing and The Good Doctor's medical advice thrown in, over at Pancho's in Puna. All in all, Princess is our strongest mount except for Herc.

Livia blushed, glancing up at Margaret and Princess, giving Tim a simple yet hearty "Mahalo." Even her own Hokulani was a bit shorter and narrower than any of her previous mounts. So much more comfortable, and her back and hips would thank Tim tomorrow too. All a sudden, she remembered a question she needed to ask. "My jeep got serviced down there. Does Mr. Rivera have a parts problem down there?"

Tim shook his head no, explaining that Mr. Rivera recently had been a bit overwhelmed, with some bad health and financing his college bound twin's freshman year — when Mina interrupted.

Preening, in her new red-and-white NHL Aloha Shirt that flapped open across her candy stripe swimsuit, she flashed her watch, adding, "Couldn't be a better morning for a ride. I'm all set! How about we get going?"

Hercules jerked his massive head at Mina's pinched complaint. Tim reined him in and gave his customer full attention. He even offered to lead Captain to the trailhead.

"Oh– no! I am perfectly capable," snipped Mina. She attempted to contain herself, as Tim quickly re-wound the lead rope on Hercules' saddle horn. He gave a quick glance back to Livia, on the far end, and they were off.

She did her best to occupy Mina by poking fun at herself. "Remember way back when Guy called me Rose? He always teased that I grew up in St. Olaf. Actually, I always took it in jest –and as a compliment."

Mina laughed. "Yeah; he still does. You grew up in Southern Indiana, somewhere near South Bend — right?"

Livia flinched and mumbled, "Yeah, right." She switched subjects, settling on hockey and golf. Years ago, she learned there was no right answer, and that Mina was known to take quick offense to correction. Even thoughtful debate rarely made any lasting impression. One thing you could say was that she knew her own mind. So, Livia tried one of Luke's tactics and said, "Isn't this sun great? I checked the national weather reports, and Michigan has had the wettest December since the 1870s. So, aren't we lucky we're in Kona?"

She breathed easier when Margaret carried the conversation. Livia could not help notice, as Mina critically eyed Margaret's horsemanship. Heady rivals, on the ice, the equestrian queen might look for an opening to prove her prowess on the trail. Then Margaret kept her place away from Captain, one hand loosening the belt to her jeans. After an easy mount, she leaned forward, ever so slightly forward, and stroked Princess' creamy mane and tawny withers. Mina's head bobbed rhythmically, as Captain altered his gait, in time with every bounce or reseat she took. Margaret graciously accepted Tim's help to lead her mount to the space between Hercules and Captain.

Again, Margaret gently patted both sides along Princess' saddle then told Tim, "Livy is very athletic, and if I am not mistaken, you may be roping in a new student. Just a hint: She can be quite nervous around big animals. I hope she does well and takes a liking to your little Hokulani."

Mina cleared her throat, obviously irritated by the mount selected for her. She was to ride the younger Hokulani; however, only minutes ago, Tim asked her to ride Captain. She was a little taller and lighter than Margaret was, and Captain was getting up in years. Tim explained that the horse seemed a bit weary after his morning exercise. Impressed by Captain's burnished and ornate tack, and always up for a challenge, Mina accepted Tim's request.

Livia faced the late morning sun as she paced her horse in wide circles. Her thoughts wandered to the big monument below, as she drank in the clear warmth and considered how nice it was that Margaret finally had an entire day to swim the bay and explore the entire landscape around the Captain Cook obelisk. Normally, Margaret's work schedule did not allow her to ride weekday mornings. Another attending physician had requested she trade this week's schedules with him. Blessed with the patience of Job, Margaret won out this time and got a rare opportunity to bask in the sun. Livia envisioned the lower portion of the trail - and depending on temperature, cloud cover and angle of light, each familiar twist and turn offered its own glorious vista.

Her gaze fell to Captain's martingale and snaffle bit. Mina owned three horses but, from previous experience, Livia knew he was a handful. He could be very persnickety about his riders. Livia's rein hand barely tightened and her mount pulled up. Waiting patiently, Livia mulled over Hokulani's Hawaiian name. She leaned forward and whispered in the horse's ear. "Okay, 'Stars in the Sky' suits you well." An equine ear flick brought more kudos: "What a gallant little Arabian you are today." Both thoroughly relaxed, Hokulani shifted weight and Livia stretched in the sun.

Tim phoned for one last weather report. Sea storms and lightning notoriously buffeted this trail along the raw cliffs.

Mina had a stage whisper, too. She leaned forward, snatching Captain's mane, and twirling it through her fingers. He whinnied and began matching Hercules' stomps. Failing to sit her horse, Mina hissed, "You want to get started, don't you, Captain, old buddy? In a shrill, nasal moan, she turned to Livia, "What time did you say the luau started? Do they eat and dance any earlier, this time of year? You know — how Guy likes arriving early."

Livia cringed. "No, not really. The daylight hours, for all seasons, are give and take an hour. We're barely over ten degrees, from the equator. Tim is extra careful; any storm can bring lightning and down drafts along here. Would you like some of my sunscreen? There's plenty." She watched Mina apply plenty sunscreen during the car ride. Her impeccably groomed red nails set off her tawny olive brown hands.

Tim snapped the cell phone shut announcing, "Weather's fine," and they were off across the grassy section of high meadow. At the trailhead, Margaret commented that she expected the gradient might be a bit steeper and was surprised how gently the trail wound through the livestock fields. Hundred more feet and her comments came true as the short horse train wound along the ten-foot wide ledge, which seemed to go right off into nowhere. Livia heard her praise Princess, as well as cinched up the rein – Margaret having taken the northern approach was not overly familiar with this top portion of the trail seemed excited but more cautious than usual.

As always, Possum knew his job - that of never leaving the shadow of Hokulani's left rear hoof. With the rear well taken care of, Livia's attention began to focus on the horses in front of her. The agile Arabian's small hooves quietly cut into the trail carefully sidestepping each set of rocks, roots, or both. Following Captain, Hokulani fell into a comfortable pace, and she kept a good distance from him — never needing her path corrected. That put Livia a bit more at ease, as she quickly replayed the scenario of her first ride down and up these cliffs. After the first 400 feet, of making her duck every tree limb, Captain continued his errant behavior and jerked the lead-rope that Tim attached to his bridle; although, she was freed from Mr. Pestication's intentions, to enjoy the surroundings. Today, the old poot wore a new bit - and possibly Mina would fair better.

In addition, that was not the whole of it. One their last trip, the ornery paniolo horse, got his muzzle swatted good for barely touching Herc's hindquarters – and these last few minutes, his old tricks were beginning to surface. Livia wondered if he had been less bored at his previous job herding cattle. Possibly this nose-to-tail stuff gave him too much reason to get testy. He sat a pretty good ride; however, she warned Margaret and Mina to wear heavy pants. Any rider who drew his lot might be scraped through the bushes.

Halfway down the two miles of 1,300-foot direct descent, the trail flattened and cut a wide path across a tiny meadow. Tim stopped, released Captain's lead, and lined them up, horses' rears to the bay. After taking his Nikon from his saddlebag Tim stood tall, in Herc's shortened stirrups, and snapped pictures - as he extolled the intoxicating beauty and history of Kealakekua Bay. Behind them shimmered a ten-mile panorama - one of the finest in all the islands. An eight-by-ten photo of three women, on horseback, framed by stark cliffs leading to a distant and perfectly matched horizon, of lipid blue, would most certainly crown any massive coffee table or gauche two-story entrance wall.

Well choreographed, the horses turned and lined up in unison. Livia handed out bottled water, and everyone soaked in the view, as Tim gave his standard tourist spiel about the sheer cliffs to their far left. Supposedly, it was an honor: accompanying baskets of sacred bones, and being lowered to the remote caves hidden there - and on occasion, having completed their work, the person had been cut loose and fell to his or her death. To that comment, Captain shook off Mina's hawked up mouthful of water.

For the final descent, Tim once again secured the lead rope to Captain's halter, to which Mina immediately objected.

Margaret — having heard enough of Mina's consistent hassling, added some rare kindling to the free-for-all. "Hey Tim, Livia told me that you tied a lead on Captain when she rode him down here four years ago?"

He chuckled, "Yep, I did, and – well, he's same old goat. Even with the jingle of my spurs, both these patoots like to show off for the girls. If I put Princess or Hokulani between them, it gets even worse."

Mina shrugged. "Well, I am a bit more horse-worthy than Livia."

Hokulani shuddered, as Livia gently patted her withers and considered Mina's actions. *Same as ever; hasn't changed a bit. So humble.* In Tim's defense, Livia piped up. "Well, I was ever so glad to have Tim lead Captain. With nothing more to do than sit the saddle, I just drank in the scenery. Otherwise, I'd be eyeing Captain and correcting his every move. Tom says this old cusser was a good ole cow rustler. I know he knows every inch of this trail, but – holy-mole– he's headstrong. Had me watching for every next branch or boulder, thinking I'd have to duck or lean. The very last inch, he'd veer back to center path. See that? His ear twitched. He knows exactly what I'm saying."

Mina's hand raked her hair, as it fluttered in the breeze. "Oh, our Rose — she's so dramatic and so prone to exaggeration."

Livia kept pursing her lips hard shut. Drama was life — but, she, an exaggerator? Never! Sure enough, another 100 feet with Tim's ears burning - he acquiesced and removed Captain's lead. Repeatedly, the ornery patoot swished his tail and tried his tricks giving Mina good cause for chaps and a helmet. Good thing - the snaffle bit held. Mina reined him in, and Captain kept his head.

Livia snickered. She was no equestrian, but common sense told her no man or animal should never risk an upper cut of Herc's draft-size horseshoes. She grinned impishly, and twisting her head around she crossed her eyes and stuck her tongue flat out at Margaret.

Amused, at Livia's sideshow, and once again faced with two rear ends - Margaret chuckled and purred, "Good girl, Princess. What a good girl you are.", while scratching and ruffling her mane for minding her own business. "When we get home, we'll ask around to find a cheap lady friend to be your trail-mate when you and Hokulani ride with Hercules. Then we can leave Captain home." Princess whinnied and jerked her neck up and down, leaving Margaret to dodge a branch.

"All my hockey fools - Okay back there?" called Tim.

"Oh – we're – just – mighty – ducky!" chirped Margaret.

Livia laughed. "Second pun of the day. Boy, I wish Cate could be here; she'd have loved this."

Margaret snorted, Tim cleared his throat but Mina whipped around snapping, "What did you say?" Captain immediately planted all four hooves, as would any barrel-racing quarter horse. Quick reflexes and a skater's balance saved her from toppling off her saddle.

Livia deliberately and slowly called out the wonders of the afternoon. "Oh, my– just to witness this incredible view again. Cate so loves this view of the sea. She says this blue is the most– awesome– cerulean—"

Mina huffed, "Really? Any fool can see it's damn blue!" As if she could not tell if Livia had heard her, she hissed, "Livia! Why not stop talking and go write a… Oh– just stick a pencil where the light don't shine!"

Livia's teeth on tongue and icy stare goaded even more aggravation.

The trail continued its steep descent. About the time she could see the where the trail leveled out, they passed Old Cart Road. You could have heard a pin drop. Livia felt something begin to brew, and Mina began to turn around — but before they could start again, Tim deftly pulled off his shirt. Rolling it neatly, he reached back and laid it between hips and cantle. Mina straightened up and leaned a bit for a better view. Margaret was too quiet, and Livia wished she could feel the wind and sun on her back and chest too, as he stretched grandly– first to one side, then to the other, and finally commanding everyone's attention he said: "Ladies – you cannot see it yet but directly ahead is a twenty-foot obelisk, the Captain James Cook Monument. At the foot of our trail — yes, there it is — see the tip of it? Look 500 feet past that grove of small trees."

The tension broke as Mina pointed it out. Tim gave her liberty to keep at it, as he pulled on his vest and lilted into the canned tourist version: how the monument stood on a plot deeded by Queen Likelike to Great Britain 100 years after the captain's demise. Momentarily, they sat in shade again. Tim said, "I'll tie up the horses; however, before you hop down to go snorkeling, let me show you the best place to enter and exit the water. While you ladies swim, I'll set up your lunch and be right here with Possum when you get back. Let me know if you have any concerns or questions. Please, take all the time you want down there and enjoy yourselves."

Livia lead the way through the sand, rocks, and trees - as Tim had his hands full with all four horses. From where they sat changing to their reef shoes and flippers, she watched him twice reposition Hercules and finally tie him across the trail from Hokulani and Princess. With them settled, and knapsacks in hand, he finally found a shady smooth spot in the monument's shadow. With the women out of sight but within earshot, he read, pet Possum and chirped something about Mr. Orneriness not realizing he lost the family jewels. "We always assume a gelding is of better temperament. In my thirty-five years around paniolo horses, I've noticed just the opposite."

"Oh — Livy, Please– take a picture of me atop Great Britain!" gushed Mina, as she gently slapped her camera in Livia's hands, before trotting off and mounting one of the four cannons, which held anchor chain surrounding the obelisk's base. While Livia checked for film, recalling the time she snapped a whole roll of nothing with Mina's new-fangled 35mm camera. With plenty of space, on this digital camera, and Mina mounted fully in position, Livia opened the wide viewfinder, and snapped away, carefully discarding and editing the proofs before saving them to the camera's memory chip. Mina posed, quite animated in her glory. The shutter clicked repeatedly, as Livia hoped her model could not hear tiny snickers rising, from the small audience that noticed Mina – hands in the air rocking and straddling the four-pounder.

One last whoop: "Giddy-up," and Mina ran off to show Tim the digital proofs, Margaret sat on the sea ledge below and adjusted her swim fins. "I bet Guy will get a good chuckle from that." Leaning over the water, she snapped off morsels of Livia's beef jerky. A large parrotfish trolled within reach as Margaret dropped a tiny bit in the water. With a *gulp* and a *splat*! the fish trolled for more. Margaret pointed and asked Livia, "Did you see him grab that? Guess it's not quite as sacrilegious, as Lilo called her tuna sandwich for fish food."

Grinning, Mina walked up and said, "That was a good one. Glad my feet are covered. Wonder if he'd prefer rare or my blood-red toenail polish?" She poised briefly, then yelled, "Who knows?" and hopped in the water. Quickly climbing out, she cinched up her water waders, scooted over the edge onto the submerged ledge between Livia and Margaret, and watched them snap under water photos. "Wish I'd brought one of those. Try it again!"

This time Margaret positioned her WaterShot at the surface, with her other hand ready to drop the beef jerky – and boy, did that fish jump. It nearly took off her fingers holding the beef. More determined, Margaret whispered, "One more time - you little nipper." Handing the quick winding camera to Livia, she dropped as Livia clicked. They all laughed, as the "Dip and Click Method" came off pretty near perfect with team effort.

"Wow, this little Nemo's fast. Bet I got a good shot of him mid-air that last time. He must be ten inches long," drawled Livia.

Even Mina agreed that the guidebooks did not sell this place short as one of the best snorkeling sites in Hawaii. "Oh, did you see that one?" Mina was sorely impressed by the variety and large size of colorful fish.

Livia said, "You know, it's too bad Hanauma Bay isn't this pristine anymore. It's a wildlife preserve and underwater state park - one of my favorite places on Oahu but thank goodness, this shore is a tad more remote." Except for a couple of kayakers and the sixty-foot Lanakila-II trimaran pontoon-boat, they were alone in this gorgeous bay with the steep cliffs above them. Livia looked up, and she still could not understand what the big deal was with the bone burying. Tim did not prod them to eat lunch, so they spent more than two hours leisurely swimming, before hiking up and down the shore and heading in for their food.

Ruth's twin, Rosie, had presented each rider with a plate lunch of thick deli-style ham sandwich, garnished with homemade pickled-pink turnip slices and small bags of corn chips. Frozen drink packs kept the lunches cold and defrosted into fruity slushes. Mina chatted with Tim, as Margaret and Livia savored each tasty morsel and bird watched.

Surprised, Margaret opened her sandwich. "So, this is the reason you grew cucumbers for our guests' picnic baskets. I have never eaten them shaved on a sandwich. We must buy a few seedless cukes for our lunches."

Livia smiled and reminisced how Cate had always been such a cucumber fan. If diets allowed, there would be The Ma's sour cream, sugared ones for dinner salad too - as it were, Livia could not polish off a whole bowl.

Tim shared more folklore about Kealakekua Bay and the monument. Many locals still called the world famous explorer "Captain

Crook" followed by 'pompous tyrant' for accepting alms as the harvest deity, Lono. They did credit him for attempting to keep his crew from bedding local women; even so, his crew unleashed diseases that devastated the Hawaiians. That was not all they ruined. Plenty of flora and fauna, which a few of Cook's gentlemen cataloged, are now endangered or extinct - due to gifts of animals and plants, and poor planning and conservation. Another ten minutes, of the women sharing finds and asking questions, and he bagged all the lunch plates and wrappers. After neatly tying all provisions and trash, on Hokulani, the tiny caravan began the climb to the main highway.

Margaret said, "Trail sure seemed a lot less steep coming down. I knew Hokulani was strong and fit – but already, she is beginning to lather."

Growing impatient with Livia's mount dawdling, Possum gently nipped at Princess' hocks, prodding her within ten feet of Hokulani. With all four mounts nose-to-tail, Tim gingerly pointed out stunning views. To their right, 300 feet above, the thermals wafted, in shimmering eddies against the cliffs' rough outcroppings. The more intense the afternoon heat and light - more ledges and caves floated into prominence. Holding Captain's lead slack in his left hand, he reined in Hercules when the grand horse wandered a bit too close makai. That prompted Livia to lean left, ever so slightly, over Princess' shoulder regarding the much better mauka footing.

Livia's head popped up and Margaret's head turned, as Mina's horse whinnied and reared. Not much motion but Captain's head came down, with his muzzle barely brushing Herc's tail. That slight offense triggered one sorry undercut of massive size-04 horseshoe. Half a second as Livia's head arched up and down mirroring Captain's motion, and his hoof slipped off the trail.

Tim's deep voice bellowed, "Hold!" Lead rope dropped, he vaulted off Herc's flank. Tim's massive stallion never moved, as Mina gingerly slid down Captain and expertly sided up to Herc's shoulder expertly taking his reins. At Tim's quiet coaching, the huge horse remained motionless standing solid, on three hooves, which left one extended mid-air attached to Captain's bridle.

Calmly stroking Captain's muzzle, and with a steady grasp of the horse's bridle, Tim slowly reached down. Steadily, he pulled his field knife from his right boot. Not a breath taken, he carefully began slicing Captain's bridle from Herc's horseshoe. In a flash, the knife's blade caught the sun focusing it squarely into Captain's eye. In one sorry moment, hindquarters jerked up and down to the trail - catapulting Tim through the air. –A sharp thwack and thud– resounded below.

Livia stood, in her stirrups, peering over the edge. Deathly still, Tim laid face up. She and Margaret dismounted, exchanging leads. Leading Hokulani to Mina, Livia noticed Margaret and Possum gingerly prodding Princess forward. Leaning back in the Arabian's saddle and stirrups, sat Margaret straining sideways assessing Tim's position. Stoic wince told all. Dialing 911, she repeated her doctor's code and requested the Honolulu MEDEVAC helicopter. Waiting, for another Oahu connection, she dismounted and quietly watched Livia calmly release the last buckle to Captain's bridle. The astute paniolo horse remained motionless. Captain never once pulled, at Herc's shoe, thus allowing his lead rope to be handed to Mina, who backed away and carefully led him 200 feet up the trail, from Hokulani.

Quickly, Mina returned to gather Herc. Watching her nearly skate across the rough trail, Livia still held Princess at the right side of the trail. For her size, the mare was the strongest and most maneuverable in case the rescue team needed her help pulling a rescue basket up to the trail.

Margaret asked Livia, "Do you think you can hold the lead, so Princess can pull tight the line, and I can get to Tim?"

Livia nodded, "Yes."

With the horses situated, Mina occupied herself walking-down each of the horses according to their amount of lather. Latched onto Princess' line, Margaret rappelled down and wedged herself on the ledge finally able to keel at Tim's side. They had heard his head hit first, and she quickly checked for blood loss, which was minimal. After taking his pulse she gently rubbed his hand, and his labored breathing came more steady, so mouth-to-mouth resuscitation was not necessary. Possum side-winded, down the long way, arrived at his master's shoulder, and began licking his cheek.

Gingerly, Margaret rolled herself, and gained footing on the ledge below. That brought her chest high, near Tim's head. Once again, the Good Doctor checked for blood loss. Not moving him, she checked his spine she timed his pulse again. Barely discernable, her eyes and head moved slightly from sided to side. Now came the hardest part - to wait.

Livia did not move but contracted and relaxed her leg muscles (an old marching band trick). Their first trail ride, down here, Tim told Cate about an accident on a nearby trail to Nenue Point. The excellent MEDEVAC service extracted his mother's friend, from the base of the trail, and headed straight, for Queen's Medical Center on Oahu. She said tiny prayers that it would be the same today, unless the helicopters were otherwise engaged.

Margaret still hovered over Tim. Mina asked Livia if she needed a drink of the water before she gave it to the horses. Instinctively - their hockey knees bent and they braced their feet, as a good-sized tremor jostled the ground and brought Margaret to her feet.

"Oh-shit," said Livia, as her eyes ran to the brush that hid the old lava tunnels right above the trail - well aware, that the Honokua 1950 lava flow oozed for days, only ten miles to their south. Noticing the horses and Possum seemed calm enough, she gulped, holding tight to the lead rope. A minute later, another tiny shake was all that remained of the aftershock. Something rattled through Livia's mind that all of them were only tiny specks on the massive base of Mauna Loa. A chill wind whipped up, then abruptly it ceased as the helicopter sat down, in the tiny meadow 300 feet up hill. Good thing Mina chose the trees to the south of them for the horses.

Within twenty minutes, they lifted Tim up the twenty-foot slope. Margaret handed Tim's cell phone to Livia, ducked the rotors and climbed aboard. Couple of minutes, and they were up and off.

Livia and Mina gave the accident details to the newly arrived police; but first they phoned Cate, who in turn contacted the Mauna Loa Golf Course. The starter's helper located Guy, who had just pulled up to return his clubs. Tom got the next call. Within seconds, he was on his way to the trailhead to pick up the horses. Once they got him settled down, he called Aye, who in turn broke the news to Chakra. Livia drove Mina to the inn, and Tom followed.

They sat in the kitchen, and Cate promised Tom that she would stay put, act as dispatcher, and hold down the fort. Guy blew in the door having already chartered Big Green Helicopter's flagship, the Moana Ono.

Lotus Blossom clung to Cate's knees, as Livia reassured Tom. "Back in Michigan, we would answer our home phone, with 'Hockey Central.' Just tell us what the stables chores are, and don't give your worries, about bedding the horses down, a second thought."

Livia kept assuring Tom, as Guy kept nodding and gesturing. "I got a huge Alpha Nova, and it can whisk everyone to the Honolulu Army Base. From there, a limo can get us down there, within an hour of Tim's transport." Livia figured he probably offered to buy Big Green, thus securing the emergency inter-island trip.

Somehow, the afternoon continued smoothly in fast-forward. After she settled down next to Tom on the helicopter seat, Livia noticed him shuffling a blue packet of legal-length papers. His coinciding phone call, to the lawyer, conferred her suspicions that he may have problems enforcing Tim's medical Power-of-Attorney. Her thoughts churned out a few scenarios. "Well, Princess is not the only warrior today. I'm not a lawyer but I've plenty of experience with hospital and legal papers as Attorney-in-Fact, for my parents and Pearl." With her help and Margaret's expertise - if any situation presented itself, Tom would be quarterback of one formidable team.

Everyone sat quietly in the outer waiting room. Finally, Margaret strode across, to Tom, and started through her list of questions. She checked his paperwork before escorting him to see Tim. Within five minutes, Tom quietly sat between Livia and Aye. She took his hands in hers. For a bit, his fingers traced her trillium diamond rings as he stared at the floor. She could feel his hands warming, until he pulled free and spoke. "They say he may not make it through the night. It all depends, if they can curtail the swelling at the back of his brain. Dr. Brown says she will notify us, of his CAT scan's availability - then I can go sit with him. She's even offered to stay the night with us." Forty-minutes crept by, until a nurse led him back to Tim.

Livia whispered, "Always keep that paper on you, and only let the hospital keep a paper copy." He nodded, before she released his hand. Aye sat, as if in a trance; there was nothing to add.

Livia attempted small talk. She talked of Tim's photo of him, full out – above a three meter board, with Diamondback Mountain in the background.

"Yeah, I studied two years at Arizona State student. That swan dive was taken in Phoenix, at the state diving championships.

Livia could not believe the coincidence and said. "No way! My cousin, Annie, was Arizona state diving champ out there."

Tom brightened, for a moment, stammering, "She lives in Arizona?"

"She lived in Phoenix and Mesa, and she was three-meter springboard champ when I started grade school." She watched his grin, until it faded. She brought water from the kitchen. This was the hard part - much more than being here. Little, she said or could do, would help him.

By eight, Aye's younger brother and nephew arrived. Standing, to greet them, he introduced them as Kaloki Noe and his son, Ethan. These men were Tim's estranged father and brother. Indignantly, their voices rose, as they demanded to see Tim. Aye nodded to the nurse, as Tom moved to the bench near Livia and the elevator. Neither man would recognize him. She watched Tom's eyes glass over; however, by the time Aye offered him a soda and some cheese crackers, he ate quietly only to once again stare into the distance. Four nerve-racking hours passed. Finally, Tim's brother came out, and he gave Aye the number and the address of their hotel.

Tom voice sliced the air. "Neither of you have talked to Tim in the past five years. It is my place to sit beside him tonight. He appointed me as his guardian, on these papers right here."

Ethan turned on him and railed, "Those papers and your wishes mean nothing to us. I must return, to watch my brother, later tonight -when I take my father to the hotel and get him settled for the night."

Livia cleared her throat. Luke had coached her well — made her quite aware that; whenever possible, one must use patience and good manners, in order to gain the high road concerning legal matters, especially with family. He always told her: "Never threaten to sue someone; enforcing the law is always the last resort." When Ethan did return, she joined the men and positioned herself between Tom and Ethan, calmly staring at him every time he raised his voice. She fawned over Ethan's tattoos and brought everyone food thus bogging down various conversations, well knowing that no one would enforce any legal papers this late at night. Margaret donned her white coat and stood above her friends. A heated discussion ensued. Guy and Mina did not budge, Aye remained cool, and Livia applied her best schoolmarm stare. That, and Tom towering over him - Ethan realized he was royally outnumbered.

Aye finally said, "I think not. You and your father may return tomorrow, and Tom will stay this night, along with Livia and me - and of course Good Doctor Brown. If not…" He stopped mid-sentence and turning his shoulder to them, gazed past Diamondhead.

A phone call interrupted them, and it was Chakra. That was it; no more was said. Within ten minutes, Ethan returned with his father. Aye rose, walked them downstairs - returned alone and sat quietly. He caught Livia's eye and reminded her that she needed to eat again. They figured now was as good a time as ever, so Mina and Guy accompanied her to the cafeteria. She too returned alone - saying, "I got a lamb and chicken shawarma sandwich. Finished half of it, down there, and brought this half for later. Guy and Mina took their supper, to go, and called for a room. They're on their way, to the Hilton right now." Aye stifled a chuckle, by clearing his throat, and said, "Guy had no problem reserving a room — said the concierge's dad was the Hawaii Kai Course Pro. Your coach bent the man's ear and got a quick nine holes first thing tomorrow morning. Mina has her eyes on revisiting a few Waikiki shops – said something about wedding favors for next spring's events. Both seem as content as Tallulah in wet sand."

Aye smiled. He patted Livia's back and rubbed it a while before closing his eyes, resuming a bit of shut-eye. Within half-an-hour, a nursing assistant lightly shook his shoulder and asked him to take a phone call. Upon his return, he announced that it was merely Chakra keeping tabs on everything. Aye gave the details: "Evidently — Kaloki called her, and he was sorely disappointed to find that she supported my decision. I doubt that Tom will have any more problems from them, at least while Tim is here. We have immediate family near Honolulu, too." That said - Livia decided to file away those last few comments. To subdue her over-active imagination, she would phone Cate later, and ask about Tim's relatives.

Sometime before 5:00 AM, Margaret pushed open the wide Intensive Care Unit doors and headed straight to Aye. "Tom gave us permission, to place a shunt, at the base of Tim's brain. The doctors will know whether, or not, the surgery has been successful, within the next couple of hours. I will stay with him, in the ICU, and come back here as soon as I have any more news. This is a far-cry from my specialty, so if you don't mind, I will bunk over at least a few days." That said - Livia took none of it, as a good sign.

Four people waiting in Honolulu was quite enough. Given that she was no relative of Tim's, her love for hospitals, and the crowded quarters, Livia agreed to fly home. Cate would rarely ask, even if she needed help — Livia volunteered to work at the stables. After she phoned, for a taxicab, Aye accompanied her to the admission lobby. In the taxicab's backseat, they hugged, and Livia said, "Seems weird. I've never flown without baggage."

As Aye paid the airport parking lot attendant, Livia told him: "I'll get in contact with their friends, Tom said, 'Just ask if I need anybody's help with the horses.' Some have already picked up their boarded horses till he gets back." Once past the TSA frisk, she waved goodbye through the metal grille.

Back home, Livia started every morning by feeding the animals and answering the phone messages for riding reservations. Later in the week, she contacted all of Tim's blacksmith and farrier accounts. Most customers asked that she find out, if there was anything, they could do to help. Every few days they checked about his progress. After a few weeks, Margaret described Tim's injuries and progress in more detail. It shocked Livia and Cate when The Good Doctor said she had not expected Tim to survive his first surgery. The chief army neurosurgeon gave him only a fifteen percent chance of waking in the ICU that first morning. Oddly enough, during that time, no one heard a thing from Kaloki or Ethan.

Chapter 15: **Fantasy Auction**

One sultry afternoon, Livia stomped across the kitchen floor and stopped short. Following Cate's stare to the floor, she felt it nearly burn a hole in her muddy old cowboy boots. Usually a fastidious housekeeper, removing them somehow escaped her attention. "Had these a good twenty years, and something just told me to yank them off our Michigan garage sale table."

She fussed as she pulled them off and chipped at the mud. Scooting further down the back steps she noticed as Cate glanced away. Attempting not to smirk, she wrinkled her pug nose and drawled, "Yeah, at least they're small boots." Smirk faded, to a sideways chin wiggle, as she wiped boots and steps.

Cate looked at the gritty mess. "Awful short work of piglet tracks." She grinned, and Livia's smirk spread to smile. She considered teasing: "Be nice, or you can compost that lovely ripe straw from the horsey stalls." After stretching and noticing that her biceps and back ached less, than when her chores were mere errands and gardening – she found quiet satisfaction.

Cate rolled her eyes to the ceiling. She sighed and complimented Livia, about developing a warm golden tan. That brought an easy truce.

The week after the women took over the stable chores, two fancy wicker baskets sat near the kitchen door. Each was covered, with two crisply starched gold napkins embroidered with bright gold **SAMMO'S**. One held a nice chilled bottle of wine and desserts; the other held two warm and tasty three-course diners.

The following morning Livia showered before returning the baskets to the restaurant. Only once was this necessary, for she met the busy bar manager - who winked and feigned his indifference saying, "Oh my word — just place it at your door, as they do at the Outrigger Royale Resort. All baskets are picked up before dawn." He took off, to the busy kitchen, and Livia mimicked his walk - sashaying back to her Jeep. Lighting wiggling her head, side to side, she flicked, flipped and dropped her wrist saying, "Just place it… at your door… picked up before dawn…"

Sure enough – two more baskets heaped with their supper and a fine bottle of Beaujolais was beside the kitchen door promptly at six the next evening. It seemed to have come with the wind, which spurred a discussion as to whether or not Aye was involved. Cate took the lead and told Margaret: "He's the only one who knows our schedule. Chakra covers for me when I make my late afternoon errands. Livia showers, and you hightail it to the office right after your hospital shift."

Livia shot in a comment. "Whatever! The food is wonderful. I cannot tell you the amount of time it saves us, in shopping, prep, and clean-up."

Margaret said, "Well — we will count it as a blessing. I have to tell you that Guy and Mina get a courtesy room service dinner also – every evening since they've been at the Hilton Hawaiian Village." That comment brought a hard swallow from Livia and Cate, at the same time.

The weeks passed more quickly as they settled into a more familiar routine. Once again, Cate noticed Livia - as she stood before the stove, dirty boots and all. It was just before noon, and the kitchen chemist was lining up five cans of ingredients next to her Dutch oven.

Cate chided, "There's plenty of leftovers."

Livia kept chopping chicken, "I'm not the leftover queen. I've got a hankering for some white chili and no time, to simmer it in the crock pot." Cate popped leftover diced chicken, in her mouth, as Livia added four cans of diced Italian tomatoes, two cans of white beans, and sprinkled in a box of dry falafel mix across the large pot of chili. The last shreds of chicken devoured, she scissored curled parsley into the mix, followed by a hefty dash of Mr. Shakee's spicy blend and a barely a pinch of white pepper. "Hand me a slotted spoon, please. These two halves of potatoe have got to come out."

"Eww – I hate pepper. It's way too hot for me," grumbled Cate, "and please, for the last time, do take off those boots."

"You ate it before, and you like it!" On her way to the pantry Livia flipped her boots, onto the porch. Returning, with deep soup bowls and a bottle of white cooking wine, she threw the last ingredients into the mix. It bubbled, while Livia tossed a salad, and Cate set the table. Passing a sleeve of saltines Livia chirped, "How is?"

"Not– too– damn bad. Would you please hand me my recipe box?" She quickly jotted the ingredients between bites of crackers, soup and salad.

Livia finished a bowl, and half another, before pushing back from the table. "That ought to hold me. Especially, if I pack one of your walnut oatmeal cookies for mid-afternoon. Margaret is meeting me at the stable. She's got her heart set on riding Aunt Gertie, and Dr. Header is bringing Knockabout. I promised to tag along on Hercules – play a chaperone – you know, in case the horses get frisky. I do hope she'll talk to me afterwards. Tom says she will be fine; the trick is to stay down wind on the trail. Rinsing soup and salad bowl, Livia started digging through the junk drawer.

"A tad to spicy – hum?"

"Yeah, I best take a few Tums. I'll change the recipe to a *small* pinch each, of Mr. Shakiee's and pepper."

Cate chuckled, as she added antacid tablets to her shopping list. "I baked a huge oatmeal cookie, and packed a half-frozen pint of milk.

What you don't finish, you can give to Possum and Army." Big hug and Livia remembered all the cold Michigan mornings that she added a little treats to Cate's lunch bags. Now Cate worked from home, and she scurried out and about. So far, their roles had reversed four times. Though, this time best not be a long-term arrangement.

As they unpacked dinner baskets, Livia chattered and found Cate returning to good humor. However, something was up. She quickly noticed Margaret overly quiet. Maybe, she had been overly eager, in keeping an eye on The Good Doctor and her doctor. She gave them plenty of space. Actually - they rode alone, for an hour, and neither seemed the worse for it.

Cate spat, "You didn't?"

"What?" Livia answered, and then quickly glanced from Cate, to Margaret.

Margaret hesitated. Then she slowly admitted that she had accepted Richard's invitation to Waipio Valley for the first weekend in April. "He says he's to birth a high risk mare over there, and he would like it very much if I could be his guest at the Cliffside Bed and Breakfast for those couple days."

Livia read Cate's ever-so-slight nod (signifying this was not the time to disagree or lock horns with Margaret). "Oh, that is a gorgeous coastline all along Waipio Valley. April – now that could be a wee bit wet."

She caught Cate's "that was way too much information" glare and said, "But, Cate, you remember when we saw the waterfalls, north of Hilo, after that ten-inch tropical rain storm. They can be so– gorgeous."

Saved by the phone. Cate rushed to the front desk and caught it on the third ring. Handing it to Margaret, she and Livia held their breath grabbing each other's hand. Momentarily, Margaret covered the phone. "It's Guy; he's with Tom." Uncovering the receiver, she continued. "That's wonderful; let me speak with the resident on duty."

As she talked shop, Livia and Cate's hands released - as both exhaled and sat down. "Makes our piddlely problems - pretty small by comparison," whispered Livia, as Cate nodded.

Margaret cleared her throat and announced Guy's plane landed at 9:30 in the morning. She asked if either of could pick him up from the airport. Cate nodded. Margaret told Guy Cate would be there, and they would alert Aye. As soon as she set the phone down, a group hug ensued followed, by a good five minutes of planning the rest of tomorrow. All three snapped to attention noticing Aye standing quietly at the door with arms folded, grinning from ear to ear.

Five more weeks, of Tim in the hospital, and Tom returned home. Not two hours and he sat, in the inn's kitchen, complimenting Cate on the stable's bookkeeping and Livia on the rest of the general upkeep. Neither did he forget about complimenting Margaret, for exercising the horses. Always self-effacing, Cate stood, asking, "Anyone for another raspberry iced tea?"

Gently catching her by the arm, he crooned, "Not so fast. You've been helping us, every since the very first week we met you, and I can serve myself tea. You realize — Tim was sure that we would be filing bankruptcy papers by now. Probably so, if you had not taken over our books that very first week."

Cate blushed three-shades of purple and looked down, as her tiny mouth twisted, to the side. As she wiped her eyes, Tom hugged her and apologized, for upsetting her. He daubed her tears, with a tissue Livia handed him. Then he sat Cate down and refilled everyone's tea.

That weekend the women waved, from the tarmac, as Tom's plane took off again for Honolulu. For the past couple days, two of Chakra's nephews had taken turns tending Tim's bedside. The Queens Medical Center doctors announced - he might be transferred to Kona Hospital, in a week or so.

Tim had a couple setbacks, and the weeks passed as everyone mustered up. Aye managed the stables for a few days, so Livia could have some time off. Cate was balancing the inn and the stable's ledgers - when a phone call forced her to drop everything, and fetch Livia from the airport. Carrying only a backpack and a carry-on bag, she waited curbside near the open air terminal.

Cate jumped out, threw her arms around Livia and said, "Missed you so much." Still embraced, Livia nearly swooned as Cate concluded: "I never knew how much you do, till you were gone. Thanks for coming home to help. I know you could have stayed a couple more days – if only to see the gardens." She slowly released Livia, continuing to ask about their friends in Honolulu. Cate took the huge backpack and bag and set them then in the trunk, as Livia sighed to herself, "I've known her for fifteen years, and she's still ever on-guard. No wonder she was such a damn good goalie."

Passenger door wide open Livia climbed up and sat, like a lady - then she followed through, gracefully pivoting her legs to the floorboard. Noticing Cate's eyes on her, and she turned and said, "What? Don't look at me – like I should hop onboard, like a cowpoke. Anyway, I need to guard my aching back, because I want to keep up with all the other cowpoke chores. Tim's not doing so well yet, and his doctors won't say when they'll release him. Guy and Mina have flown to Honolulu twice and are staying till he gets a better prognosis. Margaret's coming home tomorrow." She turned from Cate, and surveyed the familiar dark rocks, from the airport to the high misty mountains. "Oh, I forgot — we're supposed to air-express some luggage to Guy and Mina."

Stepping back, Cate shook her head and said. "Maybe she's feeling guilty - but somehow, that woman always knows how to land on her feet. There won't be a corner, of a Honolulu or a Waikiki shop, that won't go unexplored. Mind my words: next year, every Christmas present will be from Oahu."

Livia said, "In all fairness, it wasn't really Mina's fault," but she chuckled to herself, recalling how Mina always made the best of every situation, and in this case was playing Guy's personal shopper to the hilt – selecting family, business, and hockey team presents for the next couple years. Rubbing Cate's neck, she chuckled to herself and added, "I'll gather their clothes and personal items and send their bags to the Hilton. Later, this evening I'll get everything lined up at the stables."

Once again, Livia continued to rise before sunrise, feed herself and the animals, and return phone messages, for riding reservations. A few more weeks, and Margaret described Tim's injuries and progress in more detail. It shocked Livia and Cate when The Good Doctor explained that she had not expected him to make it, through the first night after the accident.

Tom escorted Chakra and Aye home one evening. Afterwards, he helped Livia empty the dishwasher and collected his plastic container of leftovers, from Cate's fine supper, before leaving to bed down the animals at the stables. Margaret's fingers tapped the table, as she watched Livia's pink highlighter glide across the newsprint circling TV programs, until she reached to the counter for two days worth of mail. Livia kept circling, as Margaret spread out magazines and envelopes. Tossing bills to one side, she selected a fancy envelope and sliced it open with and old scalpel. Unfolding the tri-folded rag paper she sharply took notice, waved it in the air, and yelped, "Ladies look here! We have very cordially been invited to the 8th Annual Kamuela Fantasy Auction – on February 15th, at 7:00pm."

They looked over her shoulder at the insert, which listed two columns of beneficiaries: three AIDS projects, Wheeled Meals, two women's shelters, and five children's and the indigent food banks that net 90% of the proceeds. Margaret said, "You know, I bet one of those might benefit patients like Tim."

"The $80.00 donation includes Tony Roma's champagne fountain, open bar, heavy pūpūs, and petite desserts. Dance tunes by Esmeralda. R.S.V.P. by February 5th." She read the insert. "Anyone may submit a friend, as an auction item, by February10th. Entry fee of $125 is suggested." Her thumb slid down the sheet to the postscript: "Aloha Wear or Formal Attire."

Livia grabbed an air guitar and boogied a few steps back. "Haven't got all gussied up since one of Guy's office Christmas parties. Sounds like fun."

Cate rolled her eyes. "Heck, yeah! It couldn't hurt business much. We could write off donations to any one of these charities. We could buy tickets with the money from the inn's slush accounts." She let slip, with one of Livia's, "'Holy Cannoli!' Damn, that's only two weeks away!"

Margaret agreed and suggested that they purchase a couple extra tickets for Guy and Mina. "If, for some reason, they can't make it, we could ask some friends." Dr. Header's profile flashed through Livia's mind but she answered, "It really doesn't seem to be the best timing, but chins up – maybe we'll get good news about Tim coming home and can celebrate at the auction. Yeah — I know, 'What's meant to be, is meant to be.' Maybe some of the charity funds could in some way benefit Tim?"

They all shrugged, till Cate said, "While we are on the subject of money-making; we've lost business since the accident. I never considered quite how much the Saturday pony rides and Tom's trail reservations brought in, as additional business. We need to stay more liquid here, and I need some suggestions."

Livia slowly raised her hand. "We had a local grand opening. Now -since we've almost got our second year under our belts, could we send announcement fliers to all our paradise-starved friends and old business associates on the mainland?"

Margaret was the first to nod. "I agree. Maybe we need to take a couple days and each make a list of prospective guests including addresses, and if possible, phone numbers." All three agreed not to enlist Internet support wherever possible. They each listed special enticements – and agreed on offering a coupon, for 20% off the rack rate, for any reservations longer than a week, which might entice new and return customers. Also, a new petty cash was established, for complimentary transfers, to and from Kona airport. Livia's idea of extending the offer, to Hilo's airport, was tabled for another meeting. Cate told Livia to pen the announcement. They would meet again Thursday after dinner to review her rough draft and make a shopping list for snail-mail supplies. Among them, they wrote a mailing list of 206 mainland acquaintances in addition to 43 kama'āina specials offered to islanders. Within ten days, all envelopes had been posted.

At first, only three solicited reservations came back, and those were word-of-mouth referrals – mostly for the romantic weekend special, which included two red roses, homemade brownies and soft pretzels, and a bottle of non-alcoholic wine. Besides their disappointment, they worked with a renewed fervor, on new retail items, and the weeks passed quickly as they once more settled into a semi-familiar routine.

Livia kept mucking stalls. One morning Cate brought up the rear after grabbing the mail, and called Livia Miss Cowboy Boots, for finally remembering to leave her boots outside. Mail sorted, she showed Livia two envelopes, both with the Kamuela postmark, and stated, "Know anyone from up there? One's to us, and the other's to you."

Livia tore hers open and shoved it back, at Cate, who spluttered, "No kidding? Someone's paid a $125 entry fee to submit your name, as an auction candidate."

"Guess so, that's what it says — with my permission, of course. For the life of me, who the hell would do that?"

Cate, who protested: "Sorry to disappoint — but it wasn't me. Our corporation can't write that off on taxes."

Livia squinted. "Thanks. Actually, it could." Nose in the air, she squared her shoulders. "Well, it couldn't be Guy. We decided not to tell them about the auction, well– not yet. Maybe it's someone local who met us. You know, someone whose attempting to add some variety to the auction."

Cate shot back, "Oh, yeah? Well, someone's in for a well-earned surprise, if you accept."

Livia blew her a raspberry, twirled around and muttered, "Anyway, I will definitely think about it. The proceeds do go to charity, you know."

She noticed Cate facing off with Margaret, who hesitated before slowly admitting she finally accepted Richard's invitation to Waipio Valley, adding, "He asked me to be his guest at the Cliffside Bed and Breakfast."

Cate's red-hot glare held Livia's tongue only briefly. She muttered something about April, and it could get pretty damn wet over there. Cate's glare still intense; Livia nervously said, "Well, Cate says Akaka Falls is —"

Cate grabbed Margaret's cell phone. It rang as she handed it over.

She listened with a few, "Okays" and a few other brief sentences before hanging up. Clearing her throat, she filled them in. "Tom says Guy and Mina are heading back to Michigan tomorrow. He will fly into to Kona. One of is to pick him up tomorrow, and we need to tell Aye." Hands in the air and she said, "Party time! Well— maybe just one."

Their group hug ended quickly enough, as an audience of one filled the hall door. Aye stood grinning from ear to ear. "Chakra got a call from Tom and asked me to come down. We're so pleased; thank you for all you've done."

Margaret approached him cautiously. And with her hand on his shoulder, she sternly explained that Tim, though awake from the coma, remained in very serious condition. She explained that it could be rough months ahead until Tim could be moved to Kona; although, the resident said he would most likely be stepped downed from intensive care in a couple days.

Calmly but adamantly Aye continued, "That is as much as we hoped for. Chakra will send someone to sit in, for Tom's occasional relief, until Tim gets up for therapy."

Margaret patted his back and chuckled "Sounds like a plan; let's go see the grand lady."

So, everyone did their part for the next few weeks. One evening when Cate was throwing together supper, and Livia was rubbing her tired feet - Margaret rushed through the door. Finger pressed to her mouth, for quiet, she took Cate by the shoulders and sat her down, next to Livia, then rushed to the pantry. Out her head poked, and in sock feet, she quickly shuffled to the table with a bottle and three crystal glasses. Popping-open her best bottle of French wine, she filled glasses before leaning into their incredulous faces and saying, "He's being transferred to Kona Hospital tomorrow." She leaned back, leaving Cate and Livia speechless, until they noisily clanged a toast to Tim's health.

Two nights later, the phone rang. Since the Red Wings had Cate's nose glued to the TV, so Livia answered and listened intently. Tom chattered how Tim squeezed his hand and sipped a bit of water. "I hate to ask', Livia finally edged in, "But can you tell me where I can find Tim's business papers? His attorney asked me for them."

A long silence.

Margaret came down the back stairs, as Livia sat down hard. "What's up? Is there a problem?"

"Sort of but not anything with Tim's recovery but Tom just confessed that Tim's mother held the deed to their stables and when she died, there had been no quitclaim deed to Tim for it. On top of that, there's only a medical power of attorney – not one for Tim's business affairs."

"Okay, I'm a medical doctor. Translate the legalese, please."

"It means that, until Tim gets up and can take care of himself, the stables legally belong to his mother's closest relative, and that happens to be his father. I might take a stab in the dark, but either he is not aware of this, or they had a common law marriage - and I don't believe this state recognizes such an arrangement. All in all, I assured Tom that I'd contact their lawyer first thing in the morning. Somehow, as long as

Tim's in the hospital, it's hands off from his family." "We'll have to see about that, too," answered Margaret.

Cate rushed downstairs, in her pajamas, and asked if she had missed a pow-wow.

"Not really. Tom just called to say Tim is standing."

Cate jerked elbow to waist, with an explosive, "Yes!"

They briefly clapped, as Margaret played referee raising both arms in the air. "Third-point for our team!"

Cate looked at Livia's wide eyes but merely chided Margaret - warning her to be careful what she said, for it could end up in Livia's editorials.

None of it was published; although, Livia kept a log of each step and every increment of added weight for strength training. She explained that it was too personal, and she did not want Cate privy to a story, which might jinx Tim's progress.

And he surprised everyone with the progress he made. Everything went along, so smoothly, that the charity auction day crept up in no time.

That morning Livia felt a bit unsettled, and she lay on the daybed that Luke had bought for her. Since early morning, smoke hung in the air. She wondered if it drifted across, from the Maui sugarcane fields, and kept her hand on an over-the-counter inhaler. A few puffs helped, and she felt better until a letter arrived. The return address showed a new address, that of her first love at college. She stayed put and read the letter stating there was a trip planned, in lieu of washing dishes, on an Olivia cruise liner. Only an estimated arrival date was given, for the ship would circle the main Hawaiian islands. Livia did not mention the letter, or its particulars, and made a point of circling the arrival week, in the inn's reservation book. She filed the letter and would deal with the details later.

She must have fallen asleep. Another puff, from the inhaler, and she pulled herself off the daybed. Sitting tall before the huge round mirror, of Annabelle's walnut dressing vanity – she made ready for the party and auction.

Three Christmases marched by, since she really got all gussied up. Luke was gone, but his Lionel Holiday Express train clacked along, circling tree and presents, as Annabelle watched her twirl about in a new outfit. Cate always dressed semi-formally for the Guy-Mel Christmas Party. That last year - they donned Aloha Wear, for the New Year's Eve party. Now, the train sat in its box, and she wondered whether her present this year would be that gorgeous Hilo Hatties Christmas Aloha shirt, with columns of red poinsettias down the front. Tonight would prove her greatest effort at dolling-up, for what she hoped to make a splendid evening. Waimea's Kamuela Auction affair would draw out the high rollers and possibly some great bids; and to that end, she was ready to kick out the jams. Her steady eye-lining hand was well-practiced since the seventh grade. Peering into the mirror, she outlined each eye, with silky-smooth kohl paste, and noticed her gray silk tuxedo and shirt hanging, from the open wardrobe door - fluttering in the breeze.

Beyond the bedroom's tall windows, taupe clouds crowned misty green mountains. The inn's view gave way to an earlier one, back in Camp Fortson. Those second-story windows gave a wonderful vantage but nipped the view, into a much nicer one that was quite misleading. The nicely trimmed out window sashes showed an old landscape, of roof tops buffed with lovely fluffy oaks and maples - but hid two ugly senior citizen high-rises, automotive buildings, and crowded streets below. Lilinoe's breeze dried the pliable eyeliner, to steel grey, and exposed the real view.

She drew up the dressing robe's Peter Pan collar and brushed her long hair. Rosebud Salve rubbed, into her fingertips, and smoothed the ends, as she combed behind her left ear. More salve applied - she braided a smooth plait and pulled it high into a tiara-shaped do. After anchoring it with a rhinestone clip, at the opposite ear, she selected two intensely dyed red orchids, from Annabelle's hand-painted china daisy vase, and placed one above each ear.

Black cloisonné cufflinks and studs finished off her light pink silk shirt. She slipped on silk stockings, suited up, and wriggled her toes into finely stitched size-six patent leather shoes. Bow tie and cummerbund tightened, she stood tall pulling down the jacket's nipped waist. Then she buttoned in Luke's watch fob, draped it across, and dropped her Great-grandmother Scheffer's tiny timepiece into a small inside pocket. She pulled it out again - checking the time. Patting tiny keys leading to the watch, she selected an embroidered linen handkerchief. All pinched up by its center, and folded over once - its crisp points peeked-out from her breast pocket. Seated once more, she poked-through trillium diamond earrings, two in each ear. She glanced down at her polished matching rings, which nicely set off the black designs across her hands. Leaning forward – she licked in a dab of lipstick before hopping up. A huff and a sigh followed chores nearly done. Standing, as straight as she could, she slipped driver's license, insurance card, and two $20.00 bills in her hip pocket. Full stance, at the door mirror, she turned glancing from heel to hip. Each satin stripe matched its trouser crease, and she marched down the hall.

As usual, Cate and Margaret flanked the newel post quietly looking up. Cate knew the drill: to start a half-hour early, so as not to rush Livia. Margaret had the drill down pat after two weeks in residence. The moment, Livia paused on the landing, both women's jaws slacked.

Cate smiled and said, "You look stunning." Margaret gave a hearty nod before pealing off a two-finger whistle — and they were off to the auction.

They made the short trip to Waimea in record time. Standing, beside the Kahilu Theatre, they drank in the crisp mountain air and smooth sunset. Sparkling patrons crowded under the marquee, as the moon cleared the mountains lighting their faces. Livia hung back near the doors. She found it gut wrenching, to watch all the rail thin participants milling about the parking lot sucking on cigars and cigarettes.

Inside the main doors, a mural filled the left wall with a Parisian street scene lushly paved with real money trees. Opposite that, a photographer and assistants flanked two plasma monitors that flashed a new set of dazzling photos every ten seconds. Livia stood back, from huge faces flashing before her, as an usher pinned a solid gold disk on her shoulder indicating she was Item #8. She followed Cate and Margaret past the back wall, of tables, where they sampled pupus and drinks until another usher whisked her away to an area cordoned off, with velvet ropes. There, the participants were asked to smile and strut about a bit. Twenty minutes of them milling about and her mouth feeling tired, a light orchestra pleasantly interrupted them for a nice half hour of dancing.

After a few selections, the women split up and visited various friends. Cate talked sports, and Margaret gave a few brief hellos before leading Livia to the corner, where she properly introduced her to Ma Loa - never realizing the two had met before. Cate joined them, and all four agreed on one thing: it was no real party without Tim and Tom. Margaret answered her pager, and Livia excused herself, from Cate and Ma, and made haste to the bathroom. On her way back, to find Cate, Livia brushed shoulders with Ma. They walked past the bar where a dapper middle-age man caught Livia's eye. Cate not in sight - they selected fresh drinks, and crossed paths with the man again. This time, it was unmistakable - that definite wag of his index finger beckoned her closer.

Not stopping, to get friendly, she chimed out a carefully enunciated phrase: "I *don't* respond to any man's finger."

Ma blew hard across her drink, finely showering the next woman's low-cut dress. Exhaling a second hard cough, she shut her mouth with a hard, "I see," before softening a bit and offering the doused woman her napkin.

Livia blushed but vamped a good descent when the man tipped his top hat to her. Ma composed herself, smiled, and pointed across the room to Margaret who was motioning them to the lobby, for a photo session.

They purchased a nice group photo. No sooner than Margaret read aloud, "Short Program," from the billboard adjacent the money trees - they heard a low drum roll, which came from beyond the inner theater doors. Herded along, with the rest of the crowd, they sat before a small elegant stage dimly lit with footlights. The doors shut behind then, as huge spotlights converged on the velvet curtains. Baton poised, the conductor faced the right wing - as someone paced in the shadows and repeatedly dipped a bow at him. This continued, as the crowd began to murmur, and the conductor allowed a few light bars of music then lowered his arms, as the scenario repeated itself. Finally, the figure in the wing took a jump and a muted trumpet moaned: "Ta–da, Ta–da, Ta–da—dah…" The muted refrain repeated until out popped the Garland's - Little Tramp - and with a tiptoed trot, he ran to the spotlight.

The Tramp bowed, then stood, and brushed the flower dangling from his black hat back off his face. He smiled, lowered his chin and pretended to blush – as a dimple appeared in his lightly chalked face. One tiny step forward — he hugged himself and emoted: "I love New York! I am so excited — I love it!" The crowd roared, and the tramp burst into *New York, New York*.

"That's Guy doing Ol' Blue Eyes!" exclaimed Livia.

Cate and Margaret nodded and said it had been harder-than-hell to keep it secret. Oh, how wonderful his favorite song rolled out. He must have hired a voice coach, for he pulled it off with excellence. Next, he covered his heart with his hands, looked to the ceiling, and then down at his audience, and crooned *Swanee* "How I love you, how I love you, My dear old Swanee…" Finishing every verse, he punched out "–When I get to that Swan-ne shore!" and he kneeled with arms wide out.

Someone shouted, "Hello— Al, Judy and Albee! Oh, how the crowd ate it up.

To that, Livia shouted, "Frankie!" and she clapped her hands till they hurt; although, she couldn't stop thinking about Indiana University's student drama group traveling the Ohio River, on an old paddle-wheeler, docking along shore, and performing wonderful old minstrel shows. That was - until the late 1960's when most of its songs, were labeled as politically incorrect. During the next five years - movies, such as *Song Of the South,* were shelved. She never believed in banning books or anything else. With a PG-13 rating the 1946 masterpiece, of real actors mingled with awesome animation, could at least be offered as a DVD rental. She believed the phrase: forgetting any portion of history leads to repeating it.

The Tramp caught her attention, as he pulled himself up, and ran to the wings nearly tripping on his floppy clown shoes than a minute, and he took center stage sporting a fine Uomo tuxedo and no makeup. The Vamp's heavily lined eyes twinkled and blinked, as he said, "Thank you. Thank you so very much." His head nodded, in time to the audience's consistent light applause, and he mouthed one last "Thank you," as his eyes glazed over. Speaking a few quiet sentences, he finally raised his voice a little – and said, "You know why we're here." With an elongated nod to the conductor — The Vamp hugged himself, took one deep breath and hit a perfectly smooth pitched note ending in *"Somewhere Over the Rainbow..."* soaring above the crowd. Well, one could hear a pin drop and every handkerchief came out. The song ended; The Vamp bowed deeply and threw kisses to everyone before ducking between the curtains and the spotlight snapped off. The crowd chanted: "Encore. Encore..." but none came.

The stage lights dimmed and then grew to a rosy pink followed by a half-as-bright spotlight. The master of ceremonies walked to center stage, and he asked the crowd to ready their purses for those who were less fortunate.

A brief light from the lobby and Guy walked-in, with Mina on his arm, and joined the women. He said, "No way – could I miss a chance to do 'Swoonatra' — well that, and the fact Mina has her heart set on a couple second-honeymoon nights, at The Four Seasons Hualalai." He winked, "Her treat." He sipped wine and explained he and Mina would not bid tonight but they would cut a check, in the morning, before they left for Detroit. A team again, five Bears stood together – ready for the auction.

And what was to come - Livia would have never expected. A few celebrities (of whom few locals recognized) spent thousands on evenings with gorgeous younger men and women. And when there were only three more 'Items' to go, Livia stepped on stage. Margaret smiled, raised paddle-91, and set the bid at $300; to that offer, Richard chimed-in and paddle-66 boosted the bid to $1000. Livia gulped and looked down at the crowd. Figuring there was little to lose by hamming it up - she stepped forward, released the button on her cutaway and slid her hand to her hip. Smiling grandly she pivoted smoothly, and looked back over one shoulder before facing the audience. Margaret whistled, the crowd cheered, and the man at the bar threw his top hat in the air. Ma raised paddle-69, said $5,000 and caught the hat. Livia gulped harder. Not to be outdone, Richard bid $8,000 and got elbowed by Margaret. Ma countered with $10,000 and the gavel came down – and nearly did Livia.

All she remembered, from then on, was a quick champagne toast to all the participants and patrons and a quiet ride home.

Chapter 16: Orchid Of Hilo

Nearly sunrise, and Aye leaned hard against the back bumper of Livia's little red Jeep loading small orchids behind the front seats, and placing crumpled newsprint and pop cans between each of the boxes. They needed protection, from the open air, and bumpy winding Saddle Road. He always said that damn road could jostle anyone's fillings loose.

Still reeling from the auction, Livia stood inhaling her coffee and fantasized about the good use of the money. Repeatedly, she fiddled with the band on her ponytail, pretending to adjust it. She offered to help him but he declined and grabbed the last aluminum can from the grocery bag wedging it between the last cardboard boxes.

Drumming her fingers on the steering wheel, she focused on the inn's red hibiscus hedge along the driveway. Although she had been halfway across Saddle Road, in a diesel tour van, this was her first expedition to Hilo on the infamous road on the high divide between Mauna Kea and Mauna Loa. It crossed the Pohakuloa Military Reservation where an enlisted man had been killed, during training practice last week. Quick to remind herself that Kona wasn't the hustle and bustle of Detroit, she kept repeating, "Aloha Time, Aloha Time…" Her grandmother's stage whisper broke through, "It's not nitroglycerine – could we pul-lease get a move on?"

Recalling the first leg of her first trip up the high pass, she patted the aspirin in her pocket softly chuckling at the way Cate always called them her 'asp tabs'. Anyway, she might need them when they got to the high country. For now, she tried patience – between Aye and the Francolin Fowl chicks with their mama crossing the highway kept the Wrangler at a halt. The last chick hidden in the mound of dry fire grass, Aye proceeded into the highlands.

Terrain and wildlife never disappointed up there, as on her first trip with Cate – when just past the ten-mile marker Livia had yanked her head back as pueo (owl) nearly clipped the tour van's right windshield.

Tour books glorified the 5,000-foot high pass, as raw and dangerous, and well advertised the fact that most car rental companies would not insure anyone driving along it. Livia figured county officials needed the narrow two-lane road clear, of liquored-up locals and tourists, and she was pretty sure the military could do without the gawkers. As usual, legends and rules enticed more people.

"All done!" Aye pushed himself away from the bumper and pressed down the lift gate. Striding to the passenger's side, he grabbed the Wrangler's assist handle plopped his derriere firmly on the seat. Livia's right knee jingled the ignition keys. Grinning widely he patted her knee. "I'm ready – finally. Sorry, it took so long. I know you are anxious. These orchids will not fetch a decent price, if the spongy leaves or blooms are bruised. Mahalo for waiting."

They breezed along North Kona Belt Road, its shoulder rimming the base of Lowe's new thirty-foot boulder wall. Dark dull stones hid the two-story Border's bookstore and offices beside it. Barely braking, for a Detroit Stop, she turned right on Henry Street and headed to upper Palani Road to another right at the stoplight. Heavy construction machinery lined nearly every driveway on the way up to Mamalahoa Highway. Most weekdays, workers busily chopped half parcels into condominiums, home lots, and mom-and-pop businesses – neither sign of progress enhanced the views of mountains or sea.

Developers had yet to scrape the scant forest reserves of Hanoa Crater. She scanned Kaloko Drive, residential perches came a tad too expensive for her taste, but the weather up here was enticingly cool. A bit further, on the left, sat the 200-foot wide parcel she nearly purchased for a house. She and Cate were greatly relieved when she caught the dishonest realtor's and mortgage broker's scam before closing the deal.

Not long after she had been lucky to overhear a nice conversation at Mrs. Shetima's restaurant. Over dessert, the ninety-year-old spitfire confided to Cate, "The hills of South Kona are still the best place to live."

The car cut through Lilinoe's mists, and Aye turned around occasionally keeping an eye on his orchids. With no air conditioning, windburn was his immediate concern. Livia hit the vent controls and rolled the windows up halfway saying, "You know, those plants are worse than babies."

He snorted gently, "Nearly so." Easing his back up against the passenger seat, he turned his face to the mist and the morning's first rays.

Sighing and humming, she patted the roof, then angled her left hand to guide in the warm winter air. Coffee droplets clung, to her steel mug, and she gently rolled it onto the floorboard - all the while musing how she filled it, at her parents' house - those six years she walked to work.

Suddenly, the flank of Mauna Moanuiahea gave way to the far distant White Mountain. Livia gasped at its brightness from thirty-five miles away.

Might Mauna Kea, lolling in the morning sun, gave sharply contrast to the cloaked Kona lowlands. Postcard or book - neither gave justice to her first view, of pristine tropical snowcap. Silently, she wiped her bottom lip. When she could stare no longer, her thoughts turned to Hilo. The road hugged the ranch land, and she pointed at the makai meadow with big wooden sign. "That, whatever it is, always reminded me of an odd Polynesian sail."

Aye strained near the steering wheel, for a better view. "I've wondered that too. Not quite a totem – and definitely not a Hawaiian sail. It is probably a marker, for Waikoloa Road."

Livia asked, "Didn't they recently parcel some acreage, from the Kiper Ranch, to develop another golf resort adjacent to that tiny town? Some Hilton employees told Cate - it was to provide them more accessible housing. Don't people know most of this land is arid flood plains? Four times last year, brush fires and heavy rains shut down Queen Ka'ahumanu highway."

Aye nodded. "I love this Gorgeous God's Country but the heat and the gully washers keep me from living out here. Now, I hear the military will buy the land adjacent to all sides – where this road intersects with Saddle Road."

"Speaking of adjacent and buying – get this one: I've heard that council members hired a planning specialist and he plans to pose an amendment, to the General Plan Land Use Pattern, that some 100 acres our lovely Kealakekua be changed from Important Agricultural Designation to Rural. Nice – huh? Oh, gee – help me out here." She needed him to verify the route she was about to take.

All he said was: "Same old, same old – plantations, now real estate." Then he took a deep breath and reviewed the directions: "The turnoff to Saddle Road is on the right up here." Lightly tapping his right index finger to the corner of the windshield he said, "Turn East on Saddle Road. You know, after ten miles or so – we will pass the firing range, from there I will tell you more every couple of miles."

She kept her eye on the road for the mountain loomed even more majestic than before. Aye previewed every turn in the road. They chatted, and he surmised - they could supply fifty, or sixty, orchids every three weeks.

The shopkeeper they were visiting today thinks she can sell about thirty plants a month. Also, she will distribute plants along the Hamakua Coast. Usually twice a year, she would leave, on buying trips. Those months, they would need to fill their own orders along the northern route. In that case, it would be easier to drive to Waimea then head south almost to Hilo.

Livia knew that Aye occasionally delivered orchids south of Hilo, from Puna to Volcano village. Once, he warned her not to sell any in Kailua or at the Kohala Coast resorts. He wanted no one to suspect the cove as his source. Wednesday mornings were perfect for their Hilo trips. Most guests left or arrived Friday through Monday. Today, Aye suggested they would later buy lettuce and tomatoes from Nakagawa Farms before heading home. With repeated trips, she hoped she could do more errands there.

They wound their way through the Hilo subdivisions. Pointing to the next intersection, Aye reminded her that Saddle Road was the same as Highway 200. Past the hospital and the library was Ululani Street. Past that, they would turn left at the next stoplight. Kinoole Street led into town.

"Not bad directions; you make a good copilot," said Livia the first couple of times she found a street sign or landmark exactly, per his descriptions.

Aye pointed. "One more block and we come to Kalakua Street. Turn left in there. It's the Cultural Center."

The streets were nearly deserted as Livia pulled into the alley, and Aye pointed to a parking spot, next to a midnight-green Mustang convertible. He quipped, "Yes, a big old building — just like you described back in Michigan." Pointing overhead, to a set of big doors, he asked her to back the car close to the loading dock. Before she could turn off the engine, he hopped to the pavement. Stretching, he touched both knees and pulled himself tall again. After a deep breath, he gave a whimsical, "A bit humid — but I do so miss the place. A slight movement, in one of the tall windows above, brought his eyes up and he waved - while telling Livia: "I was born down that street over there, though my mother was from the Kau District."

Oh, wonderful – my favorite district, thought Livia. Somewhere - she read that Hawaii's districts were the equivalent, of the mainland's counties and parishes. The Kau was birthplace of High Chieftess Kapiolani, and before her Queen Keopuolani may have been raised there. She watched Aye scoot about grabbing and lifting boxes – remarkably spry for his age and this time of day. This morning came closest to her first one on Oahu's windward coast — calm, soothing and glorious like all the six days of that trip. She would rise at 5:30 every morning and rush to the balcony, sipping coffee in the sun. Perched high above the Marine Base, she could snap photos between high-power lines. Somehow, Hilo's rain seemed a tad more damp and permanent.

"You coming?" called Aye.

"Yeah, sure. Just day-dreaming. Be right there."

Climbing the tall flight of stairs, Aye opened the back door to the shop, and a tiny Corgi pup waddled down them to Livia. With a diminutive, but insistent, "Woof, woof!" he nosed her hand. Lightly scratching his ears, she heard a woman's voice ring out, "Come on in! I will be right there. By the way – his name is Spartacus, and he really likes his ears scratched."

Aye scratched the little scutter under the chin, and on the chest, as Livia mouthed the pup's cute name. Quite still she stood, with her hand held out, so he could sniff. He rolled over, as she made kissy noises, and purred, "Such a big – boy–. Yes, I'm a sucker for tummy rubs too." Her eyebrows shot up, and more words came to mind - as Sparty's back legs wiggled, and he sprinkled.

Distant polite conversation continued, then the voice came closer: "He *is* a very good boy– brings good juju every time he visits. I am watching him until his owner, the shopkeep below, returns tomorrow from tending to his uncle on Maui. Oh – and Little Sparty has a littermate, a big dude named Agador. Another friend's watching Agy; anyway, I'll be right back there in a moment."

So Sparty fell asleep in Livia's arms as she watched him wondering what Agy looked like. Her back was tight from the day before, so Aye transferred the orchids without her. He took his time, and she heard him tell the little flowers they would be very happy, in the big store windows facing the morning sun. A few minutes later, the shopkeeper's bell jingled, followed by a gentle click of the front door. Barely audible footsteps fell down the hall. "Okay! I'm back – and I'm all yours!" As the voice rang out, footsteps got louder rounding the stock room door.

Face-to-face, Livia gulped air. Less than two feet away stood the stately woman, auction winner and her guide to the temple and Ulupo Gardens. More silence — until she found her voice, and stammered, "So– you live here?" That was all she could think of, as she forced some semblance of composure.

Her eyes followed the tall woman's almond eyes, looking up at the huge mural of a flock of redheaded cranes. A tiny scrape of nails and they glanced down, as Little Sparty skidded between them, his mouth full of glossy newspaper inserts. Ears rubbed, away he scampered – banging and scraping the paper along the far wall of the hallway. Livia followed, taking the papers and giving him a gentle tap on the nose, with a stern and extended, "No."

Noticing a small, heavy corrugated packing box near the back door, she pointed and asked, "May I give him that empty box?"

That met with raised eyebrows and a firm answer: "Sure, it's only going to the trash." She smiled, looked her up and down, and handed it over.

Livia sat on the floor beside him - ripping off the top flaps, and scooting the box on its side near the puppy. Leaning closer, she whispered, "Only cardboard Little Boo. Let's refine our taste."

Aye joined them and apologized, for not having introduced Livia to Ma Loa. As he did so, he winked at Ma who bent down and touched cheeks with her then scratched Sparty's tummy, as he sat in Livia's lap. She wondered if colored ink had a taste that attracted puppies. Attempting to shake off the confusion, she reminded Ma to encourage Sparty's owner, to allow him to teethe on plain cardboard.

Ma quickly replied, "Sounds good, but this little chap does get around." Livia scooted back and set the puppy off her lap, as Ma continued, "Come, sit. Would you like hot tea or cold soda? Uncle Aye can putter forever - arranging his orchids. Only he knows where they will thrive."

"Uncle Aye?" Livia's word tumbled out. "Is that a respectful address such as 'Auntie' - Hawaiian style? Yes, I'll have a diet cola, if you have it." Somehow, her thoughts came out all jumbled.

"No. Uncle – as in we are related," Ma called out – head in the refrigerator. She returned with a tray of drinks, and Livia watched her long, buffed nails touch the crystal glasses, as she set them on the table. Her graceful head turned, as she gazed lovingly at Aye.

No rings thought Livia. Lovely jade earrings, of green dragons, with talons latched onto lavender jade circles, rocked with Ma's every gesture. A tiny wooden Iolani (hawk) was cleverly attached, to the top of Ma's left ear. Odd combination - was the jewelry crafted locally?

Ma chuckled. "So serious you are. Well, Uncle gets excited too."

Livia said, "Oh, sorry. How impolite. I was staring at your earrings."

Ma smiled and handed Livia a chilled glass filled with cola garnished with a huge slice of lime. Livia turned toward the scraping, of the huge window being raised. Without her noticing, Aye had left. Now, he rounded the corner and accepted tea and sliced mango. Odd - that he and Ma withheld the very fruit that made her itch. Her favorite cola garnish had been offered, which was normally served as an afternoon or evening drink.

Wiping freshly washed hands, Aye's distinct scent of cinnamon jasmine wafted through the morning air. "Good thing you washed; I always worry about lead in the old storefront paint. Almost every customer has commented about those lovely glass shelves, which you installed last week," complimented Ma. "They are nice. In the late 1960s, my parents took twenty-four glass shelves down from in our tall Indiana sunroom windows. I can't forget cleaning those damn shelves and the windows inside and out."

"All right — we've got a dyed-in-the-wool Hoosier — too sweet."

Livia cringed. Sucked back, to her Southfield Engine cubicle, she had heard way too many "sweets" and "robusts" from everyone — both management and young tech wizards. Although she used slang, she abhorred buzzwords — one tiny reason, among big ones, for fleeing Detroit's Big Three. Actually, they and St. Seaton's expected that she not only work hard for them, but be beholden to them - and that was never gonna be.

"What? Did I say something offensive?" asked Ma, as she touched Livia's arm ever so slightly.

Livia merely said, "Too many buzz words."

Ma chuckled, "I am so sorry about your career problem." She chuckled and explained that a friend's son had said 'Sweet!' in California – before adding, "You must be really glad to have moved here."

Aye sipped the last of his water as Ma sucked ice from her glass. "I've met The Good Doctor. Her reputation precedes her at Hilo Keiki Clinic." He watched Livia swallow hard, and he chuckled. "From what I've seen of this one, she wouldn't put up with either one of them, if they weren't."

Ma glanced down at Livia's premium lightweight walking shoes, and said, "Just this time, let me lock up shop and let's continue over lunch at Ali`i Court." The Hilo Hawaiian Hotel on Banyan Drive was well worth little over a half-mile walk. With Livia firmly wedged between them, Ma and Aye ducked in the back door to the kitchen. "Teeny Man!" Ma called out. "May we have the bayside window while you set up the buffet?"

A not-too-tiny chef dropped his pastry-icing bag and approached with a beaming smile. He bowed, and with a grand flourish, he swept his hand at the far end of the back dining room. "Anything for my princess." Turning slightly he quipped, "Uncle Aye!" He stood a minute, wiping his hand on his apron, and then he grabbed both of Aye's hands, pulling him closer to rub noses – then followed suit with Ma.

Livia looked down and noticed her feet were riveted to the floor, and quickly stepped forward for a hug. Then, she shrugged and followed everyone to the table, in quick tiny steps announcing, "Guess we're in for a treat. This really looks lovely."

Aye whispered, "She's paying, and the food's sumptuous."

Livia could just barely see Mauna Kea, from the left corner of the dining room window, as it graced the high panorama of Hilo's hilly coastline fronted by Puhi Bay. Teeny backed away, so the incoming waiter could command their full attention.

The waiter rushed to them. "Hi, my name is David, and I'll be your waiter today. If you are ready - may I suggest a pitcher of Mehana Beer and some sautéed calamari?" Aye cringed, stating the pitcher was fine but they would have the lightly battered platter of local vegetables and shiitake mushrooms. They settled on fresh-baked Hawaiian bread and rosemary roasted chicken carved at the table, topped off by an exquisite dark chocolate mousse.

Their meal ended too soon with Ma admitting that she needed to return to the shop to tend to the puppy. Weathering the steamy walk to the center of town - a brief shower ensued, as Aye apologized, "They needed to start for home." Ma touched noses with him, and she gave Livia a hug. The Jeep was loaded with free produce. Teeny convinced them to take more, shaking his head, muttering, "Bountiful - much too much produce for us here."

Another three hours and Livia recalled the highlights of the day — not as impressed with their return trip across the mountain pass. Although, she wore her best pair of sunglasses and the windshield was tinted dark enough, the sun nearly seared her brain. There was no way she would choose this route, if they were not in such a hurry to get back and check on Chakra. All a sudden she remembered Margaret's tiny spare cell phone in her vest pocket. A couple miles, and she pulled off the road. "We can check to see if Chakra is well, and if Cate will make sure she's got some supper - we could take the northern route up the coast and through Waimea, and grab a bite to eat up there."

A stop in Waimea brought Aye's head up. He said, "Oh, no, not a problem." Then he asked, if Livia could show him how to dial a number.

She would be happy to, and she had not realized he never operated a cell phone. Just as she had, with Annabelle, she explained it, as a type of radio. Aye turned it on, and it connected the very first time. He seemed quite surprised, to hear Chakra's voice so clear - who, by the way, was just fine.

Livia phoned Cate. "Why not share some Rooskie potato salad with Chakra this evening? Aye wants to be back by sunset." Flipping the phone shut, she wheeled around to Aye. "Great – then it's settled. Where would you like to stop for supper?" Barely taking a breath, she answered her own question. "I know. We could eat in Waimea, then take the high road home."

"Sure, we will take Route-19 next time and 190 tonight," said Aye.

Livia made her offer. "How about the Oriental restaurants, in the food court? They're pretty good, or we could have a burger or a steak at the Kiper Ranch Grill – your choice is my treat."

Aye scratched his chin, so she continued, "The food court's got a really neat pass-through fireplace, and both have good views." He chose the food court, adding that he would like a thick Orange Juiciest for dessert.

"Good, I can people-watch there. Got that fascinating habit sitting with my Grandmother Etter, in the nursing home lobby, or the shopping mall, when my mother was busy or shopping. Guess that's why I eventually earned a minor in psychology." She got gabby. She wondered if Aye chuckled, because he realized she was tired and hungry. She listened to him talk, about his blood sugar test. It fell, within the normal range, even though he was over twenty-five years her senior.

The air was warm but she shivered. For some reason, she could not shake the feeling of being watched. She set her chopsticks to work on her noodle bowl, as Aye munched stir-fry and quickly settled back savoring mouthfuls of his tangy dessert. He seemed relaxed and not worried about Chakra - or maybe, he chose not to be. After dinner, they took a quick walking tour around the parking lot, peeking in various store windows. "It certainly has changed a lot since I've been up here," was all he said.

The sun set, and soon they headed down the road. The dashboard's digital clock glowed, as Livia mused, about arriving home by 8:30. Comfortably full, she found the drive pleasant. They passed Kalaoa's few streets - high above the quiet sea. Little by little, Kailua's golden streetlights flickered on. At Palani junction, she wondered: *Why have them so dim?* Past Aye's shoulder gleamed the ballparks' bright white lights – even nearer Mauna Kea than Kailua. Well, there were those who did not want the observatories.

Aye snored lightly, as she headed down Henry Street. Gliding past the stoplight she pulled, to the right shoulder, and jostled him awake. He stretched a moment, got out, and took two bags, of six plate lunches, from the backseat. After setting them next to the high brush, for the homeless, then settled himself once more beside Livia. Half a mile and he snoozed again. Passing car dealerships, she noticed his head settle, against the window pillow - as though he had never awakened, since they passed 'the pseudo-Polynesian sign'. She passed Kealakekua, and Aye's snorting awake interrupted her thoughts. Jostled by the inn's driveway - his head popped up - giving her a hearty chuckle.

A bit startled - he said, "Home already?"

"That we are - sir." She followed the old logging lane, which ran past inn and cottage. Watching him amble toward the door and turn off the light, she leaned out and said, "Take all the time you need in the morning." Even though the sun was long gone, she enjoyed the lingering warmth before backing up and circling the inn to the carport.

Cate sat peacefully at the brightly lit kitchen table. Looking up she gave a cheery, "Hey, you're home already. Chakra and I ate, and we had a nice visit. We put our heads together and planned the inn's quilt shop. What would you think if we renovated the south side of the lanai, for an enclosed room?"

"Fine by me, as long as there's a corner to sit and have coffee. You might run the details past Margaret, but I have no problem with whatever you-all decide. A quilt shop's always been in your plans, and Chakra probably could form a good cottage industry. Oh– poor choice of words — that's not how I meant it–"

Cate was quick on the uptake: "I know what you meant: more of a consignment type setup, and we would need to buy wholesale too. Well– it sounds like you had a satisfying day; I know how long you've waited for it."

"Oh, I forgot - you would have loved this tiny dog Ma was puppy sitting. Well, you'll get to see him someday. And the drive home was nearly perfect – except for driving directly into the sun for a bit." Selecting a chilled beer, she told Cate about little Spartacus, the big mountain's snow, and Aye's meal and snooze - ending with the fact: she really could forego more trips to Hilo. She was just glad to be home.

Cate got that dreamy look on her face. "I bet the stars are fabulous from up at Mauna Keas right now. That book we had, with those cloud pictures taken up there. You know – the one that looked like a huge flying saucer ready to touch down? That must be simply awesome, to see. It is something for us, to look forward to – someday."

"Yes – we did see low clouds, but nothing like that."

A couple weeks later, Livia got the call to make good on the deal from the charity auction. Dreading the drive, she headed back to Hilo late one afternoon, to arrive by the end of Ma Loa's workday. This time she drove the northern route: up past Waimea and down the misty and gorgeous Hamakua coastline. Akaka Falls on the right and not far to the city limits she recalled having read about surfing along here. Ma had also mailed a sketched street map; however, Livia feigned stopping short of the place. In reality, she left her car parked a couple blocks down the road and walked to Ma's house.

They shared a nearly perfect supper and faint pink sunset. After rinsing and setting plates and utensils on the drain board, Ma changed into a swimsuit. Livia watched her pull down the big long board then hop and skip over a set of low waves. First, she straddled the big sucker but was soon lying down on the board and paddling what Livia guessed to be 300-or-so yards before ducking through a medium-size roller. Walking barefoot along the only stretch of sand, she watched Ma get smaller, until she nearly disappeared. She popped up again and walked the board. Making a few more runs - the waves cooperated. Livia stood in awe wondering what exactly 'hang-ten' meant. She reasoned it might mean: toes being licked, by the waves, at the tip of the board. By the various positions Ma exhibited, Livia soon realized Ma was no novice.

The moonlight trailed into Hilo and she seemed to ride it. Worrying a bit about murky water and sharks, Livia noticed the sand pulling her toes down as she watched Ma come closer and closer. Heart pounding, Livia sat and strained to pull them to her chest as the rough water lapped above her knees. With a gasp, she pulled free.

The air cooled, as Ma came ashore, and Livia couldn't help but notice the triangles and wide zigzag dashes flex along Ma's long thighs as she carried the board. Did those markings protect her from sharks and such? Sometimes, they frequented murky waters - especially at dawn and dusk. Ma's tattoos differed from designs signifying the shark clan. Local legends described similar designs as a man's, or a shark's bite — similar to those she had seen, on Aye's ankles and some hula dancers. With only their tops outlined, these tattoos reminded her of mountain tops. No longer able, to contain her curiosity, she asked Ma, "Are your upper arm tattoos, with triangles and intricate dashes, similar to that of a man or a shark?"

"Neither. They represent 'Iolani – that being the royal hawk, and Mauna Kea of my one ancestor." Leaning her board against the lanai, she leaned to one side and patted dry her waist-length hair. Livia watched the bluish black cascade shimmer in the moonlight and breeze, as Ma poured cognac. They each sipped a small glass full, licked the rim. Another slid down even more smoothly, as they relaxed on the east lanai until the evening breezes grew cooler.

Moving inside, Livia glanced around the library. "What a lovely handmade antique doll." She did not ask but wondered if its hair was fashioned from coconut fibers. "I have a doll collection that my grandmother brought from her NEA tours. She collected more than a dozen as souvenirs when she traveled abroad. Is your doll from around here? It looks very old."

Ma shrugged, saying that she found it in the attic of her store. "I found it with an old box of paper dolls and fancy paper clothing for them. Some were inscribed, with the childish hand of my Great-grandmother Lana. Her mother, Lily, ran a thriving business from the Kalanikoa Street building you visited."

Her hostess quickly showered, and changed into a glistening red silk kimono. She then presented Livia with a choice, of a lovely blue silk kimono or a fresh-white linen caftan. After running her fingers across both, Livia said that she preferred the later. She slipped it on and her clothes off, and in amazement she watched as Ma leaned across a large silver bowl of water and painted on wide elongated lines of green eyeliner. It gleamed in the moonlight - as did Livia's white gossamer linen, which remind her of ancient Egyptians' robes in *National Geographic*.

Soon, they could not restrain their laughter, and after a few more drinks, they drifted from one room to another, finally settling in the study near one end of the bedroom where Ma built a cozy fire in a small isinglass stove. Livia watched the flames jump wildly, and she rubbed her friend's delicate shoulders, thinking of Cate's and resting her chin on Ma's shoulder. Their lips brushed, and Livia yanked back with full certainty Ma had nipped her lip.

Ma's robe reflected the fire. As it began mesmerizing Livia, she flicked on a tiny red lamp saying she would return momentarily. She crossed the fine smooth floor to the barely lit storage room. A slight click - and from the dark alcove Livia noticed two gold balls reflecting the light from Ma's cleavage.

A cold but refreshing breeze drifted in from the door wall that framed moonlit Mauna Kea. Holding her elbow quite still - Ma selected a pair of foot-long steel sais, from the martial arts display case, and sliding them beneath the balls she flicked them out the door. Two smoking gray streaks marked the boards where they struck before falling to the beach. Seemingly unscathed, Ma calmly returned the weapons, to their display plaque. Livia willed away the tightness, in her chest, and quietly awaited Ma's intentions.

Ma moved across the floor, and selecting a booklet from matching bookcases above the stove she said, "Here it is." She stood quietly, no more that a few inches from the stove's heat, with her left hand flat on its cover - before stooping to dampen the ashes. She rose and placed the old manuscript on the couch between them, and Livia began to survey the handwriting on its cover and slender spine.

Ma thumbed the first page open, to Lana's childlike script that introduced the diary of her mother, Lily. She was Ma's Great-great-grandmother, and her journal held her memoirs and lay detail to her tropical affairs. From the fourth page, Ma read aloud her dedication: "To all my granddaughters, with all my love and any bits of wisdom. —Lily Hakkalani."

Ma quoted her mother: "We call it 'The Sugar Mountain Legend'." Then she gingerly turned the next page and reading, as Livia looked over her shoulder and smelled Ma's jasmine perfume laced with musty old manuscript.

Lily's words began: "It has been a most amazing day; and as follows, I shall attempt to describe it.

Today's afternoon sweltered all, who lingered in Hilo Bay Park, as most our air has been sucked offshore, by Trickster Maui. The heat especially affects me, as my body swells hidden under the New People's garb."

The story detailed Ma's lineage, to Great Kapiolani, and her ancestor Lily's brief and tawdry relationship with Ting Lee. Their lusty affair had him working her over, and over again, in the roiling eddies of Honolii Stream - culminating in lust child, Lana Hakkalani. Lily's last entries described a separate wonderful life, with soul mate, Tehani. Both women lived together, well into their mid-eighties, and they managed an empire of brothels - channeling their wealth to Hilo and Puna's poor.

Well after 1:00, Ma cleared away tall iced tea glasses, adding that, from this journal on, the windward coast's historical records supported most aspects of Lily's Sugar Mountain Legend. As a couple, Lily and Nikki raised their daughters. Ting never returned, and they bought the big general store and ran most of Hilo's Rouge Street District.

Livia sat wondering about her own recent Internet search. There was a slight chance that her own ancestor, Hinman, who may have landed on the Puna coast in 1820. Did she have any long-lost relatives along this coast? Doubtfully – but she had read notes about a captain's grandson sailing back to England and returning to New Hampshire taking the 'long' way home. That could have put him here, or elsewhere, with the first missionaries a good sixty years before Ma's Chinese ancestor arrived at the sugar plantation. She was shaking away these fantastical thoughts when Ma came to her side.

Livia dodged the bullet saying, "But - how did Lily get started in her line of work?"

Ma answered, "All I can find out is that Lily's mother came here as a married woman from Oahu. She was forced, into prostitution, and brought to the Big Island around the same time the plantations began producing sugar. Her husband contracted leprosy and was shipped to Molokai. She followed him but returned after he died. Also, local records say Lily and Nikki lived a full and satisfying life, 'sans Ting' in Lily's later words." Livia figured Ma meant both women helped him put his cockles on a one-way trip back to China.

Livia stayed seated for two reasons. Ma Loa anted up some mighty good charity money for her; and before the auction, she had promised herself she would honor the winning bid. A third reason presented itself tonight. If ever she had ever been hard up, for a hot and steamy local story, she just got it. Then, another big surprise came. Ma confessed that she too had a daughter. Her little girl was given, as hanai, to Ma's distant cousin, Mabel, in Seattle. Oddly enough - a legal adoption had been arranged, to accompany the less formal one. It better enforced Ma's ideals regarding Mabel's equality. That had been almost twenty-five years ago, and mother and daughter only visited twice, once when the girl began kindergarten, and again upon her graduation from college.

Livia began to wonder, if she seemed to wear a white collar. Why else was she privy to all this? Her fingers touched her neck – nope, not there. Finally, she justified that she had given one full evening of service, and on her way to the bathroom, she began implementing her method of exit.

Before Livia left Kona, Margaret had given her a way out. If she called Margaret's private pager, she would connect to Tom's friend, and he would return her call - displaying an impressive need for a place to stay in Hilo, for the night. Margaret's answering service connected and re-connected in seconds. Livia flushed the toilet - and no sooner than it had stopped running, Ma's phone rang and she answered.

Livia combed her hair, primped a bit, and walked to the end of the hall overhearing the call. Leaning against the kitchen's doorframe, she politely asked for a sandwich. The perfect hostess, Ma quickly assembled an assortment of carbohydrates and proteins. Livia decided that oral diarrhea was the preferred course of action. She ate slowly and said, "When I was little, my mother told me never to ask for more than a glass of water, but she didn't have low blood sugar. It must be all the excitement, or something. Sorry for babbling — as the women on my hockey team have noticed for years - when I'm hungry, I tend to chatter about most anything."

Ma settled her at the kitchen table and poured her a glass of water. She squeezed a slice of lime in it, as she sat and sucked another piece of it. After waiting patiently, she turned on some mood music and returned to Livia rubbing her back while she ate. Deliberate bites of delicious bean dip, with crisp veggies and chips, and she cooed, "What's with all this back and shoulder rubbing? Haven't had a good massage, since the nurses in college."

It was perfect timing, and twenty minutes later, Tom's friend was at the door, with a sob a story about how Bernard had dumped him at the Yellow Bandanna. Wringing his hands together, Eddie whined, "If I can just stay the night, I'm sure I can get a ride first thing in the morning to my brother's condo in Waikoloa. Damn that Bernard, he called me, and I got so excited that I forgot my wallet. Tom's been my buddy since grade school, in Tucson." Rolling his eyes, he added, "I only moved here a couple months ago. He was such a dear to give me his number, telling me if I ever needed it just to call."

Livia realized Ma held Tom, in high esteem, but it did not keep her from droning out, "I can see why."

Sniffing, Eddie spat a sloppy, "What?"

Ma answered, "Oh, he's nice."

Another minute of his slobbery sob story and Livia had heard enough. "It's really nice of Ma letting you stay over, but if you want a ride home, I can drive back to Kona tonight and drop you off in Waikoloa. It's just an idea. Ma — what do you think?" Either way, Eddie was in the middle of the mix - and Livia figured her duties were over for the night. She also realized that she was not on her home turf, and that could present any number of problems. Ma was no dummy. Sure enough, she played it out and threw everything back in their laps — but not all at once.

What Livia witnessed was action worthy of Caesar's 'Divide and conquer.' In two tiny steps, Ma sidled up to Eddie, held out the back of her hand, and waited for him to accept it and give it a kiss. He did kiss back, and she slowly turned it over, running a long index finger from his throat to the tip of his chin. She came up for air and leaned a bit closer — all the while blinking demurely. Finally, she complimented him. "Well, Eddie, that was good and you are mighty cute." As he blushed, she drew him closer, planting a breathy kiss near his ear. Encircling his waist with her other arm, she turned and escorted him to the lanai.

Livia fed the last bit of food to the cat, barely hearing their laughter, but her eyebrows shot up at Ma's last comment: "Maybe you'd like to get it on with Livia and me." Right then, and there - she called trump by holding her breath and keeping her legs rigid. If she passed out, and if Ma truly cared - she would dump Eddie and hurry to her side. Livia decided she would allow herself, to bring up her dark side, just in case she awakened to them both taking advantage of her. Her mainland martial arts classmates nicknamed her 'Snap' because she could startle or drop The Dragon so easily. Her pulse ebbed, the room faded, and she dropped to her knees.

Her face was being patted. "What happened?" She played at sitting up. Dispersing deep breaths and feigning a thick tongue she puffed, "What–? I can't understand it. Blood sugar must have dropped." Her mind raced. *Good.* She had managed, to relax her jaw adequately, so as not to bite her tongue or break her teeth. Yup, that old hockey trick sure worked, of keeping your teeth apart when your mouth guard fell out on the ice."

They stood her up and set her down gently, on the couch facing Ma - who supported her head with her shoulder, and held a cool wet towel on her forehead. Eddie was making some sort of noise in the kitchen. Livia leaned back, swallowing hard, and playing it for all it was worth – said, "Guess eating carbohydrates wasn't enough; maybe I need more than a couple hours of sleep too." Her eyelids fluttered shut until Eddie brought orange juice and apologized for her feeling bad. "Tom says you've got low blood sugar. Here's some juice with a little sugar added." Livia sipped it slowly and worked it, for all it was worth, at managing to collect herself.

She asked, "May I have a small bit of tuna or some meat?" Ma was vegetarian, and that ought to assure no more mouth sports for the night.

Ma sighed, "Sure. You can snooze here on the couch. Eddie — you can hit the floor or bunk with me. When you wake up, he can drive you home."

Livia forced an anemic smile. "Oh, thanks. I'm so sorry for ruining your evening."

Eddie woke her early saying, "My real name is Simon. She is one hard sleeper, or she is playing me, for a bigger fool, than you played her. You owe me and Tom a big one."

"Well, I do appreciate—"

Simon interrupted her and continued to whisper. "After you fell asleep, she started a drinking contest. I noticed the scotch, so I kept asking for refill of that nasty swill and some water. For some time, we plowed them down. But every time she got up, for the bathroom, I refilled mine with the tea that I'd stashed under the lanai before I came in."

"That's pretty smart," whispered Livia.

"Not really," he grinned. "I was mighty thirsty, plus I used to be a narc, till I hit a big jackpot, out in Reno." Flicking his wrist, he added a lilting, "Girl– you wait here. I will get some paper. Write a note, and we're outta here."

They got down the road, to their cars, where she thanked him profusely and followed him up the coast to his home at Maumau Point. The vistas on this coast were every bit as awesome, as Livia's favorites, but she chose not to backtrack to Saddle Road. The weather was clear, and she motored on home through Waimea. The further the road wound north, around and behind Mauna Kea, the more she relaxed she became. Yes, she seemed to be in her element up here. If she was younger, it might be worth a move to one of these remote ranchettes. For a treat, she stopped at the Kiper Ranch Gift Shop and bought a pair of red cowboy boots. Lucky match for her red riding vest when she rode Hercules, with Margaret and Princess. Correctly sitting the horse bothered her back less than expected, and the extra business helped Tim and Tom.

Late that afternoon, she told Cate all about Ma. Then Margaret and Tom called, and she gave them the short version. They had great news: Tim managed to wiggle his toes again — on the left side yesterday, followed by the right side today. Livia grabbed Cate's hands, and they jumped up and down -just like old hockey teammates do after winning a rough and tumble game.

Chapter 17: **Power Of Attorney**

The next orchid delivery trip to Hilo, Ma settled Aye and Livia, at the table, with a nice tea and coffee. The front doorbell rang and she collected three boxed breakfasts from The Queen's Court. After filling three teal china plates, she picked at hers - as her ravenous guests made quick work of theirs.

Finished first, Livia sipped the last of her coffee and filled the empty air, with a few of Cate's old hockey stories. The best one was their first year, of play, when the red-and-white Kick Ice Bears still called themselves the Hockey Honeys. All decked-out in hot pink, on black jerseys and socks, they stormed Route 401 toward their first big tournament hosted by the Brampton Candadettes.

The Honey's stick handling was not too awfully bad, in their first game against the Moo Moos of Livestock Trucking; however - their second game was something else. The Honeys faced off with an experienced team, from Prince Edward Island, which quickly initiated then to clean but searing Canadian play. To make matters worse, during an early time-out a Honey overheard an opponent say, "It's so nice to play here, with other women. Our island is so remote; we only have men's teams to scrimmage." Well, PEI scored lots and the Honeys did not; therefore, the Canadien tournament rules called for the remaining three minutes of play, with a running clock. Once again, the face-off came to the Honey's zone, and Cate motioned her teammates to get into the net behind her. Four teammates climbed in, as the other team circled the blue line and quizzically scanned the bench and their coaches' faces. The clock kept running - as the Honey's remaining forward, Brandy, skated circles at the far blue line cackling like a banshee; that was, until both referees blew down the play.

All was taken, in good humor, but the referees did throw one of Cate's teammates in the box, as they do for goalies, until the game ended —with and embarrassing score: 16-0. Both teams shook hands in the line-off. The Prince Edward team — being the best of sports — asked if the Honeys had team pins to trade, because they loved Yankee collectibles. Sitting the bench, with a torn hip tendon, goalie #8 leaned across the divider and whispered to the Canadienne assistant coach, "Please be careful calling all of us 'Yanks' – people down south don't take lightly to it." That got her a big hug. He told her he got a taste of that during his last visit, with his in-laws, who wintered at Hilton Head.

In the locker room, the Honeys waited quietly for the usual pep talk, and they pinned their coaches to the wall. What were they thinking? Coach John and Coach Ned explained that Brampton registered more than 250 teams, in 12 levels. They registered the Honeys; in a pool, at least two levels above their skill level, so they and Fraser's B-team could play C-level at the same rink. Needless to say, the coaches barely made it home alive. Having learned their hockey well in Canada, The Honeys changed their name and skated on new home ice the next fall.

Two stories later, they settled down by sucking breaths, clearing their throats, and asking for another story. Livia explained how tiny Cheboygan, Michigan built and managed their new rink. Confessing that she and Margaret had once envisioned an ice rink in the cool air, of Mauna Kea's southern flank, she noted that was no longer their location of choice; however, they would still need plenty of contributors and volunteers.

Ma shrugged. Looking to Aye, "Maybe when we get a bit more time, we'll do a little brainstorming with a Realtor. You know some entrepreneurs up there, don't you?"

Aye nodded. "Might be something to consider. But first, can we have one more story?"

Livia set the stage, once more, stating that the Hockey Honeys were the first team in their league. In the Detroit Metro Area, the city and some sixty suburbs that supported one rough and tumble girls' league, but no senior women's league. That was the late 1980s, and women over twenty had no place to play — plus the fact: very few colleges or universities had teams, except along the Eastern Seaboard. Her girlfriend, Brandy, while playing golf, found a hockey notice, which Mina tacked-up on the clubhouse bulletin board. Those two plus eight more women, mostly over thirty, practiced twice a week, at 6:00 AM. After a year of scrimmaging one local private high school and a few university club teams, they organized five teams into the Metro Skaters' Hockey League. "Nowadays the league is known as the Michigan Senior Women's Hockey League with over forty teams in five divisions. And to think, when I first sketched the Bear's logo – I had to fight my own team, to get 'Women's Hockey' stitched, into our chenille emblems. At first our captain argued with me, so I asked her –'Do you wanna explain why your name is on your son's or husband's hockey jacket?' That settled it, and I got my lettering."

Ice time was extremely hard to secure, in that most the rinks favored beer-guzzling men, or most evenings were busy with kids. Eventually, more rinks were built. The women promoted themselves better, cajoled well-heeled sponsors, and secured ice time in various matronly ways. In early 1992, when all was beginning to roll along pretty freaking fine, Michigan's governing board deemed all senior women's teams as rostering B-level players. –Not!

"Yep, MAHA's gavel, rather than a good ole hockey stick, blew the back-end out of most every player's panties. Before 1992, a ringer signed up with Howell's fledgling team. Her specialties were a wrap the net score, or falling down and drawing penalties for a larger player – whom she fell under. One player sat out a year, per league regulations, before stepping down a level of play. With only two tiers of players, most teams got greedy and scouted. The candidates were mostly aging Inter-City League players, who tired of being thumped on, wanted more civil play. A few more years, and they poured into every team – except maybe two. The next winter an upper level team, The Blade Runners, picked up a woman called Chuckie – well, we called her Truckie. I never understood, with her talent, why she played us beginning players. What was that all about? I mean – what is the sport in that? Nice woman, but her shots could knock a hole in a brick wall. Although, for many a game, Cate held her and the Runners off at 1:1. In one local tournament, she went down and we lost –after four overtimes." Livia noticed her audience sagging a bit and wound it up: "The league finally registered enough teams, to pull off five divisions, and leveled the playing field a bit better."

Ma admitted that sounded like terrible fun. "Wasn't it dangerous?"

"Yeah – right! Like you mean surfing and shark bites aren't?" Livia got a really good chuckle before admitting, "I guess so. My hip injury makes for a mighty fine barometer, and a teammate skated backwards and fell on my back in practice. My skates were jammed, blades tight against the boards, and she nearly broke my knee. Oh - and I broke two fillings, even with a mouth guard in. Cate tops the cake — she played her last nine seasons wearing two $700 Graphite knee braces. There were painfully silly times too. There were jokes about the blue line grabbing someone's skates; i.e., toe picking or falling backwards mid-ice where there's nothing there but thin ice over blue paint. Worst accident I ever saw was a teammate in a nondescript scuffle. Five-feet behind my net, her skate blade wedged in an ungroomed crevice at the boards. She slumped to the ice and barely moaned – her ankle having snapped above the boot. The tournament stopped – till they carried her off, on a stretcher. Not me — I bellowed like a calf when my shoulder got shoved a bit out of socket."

Aye and Ma swallowed hard. They chose not to one-up Livia, with surfing disasters. She helped Ma carry breakfast boxes down the back stairs, to the dumpster, when Ma's cell phone chirped. She retrieved it from her apron pocket, as Aye rounded the corner with the last armload of orchids. Covering the receiver, she whispered, with her lips nearly touching Livia's ear, "It is Cate. She needs you back, as quickly as possible."

Aye and Livia packed, as Ma quietly the details. "Kona Hospital called. Tim will be released this afternoon, as soon as a family member can get there and sign him out. An ambulance has been scheduled to take him home. Margaret will be on call and can meet you. Page her as soon as you get there."

Most everyone knew Tom's situation from having attempted to sign Tim's release papers. The resident in charge told Tom that the hospital's legal department stipulated a blood relative must sign a patient out. As luck would have it, two days ago, the island grapevine placed Tim's father, Kaloki, in Kauai. Actually, he had been there a few weeks for business. Cate told Ma they had been notified, only moments ago. Chakra was not a blood relative, or else she would have signed the release. Livia figured if they left for Kona immediately, Aye could get to the hospital first. If they could get Tim home, without all the painkillers - then he could sign new documents, in Tom's behalf, for the circuit court judge to review.

His signature would avert a major confrontation, which had surfaced nearly two weeks prior; when Kaloki had Tom served with papers stating that he was to be off, of the Queens' Stables property, within twenty days. Also delivered was a fifteen-year-old Durable Power Of Attorney. Tom's lawyer confirmed the documents were enforceable for business and real estate purposes. Tim had rewritten his medical papers thus naming Tom, as his attorney in fact; although, he failed to list him in any other documents. In theory - once Tim was released from the hospital, Kaloki could control his every asset and property. If he chose to place his son, in a convalescent center, Tim might be kept too drugged to make his own decisions. Without a circuit court judge's prompt reversal, or approval of a new document, Tim and Tom might permanently loose the stables.

After the accident the women assured Tom he was free, to sleep on the couch, or pay housekeeping and sleep in guest suite. Livia helped him locate Tim's father - whose Internet business correspondence placed him, in Kauai. The past few months, Kaloki did not return Tim or Aye's phone messages.

Ma gave quick hugs, before they rushed off to Kona. For a few hours, the sun would still be at their back. The ride home was a solemn one. Aye broke the silence. "You know, I just can't help thinking I could have done more for him," conceded Aye.

Livia swallowed hard then adamantly shook her finger at him. "Don't you say such a thing! It is never easy when it's family, plus it was in a dire circumstance."

To that, he hung his head. "No. I meant years ago, when Tim was only a baby. Hawaiians have a custom, 'hanai,' by which we adopt relatives out. I was the oldest brother, and I could have sent him to another island when everyone assumed he was my son."

"You mean illegitimate son."

"Yes. Everyone saw the resemblance, and because of my early years of carousing, they assumed Tim was mine - but he was my brother Keno's son. It was a secret that I kept, from all except Chakra. Keno, my youngest brother, looked up to me. As an undercover police officer, he easily became addicted to drugs. His one night indiscretion, with a red-light madam, resulted in Tim's birth; that is how he is a cousin to Ma. After Keno overdosed repeatedly, I thought I was helping everyone by keeping the truth from his wife. Somehow, for the longest time, I figured that Keno strayed and had problems because I had not given him enough attention. After his death, I asked Kaloki to adopt Tim. Actually, all I wanted was for him to keep an eye on Tim. I disregarded our customs of sending him to relatives on another island. Living here, he missed a proper new start. Oh – if hindsight were foresight; I should have kept Tim and done my best for him."

Livia patted his shoulder, admitting, "Yeah, life can be a real heartbreaker; I know about families. My mother died wondering what she had done, because her family split apart over various estates. I told her that she was in the wrong place at the wrong time. She got between her relatives and money. 'So sad,' she would say. Then, let them have it. I guess I don't know them.' She wasn't rich, but she had enough assets to keep her dignity and mine."

Aye patted her on the shoulder and said, "Chakra says, 'Sometimes humility precedes greatness.' I think most people would forego greatness for true love." In a few minutes, he continued. "Kaloki was the perfect father figure until he lost his job because of a gambling venture, at one of the major resorts. With loss of income, his greed surfaced. Passed over in the family trust fund, he wanted the Kona stables for development property. He will rezone the land and ruin those makai pastures in a heartbeat. The soil up there will not take the bulldozing — you know that. All along here, you've seen it."

"Whoa!" spat Livia. Slow down. I am still processing the fact that Kaloki is not Tim's father. Although the land is not from your family, once Tim gained ownership of the stables, as his blood uncle, you have as much right to oversee his estate, as does Kaloki – maybe even more so. Petition the court. If Tom is not Tim's next of kin, then you must be - at least for the time being. I'll loan you the money if you need legal counsel."

"Money is not necessary. So many years, so many ruined relationships – I just hate dredging up the memories."

His chest heaved heavily. Livia worried about him, having started a new regime of medications, since his last blood test. She probably should not have - but she said, "Sometimes I wonder if maybe we are given responsibilities to test our merit." Chiding herself, she switched gears: "Oh, well — times have changed, at least a little bit. I say let the dead rest; you did what you could while Tim's mother was still alive.

Just be glad that you are here for him now. Give him your best, at least till Tom is allowed to take up the slack."

They bumped down the final half of Saddle Road, and her eyes darted, from Mauna Loa to Mauna Kea, and back again. She could not seem to keep her mouth shut. "You know, why not go for it all? Ask the court to appoint you along with Tom, as Tim's conservator – till he gets well. That shouldn't ruffle as many feathers. Who knows? Tom's holding of Tim's medical power of attorney and your standing in the community may sway the judge's opinion in your favor." Noticing a far away look in Aye's eyes she concluded, "Okay– well, I'll hush up now."

He turned and stared at her. "Were you an attorney in Michigan?"

"No," moaned Livia, "But my father was one back in Indiana."

"Well, where do you get these ideas?"

Her chin dropped but she kept her eyes on the road. "I read a lot, in addition to some awful family experiences – not my parents, mind you. Plus - I went to a lot of meetings, and I listened in, on a lot of legal advice that was given on the phone. I wonder if he noticed my little ears pricked up, in the background." She saw her father's bright eyes and considered that he was no doofus, so maybe he did.

Aye cleared his throat and said, "Oh– most likely–."

She smiled and chuckled to herself, hearing Margaret's 'no answer is ever simple…' as they headed up the hill to Honalo. She considered her formative years as the miles passed quickly.

Aye grinned, leaning closer. "And, anything else?"

She glanced, in the rearview mirror. Squinting from the tropical sun she said, "Well – my favorite book and movie was…"

"*To Kill a Mockingbird*?"

"How did you know?"

A left turn, at the stoplight, and the car chugged up the hill to the hospital; Aye finished his thought. "Oh — just, getting to know– you." They both enjoyed a moment of quiet, until recognizing Kaloki's car in the lot.

Stepping up to the ER entrance, Livia punched the door touch pad. "All right, Clyde, here we go; we're gonna spring Tim from the authorities."

"Right after you, Bonnie," said Aye in his best John Wayne - and they swaggered through the sliding doors.

"Damn! How'd you let me leave my derringer, in our Ford sedan? Well, we'll just have to take the place by storm." Livia dialed Margaret's pager muttering, "Oh, yeah– every goalie loves one helluva good shootout."

Aye quickened his pace to keep up. They rounded the corner and heard a faint trumpet charge: Tah, da-da, da, da-dah–! go off, on Margaret's pager. She and her huge physician's assistant, Terry, pinched them between their shoulders, as The Good Doctor leaned closer. "Good going – Kiddo. You arrived, in record time. Cate is on her way; she has my parking pass."

Livia whispered back, "Never seen our team get dressed, so fast."

Aye nodded. "Yes - well, we may need them. That is Kaloki and his lawyer right there."

Margaret grinned. "All– righty! They are heading around, to the ambulance bay. We will head them off, at the pass." She patted an orderly's back and posted him, at the doctors' entrance, telling him, "Wait here for Cate and Tom." Pointing Aye and Livia to the smaller door, she said, "Follow me, we are taking the short cut. Don't forget, once Kaloki and company enter the ER, the puck has been dropped."

Aye fell in step, beside Livia, and he whispered, "I think she means 'their arses are mine'." On their way to the ER, she heard all sorts of muffled ill-natured bantering – as the EMS rolled Tim in, through the visitors' door.

Margaret hovered and cooed, "How are you darling?" Turning to Livia and Aye, she snapped her fingers and said, "Oh, darn — those maintenance papers, I filled out, must have finally gone through to fix the doors. You know how finicky automatic doors can be."

Livia smirked, as Aye tucked the lovely azure quilt, with appliquéd deep raspberry triangles, around Tim's neck before gesturing and invoking something Hawaiian.

In a pinch, Livia could bat her brown eyes and lie with the best of them. However, today Cate came off, as the heavy hitter. Apparently, she had contacted Benkins back in Detroit. Obviously, he had rustled up a bit, of the Aloha State's legal assistance. Briefcase in hand, a well-dressed man marched up to Aye, and with a firm handshake - he introduced himself. "Pleased to meet you. I am Akamu Harrington, ACLU champ – if I don't mind saying so."

Kaloki and his lawyer eventually gained access, through the hospital's main entrance, and arrived at Tim's bedside after everyone had assembled. The big-city lawyer took a step back, as Tim's wide eyes followed Mr. Harrington's briefcase being set head-level on his bedside tray.

At Mr. Harrington's insistence, and a little hustle from Margaret, Tim was discharged and quickly transferred to the ambulance bay. In less than thirty minutes, his tiny entourage followed his gurney up the hillside walkway to Queens' Stables. Four mighty strapping Hawaiians, three men and one formidable-looking woman, flanked Tim and Tom's apartment entrance.

Livia glanced sideways at Cate. "Umm, Chakra must have called in some help." At least they did not sport black shirts and ties. Short of step, she strode off muttering, "The more you know, the less you wanna know."

"Guess we can go home now," was all she could muster, as she nodded from Aye to the Jeep. "I need it later this evening. Please bring it back when you're done."

Sporting a grin, he thanked her, adding, "Please I'll check on Chakra, and I won't be too long." He nodded at the tattooed guards. Arms crossed over their chests. "Cousin Beulah, from Kohala, grows them big."

Livia grinned. "Uh, yeah, Paniolo Patrol – wouldn't want to meet up with these four in a dark alley."

Aye returned to sit with Tim, and Livia and Cate headed home. They warmed up some leftover and Livia quipped, "See, I told you this was a good idea, years ago. But no, it takes someone else's prodding for a plate lunch of cabbage rolls." Not waiting for the microwave to heat, she swirled a roll, in tomato sauce, and nibbled it from her fingers.

"Fine. You made your point. They were all I had, so Chakra and I ate them for supper. Your peachy salsa dumped in the sauce made them an instant favorite. I may market them. Do you mind if I give them a kitschy name?"

Livia shook her head no. "I would expect no less. Something really Russian would be cute. What's the name that your family calls them?"

"Golubtsy. So– what sounds good with that? How about something that rolls off the tongue, like Golubtsy Nui or `Oi Loa Golubtsy? Guess we'd need a real translator for that. We could stuff tiny cabbage or ti leaves with rice mixed with fish, turkey sausage, or some vegan filling. I never told you about my Ojibwa great-grandmother from up past Marquette. She stuffed them with venison mixed with wild turkey. She also used turtle, but I couldn't do that."

These were rare glimpses – but Cate's family stories never failed to amaze Livia. They gave up agreeing on a meat filling, but decided on a popping open a couple of beers. Keeping busy until Margaret's arrival, she hauled out several cookbooks and scribed, as Cate checked on recipes and NHL playoffs on the Internet. Livia asked, "Anything else in our e-mail?"

"Nah – just the usual."

Light woofs and the kitch-kitch of Lotus' nails sent them scrambling through the pantry and out the door, to the side lanai.

The lanai light caught Aye seated on the path below, jamming his boots against the inn's foundation. Repositioning and tugging on his crowbar he pulled against the ground fault outlet, seated between carport and back steps.

Livia gasped, "What the…?" as Cate completed her thought. "No, really. In all seriousness — what in the world are you doing?"

He said, "Well, Chakra is fine, Tim's asleep, and this outlet needed fixing for some time."

Exchanging glances, with Livia, Cate said, "And I thought we were bad at keeping busy." Then she took no prisoners, as she said, "Get IN the kitchen!" pointing the way, with the neck of her bottle.

Livia pointed hers too, then set it right down, and boosted Aye to his feet. "Worrying is unproductive. You don't drink, but it's high time you did. Do you realize what an exceptional set of bartenders you have here? Catie Pat's gonna fix you a Ukraine Hammer, and she doesn't do that for just anybody."

In Cate's clutches, he was escorted to the kitchen table. Seated across from him, Livia deftly stared down her prey. He sat still, except for fingering the red-and-white checkered tablecloth.

Cate called off the ingredients. "Here goes. An iced tea glass, crushed ice, jigger and a half of snappy citrus Stoli, juice half a lime; fill her up with ginger ale. Livia, please bring me a few springs of mint and lavender.

Livia made a face and jumped halfway to the silverware drawer. Grabbing a knife, she pointed it across the room at Aye's nose. Leveling her sights at him she hissed, "Don't move an inch; I'll be right back." In a flash, she reappeared with a fistful of herbs.

"Geez o Pete, Little Miss — I'm not making drinks for an army. While you're up, grab another Labatt's for me."

Aye sat nose-to-nose with the awesome concoction. Both women leaned in, as he gingerly sipped it through a real bamboo straw. About the time Margaret opened the door, he was grinning to beat the band. Wiggling his glass at Cate, he said, "Not quite shabby. Got another?"

The screen door slapped shut, nearly missing Margaret's feet, as she set down her briefcases. "What the hell have you been doing to him?"

Livia and Cate shrugged and both replied, "What?" Livia raised her glass. "Two toasts: to our good friend, Aye, and to Tim's safe return."

Margaret nodded deeply before making a beeline for the fridge.

Another drink and they headed down the path, like moths to the porch light. Cate checked on Chakra, as Aye showed Livia a freshly potted rose. Eyeing Cate through the window, she also noticed a batch of new baby orchids poking out from under the deck. She knelt at the cottage's northeast corner post, and pulled them out for a better look. Rotating the sealed clear plastic bag she examined pieces, of finger sized grayish-white aerial roots, wrapped in dark cloth, as Aye's shadow fell across her.

"Felt a bit restless, so I went to the cove after lunch. You were busy cooking something, and I hated to interrupt because it smelled so good."

More facts were good; although, it did not deter her. She lay the bag down. These objects resembled old chicken thigh or finger bones. She looked up and whispered, "The old junior high teacher don't buy that one. Try again." She gingerly lifted the bag to the porch light. "What's in here?"

"A few small bones."

Livia never flinched, quizzically asking, "Mana? So you can get Chakra better?"

He just shrugged and smiled.

Obviously, he steered clear of the subject, by explaining, they would soon be returned to their resting place. Livia did not interrupt. He told her details, of helping raise Tim - whom everyone assumed to be his own son. That lie had nearly ruined his marriage, for the love of his life: his wife, Lena, figured he had an affair with Tim's mother. Tim was his brother's child, and Aye kept the secret, ultimately garnering his wife's doubts, for an act not his own. He added that most, of his family, and Lena's, basically disowned him. Though he had no time to test her words, on the morning of the tsunami, Lena professed her forgiveness to him. Livia patted Aye's hand. From where he worked, he watched the nearly twenty-foot wave surge up Hilo River, taking out the railroad, and realized most of his family was lost. He buried his wife and half his children. The others soon ostracized him. Only Tim and Chakra stayed by his side.

They brought Tim down from master bedroom, to the lanai, on the eve of Good Friday. Livia could see Tom watching over him, as she futzed about the stables spreading fresh hay and pouring milk over the barn cats' supper. With that done, she headed to the house and turned on a few lights before heading home. Possum followed, gently nipping at her heels. It was his playful little game, probably taught by his older mate, Gabby. Tim encouraged the dogs' herding instincts, which came in handy, to keep guest riders on the steep trails. Gabby or Army had always followed the rear horse - the job now left to Possum. When he and Livia crossed the front paddock, they found Aye leaning forward, on the rattan rocker, scratching Army's white ruff. He looked up and told her that he and Chakra were satisfied with Tim's progress.

Every evening, the women gathered for a few brief minutes, as Margaret kept them abreast of Tim's health. The months that followed were productive, in that Tim rapidly improved. The physical therapy sessions helped his coordination and strength, and his mind was exceptionally clearer. He no longer required his evening sedatives. Without them, he immediately began scribbling a few messages. That greatly assured Tom but he began to show signs of exhaustion. Livia and Cate took turns watching Tim, so Tom could get a full night's sleep. When they stayed over, Tim seemed to relax a little too – that was, until it was bath time. Both women assured him that he had nothing they had not seen before, and he accepted their help. They joked and kidded around, for what else could you do? Mother Demi and Cate took care of Ursula after a horrible traffic accident that left her impaired for nearly three years. Livia told Tim, over and over again, how she often commented, "I'm not a nurse," as she tended her father and mother those last years.

Tim laughed until he hiccupped, and required a good dose of Thorazine, followed by Cate's rendition of Livia's jingle: "Depend on Depends." She stopped when tears welled in his eyes, and Thorazine could not cure that. Cate rubbed his back and joked. "Would have been nice, if Kimberly Clark had bought her lyrics. She tried so hard to market them, but they said so many satisfied customers sent them songs."

To that, Tim politely asked them both, "Shut up." He was back.

The Good Doctor still checked on him before going to work - at least a couple times a week. Sometimes Livia would just walk down to help Tom with chores while Tim walked the inner border of the outer paddock. By sharing teaching stories, she found it greatly helped to get Tom's mind off things. Both had some doozies. His favorite was Livia's - cheerleader and the cockroach story, and hers was Tom's 'Teacher and the Law' graduate paper in which he fabricated asinine situations, to limit liability, and stave off lawsuit-happy parents. The main point they agreed on, was that the general public would never fully appreciate their stories.

Livia laughed, saying her faculty nicknames ranged from Biker Babe and Sr. Celestial, to well - worse. "One day I wore a black-leather vest, and my students teased me, 'Where's your motorcycle'?" She sat quietly, then said, "Eleven years I devoted to them, and I wasn't even Catholic. You'd think a light would have gone on, somewhere in my head, when the parish council began downsizing my school. Later my analyst said, 'What were you thinking? Even the un-nuns jumped ship'."

Tom said, "And those parent-teacher conferences – weren't they to die for?" I had this one little darling who was doing her damnedest to run, I mean ruin, my 6th period class. Not till her father unexpectedly stuck his nose to the tiny window, in the classroom door, did he set her in the hallway. Said her bossiness had never surfaced at home, and that one time I got an apology. There was a boy, who did the same; to this day, I think they put him up to it."

Before Livia left for college at seventeen, Annabelle reminded her of two things: "Teaching had definitely changed, in the past twenty-five years," and "The principal sets the flavor of the school; get a weak one and you might as well look for a new job." All Livia's book-learning never trumped her mother's words – well, that and her own liberal generation of parents who often just did not spend enough quality time with their children. "Why have children if you could not, or would not, stay home and raise them?"

Tom agreed. That was the only reason that he and Tim had not adopted or hired a surrogate – well that, and they would have to find day care. Livia agreed, saying that she had no children, because St. Seaton's never paid enough, and they kept 80-days worth of her sick leave pay. Although, she enjoyed her automotive work and loved being able to check in on her parents – hard work and diligence never equaled any job stability. Tom laughed and cried with her, and the next day they started a new project instead of stories.

Chapter 18: `Ohana

Livia pulled her long hair high into a high ponytail and hurried home from the stables, to share Tim's stories with Cate. Stepping off the highway, she leaned hard into the blustery wind. Hands smoothed across the cool front desk - she followed faint country music upstairs. Two Pullman suitcases sat empty, as Willie crooned *On the Road Again*.

"Is there a problem – something I should know?"

Cate's small shoulders lifted and fell, and she slowly turned around.

"Mom called." Cate sighed. "Her dentist found gum disease, and she needs weeks of a specialist's work - around nearly every tooth. You know, with Daddy's diabetes, he cannot drive her every day and stay any length of time across town, because The Ma fell with the laundry basket – second time this month, and broke three ribs. Heimi said, 'It's finally come; they're a mess'."

"I barely made out the details with Mom sobbing and all. I knew this would happen, if she got sick again. Ma and Daddy's internist sat them down, as he did three years ago, and he insisted they move to an assisted living facility – that or she must move them to her house. Mom said she figured they would grumble: 'You're shipping us off, to and old-age home!' Surprise, surprise– they agreed to list their quad-level again, and it sold. Now, they have less than 90 days to move, and it looks I must return to Michigan for a while."

Livia's hands got cold. All she could think of was her first years in Hawaii. Finally, she eked out, "Okay" but she could not look at Cate. "Guess we'll take care of the place without you - for a while."

"You mean *you* can run it for a while. Margaret's heart is as big as her checkbook, but between Richard and work - she won't be much help."

"Yeah, you're right." She looked at her toes. It was not, as though she had not prepared for this. Arms tightly crossed, at her waist, Livia kept quiet, as Cate reiterated how, two years ago, she and Demi moved the seniors to a historic Fortson bungalow. Months later, they hated it. Their quad-level had not sold, so they moved back home. Livia listened and appreciated her parent's ability to adapt. Aging presented them with hardships, but they rarely lived life in the shadows. She chuckled at her mother's words: "I'm not sitting around waiting, for any Grim Reaper. He's gonna have to catch me!"

Cate interrupted, "It's not funny! The house I was raised in sold yesterday - and you're smiling?" Mom told me to come home and help Ma and Daddy pack. She is moving them into her house.

"Sorry." Livia knew Demi did not want Cate tied down. Yet, she never functioned, as well, without her.

"Well, shit. You know how Ursula can be. My baby sister: Miss Ego Supreme – come to think of it: the acorn does fall far from the oak or sapling. She gets around Mom, heads butt – and Ursula walks. Ten miles away, and it can be half a year before she calls again."

Livia rubbed her throat so she could breathe. She fought back the tears, but frankly — most of this did not involve her. Arguing only hurt Cate; so as usual, she would hold everything else together. She caught Cate, on the upbeat, and met little resistance leading her to the fridge.

Cate kept talking and Livia kept serving. After putting Cate to bed, she switched off the house phone and explained the predicament to Margaret. An hour later, they looked up. Cate's cell phone was ringing again. When Mother Demi got upset, the time difference meant nothing. The phone woke them three more times that night. They sat up and snoozed, and it repeated. Sometime around 5:00, both squinted, as the house phone slammed down.

Livia whispered, "Valium?"

"You want some?" asked Margaret.

"No! For Demi! All this and she still hangs up on Cate."

Two hours of quiet and they poured a hot tea and coffee.

Mid-morning Cate came to the table. She snapped a sugar cookie in half and said, "What would you think if I tell my mom I'll come home for six months?"

Livia rolled her eyes and handed her a mug of tea. "Thanks for asking, but I can't give the answer you want to hear. –Do what you must. I'll be here."

Cate's family had very few close friends so there was no backup. Livia tried not to let it upset her. She figured the best way, to support Cate, was hard plus a little fun, in her own life.

That was it. In a week Cate was gone.

Back at home, Livia could not forget Cate touching her hand through the barrier at the airport. All that week, she had nightmares. Cate's image receded, into a distant forest, at the edge of which Mother Demi's face became more distinct. Who would fill her place, as caretaker of Cate's relatives? Not Ursula. Livia could not complain; she and Jonathan had not kept close tabs on his family back in Indiana. Well, it was different now. They purchased the inn with plans, for adding an Ohana wing for Cate's family. Livia tossed back another sleeping tablet and shifted Lotus to the corner, of her bed - where they usually woke in a tangle when Margaret knocked, on the door each morning.

During the next two months, Cate called every other day. Margaret took Livia to Shetima's, for beef teriyaki every Friday – except for an occasional lobster and filet at The Outback. Their fun Friday nights ended once business picked up mid-October. November and the whales came; so did more tourists. For some reason, the humpbacks mesmerized mainlanders. Retirees would book Maui condos, for a couple weeks, then follow the whale migration to The Big Island. Senior flight attendants, on layovers, compared this piece of Old Hawaiiana right up there, with working late evening flights.

Relishing the regular guests' company Livia walked, to the mailbox, and remembered the little surprises Cate always planned for holidays and birthdays. Without cookies, hiding presents, and toasts of Brut champagne – the memories brought a rare nagging headache. She began carrying the shopping list, to the mailbox – especially at Christmas, birthdays, and Easter.

The phone calls always came, from Cate's end - after Livia dialed, let it ring three times and hung up; in as much as, Granny Alexia resurrected her old habit, of grabbing the phone and setting it down - if it took too long to connect. When Cate did get through, Mother Demi consistently interrupted their conversations. Late-evening calls, to Cate's cell phone, found both her and the phone worn out, from everyone's calling rituals and her own chores. Livia hated phone conversations, and instead she wrote letters once a week.

Mid-July, Livia sorted mail ditching the junk and separating the bills. Underneath the mess was a letter from Cherise. Fingering the pink envelope most the morning, she dropped it on the kitchen table. Since Cherise's first arrival times passed, without incidence, the letter slipped Livia's mind.

A couple days later Margaret found the pink envelope, and after lunch, Livia sat quietly and read the letter.

My Dearest Livia,

Thanks for sending your inn's advertisement flyer. Sorry for my untimely response. I had waiting on five graduate schools' acceptance letters, and I never whole-heartedly considered University of Hawaii, until you wrote.

I called U of H – Manoa, and I was immediately accepted. Although their Web site shows plans of a new community college near the Kona airport, my graduate program demands that I be on the Hilo campus twice a week.

I am still hitching a ride, on an Olivia cruise ship, and wondered if I might bunk at your inn. I will work for room and board. If not, please suggest lodgings. Let me know. (614) 711- 4211. Either way - I hope to see you soon.

All My Love, Cherise

Livia's jaw dropped. They had not seen each other for nearly twenty years. The spring after her divorce, Livia spent an Easter weekend with her in Columbus. Having quit college late in her junior year, when her father died, Cherise switched gears and graduated in social work from Ohio State – then she finished another degree in accounting. The early 1980s were all about money, but later social work was her love. A few years back, she wrote and said medication for lupus and a rare arthritis kept her from adequately tending her caseload. Now, after a short stint in Lexington, as a bluegrass stable manager, she decided to study astronomy at the University of Hawaii. She would like to visit Kona and possibly work for board. Livia's Achilles' Heel was that she always idolized Cherise's free spirit.

Livia discussed Cherise's letter with Margaret. She agreed to a free room and to share food expenses, when and if, she stayed for more than two weeks. Livia called her longtime friend. It was agreed. She would be an asset at the inn, at least until Cate returned.

This time, Cherise included details. Leaving Long Beach the ship would arrive, in two weeks. She intended to phone, when they cast off from Hilo, so Livia could pick her up from Kailua. Cherise listed details about the voyage and listed all the Hawaii ports of call: Honolulu and Turtle Bay on Oahu, Lihue and Princeville on Kauai, Lahaina and Wailuku on Maui – even Kaluaaha on Molokai, then

Hilo and Kailua. Boy – she could get a grand first impression of the islands.

The day came, and they got her to the inn with two beat-up pieces of luggage. After a couple of hours of food, drinks, and song - she wandered off to bed. Margaret had another drink and said her face reminded her of Eleanor Roosevelt's voice. Truth was - she never aged as well as Livia had.

The next morning, Livia's keen nose led her to the kitchen where Cherise stood over a frying pan of bacon and eggs. They plopped down, to full plates, and thumbed through an old pamphlet: *Thangs Yankees Don' Know.*

In addition, Cherise kept a steady flow of cooking on the table – both morning and evening. One morning it was fried ham, hominy and tomato gravy; that night it was fried chicken, buttermilk biscuits and Poke Sallet. A bottle of wine and thangs got a whole lot more friendly.

They talked about - how earlier that morning Livia watched the cottage for any stirrings, then she sent Aye poke hunting. With a freshly printed botanical description in hand, he set out on his mission. Early afternoon he handed over the plant and watched, as Cherise nibbled leaves testing the poke for allergic reactions. She once read that pokeberries and any red stems were poisonous. Aye eyed both women and went home muttering something, about how much quicker he could have located the plant, if he had known they wanted common inkberry. Cherise swallowed, and with her usual Mona Lisa smile she announced, "This was my dad's favorite vegetable when we lived in Tennessee. Two years we were in Knoxville - before moving to Missouri."

Livia met the Methodist minister only once. A very likable chap, he scared the pants off her and Cherise - driving up and down Cincinnati's hilly slums and nearly clipping off car door handles. Soon after that visit, he died suddenly from a heart attack. Cherise was twenty - and being the youngest of four children, she moved back home to help her mother. Livia had barely turned eighteen when she began dating Jonathan Easinus. Young love. Perfectly oblivious – she married, at twenty, and waltzed through five faithful years, of country living, followed by two more in Michigan. She washed underwear and helped John rise through the corporate ranks. Live and learn.

Watching the driveway, for the usual Thursday rush, Livia listened as Cherise teased about how they first met in college. Livia nervously reminded Cherise, about hitting on her, after her divorce ten years later. They ate a fine diner of home fries, coleslaw, and baked mahi mahi, and Cherise revisited old college days. "You only turned eighteen when we broke up, and you landed in the hospital with double pneumonia. Three weeks later, you returned to school. So diligent you were about studying, just to finish that winter quarter - and I had to go ask you, to fill in, on my date with Johnny. I was hoping to end his advances, if he liked you better." That was so selfish, and I'm sorry."

"Thank you; that means a lot." Livia toyed with her water glass. "I don't think of it much but that night seems like yesterday. He graciously took me to a movie after leaving you at the dorm. The next day I wrote him an apology – which led to blah, blah, blah. Wish you hadn't played matchmaker – but it's the past now." In situations like this - Cate and Annabelle's favorite quote was 'Offense is the best defense.' Livia laid it down, "Remember the first time we met, and you took me to Miss Nancy's Teahouse? We both still lived in Brentwood Hall. I was a bit of a voyeur, watching you practice with the university's marching band across the street. Afterwards, I followed you back to your room. Even from down the hall, you looked a bit peaked, so I decided to check in on you."

Cherise chuckled, "Yeah, I was sick — stupid lovesick. I was pining over my roommate, for spending too many weekends in Indianapolis, with her boyfriend. Then this cute little freshman knocked on my door. I asked you to come in and promptly pushed you down on the bed." She hung her head and said, "How bad I feel, to this day, for leading you down the lavender lane."

Livia about died. The words 'defense strategy overkill' came to mind – and to make matters worse - "I don't think so," slipped out - followed by, "I could not have been over four, when I started fighting my mother about not wearing dresses and go-go boots.

Cherise had experienced much of the same – and she cited a recent study, by Northwestern University researchers, who labeled their behavior 'Childhood Gender Unconformity'. "The worst was a crush on my gym teacher at ten; pretty normal, except it lasted five years. At twenty-five, I went home for my mother's big auction — and there, carved in my headboard was a fourth grader's script: Maria VonaTrap. Remember how she ran across that pristine Austrian meadow? Last month, she was a guest on Larry King. Still has that infectious laugh, as she told him that famous scene was nearly not finished; in that, the film crew's helicopter rotors kept blowing her down."

As Livia looked up and noticed the first tinges of a blazing sunset, Cherise hugged her and sniffed back the tears.

Lotus followed them around the garden path. Comfortable chitchat soothed old wounds. Livia said, "Our crazy dorm life - do you remember the first Friday night we went to Miss Nancy's? We liked to wore ourselves out the rest of that weekend. Went back the next evening, to see Tippy Reese and her revue. What was it called? Oh, Yeah. 'Accent on Presentation'. Who-ee! Did our waitress *present* in skimpy serving apparel!"

Livia refocused, on some pretty foggy images, as Cherise continued from a different perspective. "Well-meaning, as your parents were – by suggesting you attend Evanburgh's small university and avoid reactionary protests, such as Kent State's, and the flower-power politics of Indiana's state universities – they sent you right into the likes of me! If they only knew their old college, turned university, still had religious ties to its Methodist founders. Who was to know that ministers' children had almost no tuition? Her parents sent her straight into the arms of a P.K." She smiled. "Yes indeed, 'Free-loving Preachers' Kids,' we called ourselves."

Cherise and Evelyn, a senior, were the only two preacher's kids on Livia's dorm floor, and they were the wildest women she ever met (well except for her Canadian and Brandy). Evelyn had a penchant for tall and dark, and Cherise enthusiastically embraced diversity. Smirking, Livia wondered if Pearl ever suspected her extracurricular activities. Probably not, or she'd have died right then and there – waiting outside, in the parking lot, ready to take her to supper every Thursday. On the other hand, she was no dummy, and never wavered, from religiously taking her to supper.

Cherise revisited their Miss Nancy's escapades, and noticing Livia's smirk she filled in some more details. There were various revues, and in all fairness, she mentioned the Townie Girls' serving apparel. "They had everyone beat on presentation. If you could call them outfits - that 'Accent on Presentation' barely included four delicately embroidered white hankies. Two lace-edged triangles folded across two slender crocheted cords: two up and two down, front and rear."

They both roared. Cherise choked out, "Probably a prelude to today's 'thong.' Didn't we get free beverages?" She slapped Livia's knee. "And for anything over twenty dollars – we even got dessert and women's lib literature that was posted throughout the upstairs halls. Why, one couldn't concentrate properly unless one climbed, to the hot and more privately guarded third-floor lounges, for more intimate suppers or banquets."

Livia laughed and shoved her back. "The food wasn't much, but that service was truly extraordinary! Well– I mean– it was after you left school."

Cherise scowled, but never one to carry a grudge, she said, "As I remember – and it is hard, after so many years – Miss Nancy's changed hands a couple times, becoming Athena's, then The Underground when I returned that one semester. A regular restaurant went in, on the ground floor, and an outside stairs to the upper floors of what had been Miss Nancy's. Can't say the proprietors did not do their best to keep the place open."

"Yeah, but that was after I graduated and you came back to finish your degree. I heard the place got so raucous that they tore it down."

Cherise nodded, "Yeah, but before it became a dirty drug house, you could pressed a discreet buzzer to get up those narrow stairs to either entertainments – what a fire trap – you're right – I believe it's torn down now. Funny, now that you thing about it, some of the best customers were the few remaining sorority debs. And to think, because of their families and money - the local law authorities had to plant the drugs, to get the place closed down."

Livia attempted to calm Cherise. "Why– didn't you attend Ohio State and finish your master's in social work?" Short answer only, Livia decided to make the best of things by whipping up a couple frozen Mai Tais. Her old friend was a lifesaver, working hard all day to earn her board at the inn so Livia figured, the proper hostess, she choose banter over badger and reminisced. "Well, with our closed campus and Evanburgh not quite ready for casinos and table dancing – the Townie Girls' sure had a unique way of serving their pop, tea and cookies, with an 'accent on presentation'."

"Oh, yeah, I remember townies popping those cookies in half, with quite an *ac cent* and damn-near helping us eat 'em too."

Livia hesitated. "Wonder what happened to the sororities? They sure weren't the thing, in our day. My mother was a Castellan, but my parents never really imposed their convictions on me." Noticing Cherise's occasional quiet sips, she admitted, "Oh, there were the exceptions. One time he did comment about me living in Canada. Right before I moved there – he told me never to forget: 'It's still a foreign country.' Windsor didn't work. Couldn't get married. Couldn't buy into the business – boy, was that a blessing, in hindsight. Most that year, in Windsor, I kept watching Detroit's skyline – and I moved back."

Cherise said, "That was right after you visited me in Columbus. Did you really like it over there?"

"Yes, I did. Windsor, London and Toronto had a nice avant-garde lifestyle. But it's still not the United States.

Cherise delved a bit further and got the skinny on the whole place being awfully British. Then she heard how Livia rented out her Fortson home, to various tenants and again recently, as a Hawaii backup plan. The professional drummer came out, and her fingers drummed a cadence, as she added, "You know, I never have been materialistic, but I do kind of miss the old Buckeye State and some of my friends down in Missouri."

Livia laughed, "Some days I miss a place — that I really never knew."

"Where is that?"

"Pleasant Hill, Kentucky."

Cherise knew of the place. "I lived real close to there – well, sort of. Just a wide place in the road - it sits in the meadows, atop the Kentucky River's rugged cliffs, southeast of Lexington. Took a couple day trips there. One time we sat, on the lawn after lunch, and watched a man whittle some poplar wood. He spread out his handiwork and let the little boys and girls choose Whimmy Dittles or Pretty Poppits. Civil War stories tell – that the Shakers there depleted their storerooms feeding soldiers of both sides. Even back then, neighboring farmers didn't have much to do with them."

Then her voice turned dead serious. "You know, I think I prefer it here; you know — big part of me is an old hippie at heart. Last Tuesday, I drove through Hilo, trailed down, along the southeast shore, and found an incredible Olympic-size pool in Pahoa. After a relaxing swim, I grabbed an awesome hot dog, and the rest of the afternoon, I finished the circle tour 'round Puna's lower half – you know, down around Kaimu and Pualaa. I had read how quite a few gentle people own hostels over there. Might buy one - as my brother's estate left me a bit of change."

"Hmm – Puna, probably the district I know the least about. Never got further than Chain of Craters Road, well, that and the highway up from Hilo. Anyway, it sounds like a plan, or at least a reason for a couple day trips. Who knows? You just might meet someone special."

Cherise grinned, "Or import some friends; like you three did."

"I'm starving," said Livia. "Would you mind terribly if we get carry-out or some of your fried chicken? I bought a couple whole fryers yesterday; I even cut them up for you."

"Fried chicken – hum? Oh, that sounds yummy. She dug in both hands, and she and Cherise both got good and messy; and for once, Livia heard not a thing about making a mess in the kitchen. Mashed potatoes and white gravy made the perfect side dish. An extra pile sat, skins and all, for breakfast home fries. "I'll take some, to Aye and Chakra, after I throw together some chicken salad, with celery, grapes and pecans for our lunches tomorrow."

It tasted wonderful. Cherise loosened her jeans, and they pushed back from the table - both nearly about to bust at the seams.

They played something similar to Twenty Questions after Livia asked if Cherise still played in a rock band.

"Didn't a friend of yours write *Sweetbreads and Hominy at the Crossroads Grill?*" asked Cherise, as she cleared the dishes and piled a plate high with leftovers for Margaret.

"No. That was my Canadian who aspired to write novels, like her north of the border favorites: *Bilhah's Story* and *Names Of Favor*. I never heard if she published anything. You know, how sinfully hard it is — getting your first novel off the ground these days. And then, there's them that gets the trashiest things printed, by merely knowing or doing someone." Livia poured the last of Cate's sweet tea and set the glasses aside twin slivers, of day-old lemon meringue pie. The first bites brought puckered lips, and that prompted more silly faces. Wrong move - for not long after, they laughed so hard, it shook the table, and Cherise reached across the table, caressing her face.

Livia withdrew, sighing, "Don't get me wrong, you were always one of my hottest flames, but as I told you when John left – it's gone and I'm not interested."

As would a chivalrous knight, Cherise blinked hard and looked down to one side. "Please accept my apology: I am so sorry. You were always worth another try." They hugged, and for the next few hours involved themselves with business chores. Livia busied herself with plans for Saturday's pony rides, while Cherise revved up the pantry's computer and tapped into her favorite search engines, to research a topic for her master's thesis concerning Polynesian ancestry. They turned in a little after twelve. Late that night, Livia doubled her sleeping tablet.

And it slowly evolved that Cherise's undaunted honesty dredged up some of Livia's suppressed desires. Following a few tense evenings of tiptoeing around, Livia drove back to Hilo. After the first night with Ma, they kept regular soirées, and she returned home every morning.

Livia's grueling commutes did not last long, for Ma announced that she was opening a new store, in the previous Wendy's restaurant building, perched above Keauhou Shopping Center. She converted half the storeroom to hold a bed, table, and chairs. The altitude was cool, and they enjoyed the best view, of distant Kailua, while planning the move downhill, to Ma's new seaside condominium, once it was decorated and air-conditioned.

Alongside a takeout plater of Los Habaneros fish nachos, Ma laid out the floor plans. Details solidified, work was to begin in four weeks. The contractor signed an agreement subtracting a thousand dollars for each week overdue. Livia leaned hard on her hand, covering her mouth. She moved it and sat up, as a smirk crept across her lips. Ma, no longer able to contain herself, and teeth still dug into a jalapeno pepper, exhaled an emphatic, "What?"

Livia swallowed, and as politely as possible, she said, "Oh, it's just a silly story, of a roommate, with whom we played hockey."

Ma swallowed and said, "I've got time - spit it out."

"Well, with your contractor and all, it reminded me of her. Brandy earned an industrial arts degree from Eastern Michigan, but instead of teaching, she started her own home maintenance business: Handy Brandy."

"And ?" Ma pressed.

"Eventually she expanded her business, to new construction, and built houses near a couple busy shopping malls. Her business grew, and she had difficulty supervising her work crews – so, she asked if I could recommend a good patent attorney; in that, she wanted to do a search for a crew leash design. Well, I took the bait and asked about the design. She grabbed a couple prunes, cupped them upside down, and said, "Like this - I need to harness a man's 'you-knows' to keep his mind on the job."

A wrinkle crept across Ma's forehead. "You're kidding?"

"Oh, no– she had a little sketch. Two tiny steel collars. The leash attached they'd fit right down, and..." Livia stopped, at Ma's hand held up.

"Got it." She finished her tea and hand rolled a lavender-and-clove cigarette. It glowed with every breath. Examining her other hand, she quietly clicked her short thumbnail between two long crimson fingernails. "I must admit, the idea's pretty cute. How about this? Index finger near her thumb, she said, "Flatten it about this wide, cover it with something fuzzy, and attach two leads for a bit more control, and ride, baby, ride!"

Livia chewed her lip and wondered how she attracted such queer folk. Must be because she always played along, and grabbing Ma's hand, she yanked her across the table scattering ashes. "How might it be popular — with him, her, or both?"

"Depends on how it's used – for giddy-ups, or for whoa-nellies!"

Well, by now, the story had lost its appeal for laughter. Ma's narrow eyes slowly shifted across the street, to her green Jaguar, and back to Livia. She whispered, "Remember that feathered *Soixante-neuf* Fun Kit we ordered?" She nodded. "In the trunk."

Their liaisons of 'Fun Time' slid, into only three times weekly, if they were lucky. Then it tapered to two, in the high tourist season. The fun took off again when Cherise finished her semester, at Hilo, and she and her gorgeous Molokini geologist, Sid, took charge of activities at the inn.

A few hard-won weeks later, Cherise confided they were 'An Item'. Livia's eyes rolled, at not having heard that term in a good twenty years. The arrangement worked out beautifully. Each morning she left Ma's, arriving in time to book the new guests, freeing Cherise around sunset for personal business. In the meantime, Sid began building two small guest bungalows and was surprised to uncover the inn's old cellar entrance behind the carport wall. Aye and Livia recognized the forty-year old yellow and black civil defense placard but never realized the metal shelving unit hinged, to reveal a doorframe leading beneath the kitchen stairs.

Early, on the Friday before Mother's Day, a vanload of surprise guests swamped the inn. Livia hung out the inn's No Vacancy sign, by noon, and it took most the next day getting everyone settled. Her evening-out with Ma came none too soon. Nearly 9:00 when she arrived on Ma's doorstep, the doorbell brought no response, so she let herself in with her key.

She slipped off her sandals and stroked a gleaming black vase chock full of yellow spider orchids. Finding the parlor empty, she headed down the long hall, intent on couple of fluffy towels from the bedroom's linen closet.

That familiar alto voice hummed from the shower. Livia played the voyeur, as Ma leaned forward, rinsing her silky black hair. "Thanks for waiting to shower with me," she set the towels out of reach on the vanity. Pretending to primp, she leaned over them, as Ma's damp arm caught her and the other touched the master panel dimming the lights. Livia's shorts ere soaked by the time she got them off in the steaming shower.

Satiated and clean, Livia wound a beige knot of hair. Stabbing it with a tiny sai, she contemplated why Ma showered so early. Thoughts evaporated, as Ma pushed a tiny frosted jade tray across the nightstand, with six frozen tequila jiggers and lime wedges stuck to it.

The sweet liquor warmed her throat, as one and then the other reclined. In no time, they tossed back their heads and relished sweet oblivion.

The moon floated on the sea, as Livia shivered deliciously, and attempted to make linger that delicious inside-out feeling.

Hunger drove them to the kitchen. Ma disappeared after popping in a rousing HDVD, and images from The Merrie Monarch Hula Festival flickered across the wide monitor. Livia ate a few cold oysters and shrimp until those familiar little metallic clicks brought her head up, and backing away from the chef's island, she tiptoed to the study. Ma stalked her, only to find her perched high on the tuxedo-armed sofa.

Livia snatched the gold balls, reclined, and deftly rolled them under her warm legs. Ma pounced and pretended to fish them out. Gently rolling them back and forth, she took her time and produced a second set. Livia sighed, "You know what? I still need a bite of something – let me just whip in the kitchen for a piece of that Kona dark chocola…"

Ma pushed her flat, and sucked her breath away. Tongues released, as hot balls crashed to the floor. Ma snapped the balls in and pinned her. Legs entwined, they tribadised gently at first. Before either new it, they moved head to toe. Time immaterial they finally rolled separate, teetering alternately through suffering and ecstasy. Before hamstrings tore, Ma moaned a code word merely for safety sake. Quick sips of liquor and her breath came hot again – this time she purred in Livia's ear the old punk rock verse: "Never say never; it might better, if we slept …"

Livia gave her own surprise ending: a melodic "Ta-daah," as she flipped Ma over.

Now it was Ma's turn. She hummed in crescendos, as she heaved her curtain of damp hair over Livia's thighs – bringing that familiar rush. As in hockey, she caught a third wind. Slowly building a rhythm, she caught Ma each time and making her gasp.

Just when Livia crept to the sofa, and her body began to soften, the deep flow of relaxation pulled her closer to sleep. Not to be - Ma pounced again, and flinging blonde hair over her shoulders she hauled Livia back to bed. Slamming her deep, in the pillow pile, it was no use to struggle, and Livia writhed; every way but which, but mirrored Ma's intentions, until adrenaline kicked-in and forced their breaths clear with every shuddering gasp.

The phone rang, and Livia's eyes peeked open slowly as sunlight crept around the midnight blue window shades. Recognizing Ma's crisp answers to a customer, she groped the bedside dresser and pulled herself vertical. Hoping the conversation held Ma's attention, Livia slipped on her clothes and tiptoed to the bathroom. A bit ungainly and barely pulled together, she made her excuses, in that she should have been at the inn by now.

Ma hung up, and gave pursuit. Breathy snickers and deft dodges brought Livia dancing, from Ma's bedchamber, grabbing her wallet and keys on her way through the front hall to the door.

Once outside she flipped Ma's hair, in back of her shoulders, as she received one last peck on her cheek. Backing the Wrangler down the steep driveway she waved before accelerating down the highway. She counted nine fingers, and this was the last.

Her cell phone rang when she pulled up to the inn. Ma was heading out to the Hilo store. She and the customer planned a meeting at eleven-thirty.

Livia wished her a safe trip knowing they would travel their separate ways. The breeze soothed her, except something about Ma' story sounded a bit off. A customer – and only minutes past dawn? Yellow orchids – Ma never cut them for display. Cell phone pulses interrupted her thoughts. Margaret asked her to a late breakfast at the hospital. Excellent idea, but first she must shower.

Heading up the highway she mulled over Margaret's treat - cited mainly for being a good Joe and putting up with her auction antics. She passed the turnoff, and she backtracked to the condo for her sunglasses. Would not take but a few minutes if she hurried. Sprinting in and out, with glasses in hand she nearly clicked the door shut – when the narrow light hit a violet envelope and caught her eye. Addressed to Lelania, it sat neatly propped against that damn vase of orchids. Livia rushed back to the Wrangler. Five minutes behind schedule – she would still arrive at Margaret's office with the least amount of questions.

The next time they met at Ma's condo, Livia sipped stiff black coffee and watched Squishy crawl along his seven-foot-tall glass tank. Wondering who the bigger voyeur, she lifted him out and placed him on the sandy end of his lower tank. There, he could rub up against his pet snail, Mary.

Ma leafed through the mail and set aside *National Geographic*. Pointing to the cover she said, "Another article about Crete. I have always wanted to visit all along those islands. Few years back, another article showed a nice crisp picture of two women poised, on tiptoes, ready to vault over a spotted bull with long horns."

Livia knew the picture well, having seen all Luke's old yellow magazines, and a few of his ancient history books too. She had shown Cate, that double-handled amphora, noting she was the women's spitting image – except for their long black curls."

Ma waited patiently as Livia chattered about seeing cows, similar to that bull, when she and Cate drove past White Sands Beach. She recognized that familiar lonely feeling – like looking up at the beautiful sky from inside a deep well. With that thought, Livia left for home.

After that, the days floated by on the summer air. With Cherise's consistent help, Livia made time to help Tim. She also outlined chapters for a children's book, about a crow's incredible journey around Lake Superior. Occasionally, Ma Loa called to ask suggestions about décor and landscaping. Livia found it much easier to help - without the burden of devotion.

The day after Labor Day, Cate phoned. The call was brief. "I'm needed home – right?"

A few calls later and Livia mentioned that Tim's short trips around the paddock got faster by the day, and Cate interrupted, "I knew he could do it!"

Finally, Livia confessed her interlude with Ma Loa.

The response came flatly. "Well, I figured things there were working out okay for you. Hey, listen– I ate lunch with three of our old teammates. Remember Carrie and Junie and their Little Harvey? Well, they want to bring him and the twins, Sunny and Moira, for a visit next fall."

Livia agreed that would be fine. At least Harvey was old enough to behave himself. A sharp screech was heard in the background, and Mother Demi yelled something at Heimi. That set off Dasher. The big Dane bellowed, at her, "Get out here!" - and all that put an end to Cate's call.

Livia snapped off the phone, and Cherise's head popped up with an abrupt stare. Both shrugged, as Livia figured Cate had had enough.

Cherise quietly said, "Miss her a lot - huh?"

Self-preservation had kept her from allowing the fact to sink in. Her toes traced the roses, in the deep Chinese parlor rug, and she said, "Sure, I do."

For nearly fifteen years, of Saturday nights, Livia wrote at home. Now, was the day to phone Cate at 2:00 in the morning. All those years, Mother Demi's household pretty much ran like clockwork. Now, Cate's grandparents quickly regressed to their weekly Saturday baths, always donning night clothes, between 8:00 and 9:00. Afterward, they and Heimi fell asleep watching sports or the classic movie channel. After that was Demi's shower time, and it was the quietest time to call.

Always allowing three rings, and Cate returned Livia's call. She exchanged a warm hello and listened, as Cate listed things she knew already.

Livia's final, "Well, thank goodness we got a private chat," brought Cate's swift, "I miss you so much."

Livia minced no words. "I want you home!"

Cate shot back, "Believe me — I am working on it!"

Cate hung up saying she might as well have breakfast now. Wide awake and feeling invigorated, Livia decided on a walk along Ali`i Drive, in Kailua. Already dressed, she tiptoed past Margaret's room, headed down the back stairs, and slipped a peanut butter sandwich, bag of chips, and bottle of water in her backpack.

Most mornings, The Hard Rock Café had wide-open parking. She headed down the upper sidewalk to the last hotel, then circled back along the ocean, relishing the moonlight on the white-capped black breakers. Almost four now, and the street was pleasantly deserted. Only a couple of lovers faced the sea behind the community building. Like many Japanese tourists it was easy to stay up late. Arm in arm they stepped back as a tiny Yorkshire scampered on the low seawall - waist high to his master strolling beside him.

Good thoughts of how she and Cate walked here - their first night in Kona. The waves were disappointingly low, so they left after noticing the *haole* bums sleeping on the makai side of the building. Only a block from their hotel, Cate spotted her first *honu*.

A sip of water and she noticed two lithe silhouettes clearing the north corner of the Windjammer Pavilion. Shimmering hair and Livia recognized Ma Loa embracing a woman of equal height, though slightly slimmer.

Livia flushed with heat. Riveted to the sidewalk, she glared at them. Steadily, she hummed "Aloha `Oe" until they turned in her direction. The younger woman gave a little smile and lifted her hand to wave, until she was quickly led behind the pavilion. Livia whispered, "Well, hello to you too, Lelania. All good things come to an end –and oh, how conveniently."

She rushed back to the car and drove home with her hand out the window, guiding in the fresh air.

Scribing till dawn, she began with Cate's "What's meant to be is what's meant to be." Then she sketched a dark silhouette carrying something and winging its way, toward a dark pine edged shore, and she formulated her Lake Superior book's first chapter.

Enough writing. She ran a hot washcloth all over. It always felt good before climbing into bed for a few hours. That smooth and lined face once again starred back. "Wrinkles – how rude!" she hissed. "Screw it! Life's too short to sleep!" Donning shorts and shirt, she grabbed Cate's old Red Wing cap and pulled her ponytail through. Rounding the wall to the carport, she yanked her little cart down the path to the gardens."

She religiously scanned the voice mail erasing Ma Loa's messages without listening. The next weekend, she noticed a familiar 'Condo for Lease' sign, and not seeing her around town, Livia figured she hired some Kona sales help. All of a sudden, it came clear that she had more business ventures than one cared to count. It had been her schedule to spend Monday, Wednesday, and Saturday at her shop in Hilo. On Farm Market days, its downtown drew more Hawaiians than it did tourists. At first, Ma Loa stayed true to habit and kept her distance. But oddly enough, she began to spend Sunday mornings plus Wednesday through early Friday evening with Chakra.

Livia figured, with Cate's absence, it was a noble thing to do. Her regular trips, from Hilo, certainly gave Aye a bit of free time. Livia seldom rode Herc, but to help Tim and Tom financially she bought Hokulani. Focusing on the inn and preparing, for Cate's return, she failed spending time with Chakra and Aye.

The inn's big PC monitor glared back with the *Detroit Free Press* headline: Walled Lake Remains Found. Cold case forensic experts pieced together the identity of a skeleton found near the village's lake shore. Evidently, a corpse was found of a young man who was last seen in 1988, leaving Mengo's, near Five Mile and Woodward. Livia gasped. Back then, she frequented that men's bar more than once a month. Her boy toys escorted her along to the best dance club between Chicago and New York. That headline was no surprise - crack and a weird sort of marijuana ran rampant back then.

The closest Livia got to illegal drugs was living with her friend, Celeste, who gave up a thriving and fashionable bistro on Windsor's Wyandotte Street. She sold out ever so fast, after finding her partners snorting up the business profits after hours. Livia figured the Big Island had its problems, but she shuddered to think what other country might quickly control Hawaii, if not for the United States.

Celeste and Canada came to mind again - one late September afternoon when she plopped down all sweaty and dirty from the garden. As she picked dog fur off her socks and grappled to force her mind, to the present, it struck her as odd: not having noticed the thick stand of short mayapples near the cottage. They stood as fresh and limey miniature Norway maples in the spring. As a kid, she had noticed plenty of mayapples scattered across the woods and, just barely visible from the roads skirting Hoosier National Forest. Shoes kicked off - she moved to the inn's bench and watched, from one lanai to the other, a strained conversation between Aye and Ma Loa. She almost got up when Margaret pulled in from work and joined them at the cottage. In no time - Ma Loa covered her mouth and walked off sullenly.

Margaret met Livia halfway on the path and asked, "Would you like to try a new drink? Ma brought us the ingredients. You can mix it with sake, or Cointreau, lemon juice, and mango paste." She named it the Hippolytan. "Let's fill half the new pitcher that Aye set in the kitchen."

After Margaret changed clothes, she tried Livia concoction and quickly ran her tongue across her teeth. Shaking her head and wiggling her lips, in her best horse imitation, she swallowed and pushed the drink and the pitcher to Livia. "Here finish this. I'll make my next one a tall scotch and water."

That set Livia back a notch. As she watched Margaret bustle around, an old phrase came to mind: "You can't race a thoroughbred every day – you'll destroy it." Margaret sipped her scotch but that stuff never touched Livia lips. What better time to break out the bourbon? She poured a slight slammer and knocked it back. "Phew!" It sure didn't taste as good as she remembered, so she took tiny tastes and dumped the other stuff from the pitcher.

They quietly sipped cold libations, until Livia began to confide about Cate's return and their hopes that Chakra's maladies would soon improve.

Margaret slowly shook her head, saying, "Medicine? When all is said and done — who the hell knows?"

Never hearing a word like that from Margaret - Livia couldn't help but stare at her sturdy wide throat. Around it hung a tiny coral cross, suspended by the frailest of white gold chains. How different from the heavy cross of nails she wore through all those years of hockey. Thick hair, nondescript earrings, plain clothes, rough clean hands - and still she faced one most elegant lady.

Cate and Margaret had always been close. As of late, Livia had the occasion to visit with here and found their good friend awesomely refreshing. After rallying from her sad fiasco with Richard, Margaret seemed to carry herself with a bit more lightness. Their late-evening conversations always centered on ideals rather than people, and Livia appreciated how Margaret never bragged about her influence on so many islanders' lives.

Livia tipped her glass. "I'm so glad you bought the inn with us." Margaret returned the toast, "Our little catalyst," as tears welled in their eyes.

True to her word, Cate headed home. A party was in the works right after Tim and Tom came home from giving ornery old Captain to an equally as ornery old *paniolo* in Waimea. After a quick nap, Tim cut lengths of green-and-white crepe paper, as Tom and Livia twisted them into streamers and hung them from the porch to the trees. Livia unpacked delicate white Japanese lanterns painted with wispy orange flowers. They were stored along with the little-used Christmas twinkle lights. After the lanterns were hung and everyone ate a bit of lunch, Aye pulled out a little cart of flowers. He lined the main steps and circled the main tree trunks, with bright pink and yellow impatiens, then headed home to point out his handiwork to Chakra.

Tom and Tim appeared after their short walk. Tim mostly feigned exhaustion, to go home for his daily nap. Margaret covered her mouth and stared at Livia, doing her best to stifle a giggle – as Tom led Tim to the truck winking twice over a to-die-for grin. Two weeks ago, Margaret was beside herself coaching Tom, to adhere to Tim's strict exercise regimen after every nap. Livia waved and told Margaret: "Yeah – right. They'll have plenty of time, for a romp and a nap, before freshening up for tonight's festivities."

Aye had supervised the inn when Margaret and Livia retrieved Lotus Blossom from the Hilo quarantine. It was costly, but Cate paid and shipped her the week preceding her own plane trip, so Lotus was released right on Margaret's Keiki Clinic Day. Of course, Livia rode along to handle the dog.

Most the way across Saddle Road, they chuckled and carried on about hockey and how they really didn't miss Cate's clutter, but they did miss her organizational skills, wry sense of humor – oh, and everything else. With very few sick kids, at the clinic, they were soon bumping along home with Lotus content, in her pet carrier near the station wagon's rear window, and gumming a fist-sized rawhide Nummy Bone that Tallulah sent along for the ride.

"They must have half-starved you," drawled Livia.

"Don't let her eat more than half of that," reminded Margaret.

They bumped and bounced another five miles. Livia realized Margaret was stalling, and shot her a quizzical look. "I'm not reaching in there. If you want the rawhide, you'll have to stop and walk her. Then I can get at it."

Twenty more miles and Margaret stopped to exercise Lotus. Small talk led, to her asking how Livia became fascinated with gardening.

Livia poured water for Lotus and explained that back in Badendale, Indiana, she and Luke explored elderly neighbor Catie's formal garden paths. "I couldn't have been more than five when she gave me some…" A projectile soared straight, for Mauna Loa - then it arced back, with an ear-piercing whine, and a huge kaboom rocked the landscape.

They covered and ducked. Livia reached out and pulled the dog closer yelling, "Dang!" She and Lotus scampered to Margaret's heels, and they ran to the Volvo. "We're in the Pohakuloa Training Area firing range. Hit the gas!"

Another loud discharge followed them, flying down the old, bumpy road, bouncing across ravines where tires barely met pavement. "Never knew all those Michigan potholes would come so handy," yelled Margaret over the din and dog whimpers.

Safely turned down Highway 190, they stared at each other, with Livia muttering. "Nice! What– the hell– was that all about?" Then she snorted. "You know? If we hadn't made it out of there, Cate would be sole proprietor." Margaret chuckled, finally setting the cruise control, and they breathed a bit more easily on the smooth road home.

By morning, they were nearly back to normal. Livia brought in the Friday newspaper and read Margaret the *Honolulu Star Observer* headline: "Too Young to Fire." The first line ran: "Aiming at Mauna Loa's northern flank, new army recruits fire weapons across Saddle Road." She skipped on to the popular political cartoon, RUNESDARY. Main character, DC, having weathered Vietnam and the first Gulf War, recently lost his right hand in Iraq. She felt guilty chuckling at his physical and mental problems – not like the belly laughing at the Emperor's clothes, the Boss' "Stay the Curse" and the silly sheep. As always, she read aloud her favorite: FOR BETTER OR FOR WORSE and wondered whatever happened to Luke's favorite: Gasoline Alley.

The weekend section featured movies and book reviews. Ben White's code breaking novel featured plenty of intrigue, with rich old men debating and fighting over whether inconvenient Mary Magdalene held more importance than more popular gospels. Some of the recent right had coined a pretty responsible: 'What would a savior do?' Livia figured that provocateurs of famine, slavery, and genocide were more worthy of assault. One recent movie's cute kid hit it on the nail head with, "Maybe if people weren't so afraid, they could just try to pay it forward." Livia shut the paper and shuddered – coaching herself: *Knock it off. Get back to work.*

Between today's news and yesterday's firing range fiasco, the chores got finished but not in record time. Finally, Margaret tooted from the driveway. Livia helped Lotus Blossom hop in the back seat, and they were off to fetch Cate from the airport. It was a quick drive, considering end-of-the-day traffic. Kona's new radio station was good but they missed a few of Detroit's good old FM stations. Margaret turned it down and mentioned hearing the date for satellite radio reception, as Livia brushed dog fur from her black shorts and noticed that unsettling cloud fall over her. A couple minutes later, it passed, along with a good case of mighty uncomfortable sweats.

Cate waved from the open-air pavilion. Margaret pulled to the curb and Livia dashed to a shop, returning with the most gorgeous lei of firm purple orchids punctuated with claw-like jade flowers. A few hugs and Cate helped load the car. Most the way home she stroked Lotus's ears, as Margaret recounted yesterday's ride on the wild side making it sound pretty darn awesome.

Lotus lay upside down, and all three were dead quiet as Margaret pulled in the driveway. Cherise finally met Cate. They and Sid seemed to hit it off quite nicely. Everyone helped drag Cate's bags to her room and they watched her stride off with Aye to see Chakra. It was almost past the grand old lady's bedtime but they chatted for almost an hour before she retired. By the time Cate got back, the party was in full swing.

Cate caught her second wind. After running upstairs to don shorts, she tiptoed down the kitchen stairs.

Livia swung around the corner, from where she'd been waiting in the pantry. She handed Cate a Labatt's, and after tipping bottles, she quietly demanded. "Okay, now spill it. How did you get Mother Demi to let you come home so soon?"

"Well, actually, I didn't; it was my great uncle Ivan. He talked everyone into coming out here, for the holidays, and that was when I seized the moment. You still don't get the fact that my family does understand one thing – I do have to earn a living."

"Everyone?" She quickly considered the fact that Demi and The Ma might do better on separate flights. She smiled. That might just be possible. She had to give Demi credit for recognizing Cate's wanderlust. Cate dreamed of moving to Hawaii, and without her mother's unwavering support, she may have never broken loose from the constant demands in Michigan.

"That's right," Cate continued, "They're all flying here the evening after Christmas. My sister chipped in on Heimi's ticket, and my grandparents are treating Mother for her Christmas present. Mom, and Heimi are flying out on the red eye flight. Uncle Ivan was out here right when he shipped back east after WWII. He's chaperoning my grandparents on a later flight that morning."

Stunned, all Livia could do was stare and blather, "Awesome." They turned, arm in arm, and walked to the lanai, with Cate commenting about her lei and asking to pick orange, pink and purple plumeria for their guests.

The lei dried to an awesome lampshade crown, and guests commented about the lush plumeria filling the front desk's vase - but Livia noticed something just wasn't right.

With Cate's return, Margaret seemed happier; although, she still wasn't fully engaged in decision-making. Cate agreed with Livia's thoughts on the matter – they'd have to ask what was up. She filled Livia's large silver bowl with water, starred in it a while before arranging lovely blue hydrangeas in it and proceeding with her inquisition.

She asked about Margaret's plans to visit Waipio Valley with Richard.

Margaret hesitated, "Umm, well, we canceled those reservations at the Waipio Trailside Motel twice. I made a grocery and wine list and everything."

Cate looked at Livia and leaned closer to Margaret, as she looked down and wiggled her fluffy yellow scuffies side to side.

Cate coaxed her. "Okay, just slow down and explain what went on."

Margaret flushed, sat straight up, and said, "I was on my way to Hilo's clinic, just driving down Waianuenue Avenue – you know, in front of the hospital." She hesitated. "Actually, I filed a child abuse report."

Cate's tiny mouth dropped open. "You did?"

"Yes – you heard me. I filed a child abuse report, with the Hilo Police, and I named Richard."

Livia swallowed hard.

Margaret sniffled, "Maybe Tim was right."

Livia's face froze, as a slow "Really?" slid out. Watching Margaret's eyes drop to the floor, she flattened her lips shut and swallowed. "Sorry. I didn't realize you were so…"

Cate interrupted, with a "Shush–," as she looked at Livia before touching Margaret's hand and carefully continuing. "You know, we've gone past where we should be. Margaret knows we support her in anything she needs to do. Right, Livia?"

Livia gasped, "Oh– most certainly we do."

Margaret interrupted. "Thanks. Let's get on, with packing our goodies for the beach." Excusing herself, she checked with her answering service before returning to a very quiet kitchen.

With the table and kitchen island cleared, Livia busily sorted items for the trash compactor and recycle bin. She moved to the pantry and pretended to scan newspaper sections, as Cate fiddled with some trays and pans in the cupboard. Following Margaret's lead they had a fine day at Hapuna Beach.

That weekend was Cate's homecoming party. She was in such a good mood that she did not much mind sharing her beach photos and cake, with Tim's coming back out festivities. She served her goodies, from the side lanai, so he could hold court from the inn's west lanai. It had the best views on the coast. The weather was no less than perfect. Only warm breezes blew from the southeast's brush land. Margaret joined them, as Cate watched the whitecaps on the sea. They could even hear them crash on the point way below. "Glad I'm home. It's hard to tell, which is the grandest party – this one or Fezziwig's."

That got a quizzical stare from Margaret, and Cate explained, "After fourteen-years at the Guy-Mel Corporation, I can say that Guy always treated his employees and their guests to a primo Christmas party at his glitzy country club. Livia accompanied me, and during one party she noticed how cheerful Guy was, and she deemed him 'Master Fezziwig'."

Margaret hugged Cate and Tim hard. Glancing down at the lower lanai she lightly called out to Livia and Tom, "Fezziwig?" She noticed Livia's grind and added, "Guess we've got another little quote, from our little Miss 'Ghost of Christmas Present'."

Tom punched Livia. "Guess that means we'll have to give Old Fezziwig a run for his money!"

Livia only shrugged and said, "We'll see - maybe next year."

Chapter 19: Death Of a Queen

At seven-thirty, almost all the breakfast dishes remained on the table. Cate and Livia quietly rocked on the side lanai swing. By nine, Aye climbed the inn's side steps and announced that Chakra was well enough to be up and at the table when he got to the kitchen. Almost giddy, he set before them an amazing story.

"I could not wait another minute to tell you. She must have sent the Waimea men home, before asking that I accompany her to the southeast corner of our lanai. Before the sun rose, she faced the high mountain. For minutes, she never blinked, slowly turning until she looked down somewhere past Kealakekua Bay. On for minutes – her quiet stare fell, ending when the sun came up.

"So radiant she was when she finally turned to me. Kissed me right on the cheek then passed me by and went inside. I helped her into bed; I do hope she's resting peacefully. Oh, would you pick some of your new roses for her?"

Livia nodded, as he turned saying, "Anyway, I'd best go check on her."

Before noon, the highway was lined with various modes of transportation. The women and Reggie cleared the parking areas so that visitors, making their way to the cottage, had a bit more privacy. Sid left first, to complete some petroglyph research, and Cherise packed their lunches before leaving for the beach. Livia and Cate kept Margaret informed and moved to the main lanai by mid-morning.

Carrying baritone ukuleles, four old gents crossed the lawn and asked to sit on the inn's front steps to sing. They wanted a bit of distance between them and the cottage. Livia and Cate could barely nod, and the songs began to drift sweetly and smoothly across the property. Livia figured that the request was twofold: Chakra loved the music, and she sent these fine gentlemen to cheer the women. Cate asked why they seemed so familiar. Livia whispered, "They may be part of the seniors' group that once gave concerts on the boardwalk deck near Bubba Gump's Shrimp House."

The whole day, a panoply of visitors continued to drift down from the highway, most carefully picking their way along the old path that crossed the woods to the cottage. A few carefully drove along the hidden logging trail, past the inn, depositing their children and elders near the lanai steps. There were so many that Livia remarked, "Where have they all parked?" Most visited briefly, and upon leaving the cottage, they threw down small woven mats, and then sat to whisper and wait. Eventually, Margaret came out the door, standing momentarily, to pat Aye's hand. As he shut the door behind her, all visitors stood until she traversed the path to the inn.

Cate ran to Sack-to-Save, returning with great quantities of food, plus paper plates and ten cases of bottled water. With that chilling, she and Margaret set up tables while Livia set out sandwiches, chips, and a huge cooler of blue Kool-Aid. Anything but cool, the nausea passed, as a wave of heat shot up her collar, provoking memories of running outside, and sucking in Michigan's bracing cold.

For the last time, Margaret climbed the steps and ran her hand down the rail to her place at the table. Cate met her with a plate of food and a glass of diet cola. Sitting heavily, she sucked a bottle of water. She nibbled sushi and leaned forward, propping open both sides of her black bag. Contents assessed, she sighed, "You know, I have had this bag since graduation, and I probably used it twice back in Michigan. Out here – it's a lifesaver."

Livia remembered the time, in the kitchen when Margaret stitched her arm up, and she watched Cate blink back the tears. Margaret repeatedly swallowed hard, and both reached for tissues. Seeing them so upset hurt way more than any seven stitches.

Margaret pulled the stethoscope away, exhaled deeply, and took tiny sips of the cola. Absent of any expression she rolled it slowly and placed it in the black bag's main compartment. Barely a breath of air stirred as they stared at their food. With only a hurried breakfast, they attempted to finish their dinner. That not accomplished, they drained small bottles of water again and again.

Hours passed, and still they sat in suspense. Margaret was first to leave the table. Retrieving her laptop, she filled out a few hospital charts and submitted them online. She looked out the window, saying, "I've never seen so many attendants. Kind of like traffic flow - it was as if they were choreographed. The whole time I was there, everything around her was completed in silence. Except once, when Aye sketched something and showed it to her. I could not see what it was. However, he set it on a table - near the heavily tattooed man who nodded, carefully took it up, and left."

Cate mirrored Livia's shrug. They patted Margaret, on the back, and Livia retreated to the service entry. Still grimacing, she peeked outside. The evening star rose near the new moon's crescent. Possibly, Aye's sketch contained something about Chakra's last wishes. For once, she did not feel the need to explain to Margaret that her observations matched details of centuries old mortuary customs.

How many visitors could that cottage hold? It had to be cramped quarters, so Livia suggested the children join her for story time on the lanai. Cate quickly threw together two pans, of party brownies, as Livia scattered palm mats and pillows. They stack trays with yellow-gold Pooh napkins, milk, water, and store-bought sugar cookies. Livia fingered her soon-to-be-published manuscript: *BugTussle Depot*. Margaret wished her luck, quickly pointing out that a real audience was better than any editor's review.

It shocked Livia how quietly the youngsters took their places. Cate's expression told her this little storytelling session could be more eventful than anything she would ever write.

Oddly enough, Tim fetched a bucket of salt water from Livia and Aye's sea urchin pool. He sprinkled it around the inn's foundation, careful not to splash it on her plants. Friends and relations left, and everyone settled in for their snacks and story time.

Nearly half these keiki she had met, at the pony rides. Quiet chatter rose, from the well-behaved youngsters, as they enjoyed their treats. A little redheaded girl seemed especially anxious, as her mother tried to settle her on a large pillow. Livia motioned the young woman forward and asked the four-year-old to sit, at her side, as she read. Brief visions of Hawaiians and Talk Story predicated her opening comments about faeries stories and a society of bugs, as a tiny finger touched her knee beckoning her a bit closer.

She paused, as the nervous little girl tugged on her sleeve and whispered, "I don't want to see the pet man."

Livia glanced around the crowd. "Why? Do you see him now?"

With a quick look, the little girl shook her head and gave a hesitant, "Not now, but he was here at supper when I came with my daddy."

Livia pressed a bit further, "Can you remember when that was?"

"This week," she whispered. "I think it was after groceries."

Livia asked, "What's your name?"

Pulling her teddy bear tight to her waist, she said, "Amy Wellbaum."

Nodding to the crowded yard, Livia asked, "Where did you see him?"

Knees tight together, Amy cupped one hand to her mouth. She barely raised her finger as she whispered, "He stood back there on the small lanai."

With that hammer blow, Livia pulled Amy close. She thought back. Margaret had not answered the kitchen door any evening that week. "Stay by me. You're safe right now, so relax." Her voice fell; she got into silly character mode and said, "You'll love this story; it's full of stretchy inchworms and skitterish tumble bugs."

Amy's little shoulders relaxed as she snuggled closer.

The keiki were not quite settled. A group of little local girls, still dressed from their hula lesson, crowded around Cate's Wibbly Wobbly Dolls. Quite enthralled with the dolls' brightly painted shawls and babushkas they opened one after another before giggling excitedly and restacking them. Finished with their snack - both boys and girls ran up to the garbage barrel dumping half-empty plates, then quietly wrestled with the tiny party favors. Finally, cookie crumbs and worn-out origami paper napkins were cleared. Moreover, Livia motioned for everyone to sit on the mats in a circle around her.

Her soothing voice drifted across the lanai. Boys and girls leaned toward her, as she complimented them about having the most lovely island traditions, of Talk Story. With impeccable timing and phrases – all eyes followed her every gesture. "When I was a little girl, I grew up in the coal fields of the Hoosierland, back in Southern Indiana. As the strip mines played out…"

She ignored the few giggles and quickened the storyline. "Oh, the black, dirty coal got way too expensive to scrape out of the deep hills, leaving the miners and their families with no food on the table – so they left town, and the railroads left sidetracks to nowhere. How many of you have walked train tracks, in the old sugarcane fields near Hilo? You know how some Kuhuna lament the changes here. Well, it happened in many a small town across the United States."

As a few children raised their hands, a few seniors shuffled their feet, took their hands from their pockets, and moved closer to the lanai.

"Well – I hope our Hawaiian *akamai* will share your memories, with kama'aina and haole alike." The children giggled as the elders smiled. "As I've heard - the coal and passenger trains were a big deal back then." Livia looked down to find wide-eyed Little Amy curled at the crook of her knee.

"Beginning the first Saturday of next month – we will be mighty happy to have everyone join us for lunch. We sure can use your help, in assembling my father's Lionel train set." She stopped a minute and explained 'assembling' to a little boy, who asked. He said something to a friend and smiles, so she continued. "The train used to run pretty good, and it just might prove a fun project - until we start the pony rides again, when Mr. Boki gets well." The adults' eyes widened, and they nodded. "There are still a few huge train stations, such as underneath downtown Chicago. Can anyone tell me what the local building is called - where people get on and off the trains?"

One little girl raised her hand. As Livia pointed to her, she stood proudly and said: "Tutu and Daddy took me to the old depot."

Livia smiled and nodded. "Yes, it's called a depot." She held up a dark-lined watercolor, which she hoped her publisher would choose for her book's cover. Handing out pencils and colored paper, she asked, "Can you tell us where you saw this depot?"

The little girl fell silent and looked up at her big brother. He said, "North of Hilo near the school they attended last year."

"That's up the Hamakua Coast, isn't it?" asked Livia.

The boy nodded yes, as he patted his sister on the back.

"Now, if any of you want to draw, as I read the story, there's plenty more paper – oh, and Cate has some crayons too. She waited a few more minutes until all the children settled down. Then she held up a windswept snowy painting of old Badendale Depot and turned the first page of her manuscript.

"The train depot in this story is very similar; although, it is not a museum - it is the subject of a couple of paintings. Long since the artist drew the scene, the building has been abandoned – " and she lowered her voice and leaned down, making definite eye contact with a couple of youngsters. "At least it was– abandoned by humans." A couple of children sucked air, mouthing little "oohs." At the head of the walk to the cottage, standing shoulder-to-shoulder near the yellow hibiscus hedge stood Livia's roomies.

Keeping her voice low, Cate leaned to Margaret's ear. "Still the teacher; she can make you think she's the bear when she reads 'Goldilocks'."

Margaret forcefully swallowed and whispered back, "No shit – wonder why she quit teaching?"

With a flourish, Livia folded back the cover page and began to read. "Most everyone in the South has a nickname," Continuing, she explained that Mayor Skittlebug was known to all his constituents as Spinner. He drew a swirling tornado under 'Tear Up Taxes,' on a huge campaign poster, and tacked it right under the town sign.

"He lost his second bid for office because he failed to fix storm damage, which ruined the Big Trestle sign. When he did win again - he spun joyously in the dust of a passing Edsel, proudly waving all six arms overhead as the tiny crowd cheered, 'Up with BugTussle! Down with taxes'!"

But his success did not last long. She paused for a moment then explained, "Like many depots, the one which became BugTussle was not used much by humans after the great war."

For over an hour, the young audience visualized the rich heritage of various bug citizens. Livia's story contained short visual tales of their happiness and sorrows. During one sunny Fourth of July parade, a fire started next to the Big Ant Store's soda shop pop bottle tower. Many nearby homes and smaller businesses burned and were rebuilt; after The Mighty Bug Insurance Company ruled the fire 'an act of nature', (the tower's soda bottle magnified sunlight that sparked confetti drifted in a windowsill). At the last moment, Livia added an attempted abduction of Timbale, the smallest pill bug child, from the wood ledge surrounding the store. The town was totally in a dither until her older sister led the authorities to the perpetrator. Of course, in the end, BugTussle rallied and prospered - before slowly drifting into the future under the spell of a wicked old troll. "Well, anyway - that's the next story."

As she turned the last page of her *BugTussle* draft, the smallest children had been asleep for half an hour. Relatives quietly began carrying them to the cars along the lane, while a few older children lingered, proudly displaying their sketches, answering questions, which provoked conversations about various railway depots, as well as toy trains.

Livia noticed Margaret and Cate flanking a young woman on the private lanai. She gave one last glance to warm glowing cottage window, and she joined them. She listened as Margaret comforted a visibly shaken Ms. Yamamoto, telling how her seven-year-old son had outlined a sketch of a tall man sporting pale tan coat and pants only coloring was light-blue above the man's eyes. Her son said the man touched him with something — that the man said would only sparkle for a while like a fairy wand.' When prompted, he repeatedly said, 'No, he was white man and not dressed in an Aloha shirt.' When she asked him how - he touched his teddy bear directly below the belt."

Cate returned carrying a folder. She spread large digital photos on the outdoor buffet for all to examine before handing copies to the boy's mother. Margaret consoled the woman, patting her hand, and advising her to write down everything she knew and report her suspicions to the Waimea Police and the sheriff in Hilo. Livia realized that they could access FBI records, and that may pull in the Honolulu officials.

Livia thought about fairy tales in general, and it came to her a quick revelation associated the pale immature characters with children and pedophiles. Her psychology studies kicked-in and gave her a swift shudder. After the mother left, she admitted to Cate, "I am really sorry. My intention was not adding a child abduction, to my story. Once I faced such a large group, of these innocent children, I just said it. Subliminally, I must have wanted them to recognize any inappropriate experiences with adults. That's it. I'm not publishing the story. I'll shred it later.

Cate hugged her and assured her she made way more of it than was needed. To that Livia said, "Well, I'll shelve the story, at least till

I research how fairy tales have been used, in interviewing child abuse victims."

Huddled together and talking quietly, the bleary-eyed women obliviously did not notice Aye headed down the path.

Up popped their heads, as he cleared his throat. "Didn't mean to interrupt, but Chakra requested - I thank each of you." Tears welling up, the women grimaced, smiled, and shrugged. Livia felt like a kid again. Pointing to the keiki, she remarked how sweet and genuinely well behaved they were. She started them singing about a magic dragon who lived north of Kauai's Canyon Land, by the sea, as Cate kidded Aye about him and Chakra being a little too old to adopt, but they considered them 'Ohana. Some old gent, in the back began strumming *This Land Is Your Land*.

Margaret walked beside Aye, escorting him to the cottage, he kidded about dragons and nearby Honalo. As they chatted, Livia followed close behind, and halfway there, something drew Livia's interest, to the May apple patch, where a plant lay uprooted. More than its roots must have been disturbed, for the plant next to it had begun to wilt. Probably Tallulah or a small child was the culprit. A young man who none of the women recognized stepped down from the west side of the cottage lanai and stood quietly before raising a huge conch shell to his lips. The sound disturbed everyone.

That was the start of the procession. They carried Chakra out the front door and honored her request: that A simple lei, of Livia's baby yellow roses, and an old lei *niho palaoa* adorn her shoulder-baring white dress. A long caravan followed Tom's truck. Their destination was the little beach shack. Cate followed at the rear of the procession. Livia watched, as Auntie M. Leily lead the way, amazed how the sandy beach was made crisp green with sweet-smelling palm mats. At the moment Chakra nodded, she was laid down on them.

The day drew out, and she seemed comfortable enough. Livia and Cate stood in the doorway, as Margaret sat beside her. Aye leaned close, placing a lei of delicate white crown flowers on the great lady's head.

The Good Doctor slid her stethoscope beneath the soft kappa cloth and listened to her heart, as Chakra died in her sleep.

A few mornings later, a very fine mist shrouded the small crowd's faces. As the first rays of sunlight cleared Hualalai and struck the ocean, everyone except Aye walked to the west edge of the beach near the ash-bearing white outrigger canoe, rocking gently between the pier and Ahu'ena Heiau. It was quiet for a while, until a child pointed and cried, "Ooh, Mommy, look!"

All faces turned north. Wide bands of pink, blue, and yellow-green stretched high into the gray mountain mists. Livia quit chewing her protein bar and watched the mountains. The upcountry pines quivered as the shimmering double ānuenue (rainbow) soared two miles overhead – from distant Hōlualoa Bay's south Kamoa Point – it warmly glowed before them at the tappa tower, in tiny Kamakahonu Bay.

Everyone turned around to the sunset, as a warm wind passed through them. Livia thought of a poem her grandmother requested for her eulogy: "— and one clear call for me, and may there be no moaning of the bar when I put out to sea…" Again, the child's voice pierced the quiet. "I'm hungry. Can we get something to eat – please?" The People started talking and wandered off to their cars.

The women ate little for supper, followed by even less conversation. Margaret excused herself to do some paperwork. Livia looked at Cate and figured they could use sturdy toothpick halves, to prop their eyelids open, as the evening news droned on. For once, there were no arguments about the kitchen TV remote. Finally, Livia chose the educational station, if only for its lack of commercials. Good thing they both liked Egyptian history, for it was the last installment of a four-hour special about the Valley of the Kings.

Interrupting the late news, the phone rang. Cate answered. "I see. Yes, I will tell her. Thanks for calling." Livia slowly glanced up, as Cate laid the remote phone on her lap. She did not look at Livia, but walked to the stairs, and quietly returned with Margaret. Livia accompanied them to the parlor.

After installing Margaret on the couch, Cate sat beside her and told her that Richard was dead. The park rangers saw a small white dog and chased it all the way back to the ʻAleʻaleʻa platform, where it suddenly dashed off south. They found it digging beneath the Kaʻahumanu Stone adjacent to his body. Cate said, "Yes, the Hilo coroner said, 'Cold the body was – a good ten hours.' Kinda strange too that one of the tourist reported his Scotty dog snapped its collar, and it's been missing ever since."

A knock at the front doors got Livia up from the writing table. Tom followed her to the kitchen as she whispered, "I've never seen anything hit Margaret so hard." More focused, they returned to the parlor, where he gave Margaret a big hug and a small glass of cognac. Ten minutes later, she turned in. Cate followed and got her settled.

Livia stood polishing three wine glasses, setting them on the island between her and Tom. When Cate returned, Tom gave a nod, and they broke out her best bottle.

First, they raised their glasses to Margaret. After a few solemn sips, they toasted Tim and a job well done. They drained their glasses in silence, relieved that the real hunt was over.

Livia selected a Charlene Tapman disc from the pantry store case. The fine deep alto voice drifted into the swaying palms background to the day's events. They settled back to watch the sunset and relax in good company.

The next morning, local newspapers were plastered with the story. Even more shocking was the Honolulu evening news. Four TV stations showed footage of federal rangers chasing something white scampering along the paths behind Puʻuhonua, before the bushes quivered behind ʻĀlealea platform. The evening news featured a cameo interview, of Livia's favorite rangerette. She explained in detail how she noticed a pale dog, atop Pōhaku o Kaʻū that morning, and followed it past the southeast corner of the platform where she found a man's body curled between the support blocks under the Ka'ahumanu Stone. Header lay mere feet from where the young queen hid over two hundred years ago.

Embedded on page D10, of the Friday paper, ran a second storyline: "Suspect Vet, Murderer's Son." The sparse details included the suspect, a veterinarian from Waimea, whose father was a physician, from Carbondale, Illinois - convicted of hacking a little girl to pieces during the mid 1960s. Livia gasped, "Richard's name was nearly the same as the doctor's, the murderer that so upset my parents."

"What?" asked Margaret.

"Well, all I remember was hushed conversations about a doctor who drove around with the body parts crossing the state lines. My father was a cartographer, in the war, and had just finished updating county maps of the tri state area. Evidently, he pointed out all the secondary roads to the FBI, and it helped catch the doctor. That little girl had been my age– six at the time. Richard would have been just a baby."

Margaret's eyes glassed over. She turned and left the room, answering, "That's about right; he would have turned forty."

Two mornings later, Livia noticed Lotus huddled in the back corner of the side lanai. She found Polynesia on the floor of her cage. As she covered what had seemed a much larger bird, Pinkie waddled closer with something stuck to his foreleg. Livia knelt and pulled off a few fluffy brown-and-white feathers. She flattened her palm to the light and examined their textures. Slipping them in her pocket, she wondered, had something sinister shortened the young bird's life, or had her owl suitor stolen her away during the night? She tucked a clean cage cover around Polynesia and went to wake Margaret.

There were no tears, and the day passed quietly. By sunset, Livia dug a larger-than-needed hole near Old Woofer. She compared the age of bird and dog. Seventeen was near ancient for a dog, but way too young for a parrot to die. Cate stood quietly touching Margaret's shoulder, as Livia set the curly maple box deep in the hole and read "A

Dust of Snow" before adding soil and planting a clump of braided ti plants between dog and bird.

That week, the pets hung close, and Margaret said less than usual. Livia mentioned she seemed way too preoccupied. Cate's comeback: "Bet it was poison — we must pay more attention to Pinkie."

That made Livia wince, but the past days had been so hectic, they put all matters aside. Tomorrow was Chakra's funeral.

The day came and went. Hundreds of mourners filed by, but all in all it was another quiet day for the dead.

That evening, Aye was nowhere to be found. The authorities kept up a vigilant search for him, for more than a week; although, no missing person report had been filed.

Early Saturday night, Livia saw the light on in the caretaker's cottage. There he was, on west side of the cottage lanai. She walked down the path and stood beside Aye. More subdued but none the worse for wear, he was fine except for a missing front tooth. Well, that was until he looked up, and she saw the raw red parallel scars on his left cheek and neck.

Seconds later, that fabulous grin spread across his face when he noticed three deep blue marquis-shaped tattoos radiating from the sides of Livia's doe-brown eyes. A bit embarrassed she mentioned overhearing Ruth and some Hawaiians and neighbors are whispering about Cate calling her 'Chakra II'.

He shook his head and said, "Oh, no. Our Cate is her own woman." Quietly pinching dead leaves from his rarely neglected orchids, he looked up to Livia. "Your yellow climbing Lady Banks rose is splendid – it has doubled in size since it came out of quarantine. Would you teach me about roses?"

She blushed and petted the leaves of her new favorite climber. "Oh, Ms. Lutea, I've always wanted you, but Michigan was too darn cold." Flicking off a few white flies - she faced Aye. "You know - she may grow better than twenty-five feet tall, if you build her a nice big trellis. My white wisteria, in Camp Fortson, was supported by six-inch square posts. Every summer I pruned twenty-feet off the runners, but Whitey still grew into a small vining tree that covered the driveway. There's at least two species of wisteria. Could they be coaxed to grow here? Rainbow trees do, and they look so similar."

Aye touched her elbow. Handing over his largest red spotted orchid, he said, "You are ready for this. We will find a spot for your wisteria. If not, at the inn; maybe mauka, where Lilinoe's mists will touch a nice deep hole filled with topsoil and worm castings."

Livia remained fixated on the huge red orchid. Red was her favorite. She had very little luck with African violets or big orchids. She smiled and thanked him. "We'll study up and order a wisteria. This is a lovely orchid; I'll give it my best. Have you ever poured old milk on the moss around your orchids? I pour what's left in my gallon watering can, throw in a handful of Epsom salts, and the roses loved it."

He wrote down her suggestion, and he let her in on a couple orchid growing secrets. Use less moss and fertilizer. Keep their aerial roots a bit drier.

Ten days later, an official report came from the coroner's office. At first, no foreign substance or evidence of foul play was found on Header's body. Then the case got some more publicity. A second report was ordered, and taking longer to publish, the Honolulu report described short fine strands of hair under a his shoelaces and a very tiny finger print, on a bit of apple peel tucked under the insole of his shoe. Both matched samples from the keiki clinic in Hilo. Because lab-testing methods continually improved, Header's personal effects had been retained for future civil court lawsuits.

Livia spelled out Chakra's surname in pencil. Ka – possibly like the queen, "ahana" could be duty or to carry out, and manu like "mana" often meant supernatural power. No, not likely – her imagination was working overtime. Anyway, Hawaiians were too precise with their genealogical spelling. But what about the historical booklet about Honaunau - it mentioned a special caste of priests: ànāànā? "Hot damn!"

She slapped her knee. "Richard died about the same time as Chakra's final diabetic shock. Had she found the strength and worn herself out willing him to die?" Livia tossed the booklet and ran to find Aye.

She chewed her tongue - recognizing that he, as Chakra's consort, had customarily secluded himself and scarred his body. All she got from him was no eye contact when he said, "Kapu." Livia stood beside him - her head keeping time, with the words *Kuhuna Nui'* rolling over-and-over in her head. Aye had kept few privileges but met his responsibilities. Her tongue rubbed flat against the roof of her mouth, and she hugged him and whispered, "Those poor, defenseless children. Your Chakra was a wise and loving woman. I am so sorry. We miss her but don't ever doubt – we will be here for you."

Burly arms returned her hug, and they snuffled back the tears. They sat sipping tea and coffee, then he confided - Tim helped Ma rappel to some nearby cave, with something bundled in black kappa cloth.

Chapter 20: **Aloha Òe**

Livia resigned her position at the *West Hawaii Sun*. Sammy Smith offered her $150, for her old OED volumes, and she dropped them off at the newspaper office. He thanked her immensely and asked, about South Kona news, before walking her to the managing editor's office. Laying her keys, on his desk, next to that afternoon's markup copy, and a note saying he left for an emergency meeting - she noticed the commotion at the water cooler. Fancying herself as the hot topic, of their hushed chitchat – she glanced back at the real reason: a picture and two full columns outlining today's special edition.

She photocopied her recent article, and skipping her errands she drove directly home. Front door wide open – Cate met her mid-hall, twirled her around, and lead her to the library table. Livia took deep breaths, spreading out the markup and explaining the gist of the forthcoming news story. "There's new evidence on Richard. There are more results from the coroner. She found traces of mica and various oxides commonly found in eye shadow under his one brow. Besides that — well, it's about his huge Black Tahitian pearl ring."

Cate quietly patted her knees. "What is?"

"Skipping probate - Richard's will was read, and Judge Jenny came for his effects. The coroner's clerk handled the evidence bag and dropped it! The ring hit the tile floor – popping the 16mm pearl open

– right in half. Everyone gathered around looking down at his stash of minuscule fingernail clippings. The coroner sent them back to Honolulu for analysis. The DNA results showed thirty-two different patterns, and six of them match those of the reported minor children from Maui. Oh, the last few paragraph published the fact that Richard and Chakra died the same early morning."

Cate paced. Heading to the door she stopped, when Livia yelled.

"That's not all! A week ago, Honolulu CSI scoured Richard's properties. The sheriff, from Hilo, and his deputies cordoned the area off, and went in again after the CSI left." She took a couple deep breaths. "Evidently, they packaged quite a lot of evidence from his office. A truly amazing substance was flushed, not from his toilets – but out of the septic tank – shreds of fine stationery made from tappa-edged parchment. After days of comparisons, the investigators are sure it was a letter, to Richard, in Chakra's handwriting. It requested that he hide her bones. Once aware of her lineage, he had to have realized that her letter sealed his death sentence. Well – who'd hold the rope for him – huh? Even if he did successfully flush the letter, grab a few supplies, and head-off to Pu'uhonua for sanctuary. Fat lot of good that accomplished. You know the rest."

Livia gulped. "Remember that mother who told us her son sketched a man with blue above his eyes? Well, Mica gives reflectance to shimmery eye shadow - and now I even remember how well scrubbed Richard's eyes were, that day of the pony rides."

Cate whispered, "Makes sense now." She carefully printed Chakra's surname, in the table's fine sea-salt dust: Kā 'anā 'anā. "See here? These first two letters describe action, and the rest are for magic. Our grand lady knew she didn't have long to live, and that we couldn't catch Header in a timely manner. Oh — my gosh — I shoulda never made light of The Ma's stories." Cate took a breath and rambled on: "Remember — how Aye told us Chakra woke before dawn and stood starring from the lanai? She did not need a hellbroth to do him in.

Elizabeth Whitmer

—And that legend you recited, to me and to Margaret: about that Ali`i woman who broke kapu. Remember how the kahuna `anā `anā put a slave to death for her transgression? Well– Richard coulda poisoned himself, being a doctor and all, and especially, after she had that letter delivered to him - requesting he deposit her bones. Oh, yeah– I bet he knew, right then and there, that he was done for."

Livia barely got the words out: "Well, hells bells– I never ever thought you listened to my–" when both their heads turned toward the driveway and Margaret's car. One kept up with the other, as they headed down the main hall, to the carport. Livia lost ground, and leaning hard to grab Cate's elbow she quietly hissed, "Well, we have to tell her! Ever since their deaths, she's not been the same. Catie Pat, you'd better tell her – she's always been closer to you."

Cate stood blocking the doorway and facing Margaret. Loaded down with laptops and briefcase The Good Doctor lumbered toward them, and Cate calmly said, "The paper has quite a lengthy news article about Richard."

Livia stood slightly behind Cate and watched Margaret's head come up, with eyes clouded over. She bent down slowly and set everything down. Holding up her hand, for silence, she walked through the pantry to the kitchen. Once seated she looked at both hands clasped on the table and said, "I know. The crime scene investigators came to the keiki clinic, in Hilo." She looked up exhaling: "Who do you think gave them the tissue samples to compare?"

Livia gasped, as Cate said, "Oh– my–," and touched Margaret's shoulder.

There was a mighty sad silence, before she continued. "We don't usually gossip, but Aye told Livia about Richard's family. His father, Rick senior, was convicted of murdering a small girl, after she disappeared for four months. Fifteen years later he was paroled from prison, when Richard was a teenager. Rick abandoned him and moved to Hawaii after some crazy incident. The records say Dr. Rick was a horse tamer too. Evidently, they were examining a litter of bunnies, and he told Richard not to handle them. Left alone one evening, he must have petted all of them, and the next day the mama bunny had eaten half the babies. Many townspeople said later that Richard was not quite the same after all that had happened. Years ago, he moved here too, to reason with his father. Rick died, before he and Richard got to talk."

Margaret sat upright. "I believe there was more to it - than that." Then her voice broke. "It is terrible! But it is no excuse! There is a good person for every bad one, from an awful upbringing." She drew out a handkerchief and composed herself. "If you don't mind— I am really tired, and I am going to my room." She pulled free, from Cate's hand - and without another word, she trudged upstairs, shaking her head.

They walked to the parlor, and Cate plopped down on the loveseat next to Livia. Huddled shoulder-to-shoulder, she told Livia, "You were right. She's way too independent, for me to soothe or reason with. Glad you're here."

Livia leaned her head to Cate's, and with a tiny shrug she said, "Me too. No glory in being right; and in this case – boy, do I wish I was wrong."

They sat awhile, until something outside the window caught Cate's attention. Pointing to the cottage, she nudged Livia. "See - Aye's on the lanai. He just went inside." She stood. "I think it's about time he had some guests."

Livia jumped up, and they tiptoed to the kitchen grabbing fruit, mozzarella and wine, before heading down the trail to their kupuna. The closer they got, they heard deep little 'boofs' from within.

The door opened with little Sparty and Agy flanking Aye. Both good boys kept squeezing his knees, as he hugged and touched noses with Livia and Cate. Hugs never ceased until he said, "Good to be back; please come in. I figured I would see you, at least by week's end." With shoulders a little more hunched than usual, he looked down at the pups and chuckled, "Hope you don't mind; they may help me sample the cheese. The little scutters' owner had an unexpected move to Maui, and his uncle's condo wouldn't accept dogs."

As Cate scratched little Agy's tan points and rubbed Sparty's little white chin - Livia wasted no time asking Aye about any news.

He ate his fill, then he rubbed his cheek and left brow. "I do remember Chakra writing something – maybe less than a week before her death. She had opened a dusty box of old stationery early one afternoon. I doubt she noticed how faded were the parchment leaves and envelopes."

Livia waited, as he leaned back and pinched a few more dead orchids. "Yes, two big nephews came from Waimea the very next morning to collect a letter plus a few odd items. The men stood extremely solemnly and did not stay to visit. I do not know why. For some reason, until now I was not able to ponder on their visit." A tear rolled down his cheek, landing on his fruit. "All that week, she had so many visitors. She had taken no water for days, and was not feeling up to par at all, so I cajoled her with fresh star fruit. She accepted it and smiled, but ate none of it. Those last few months we used that new glucose meter The Good Doctor gave us. I tested Chakra's sugar five to six times daily; most time - it was right on the mark. She displayed no fever or chill, but late that evening her eyes took on a distant look. Oh – to see her rally so, at dawn, and by evening she lay dead."

They sat quietly. Livia wiped his tears and leaned her head on his shoulder. There were few words to say except, "I am so sorry. She was a wonderful lady. You just mustn't forget we will always be here for you."

Adding the same sentiments, Cate continued, "You know, Margaret's not doing too good. No, actually she is devastated by this Richard mess. She got up sick again the other morning, and to think of it, she got sick that evening when we explained what the rangers found." Cate got up and returned with some plates and utensils. "Please, we'd be happy for you to stay and have some of our fruit, cheese, and tea."

He started for the kitchen door. "Great, I would love some tea." A noise from the parlor caught his attention, and he took a brief detour to investigate. As the women set the table, he called back, "Wow, what a train table. Is that the train set the keiki were talking about right after your BugTussle story hour?"

Livia nodded. "I did - brought it down from the attic only yesterday. We had to store some furniture to set up its eight-by-eight-foot train table. Good call, to ship it out here it - for Mother's neighbor collects Lionel Trains, and he had offered to buy it more than once." She smiled and said, "Actually, it was my father's Christmas present, a couple years before he died. He was too old to build the track and operate the transformer. I spent many a good hour at the end of a long work day with him helping me plan the layout and reminiscing about trains he bought me when I was ten." Livia watched Aye's glow, as she explained how her grandfather Hinman died in 1929. "My father was only eleven then, but he just beamed when he told me about their train sets."

Then she looked away. "I only knew one grandparent. But my mother always talked of her father fondly. He died November of 1938. Mother said she only knew of him taking two vacations, in her lifetime. By age 14, she was driving Great-grandfather and him on country house calls. Only fifty-nine when Grandfather Etter died — worked so hard that his heart gave out — him being one of the few town doctors and all. Badendale turned the schools out half-a-day on the afternoon of his funeral. A widow thirty some years, Grandmother Etter never remarried."

Livia grinned fiercely. "Maybe, I'll write a book someday. I might include stories like that and the one, with my Grandfather sitting on the steps of the big Main Street house — yelling: 'I'd know that son-of-a-bitch's bare feet anywhere!' The whole family ran outside and found him pointing and naming every name — of a whole parade of white-robed marchers. And there were funny times too, like the house race track, alley apples, and at least three crazy old car stories; I'd have to include them too."

Aye patted her knee, as he ate heartily and thanked her for the fine "nibble meats." He talked trains, and said "I will come back in the morning to play with Luke's fancy engine. Well – that was, if the guests left him any room to get near the dang thing." He shook his head at using her words.

Walking him to the door, Livia whispered, "I also have a collection of old comic books." His eyes lit up, and he followed her back to the front desk, where she opened the safe and handed him a stack. "You're welcome to read as many as you like. Read them here or take them home." She watched his calm face, as he flipped through *Turok, Little Lucy,* and *Batwoman.* The fourth comic brought a twinkle to his eye. "My son liked this one; we read it a lot." As his finger paused at the end of Classics Illustrated Junior No.551, *The Queen Bee,* he blinked a few tears and chewed his lip.

Cate and Margaret had been excused from kitchen duty. Livia cleaned up, so they could relax and spend time with Aye before walking him home. Quietly leafing through the fragile comic booklets, he scanned stories and pictures, and his eyelids fell to half-mast. Margaret's call from the hospital woke him, and he stood and excused himself once more. Somehow, he stepped a bit more spryly as Cate and Livia walked him home.

Halfway to the inn they noticed him waving, as he stood under the porch light and a halo of moths. Livia flinched as three strapping Polynesians cut through the woods, heading from highway to cottage. Aye held the door open for them, and his voice rang out, "I luna." In less than a minute, the men were on the path coming toward them, carrying Chakra's grandmother's trunk.

Aye was soon to follow, adding, "Chakra's quilts – where would you like them set?"

Cate almost lost her footing. She stammered, "No. No, what I mean is - I cannot accept all her work."

"I lalo," ordered Aye, and the men set the chest down. "Then it will go into the sea. Her wishes were that they never find their way into another *haole* museum. One of her last wishes was that Ms. Katarina open a quilt studio or shop. She loved to play with the names, until she arrived at 'Loa Kea Lole,' The Long White Cloth."

Cate stared, dumbfounded. Then she found her voice. "Very well - I guess, if it was what she wanted, then I will most gratefully accept them." She leaned slightly toward the men, asking them to please place the trunk in her bedroom. "It's at the top of the main stairs, second door on the right."

He nodded and solemnly repeated, "I luna." The men hefted the trunk past the stair landing, as the women followed. Aye watched - then went home.

The following breakfast, he joined them, accepting only a serving of Livia's cold and smooth mango-flavored egg custard. Refusing a cup of tea, he made his way to the train table.

Mid-morning, a Hilo-type rain blew in, so Livia wiped her mist covered laptop screen and carried the PC from the lanai, to the kitchen table, adjacent the train table. She kept writing until well after lunch. She and Aye sucked on beer bottles, and she kept typing and humming to Lotus. True lush puppy, she licked every last drop from both their bottles. Aye pulled up a chair; and very carefully, Livia asked him to describe Chakra's letter to Richard. After she got his synopsis she asked, "Are there plans to move her bones?"

Aye swallowed hard. "Well, I'm not the one to move them. Like I told Cate - if anyone does, it will be Ma Loa. Once the local law enforcement officers have tired, of their gravesite surveillance, my guess is that she may move something to the caves. Other than that, it is anyone's guess.

Once Cate joined them, Livia pressed him no further. After another round, she noticed how they kept licking their lips and staring into the garden, and she followed their silence. Both women were struck dumbfound when Aye mentioned that Chakra had asked her nephews, from Waimea, to build an above ground pool, near the inn's carport. If the women wished it, the men could start late December and finish early January. That settled, he yawned and pushed his chair nearer to the window, saying that he would see them in the morning – hopefully not too early.

Livia watched him make his way down the walk, as she told Cate the few details. Surprisingly, Aye returned in a few minutes, for another turn at the train set. Both women kept working, at the main desk, in order to monitor him. Looking him over, Livia remarked, "He kind of reminds you of old Mr. Granger - don't you think?" Cate nodded 'yes' and kept sorting bills. Livia entered her personal checking records on the computer's ledger and said, "At least he gave a good reason why Ma spends her weekdays in Kona."

In a low cadence, Cate snipped, "And all along, you figured she was here because of you. And you have the guts– to call me Miss Id? Speaking of Ma – oddly enough, I saw her and Margaret having lunch at Gone Fishing." She cleared her throat and nudged Livia. "They were so engrossed in conversation; they ne**v**er noticed me, as I walked down the boardwalk and back. Twice, they **r**aised their glasses in a toast. What's with that – hmm–?"

Livia scowled and quipped, "**I guess**. I really dunno. I am so past all that." Cate accepted a lingering **nudge**, as a quick closure, and left it at that.

The next morning began routine enough. Margaret lifted her head from her oatmeal and tea, as Livia bounced downstairs. Mugs were filled and emptied, and little was spoken, until Margaret left the table. Livia heard the distant sound of someone wretch and thought little of it till the following toilet flush - a bit odd, since none of them used the downstairs bathroom. Margaret returned, and Livia watched her fix then pick at dry toast. Cate took her attention, when she stumbled downstairs well after ten and sat quietly gloating - probably for having slept, so late under her pile of newly acquired quilts.

Lively bunch crossed her mind, as the teakettle's low hiss pitch rose to a shrill 'get me emptied' whistle. Cate steeped her teabag, same as usual, preferring it strong enough to dye quilt fabric. Breakfast mess cleared - she stood gazing out the door. Her nose to a second mug, she returned to the table.

Just when Livia was about to scream from boredom - Margaret began, "I wanted you both to be the first to know that I've accepted a research grant in New Zealand. It is offered, through the University of Toronto, and the program involves counting gene pools. First, I am taking an extended week in Tahiti – somewhere near Bora Bora. Ma Loa helped me realize that I needed something different for a while. I deposited some money in the inn's account. Feel free to use it for the quilt shop. Emma also mentioned opening a Serious Moonlight II Café. We will see how it goes; make note of what you spend."

Livia's mouth gaped, as Cate hawked a mouthful of tea in her mug. Both managed a civil, "Oh?" followed by Cate's, "So, you're leaving us?"

Again, Margaret said evenly, "Yes, for a while. This will be a research fellowship. I will study in Toronto, then practice in various labs – like the awesome procedure I noticed, on the university's web site. Some procedures prelude those on a space mission. It is the ultimate cutting edge."

Livia snorted, "They say puns come best - early in the day."

Cate gave her the eyeball saying, "I noticed something like that on PBS." She left it at that, and put her nose back to her tea.

"Yes. There are doctors making remote studies in the town of Churchill, near Hudson Bay, via fiber optic cable. Anyway – they called with my acceptance, and I leave in a few weeks. Not to worry; I will keep my interest in the inn. Who knows? I may be able to bring some new techniques to Hawaii. Considering my circumstances, the hospital administrator wrote a wonderful letter of recommendation. If ever I want a full staff position at Kona, or any affiliate hospital, they will honor my contract. They even found my part time replacement, for the Hilo Keiki Clinic."

Cate poured a short orange juice laced with Cointreau then followed it with good whallop of beer with a dallop of frozen Stoli. Livia figured it was a bit early to drink; but on the other hand, very rude to let Cate drink alone - so she divvied up the beer slurry and ordered up a salute: "Cheers," she toasted weakly, and swigged it down one painful gulp. That was all she said all day.

Livia next had to sit down when Cate announced she was registering for a fall course, Macro Economics. Since the University of Hawaii – Kona Campus still had not opened, per an undetermined construction delay, she would study online and take her exams in Hilo. Livia always knew that Cate had it in her. She figured what held Cate back, for nearly fifteen years, was her previous quest for the pre-med perfect grade-point.

Livia asked whether her constant nudgings, about how important education was for ones own well being, had prodded Cate back to school. A negative answer came, with explanation that her diatribes were well taken, but it had been watching wacky Cherise slogged her way through a second graduate degree that kicked her into action. *Whatever it takes* thought Livia, as she gave Cate the whole center stage.

Three months later Margaret called from Churchill. She explained how she had nearly finished her gene pool training, and that she would return to the inn for a few weeks before taking up her research post in New Zealand. "Yeah– they had some extra frozen sperm in the lab, so I got permission to buy some." Then her pager went off, and she quickly gave her good-byes before promising to call in a couple weeks.

A few hours later, Cate made reservations for her family's December holiday visit. With golf starter Frank's help, she found them an awesome condominium near Waikoloa. Livia wondered why all a sudden Cate asked to borrow her huge *Hawaii Handbook*, and listened as she made reservations for army sergeant and his wife. Lotus fell asleep in her lap, as Cate repeated the reservation information. Livia overheard – the grandmother was to take Little Eddie, for the evening, so the couple could celebrate the wife's birthday.

How could Lotus sleep so soundly with little Eddie consistent whines and staccato shouts? By the way he had carried on that afternoon, at first Livia assumed the child autistic – until he made eye contact as soon as she set out some Halloween pumpkins. With no toys and strapped in his stroller he leaned and pointed to the webs and dangly witches that she draped post to post across the lanai. Popping open a honeycomb paper spider and a glittery black cat, she offered them to him. Good half-an-hour he spent entertaining himself, as he quietly poked his fingers in and out their delicate honeycomb tissue bodies, all the while keeping an eye on her as she animatedly adjusted the decorations.

With the lanai decorated and every box set away, Livia sat with Lotus and carefully considered the fact: Miss Lotus got more interaction than did Eddie. Maybe this family did not celebrate Halloween - but neither parent pointed out colorful flowers, goldfish or birds; nor had they asked a question, or told him a story. The young mother attended her knitting, with an expressionless stare, as soft as her husband's. Plugged into his noise-reducing Talkman headphones the young father's head kept time to a beat other than his son's. Both parents had long given up their liturgies, of "shush, or be quiet" – some twenty minutes ago – so Eddie kept himself sane making his own noise. Livia jostled Lotus awake. She could move away, from the noise, but not from the thought: whether he was her wake up call to teach again. Din in the background Livia and Lotus hit the kitchen door, as Cate clicked off the phone.

Hurriedly sorting and setting away papers she busied herself assembling a picnic basket with three place settings, and as if she remembered it was just her and Livia, she removed one set before laying the basket under the counter. "Guess it's ready to go for later," she announced before she explained tomorrow's guest list and the fact she had hired Ruth's nephew, Manawal. He would carry a forty-hour week, and his job would consist of heavy cleaning and lifting - thus helping Aye with small repairs and maintenance. Hiring him qualified their corporation for a cheaper and more comprehensive health care package. She gave a few details how Manny had quit his job on a Hilo fishing boat. The scuttlebutt, according to the dockworkers, was that a group of Michigan 'boys' chartered boats. They found Manny a bit too good-looking and could not keep their hands to themselves.

Livia winced. She recognized that group, from the Detroit local newspapers, and figured its wily businessmen had relocated their escapades here, from seamy Honduras. They could write off the stiffer airfare and easily cover their tracks, in the little-known port of Hilo. She slapped her cheek - for hoping Pele would, once and for all, satiate the Michigan Boys' appetites.

Cate kept Livia busy reading to her, about the Mauna Kea Resort's spotlight that attracted giant mantas hunting plankton during the dark of the moon. Channel-10 recently showed one manta, with a fourteen-foot wingspan, gliding so fluidly over the rock lined waist deep bay." Weeks after that show Livia checking the phone book, for tides and moon phases, and pestered Cate hoping for a chance to watch the leviathans circle the resort's light.

Early Friday morning Livia sipped her coffee and leaned across the table to grab the newspaper that was propped up against a huge vase of glossy pink anthuriums. Beneath it lay a fancy envelope, addressed "Dear Livia." The familiar printed letters could only be in Cate's hand. Sliding her finger beneath the flap of fine rag paper, Livia noticed footsteps on the stairs. Facing Cate she gently waved the envelope and teased, "You're up kind of early. What's this?"

Cate opened the envelope and nonchalantly said, "It seems to be some sort of invitation. Here – you read it."

Livia put on her glasses and scanned the enclosure. "Join us on the beach of the Mauna Kea Resort." She removed two small cards and gasped, "Oh! I can't believe it – clambake tickets – they're for Saturday, September 11. That's tomorrow night!"

Cate poured a tea murmuring, "Fancy that." She stirred her tea and faced Livia. "It's been much too long, that I've postponed our big evening. You've waited so patiently — hoping to see those giant mantas." She gave Livia a moment, then she reminisced about their first Big Island trip – complimenting her, on how she found excellent snorkeling spots at Kaaha Point and nearby Hapuna and Kauna'oa Beaches, where she nearly stepped on a baby manta, in the waist-deep waves, before it fluttered to deeper water.

Livia listened and squealed, "Jellyfish!" just as Cate had, before she mistakenly pulled her ashore - never to live down - the one and only time she alone saw the baby manta.

Many a time they returned to Hapuna Beach - but Livia still missed seeing a manta. The beach had great handicap parking and access, so they talked often of bringing Heimi and Demi here someday. But each time the beach was mentioned, they retold how they spent many mornings there - never seeing another jellyfish, or manta. Nearby Waialea and Puako Bays encircled some of Kohala's best but most dangerous kayaking spots. When they included Margaret, on their fine trips, Livia always stood outlook, so they could investigate along the swift undertows and snorkel the reefs at the bays' south points. After repeatedly asking, about clambakes and mantas, Livia quit - figuring Cate was not interested or was merely too busy.

Spinning around she said. "Aw– you remembered." Planting a big kiss on Cate's cheek, she said, "Thank you" before glancing to the calendar. "7:30 - a shore side table - on a moonless night is perfect."

Cate's teacup steamed her tiny glasses. Rosebud mouth pulled to one side, she said, "Well, it's the least I could do. I missed you, and we need something to commemorate our first trip to the island. I'll never forget those gorgeous stars, from Mauna Kea, and I may never have seen them – had you not taken me there." She blew on her tea and leaned closer. "Oh – it's a high tide too."

Chapter 21: Clambake

A little after 6:30, they drove up Kohala's Gold Coast, passing the airport and the stark miles of spiky black 'a'ā. White graffiti rocks lined the road – a few brief epitaphs sprinkled among a multitude of mushy love notes.

Usually Livia was the tour book quote-aholic - but that evening Cate played guide by pointing out night birds and Kona Nightingales. It still amazed her how a tiny herd of wild jackasses, left over from turn of the twentieth-century pack trains, could still find enough food and water to live out here. A couple miles past the turnoff to Waikoloa, she turned downhill and passed through the Mauna Kea's stately gatehouse.

Felled by the view, Livia scanned the verdant golf courses. Unlike the morning, their usual time to win a public parking pass, the air was searingly clear. Lush fairways seemed to float as massive palms swayed in the breeze.

Quick stop at the pro shop, and she listened to Cate's banter with starter Steve. At the open-air entrance, they exchanged packets of brochures and waved bye as he straightened racks of high-priced golf shirts. Leaving the car in the shady lot, they ambled along the incredibly groomed walkway to Kaaha Point. Livia pointed to a pair of Kentucky cardinals preening in a boxwood type shrub, noting how they were more active and noisy at dawn.

Continuing down the walk, they breathed in the salt air. They noticed an elegant pair of peacocks and nearly ran into an incredibly huge spider's web. Cate shuddered and caught her breath, as Livia pat her shoulder and pointed out the tiki-torch entrance to the lower promenade. The muumuu-clad hostess accepted their tickets, and she smoothly motioned a young man to escort them to their table. With them seated, he wished them a wonderful evening - pointing their way to the Shell Ginger Bar nearly hidden behind huge patches of Bird of Paradise topped by crossed torches. They warmed Cate's perfume - which wafted over Livia. Relishing the heady Oscar and salt air Livia slid her hands down an icy Mai Tai and rubbed her damp neck. Fortified, with a couple swigs of whisky cocktail, Cate touched Livia's waist and escorted her to their table.

A trio strummed ukuleles lightly and sung a variety of piano bar island songs. Livia's blouse flapped in the breeze, as her second drink floated to her head. She offered a toast, to many more years in paradise. Cate sipped a fresh cocktail and found it rivaled her Oahu pink volcano. Livia noticed a stir near the bar. Amid four burly guards came an entourage centered on a flowing robed man, followed by a small group of veiled women. Fixated on their garb, she counted her breaths and tried to refocus on salad trays mounded with choices of dip for fresh fruit and veggies. Cate did not seem to notice, looking only at the paper napkin on which she jotted the ingredients of the mango mint dressing. Slowly, Livia drew her lobster bib to the crown of her head, pulling its ties behind her ears. Her glass long since empty, she chirped, "Wimple, hijab, or should I tear this in half for an Amish cap? Why do women cover heads, and men do not? They even allowed that man to seat them."

"Stop that–" hissed Cate. Cautiously yanking the bib, off Livia's head, her lips did not move as she coached, "Please– just try to behave yourself."

"I am trying."

"Oh— you certainly are!" She mopped her brow. "What am I ever going to do with you?"

The answer came from Livia's smirk, as she sat quite prim. The salad bar and a few huge steamed Manila clams held her off, until she pointed to a sous chef setting out fresh Keahole lobster tails. Then, the executive chef caught Cate's attention as he began carving prime rib.

A few more songs gave them space for digestion and dessert. They watched Maui's mountain clouds change colors, and talked of visiting Kauai's canyons and a boat ride to Hanalei. The air grew so still and perfectly clear; they nearly jumped as a deep gold crowned the great resort's roofline. Just as suddenly, it changed to searingly bright orange. Livia's hand touched Cate's face, shielding her eyes, and she pointed. "Awesome orange, but look – out past the high rocks." Facing the deep rosy cloudbanks, they squinted as a wide silver line beamed in front of Maui's gray mountains and Haleakala. Leaning together, their eyes followed the silver to the evening star. The moment the sun dipped into the sea, a green flash took its place and the crowd moaned; after which, everyone grew unusually still.

A sky full of sparkling stars found them making short work of the coconut cake and sampler tray of bite-sized desserts. Livia could not help but comment that the Evening Star was really Venus chasing the sun.

A faint quiver pulsed near the horizon. As she reached for Cate, she heard her say, "Be careful saying who's chasing whom. A star is pretty big to fall in your lap."

The guests herded back to the serving tables. After sampling the dessert trays, Livia turned once more, to the tiki bar, and noticed a barely discernable sliver of moon rising in the east. Rushing back to Cate, she pointed. "Look there – to the right of Mauna Kea's observatories."

Cate soaked up the moonlight and mentioned the evening was all she had expected. Livia had already turned around. Eyes leveled at the horizon - she pointed to the blip, of cruise ship, bound for Honolulu.

Cate said, "Reminds me of the time we took your mother, on that Diamond Head Dinner Cruise."

"Yeah."

"Aw, sweetie– I'm sorry you couldn't get her hospice moved out here."

"I did try."

"Yes you did, and you stayed with her, and you did your very best."

"I know."

Cate smiled. "Okay then. Shush up and go eat your pudding."

They finished dessert, and the sky turned ebony. A few guests folded their napkins and climbed the steps from the beach. Cate and Livia followed the railing, along the resort's high promenade, and made their way to an overlook above a curved inlet. Thankful, for the cooler breeze, Livia daubed her throat. She and the rock wall cooled, as the Kohala Mountain breezes remained and ruffled everyone's hair. Cate stood behind her, so she could lean harder on the wall - watching the illuminated water below. She pointed and whispered. "I've never seen the star reflections so sparkly. Oh! You can even see to the bottom. Look over there; something barely skimmed the surface." Glancing up, she asked, "Do you think they mind us watching them?"

Cate sucked a breath of fresh air and gave Livia a big hug. Pointing to the pool of light, she said, "Aw, my *Hoaloha,* they don't mind us. See there? That one brought her pup."

Once again, it was night by the sea. They huddled close, mesmerized by the shifting shapes of manta wings.

Epilogue:

Life with Livia continues.

Aloha Rainbow's spicy prequel continues in Michigan and Hawaii. It reveals how Livia, Cate, and Margaret became teammates on and off the ice. Families, coworkers, the Kick Ice Bears and The Metro Skaters' Hockey League promise more fun.

Aloha continues in a sequel. Chakra left Cate more than quilts. Margaret returns from New Zealand with her twins and a pie-in-the-sky scheme to build a solar ice rink. Oddly enough, the twins resemble Livia. Yes - there's more to come about Ma, Tim and Tom.

Have fun and work together.

Aloha and Mahalo - E.W.

Author at home with pet corgis.